Praise for the Mrs. Murphy Series

PROBABLE CLAWS

"The animal crew, joined by a surprising new addition, is in rare form. . . . Beautiful illustrations bring the pet personalities to life." —*Kirkus Reviews*

"Series fans will know exactly what to expect: animals who talk to one another, Brown's personal views on an array of topics, and a healthy dose of Virginia history."
—*Publishers Weekly*

A HISS BEFORE DYING

"The staccato conversation style of the contemporary chapters contrasts nicely with the more fluid prose of those set in the eighteenth century. Brown's signature asides—on such subjects as local and national politics, traditional art, race, God, and just about anything else that strikes her fancy—give readers plenty to think about." —*Publishers Weekly*

"Clearly the cat's meow." —*Library Journal*

TAIL GAIT

"[Brown] successfully weaves mystery, history, real estate and romance into her latest novel. The blend is unusual but gripping, and combined with bipedal and quadrupedal characters who constitute old friends, it shines as imaginative and educational entertainment." —*Richmond Times-Dispatch*

"A cute premise . . . [with] a clever plot twist."
—*RT Book Reviews*

THE BIG CAT NAP

"[A] charming and enchanting mystery that affirms the Crozet cozies remain fun tales as Harry and her Puss 'n Cahoots squad investigate the homicides. . . . Fans will appreciate this engaging anthropomorphic whodunit."
—*Futures Mystery Anthology Magazine*

"Top honors go to the author's love for her beloved Virginia countryside and for her animal characters, who as usual steal the show." —*Kirkus Reviews*

"A welcome return to cozy form . . . Amusing exchanges among the cats and dog and their commentary on the humans around them will please series fans." —*Publishers Weekly*

HISS OF DEATH

"[Rita Mae] Brown ratchets up the tension in a conclusion that brings Harry, the killer, both cats, the dog and two horses into the final showdown. Brown . . . reunites the reader with beloved characters, supplies a wealth of local color and creates a killer whose identity and crimes are shocking (in one case, particularly so)."
—*Richmond Times-Dispatch*

"As explained on the book's cover, it takes a cat to write the *purr*-fect mystery. Indeed. . . . With a baffling mystery at hand (or paw), it might just prove to be one of [Harry's] most perplexing cases." —*Tucson Citizen*

"Brown sensitively depicts Harry's cancer treatment as the paw-biting action . . . builds to the revelation of a surprising killer." —*Publishers Weekly*

CAT OF THE CENTURY

"[Rita Mae Brown's] animals are as witty as ever."
—*Kirkus Reviews*

"There are plenty of suspects with motives in a well-constructed cozy that readers will enjoy in this one sitting read." —*The Mystery Gazette*

"The mystery part of *Cat of the Century* is quite good. The clues are there but the reader is still left guessing."
—*Jandy's Reading Room*

SANTA CLAWED

"Fun and satisfying . . . an essential purchase for all mystery collections." —*Booklist*

"[A] whodunit . . . that fans of the furry detectives and their two-legged pals will appreciate." —*Publishers Weekly*

"Fearless feline and clever canine sleuths." —*Kirkus Reviews*

"For all mystery collections and essential for series fans."
—*Library Journal*

"Captivating . . . will keep readers guessing whodunit to the very end. A delightful Christmas present indeed."
—*The Free Lance Star*

"Anyone who's a sucker for talking animals or who simply enjoys fantasizing about the thoughts running through a beloved pet's brain will find heaps of guilty pleasure in Brown's latest addition to the Mrs. Murphy series."
—*Rocky Mountain News*

"The animals once again provide ... the best comic moments." —*Alfred Hitchcock's Mystery Magazine*

"[A] satisfying whodunit with a wealth of Virginia color. And, as always, the real fun comes from Tee Tucker, Mrs. Murphy and Pewter.... In *Santa Clawed*, they're the true Christmas angels." —*Richmond Times-Dispatch*

THE PURRFECT MURDER

"Brown provides a perfect diversion for a cold night, complete with a cat or a dog on your lap." —*Richmond Times-Dispatch*

"Veteran readers ... will not be disappointed in this outing."
—*Winston-Salem Journal*

"The well-paced plot builds to an unpredictable and complex conclusion." —*Publishers Weekly*

"The pets steal the limelight ... [and] offer pleasure to fans of animal sleuths." —*Kirkus Reviews*

"The plot moves easily and those nonhumans who speak to each other, if not to their people, are a real pleasure and well worth one's time." —*iloveamystery.com*

PUSS 'N CAHOOTS

"Such a delight to read." —*Albuquerque Journal*

"The novel's tight pacing, combined with intriguing local color, make this mystery a blue-ribbon winner."
—*Publishers Weekly*

"This clever mystery strikes a comfortable balance between suspense and silliness." —*Booklist*

"Fans of the cunning animal sleuths will enjoy their antics and the spot-on descriptions of the horse-show circuit."
—*Kirkus Reviews*

"[Rita Mae Brown has] readers guessing whodunit until the very end." —*The Free Lance Star*

SOUR PUSS

"*Sour Puss* makes for a sweet read. . . . Brown has a devilish sense of humor." —*The Free Lance Star*

"One of my all-time favorite cozy series . . . This series is just plain charming." —*The Kingston Observer*

"[The authors] have once again pounced upon just the right ideas to keep this delightful mystery series as fresh as catnip in spring. . . . These are books written about and for animal lovers. . . . One of the best books in a good series, *Sour Puss* should leave fans purring." —*Winston-Salem Journal*

"A captivating look at grape growing and the passionate dedication it requires." —*Publishers Weekly*

"This venerable mystery series has been on a good run of late. Brown does everything right here. . . . Wine fanciers or not, readers will happily toast the animal-loving author for creating this robust and flavorful tale." —*Booklist*

CAT'S EYEWITNESS

"Thirteen is good luck for the writing team of Rita Mae Brown and her cat Sneaky Pie—and for their many fans. The Browns know how to keep a mystery series fresh and fun."
—*Winston-Salem Journal*

"This mystery, more than the others, has depth—more character development, a more intricate plot, greater exploration of the big topics. I give it nine out of ten stars."
—*Chicago Free Press*

"This book could not have arrived at a better time, the day before a snowstorm, so I had the perfect excuse to curl up by the fire and devour *Cat's Eyewitness* virtually at a sitting. . . . Entertaining, just the thing for a snowy afternoon . . . well worth reading." —*The Roanoke Times*

"It is always a pleasure to read a book starring Harry and Mrs. Murphy but *Cat's Eyewitness* is particularly good. . . . Rita Mae Brown delights her fans with this fantastic feline mystery."
—*Midwest Book Review*

"It's terrific like all those that preceded it. . . . Brew the tea, get cozy, and enjoy. This series is altogether delightful."
—*The Kingston Observer*

"Frothy mayhem." —*Omaha Sunday World-Herald*

"[An] irresistible mix of talking animals and a baffling murder or two . . . the animals' wry observations on human nature and beliefs amuse as ever." —*Publishers Weekly*

"Delightful . . . Grade A." —*Deadly Pleasures Mystery Magazine*

WHISKER OF EVIL

"A page-turner . . . A welcome sign of early spring is the latest sprightly Mrs. Murphy mystery. . . . There's plenty of fresh material to keep readers entertained. For one thing, the mystery is a real puzzler, with some subtle clues and credible false leads. . . . [They] have done it again. Give them a toast with a sprig of catnip." —*Winston-Salem Journal*

"Rita Mae Brown and Sneaky Pie Brown fans will gladly settle in for a good long read and a well-spun yarn while Harry and her cronies get to the bottom of the mystery. . . . The series is worthy of attention." —*Wichita Falls Times Record News*

"Another winsome tale of endearing talking animals and fallible, occasionally homicidal humans." —*Publishers Weekly*

"The gang from Crozet, Virginia, is back in a book that really advances the lives of the characters. . . . Readers of this series will be interested in the developments, and will anxiously be awaiting the next installment, as is this reader."
—*Deadly Pleasures Mystery Magazine*

"An intriguing new adventure . . . suspenseful . . . Brown comes into her own here; never has she seemed more comfortable with her characters." —*Booklist*

"Another fabulous tale . . . wonderful . . . The book is delightful and vastly entertaining with a tightly created mystery."
—*Old Book Barn Gazette*

"Undoubtedly one of the best books of the Mrs. Murphy series . . . a satisfying read." —*Florence Times Daily*

Books by Rita Mae Brown & Sneaky Pie Brown

Wish You Were Here • Rest in Pieces • Murder at Monticello
Pay Dirt • Murder, She Meowed • Murder on the Prowl • Cat on the Scent
Sneaky Pie's Cookbook for Mystery Lovers • Pawing Through the Past
Claws and Effect • Catch as Cat Can • The Tail of the Tip-Off
Whisker of Evil • Cat's Eyewitness • Sour Puss • Puss 'N Cahoots
The Purrfect Murder • Santa Clawed • Cat of the Century
Hiss of Death • The Big Cat Nap • Sneaky Pie for President
The Litter of the Law • Nine Lives to Die • Tail Gait • Tall Tail
A Hiss Before Dying • Probable Claws

Books by Rita Mae Brown featuring "Sister" Jane Arnold

Outfoxed • Hotspur • Full Cry • The Hunt Ball
The Hounds and the Fury • The Tell-Tale Horse • Hounded to Death
Fox Tracks • Let Sleeping Dogs Lie • Crazy Like a Fox

The Mags Rogers Books

Murder Unleashed • A Nose for Justice

Books by Rita Mae Brown

Animal Magnetism: My Life with Creatures Great and Small
The Hand that Cradles the Rock • Songs to a Handsome Woman
The Plain Brown Rapper • Rubyfruit Jungle • In Her Day • Six of One
Southern Discomfort • Sudden Death • High Hearts
Started from Scratch: A Different Kind of Writer's Manual • Bingo
Venus Envy • Dolley: A Novel of Dolley Madison in Love and War
Riding Shotgun • Rita Will: Memoir of a Literary Rabble-Rouser
Loose Lips • Alma Mater • Sand Castle • Cakewalk

A MRS. MURPHY MYSTERY

Probable Claws

RITA MAE BROWN & SNEAKY PIE BROWN

Illustrated by Michael Gellatly

BANTAM BOOKS • NEW YORK

2019 Bantam Books Mass Market Edition

Copyright © 2018 by American Artists, Inc.
Illustrations copyright © 2018 by Michael Gellatly
Excerpt from *Whiskers in the Dark* by Rita Mae Brown
copyright © 2018 by American Artists, Inc.

Published in the United States by Bantam Books,
an imprint of Random House, a division of
Penguin Random House LLC, New York.

BANTAM BOOKS and the HOUSE colophon are registered trademarks of
Penguin Random House LLC.

Originally published in hardcover in the United States
by Bantam Books, an imprint of Random House,
a division of Penguin Random House LLC, in 2018.

This book contains an excerpt from the forthcoming book *Whiskers in the Dark*
by Rita Mae Brown. This excerpt has been set for this edition only and may
not reflect the final content of the forthcoming edition.

ISBN 978-0-425-28717-0
Ebook ISBN 978-0-425-28716-3

Cover design: Victoria Allen
Cover illustration and hand lettering: Sara Mulvanny

Printed in the United States of America

randomhousebooks.com

6 8 9 7 5

Bantam Books mass market edition: April 2019

Dedicated with love
to
Carolyn Maki,
who knows value can't be assigned,
it's intrinsic

THE CAST OF CHARACTERS

THE PRESENT

Mary Minor Haristeen, "Harry"—Hardworking, task-oriented, she runs the old family farm in Crozet, Virginia. A loyal friend to both human and animal, a quality not lost on those who care for her. If she has a weakness—perhaps best explained as a personality trait—it is that psychology has no interest for her. Harry doesn't care why you do anything. She simply deals with the result.

Pharamond Haristeen, DVM, "Fair"—Tall, powerfully built, at forty-three he is one year older than his wife, Harry. His equine patients trust him as do most humans. He is more sensitive, more introspective than his wife.

Susan Tucker—Harry's friend since cradle days, she loves Harry as only an old friend can. The two can disagree but will always come to each other's aid. Susan's deceased grandfather was a former governor of Virginia. Her husband, Ned, is a representative to the House of Delegates.

BoomBoom Craycroft—Another childhood friend who can find herself swept up into one of Harry's messes. BoomBoom often asks the obvious question. Obvious to her.

Deputy Cynthia Cooper—She rents the old Jones homeplace, a farm next to Harry's. As she was not raised in the country, Harry and Fair are a great help to her. She does her best to deflect Harry's curiosity. If Susan and Fair can't contain Harry, it's a sure bet Coop can't, despite her shiny law enforcement badge.

Reverend Herbert Jones—He's known Harry all her life. She is a faithful congregant of St. Luke's Lutheran Church. He learned to lead men as a young combat captain in Vietnam. On his return after the seminary, he did his best to lead women, too—to faith, charity, and peace. He is a good pastor to his flock.

Lisa Roudabush—Heads Nature First's Charlottesville, Virginia, office. Nature First is a statewide environmental group growing in power. She's in her mid-thirties, married to her work.

Raynell Archer—Assists Lisa. She worked her way to Nature First through other nonprofits.

Felipe Zaldivar—The second-in-command at Nature First. He's intelligent, steady, devoted to Lisa and the cause.

Gary Gardner—A local architect with good sense, who is able to keep costs down and loves to work.

Marvella Rice Lawson—In her sixties, she will never be described as easygoing. She's one of the powers-that-be at the Virginia Museum of Fine Arts. She and her late brother Pierre, each an art collector of vastly different tastes, amassed art worth a small fortune. When the highly intelligent Marvella walks into a room, she parts people like the Red Sea.

NOTE: Harry was an Art History major at Smith College, Northampton, Massachusetts. Her father couldn't believe she'd major in something so useless. Her retort was that this was her only chance in life to do so, as once she was out of college she would need to work. Both parents were killed when she was in college, before her father had the chance to appreciate the woman she became. Now, at forty-two, some lights are being turned on upstairs.

THE EIGHTEENTH CENTURY

Catherine Schuyler—At twenty-two, intelligent, level-headed, and impossibly beautiful, she is learning from her brilliant father about business. She already has a reputation as a leading horsewoman.

John Schuyler—A former major in the Revolutionary War, only a few years older than his smashing wife, he is powerfully built and works hard. As he is from Massachusetts he can miss some of the undercurrents of Virginia society.

Rachel West—Two years younger than her sister, Catherine, she, too, is beautiful, but her beauty is softer, sweeter. She's easy to please, ready to help, and possessed of deep moral conviction.

Charles West—Captured by John Schuyler at the Battle of Saratoga, the then nineteen-year-old marched all the way to The Barracks prisoner-of-war camp outside Charlottesville. The second son of a baron in England, he had the good sense to stay in America. Like John, he is dazzled by his wife and knows how lucky he is.

Karl Ix—A Hessian also captured. He and Charles became friends in the camp and continued working together after the war.

Maureen Selisse—The daughter of a Caribbean banker, she was a great catch for her ruthless late husband, Francisco. Keenly aware of her social position, she is also accustomed to getting her way. She hated that he carried on with a beautiful slave, making little attempt to hide it.

Ewing Garth—The father of Catherine and Rachel, a loving man, brilliant in business. He is a creature of his time, but one who can learn. He helped finance the war and hopes the new nation can hold together. A widower, he misses his wife, a true partner. The economic chaos of the Articles of Confederation affect his business as well as everyone else's. He sees doom ahead for the new nation and no way out.

Jeffrey Holloway—Young, not well born but divinely handsome, he married the widowed Maureen Selisse to everyone's shock.

Yancy Grant—Infuriated more than anyone by the above hasty marriage, he hates Jeffrey. Being challenged to a duel by Jeffrey wounded both men, yet a respect resulted from this.

THE SLAVES: BIG RAWLY

Sheba—Maureen Selisse's lady-in-waiting. Really, she's Maureen's right hand and she enjoys the power. She'll destroy anyone who stands in her way. She is believed to have run away after stealing jewelry. No one knows where she is.

DoRe Durkin—He works in the stable and limps from an old fall from a horse. He mourns his son Moses, after Moses's flight up North in the wake of the death of Francisco Selisse, who brutalized Moses's love, the beautiful Ailee.

William—Works with DoRe. Has riding talent but not as much as he thinks he has.

THE SLAVES: CLOVERFIELDS

Bettina—A cook of fabulous abilities. She's the head woman of the slaves, thanks to her fame, her wisdom, and her wondrous warmth. She also has a beautiful voice. Bettina's view: "I could be a queen in Africa, but I'm not in Africa. I'm here." She made a vow to Isabelle, Ewing's wife, as she died. Bettina vowed to take care of Catherine and Rachel. She has kept her pledge.

Serena—A young woman, learning from Bettina both in the kitchen and out. She has uncommon good sense and will, in the future, wield power among her people.

Jeddie Rice—At nineteen, he is a natural with horses. He loves them. He's been riding, working, and studying bloodlines with Catherine since they were children. Like Serena, Jeddie has all the qualities of someone who will rise, difficult though the world they live in is.

Tulli—A little fellow at the stables who tries hard to learn.

Ralston—Nearly sixteen and thin, he, too, is at the stables. He works hard.

Father Gabe—Old, calm, and watchful, he accepts Christianity but practices the old religion. Many believe he can conjure spirits. No matter if he can or can't, he is a healer.

Roger—Ewing's house butler, the most powerful position a male slave can have. He has a sure touch with people, black or white.

Weymouth—Roger's son, in his middle twenties. The hope is he will inherit his father's position someday, but for now he's fine with being second banana. He's a good barber and in truth not very ambitious.

Barker O.—Powerful, quiet, he drives the majestic coach-in-four. He's known throughout Virginia for his ability.

Bumbee—Fights with her husband. Finally she moves into the weaving cabin to get away from him and to comfort a lost soul.

Ruth—Mother to a two-year-old and a new baby. How she loves any baby, kitten, puppy, as well as the master's grandchildren.

RICHMOND

Georgina—Early middle-age, quite attractive but putting on weight, she runs a tavern that also serves ladies. She knows everything about everybody, almost. No one uses last names in this world except for the male customers, men of means, in the small city.

Sam Udall—As a dedicated customer of Georgina's, he appreciates her shrewdness. He realizes the financial world has changed since the colonists have won the war. He also understands that the old Tidewater grandees are slipping. A new man is emerging with new money if the financial chaos can be corrected.

Mignon—A runaway slave from Big Rawly, she serves in the kitchen. A tiny woman with big eyes, she eluded discovery.

Eudes—As the outstanding chef at Georgina's, he brings the customers in for the food. He is quite an independent thinker; he's a free black man who, like Georgina, doesn't blab everything he knows.

Deborah—The most expensive of the delicious offerings at Georgina's thanks to her beauty and her self-possession. She can drive a man crazy. She's a runaway slave, as are many of the girls. The white girls also ran away. Spared slavery, they were not spared brutality, unwanted sexual congress, or poverty. All of which binds the girls to Georgina, who treats them decently—plus they make good money.

THE ANIMALS

Mrs. Murphy—Harry's tiger cat who knows she has more brains than her human. She used to try to keep Harry out of trouble. She gave up, knowing all she can do is extricate her human once she's in another mess.

Pewter—A fat gray cat who believes the world began when she entered it. What a diva. But the Queen of All She Surveys does come through in a pinch, although you'll never hear the end of it.

Tee Tucker—Bred by Susan Tucker, this is one tough, resourceful corgi: She knows she has to protect Harry, work with the level-headed Mrs. Murphy, and endure Pewter.

Owen—Tucker's brother. They adore being with each other. For Tucker it's a relief to sometimes be away from the cats.

Shortro—A young Saddlebred ridden as a hunter.

Tomahawk—Harry's old Thoroughbred hunter who hotly resents being thought old.

Pirate—An Irish wolfhound puppy who loves everyone but is confused by Pewter, who does not.

THE EIGHTEENTH-CENTURY ANIMALS

Piglet—A brave, smart corgi who went through the war and imprisonment with Captain Charles West. He loves living in Virginia with the other animals and people.

Serenissima—Francisco Selisse's fabulous blooded mare whom he sent to Catherine to be bred to her stallion, Reynaldo.

Reynaldo—An up-and-comer with terrific conformation, but hot. Catherine and Jeddie can handle him.

Crown Prince—A younger half brother to Reynaldo. Both are out of Queen Esther, and fortunately, Crown Prince has her temperament.

King David—One of the driving horses. He's heavier built than Reynaldo and Crown Prince. Solomon is King David's brother. They are a flashy matched pair.

Castor and Pollux—Two Percherons who do heavy-duty work. They are such good boys.

Sweet Potato—A saucy pony teaching Tulli to ride.

Black Knight—Yancy Grant's fast Thoroughbred.

Probable Claws

1

December 23, 2016

Friday

"It's a madhouse out there." Harry leaned on the checkout counter at Over the Moon bookstore in Crozet.

"Can't complain. Business has been good." Anne de Vault, the owner, glanced up as more customers entered the store as if to prove her point.

The store, finally settled in its new location, boasted good floor display space as well as wall bookcases. Mrs. Murphy and Pewter, Harry's two cats, and Tucker, the corgi, inspected the books closest to the floor.

"No books on catnip," Pewter, the gray cat, complained.

"Who would write about catnip?" the dog wondered.

"An herbalist," Pewter replied. *"Humans drink catnip tea. It's a waste of good dried leaves but they do drink it. Catnip is meant to be chewed, inhaled, and then rolled in."* This was pronounced with authority.

Harry watched as customers picked up books, put some down, kept others. There was no accounting for taste.

"Even the post office parking lot is full. I was lucky. Just as I pulled in here a big SUV, big as in big as the state of Illinois, pulled out. Before I start browsing, did my order for Susan come in?"

"*Capability Brown*. In," Anne replied.

"Susan is getting as serious about gardening as she is about golf. Saw the book written by the Duchess of Rutland. Thought she'd like it." Harry commented on one of her best friend's deepening interest in gardening, and who better to write about it than an Englishwoman?

The English excelled at gardening. Rich, poor, in-between, they had the touch.

"The book is enormous. Lots of photographs, drawings." Anne placed it on the counter.

"Give me a minute to cruise. I need to find some other gifts and nothing is better than a book."

The door opened again.

Anne called out, "Lisa, your books are in."

Lisa Roudabush, mid-thirties, medium height, was the director of the Albemarle County office of Nature First, a statewide environmental nonprofit. The headquarters was in Richmond but small offices were in every town with a university since the young were environmentally conscious.

Raynell Archer, Lisa's assistant, began to turn the card cylinder looking for clever cards. They had walked into the store together, both lingering.

"Harry." Lisa smiled. "Come to the office after you buy

your books and I buy mine. Gary Gardner is almost finished and it's a terrific design."

Raynell, now looking at books displayed artfully on a table, added, "Harry, the walls run diagonally."

"Do they?" Harry was curious.

"Well, I need to go to his office to pick a few last plans, approve more drawings, but we are nearly finished." Lisa would be glad when the remodeling was over.

"He's doing a wor…shed for me. It's a gift from my husband. Isn't Gary fun to work with?"

"He is." Lisa looked out the large front windows, one of the best features of the store. "Are we ever going to see the sun again?"

"Spring," Anne called from the counter. "And it's supposed to start snowing again tomorrow and on Christmas. A white Christmas."

"I tell myself winter can be beautiful but I never quite believe it." Lisa walked to the counter where Anne had piled up her ordered books.

Lisa took the first one off the pile, a history of architecture in Richmond. Nature First, while primarily an environmental group, also regularly joined forces with other nonprofits to save historic buildings. The organization was also keen on the epochs before colonization, even before human life.

Lisa licked her forefinger to turn the page.

"My great-aunt used to do that." Harry laughed.

"Are you telling me I'm an old lady? I'm younger than you," Lisa fired back as she turned another page.

"Well, yes you are," Harry replied, enjoying the exchange. "But I've only ever seen old people do that."

Lisa motioned Harry over. "Look here. Pages always stick together. Licking my finger is easier than trying to slide my fingernail between pages or rubbing them together to pop them apart." She demonstrated her thesis then said, "If I buy a book I have to leaf through it for a few pages, get a glimpse of it. Then I'll read it later."

Anne seconded this, adding, "Harry, your Mixed Role Productions calendars are here, too. You're behind this year. Usually you order them in July."

"July?" Raynell asked, having joined the others at the counter. "Why order a calendar in July?"

Harry replied, "They run August to August. And they're eight and a quarter by five and a half inches so I can't overlook them. See? Perfect size. If I order them in July they arrive in time for August."

She removed shrink-wrap from the black-covered calendar with silver lettering that read 2017–2018, then demonstrated. "Big squares for each month, and then the days for the month are on lined pages, three days to a page. There's a monthly financial record, too. A special occasions page is opposite the month at a glance. I got hooked. Here. Merry Christmas."

"Harry, I can't take your calendar," Lisa demurred.

"I always order extras. You use it for a month and you'll get hooked, too. And they aren't expensive, which is the best part."

Lisa took the light green–covered calendar offered her; they came in many colors. "Thank you."

Harry examined Lisa's books, read the titles on the spines. "Let's see, *Architecture in Richmond before 1800*. Birding books and books on dinosaurs. Are you bringing them back? Nature First isn't bringing them back, are you? Have you found some DNA?"

"Funny you should bring that up. I believe the day will come when that happens. Look at the uproar over that perfectly preserved mastodon," Lisa replied.

"No need to dig. Those are in the Senate," Harry kidded.

"If you only knew some of the people we have to work with in the House of Delegates. They don't read. They deny what they don't know. They love to exercise their little bit of power. You'd think they would at least read history and political theory. I always hope the level of intelligence is higher in Washington."

"Oh, Lisa, I think the results speak for themselves." Harry shrugged.

Raynell, close to Lisa's age, piped up. "They deny climate change. They fail to realize how significant the architecture is in parts of Richmond. It's maddening to work with such limited people. All they think about is their next election."

"You're right about that," Lisa agreed as she closed the book about architecture. "There aren't many really old buildings left since Richmond was burned in 1865. A few. They are so beautiful. The new stuff, not so much. But the scarcity means we must protect them, the detail alone on some of these structures is beautiful."

"Marvella Lawson, the Virginia Museum of Fine Arts

power, has promised to take me to look at some of the newer things, including those under construction," Harry said.

"We fought the demolition of the Kushner Building," Raynell said. "Didn't do a bit of good. Big money. These tall buildings can interfere with nesting and the lights at night confuse migrating birds. Big money doesn't care about anything but more profit."

"Richmond doesn't have a good development plan. Charlottesville is even worse." Lisa sighed. "I'm beginning to think they hire the architect who will build the ugliest thing ever, like the giant pickle in London."

"That is pretty awful," Harry agreed. "I always think the English know better and now they are as bad as everyone else. Old London was so much prettier than New London."

"Well, they've mucked up Philadelphia, too. That used to be such a unique environment. Now it looks like every other city." Raynell's voice carried a hint of venom.

"Are you from Philadelphia?" Harry asked.

"I went to Swarthmore."

"Ah, good school."

"Where did you go, Harry?" Raynell asked.

"Smith."

That more or less settled the college discussion. It's hard to beat one of the Seven Sisters. But Anne thought otherwise.

"Well, I went to Denison." Anne beamed at Harry. "Not Ivy League but I am proud of my alma mater."

"Back to Richmond." Lisa tapped the architecture

books. "It's estimated that four hundred thousand people will move to the city in the next ten years. Where are we going to put them so they won't destroy natural habitats?"

"How about on riverboats?" Harry remarked.

"Why would anyone live on a boat?" Pewter, tired of being in the store, grumbled.

"Maybe they like to fish." Tucker was practical.

"Houseboats can be pretty," Mrs. Murphy said. *"Remember that old movie Harry and Fair watched? Houseboat."*

"Hollywood." Pewter sniffed. *"Of course the boat looked good. They need to make more movies about cats."*

Slyly, Tucker responded, *"I'm sure they're planning that right now."*

Pewter bared her fangs. Harry saw it just in time. "Don't you dare. I'll never bring you in this store again."

"Bother." But Pewter did close her mouth.

Anne put a bow on the large paper bag. "Here. You can reuse it." She handed it to Lisa.

"I can."

"I don't see any presents for me," Pewter complained.

"You don't read," the corgi fired at her.

"You can't read. At least I can." The fat gray cat sniffed.

"Oh, patting at the pages of a book or the computer screen isn't reading," Tucker replied.

That fast, Pewter boxed the corgi's upright ears. *"Don't you insult me, you illiterate cur."*

"Stop it. We'll get thrown out of the store. I like it here," Mrs. Murphy told them.

Both Harry and Lisa carried their treasures in large shopping bags. Harry followed Lisa and Raynell to the

Nature First office down the hall from Over the Moon, as they were both located in a new commercial building.

"Hello, Felipe," Lisa called to the number two man in the organization.

Looking up from his computer, he said, "What a haul. You must have bought out the store. You, too, Raynell, but you showed a little more restraint. Oh, hello, Harry, and your posse, too." He smiled at the pets.

"I'm here!" A nine-week-old Irish wolfhound puppy, already substantial, raced out from Lisa's office.

Pewter puffed up. "Don't touch me!"

The puppy stopped cold.

"Just ignore her," Tucker counseled the youngster. "Who are you?"

"Pirate. Lisa bought me and she is taking me to work but I have to be quiet and I have to ask to go to the bathroom."

"Good idea," commented Mrs. Murphy, who knew how big the Irish wolfhound would grow to be.

Harry set her bag on a corner table, knelt down. "Hello, puppy. Aren't you beautiful."

Pirate ambled right over, placed his head in Harry's hand. "You are a nice person. And you're walking with Lisa, you have to be a nice person. I start school after Christmas. I have a new collar and leash."

"Lisa, he's beautiful. When did you decide to have a dog?"

"I've been thinking about it. I live alone. I like dogs but I was always on the go. Now that I'm settled I thought this is the time. Well, come on, let me show you what Gary's done."

Raynell ducked into a small office near the front door.

The two walked through the changes Gary had made, which mostly involved moving or angling walls. Clever. His alterations brought in more light, taking full advantage of the many windows in the new building. Although an architect, he also guided Lisa and Felipe to interesting furniture, comfortable chairs in natural colors. Gorgeous photographs of Virginia's wonders covered the walls: the falls in Richmond, the Chesapeake Bay, the Blue Ridge Mountains, the bridges of Norfolk and Virginia Beach that ran over to the long spit of land, the Eastern Shore. The combination of bridges and tunnels traversing the bay were an engineering wonder. Then again, Virginia was home to one of the Eight Engineering Wonders of the World, the four tunnels that Claudius Crozet dug out of the Blue Ridge Mountains for the new form of transportation, railroads. He had no dynamite. It was all done by hand. Two of the tunnels remained in service. The other two were being reclaimed and rehabilitated as part of a walking tour. Another large photograph of a bald eagle soaring over the James River, sun glistening off his wings, had pride of place when you walked into Lisa's office.

"This is wonderful," Harry exclaimed.

"We're almost done. Gary wants to come make sure the cabinets fit in. You simply touch the front of them and they open."

"No kidding." Harry reached out, pressed the front and sure enough the cabinet opened noiselessly.

"They're enameled. That was expensive but it looks fabulous," Lisa enthused.

"*Do you like puppies?*" Pirate asked Mrs. Murphy.

"*I do as long as you don't slobber on me,*" the tiger answered.

"*Puppies are disgusting. They poop, they pee, they slobber, they throw up, they chew. Ugh!*" Pewter bared her fangs.

"*Ignore her,*" Tucker again told the puppy.

"*Do you live with her?*" Pirate wondered.

"*I don't have a choice.*"

"*You would be bored without me. Bored to tears. You have no new thoughts. You rely on me.*" Pewter lifted a paw to lick it, languidly.

"*What about the other kitty?*" the large puppy inquired.

"*We're friends.*" Tucker smiled as Mrs. Murphy came over to sit with the corgi while the humans babbled on.

Lisa was showing Harry her revitalized office. Sleek, the only knickknacks were little rubber dinosaurs and some detailed decoys.

The bookshelves, also enameled, reflected light. Behind a row of dinosaur and raptor books two long black legs poked out. Harry, ever curious, peeked behind the books, jumped back.

"Lifelike! What's a rubber tarantula doing here?"

"I actually had Mildred, I call her Mildred, on the shelf, but Raynell hates spiders, so I sort of hid her."

"*I hate spiders, too,*" Pewter pronounced.

Pirate asked, "*Why?*"

"*Too many legs. If you walk into a web it takes time to clean it off. Those strands are sticky,*" Pewter said.

"*Oh.*" The big-little puppy, wide-eyed, looked at the fat cat, who was always happy to be the authority.

Harry, now back at the entrance door, knelt to again pet the puppy. "Lisa, the best friends come on four feet."

"I believe it."

"Bye," Tucker and Mrs. Murphy said to the puppy while Pewter strolled out in front of everyone.

"Come back. We can play!" Pirate wagged his tail.

"We'll try. Wish we could drive." Mrs. Murphy laughed.

"Merry Christmas, Lisa. Merry Christmas, Felipe and Raynell."

"You, too," they called back.

The four hurried to Harry's Volvo station wagon as it began to sleet, now turning to snow. The precipitation wasn't heavy but it was cold. Harry wanted to get home before the roads turned slick as an eel.

"Turn on the heater," Pewter demanded.

"She will. You have a fur coat. She doesn't," Tucker reminded the fatty.

"Humans lack fur, claws, sharp teeth. They are so slow. I mean they can't run. Hearing, pfft. But their eyes are good." Pewter added something positive.

"Look at it this way, Pewter. She can use the can opener. We can't," Mrs. Murphy said.

"There is that," Pewter agreed as the snow fell a bit more heavily.

2

December 27, 2016

Tuesday

An earlier dusting of snow reflected the small round lights of various colors, strung from shops. The shopkeepers were upbeat. Even the Salvation Army bell ringers were smiling. With New Year's around the corner more sales could be expected. Bargain hunters walked briskly from shop to shop in the small Crozet downtown, more like a crossroads, really.

Bending over an old, lovely, much-used large drafting table, Harry noticed the flow of people outside the store-front windows of Gardner's Design. The shop, marked by a compass over a T-square painted on its hanging sign, was next to the well-lit art shop, and provided good parking, which was always a problem as the old stores had been built close to the road. The no-longer-used railroad station, originally the draw for business, still stood by the tracks.

Gary Gardner, trim white mustache, in his early sixties, bent over the table. Large sheets of paper were held down by tiny sandbags and his T-square, which was affixed to the top of the drafting table.

"Harry, if you'd just give me the word, I would create Le Petit Trianon for you. Imagine working in such divine surroundings? You might even decide to keep sheep." He tapped her hand with a pencil.

"Gary, I'd need to wear a bonnet. That would never do. For one thing, the cats would destroy the ribbons."

Mrs. Murphy and Pewter, sitting on the floor, quickly defended themselves. "*Never!*"

Tucker saw her moment. "*Ha. Then they'd chew the straw.*"

"*You'd herd the sheep. You'd create more havoc than we would.*" Pewter curled her lip.

"*My job is to herd,*" the corgi responded with pride.

"*Well, our job is to dispatch vermin. How do you know mice won't make a nest in a big bonnet when it's not on Harry's head? Think what might happen when she'd tie the bonnet on her head?*" Mrs. Murphy sounded perfectly serious.

"No Trianon?" Gary's eyebrows shot upward. "Harry, you disappoint me, but only a little. Your workshed, as you can see, has two large rooms, plenty of space to use the long desk against the wall, lots of windows and skylights for natural light, and an across-the-wall pegboard. You can hang up everything."

"That is useful."

"And you're sure you aren't going to buy a band saw?"

"No. I don't want to use gas- or electrical-powered

tools. They're too fast for me. Know what I mean? I'd rather do it the old way."

"The eighteenth-century way." He grinned at her.

"If it ain't broke, don't fix it." She shrugged and then looked at his one wall, built-in bookcases that he had designed, identical squares, bursting with books. "Have you read all those books?"

"I have but I've had decades to do so."

"What about those boxes on the bottom, the ones that look like fat old books? My father used to have those file boxes, as I recall," she asked.

"Building codes for the counties where I've designed a house or a barn. I can fit two per square as you see. Breaks up the visual monotony. Every file box is a year. You'd be surprised how often those codes are changed. Of course now you can download them, but I do prefer the files."

"Do you have the codes from when you worked for Rankin Construction?"

Rankin Construction was a large, third-generation company in Richmond. They had started before World War One and changed with the times. Now they built high-rises, stripped old tobacco warehouses, made pricey condominiums as well as office buildings.

"Yes, up until I left thirty years ago. I'm sure Rankin has kept everything."

"Did you like working on those large projects? You never talk about them."

"Well, I like architecture, old and new materials. I like efficiency and soundness. And Rankin is a good company but as it grew and grew, more and more layers of people meddled with my work. More and more building inspectors at every phase of the project. I learned to hate it so I packed up, moved here, and took my chances."

"You certainly hit the top. Your homes are featured in all those glossy magazines."

"Harry, I am just as happy creating the perfect work space for a good woman as I am putting together a two-million-dollar showplace. Why anyone wants to live in something like that is beyond me but hey, the commissions are good."

"You have sure helped us a lot with those old school buildings, and we are keeping the name, too, 'The Colored School.' I think it's important to be truthful."

"Me, too. Working with Tazio Chappars is a joy," he said, referring to a young architect who was making her way in the world to whom he was a mentor.

Dazzling Tazio, half Italian and half African American, took the best from both. She was also a person with a big heart. In a snowstorm years ago she had rescued a yellow Lab youngster abandoned and starving. Like most people she had no intention of owning a dog, and a big dog at that. But Tazio and Brinkley were a happy part of Crozet. If you saw one you saw the other.

Harry nodded. "She is talented, isn't she?"

"Very. Talented and practical, my two favorite qualities. Okay." He pointed back to his drawings, hand drawn. "The fireplace in the corner will heat the building up once the fire is going, but I suggest a small propane fireplace in the opposite corner diagonally kept on a low flame. Your pipes won't freeze."

"What pipes?"

"The pipes for your bathroom."

"I don't need a bathroom."

"Harry, I know you can pinch a nickle until the Indian rides the buffalo, but you do need a bathroom and you will thank me for tucking one into this structure. The other thing is I've made the ceilings fourteen feet high. A fan will push warm air down. It's not wasteful and the reason I've done that is over here; look, you have a quarter of the top space for storage. Just a small loft space. You can slide lumber up there or file boxes. It will be out of sight but protected." He paused. "Skylights in a high roofline always look good. Even the loft has a skylight."

"You can never get enough natural light."

"Trust me on the storage space and on the bathroom." His voice registered quiet command.

She sighed, sat on a high chair. "I'll have to talk to Fair."

"Your husband told me to give you the best shed in the county. And he said he wanted a cedar shake roof with clapboard siding. He swore he would keep it painted."

"He did?"

"Indeed. You married a most agreeable man." He beamed.

She beamed right back. "I did."

"I don't know why he puts up with you. He knows you don't give us enough home-cooked food. And he's a vet," Pewter complained.

"An equine vet," Tucker corrected her.

"So what. He knows how sensitive my system is."

"Pewter" was all Mrs. Murphy could say because Pewter could and did eat anything.

Her girth testified to the effectiveness of her digestive system.

"I should have fresh food. Nothing mixed into commercial food. And you don't know if that stuff came from China. Death!" Her eyes grew large.

Before the other two could vouch for the food not containing ingredients from China, a tap on the window drew their attention.

Gary motioned for Deputy Cynthia Cooper to step in.

She opened the door, closed it. "Getting colder out there." Then to Harry she said, "Saw your wagon."

"My stickers are updated." Harry smiled at her neighbor.

"Yes they are. Passing by. Another hour and I'll be off work. Gary, how are you doing? Is she being a good client?"

"Harry is always thoughtful and"—he paused—"cost conscious."

Cooper laughed. "What a nice way to say cheap."

"I am not cheap. I'm careful. Money doesn't grow on trees."

"I'm teasing you," Cooper replied. "You are tight with a buck, true, but you are generous with your time, food, your hospitality. You're always ready to pitch in and help."

Not expecting a compliment, Harry took a little time then said, "Thank you."

"She's right. You put your shoulder to the wheel," Gary agreed.

Gary, tiny sandbags in hand, lifted off the first sheet of large drawing paper, placing it under the others.

Harry's gaze wandered back to the square bookshelves covering one wall, so pleasing to the eye. He placed his treasures throughout his shelves. Snow globes had been stuck into many squares, smooth rocks from wherever he had gone rafting, one huge empty hornet's nest took up an entire square, a giant tooth reposed in another square, and tiny rubber dinosaurs peeped out from many places.

One globe always tickled Harry, a flamingo in a snow globe looking startled when you turned over the globe and snow fell on the pink bird.

Across the room hung an artillery officer's sword from the war of 1861–1865. The gilt still gleamed, the red sash with large tassels looked impressive. One could imagine them swinging when the officer walked in full dress regalia. A photograph of the fellow hung alongside the sword. This was Gary's great-great-grandfather, a slender young man with a serious mustache. How young he looked— but then, all wars are fought by the young.

"You and your snow globes." She smiled.

"Given the weather, we're in a snow globe," he replied.

"Got that right." Cooper nodded.

Harry returned to the drawings. "Forgot to ask you what else you're working on. Saw some of the redo for Nature First."

"Ah. I quite like how that is turning out. What did you think of the enameled bookshelves and cabinets?"

"Gorgeous."

He grinned. "I think so, too. It's been a fun project."

"Where did you get the idea for the slanting walls?"

"Flipping through some of the books on the shelves.

Something will jump out at me and I start to fool with the idea."

"So you saw Pirate, her puppy?"

"He's hard to miss. I'm glad she has him. Nature First goes up against some deeply vested interests. A big dog will be a deterrent if some large corporation hires a goon."

"Nature First does take them on," Cooper agreed.

"You think someone would harm her?" Harry was aghast.

"I certainly hope not but I wouldn't put it past one of these huge companies to try and scare her," Cooper replied. "Implied violence can be as effective as genuine violence."

"Harry, I didn't mean to disturb you." Gary put his hand on her shoulder. "We happen to be living through an incredibly corrupt time. Seems like every institution, including the churches, are corrupt. Ah well, perhaps we should envy Pirate and your four-legged fellow sidekicks. They have more sense than we do."

The door swung open. Tazio shut the cold air out behind her. Wearing leggings, high boots, a turtleneck peeping out from under her sheepskin coat, she looked great. Brinkley had a tiny wreath on his leather collar.

"Am I too late for the party?"

As the humans greeted one another so did the animals.

Gary motioned for Tazio and Cooper to sit in a chair. "Just in time. I was showing Harry my sketches for her shed. I want to recreate Le Petit Trianon but she won't have it."

Deadpan, Taz came back, "The Taj Mahal?"

"Too foreign. Mount Vernon would fit in." Cooper joined the play.

Harry, stroking her jaw as though in deep thought, said, "What about a yurt?"

All three at once responded, "Never. That's not Virginia."

"Who cares what it looks like?" Pewter fussed. *"She'd better have ceramic bowls with our names on them and a small refrigerator full of prime rib."*

Tucker said, *"I'm sure she'll do it just for you."*

"Taz, Gary, come on out. I made a big pot of chicken corn soup, my grandmother's recipe. Best thing for a cold day. Coop will be there. We can chew the fat."

"Literally." Tucker giggled as she stared adoringly at her human.

"Her secret is white corn, fresh parsley. I watch. She hard-boils eggs, makes the rice, she is serious about chicken corn soup. I quite like it." Mrs. Murphy twitched her whiskers.

"Thank you. I'd love to but I have a date with Paul, which really means we'll be with Big Mim, breeding papers all over the house." Tazio named Big Mim Sanborne, a wealthy woman, leader of society such as it was.

Big Mim would be breeding a few of her Thoroughbred mares in the early spring. She was breeding late but she didn't intend to race the foals. She wanted her stable manager, Paul, to turn them into foxhunters. With the exception of steeplechasing, a demanding sport for horse and jockey, Mim's flat racing days were over. It had all gotten too complicated, too expensive, and the variation of drug conditions from state to state drove her wild. She finally said, "The hell with it."

But by breeding in early spring the foals would arrive after the severe heat of a Virginia summer. Horses have an eleven-month gestation period.

"What about you, Gary?"

"I, too, must pass with regret. I told Hank Severson I'd meet him at his house to look at some flooring he took up from old granaries. Tell you what, he has a booming business. First he gets the job of dismantling old buildings then he resells the timber, hardware. He has a wonderful eye."

"Does." Harry had admired a floor Gary put in years ago at a friend's house, granary oak, how it glowed.

"Hey, Gary, see if he has any old cherry," Taz requested.

"Sure enough. If he doesn't have any, he'll find it."

They chatted, poured over the drawings again, all of them; then the little gathering broke up. They headed for the door, the animals tight behind Harry.

Opening it, a frigid wind, sharp, sliced them all in the face.

"It has gotten colder." Taz pulled up her heavy turtle-neck, as Brinkley stood next to her.

"December." Gary shrugged.

He'd run out to see the ladies off, had not pulled on a coat.

"Gary, you'll freeze to death," Cooper remarked.

A motorcycle turned the corner, slowed, making its way to the small group of people.

Brinkley barked. "I hate the sound of motorcycles."

"Another appointment?" Harry inquired.

"No." Gary, puzzled, shivered a moment.

The motorcycle, a large one, stopped. The driver, all in black leather, a tinted visor attached to the helmet, unzipped a pocket, pulled out a Glock handgun, pointed it at Gary, fired, paused a moment, the barrel of the gun visible to the three women, revved the engine, and sped off.

Gary, hand clutched to his heart, sagged. Cooper immediately put her hands under his armpits to steady him.

Harry ran out to see if she could read a license plate. She recognized the bike as a Ducati.

Taz moved over to help Cooper. "Let's get him into the warmth."

A gurgle told them it was too late.

Cooper tried to revive him. People came out of their stores. The three women managed to get him into his shop. His neighbor, Orrie Carson, rushed out, knelt down to see if he, too, could help.

"*He's dead,*" Mrs. Murphy quietly announced.

3

Shock or not the farm chores needed to be done. Home by three-thirty, Harry brought in the horses, put two scoops of grain in their feed buckets hanging in the corner of the stall, tossed in three flakes of hay.

Darkness came early. She liked to bring the horses in while light. She just made it. Large round bales dotted the various paddocks and pastures so the horses could eat when they felt like it. The large bales like shredded wheat looked coated in sugar due to the snow. Harry grew good hay, which her horses greatly appreciated. She'd place the bales together in some fields to break the wind. When eaten she'd bring in more. Some days the horses would all be next to the hay.

The top barn doors, closed against the cold, the bottom ones, too, kept the temperature pleasant for the horses.

Their ideal temperature is much lower than for humans. About fifty degrees Fahrenheit with their blankets on, fresh water in the two buckets per stall, life was good.

Pewter listened as Mrs. Murphy replayed the shooting. Tucker walked from stall to stall with Harry, who was always glad of the canine company.

"Quick," Pewter said.

"Couldn't see the killer's face, came right up to the edge of the sidewalk and boom." Mrs. Murphy sat on a saddle pad in the heated tack room.

"People kill one another like we kill mice."

Hearing Pewter, the mice came in behind the tack trunk, a small hole in the wall allowing them easy access. Their living quarters were stuffed with chewed up old towels, rag bits, and grain scattered about. They shouted, "Better not!"

"As long as you keep the deal, you're safe," the tiger cat reassured them.

"If anyone dies we should ask them to push out the body so we can bring it to Harry," Pewter suggested.

"Not now. She's too shook up," Mrs. Murphy responded.

"I mean when an old mouse dies. They seem to live forever those guys." Pewter sniffed.

"All the animals on this farm enjoy good health." Mrs. Murphy nodded.

"Hateful, hateful trips to the vet. Gives me angina. I just feel the palpitations." Pewter rolled her eyes.

"Tucker slobbers." Mrs. Murphy giggled.

"It's the needles!" Pewter's eyes now widened.

"Yeah," her buddy agreed.

"But back to people killing one another all the time. Gary must have done something wrong." Pewter inhaled the scent of cleaned leather.

"Mom told Cooper as they waited for the ambulance that years ago, like fifteen, he went through a horrible divorce. It brings out the worst in people."

"Fifteen years is a long time to wait." Pewter thought this unlikely as a cause.

"Revenge is a dish best eaten cold," Mrs. Murphy pronounced.

"I think if someone bloodies your nose you bloody them right back." Pewter appeared fierce.

"Humans, if they do that, get caught. Impulse killing. Waiting makes sense for them. All those laws perverting nature pretty much." The tiger believed humans got it all backward.

"Maybe fifteen years isn't a long time to wait ... but divorce, that's ... I don't know."

"Irrational." Mrs. Murphy affirmed Pewter's unspoken thoughts.

The tack room door opened, cold air entering with Harry and Tucker.

The corgi joined Mrs. Murphy on the saddle pad. "When the sun sets the mercury goes down with it. Going to be nasty cold tonight."

"Is," Mrs. Murphy agreed.

Harry checked her feed order, scribbled on a pad by the old landline phone, sank into her chair. She'd called her husband, who would be home from work shortly. She looked forward to Cooper joining them. Fair, sensitive to her distress, could always lift her spirits. As an equine vet his hours could be variable. One good thing about the winter was there were fewer injury calls than during the warm months, with the exception of ice. Horses, like people, could go down on ice.

"*Dad,*" Tucker barked.

The cats, too, heard the rumble of the big diesel-engine truck crunching down the driveway. Soon it stopped, the door slammed, the groan of the huge barn doors came next, then the clunk of their being shut.

The tack room door opened.

"Honey." He walked over and kissed her, pulled up a chair.

"I am so glad to see you."

"Heard a report on the local news driving home. The usual 'too early to know anything' stuff."

"Out of the blue, Fair, just out of the blue." She swiveled her chair to face his.

He slid the chair forward so his knees touched hers. "Thank God you weren't standing next to Gary."

"I was close enough to smell the gunpowder." She shivered. "He grabbed his chest, a little blood trickled through his fingers, not much at all, he groaned, and sank. There was a split second that it seemed the gun was pointed at me. It was almost like a dream. It just didn't seem real."

"*Cooper,*" Tucker barked.

Hearing the motor, Harry looked up. "I told Coop to come by for soup. Let me go in and warm it up. Won't take a minute. You fix her a drink."

They rose, animals first, closed the door behind them and hailed their friend walking up the brick walkway to the back closed-in porch. In the warm weather the wooden sides were removed and it became a screened porch that kept out the bugs.

Once inside, Fair made Cooper a hot toddy and fed the animals while Harry warmed the soup.

Sipping her drink, Cooper smiled. "Warms you better than a down jacket."

"True." He toasted her.

"Won't be a minute." Harry pulled fresh bread and butter out of the keeper on the counter.

"Well," Cooper started. "Simple .38 caliber, a handgun many people own. Unregistered, of course." She held up her hand. "I am not anti-science but I think there can be many a slip 'twixt the cup and the lip.' This will be a long, hard slog."

"Why?" Fair asked.

"No criminal record. An ugly divorce years back. No complaints against his design company at the Better Business Bureau. A member of Keswick Golf Club. Well liked. I called his old Richmond employer, Rankin Construction. He left on good terms. Had always wanted his own small design company, working with construction companies instead of working for a construction company."

"Is that awful yellow crime scene tape up?" Harry asked.

"It is. Front and back. Photographs of where he fell. The inside of his office. All done. The team, wearing latex gloves, checked drawers, cataloged mail. For now everything is in place as he left it. The forensics will be back tomorrow." She lifted her hands, palms up. "Nothing out of the ordinary, so far. But I always hope for a clue, for a pattern to emerge," Coop replied.

"I suppose you'll need to examine his projects. Talk to customers and clients." Harry tested the soup, turned down the burner.

"Yes. The most obvious problem would be if Gary ever overcharged or took a kickback from a client or construction company. That's all I can think of right now."

"He wouldn't." Harry's voice was firm. "Gary would never do anything like that."

"I hope you're right, but if there's one thing law enforcement has taught me it's that you never really know. Look at how Bernie Madoff fooled people."

"Coop," Harry said as she ladled out the fragrant soup. "Gary didn't live high on the hog like the Ponzi scheme guy. Other than golf and his annual vacations out of the country to see the architecture elsewhere, like the time he went to the Alhambra. Stuff like that. Madoff was an entirely different kind of person. Madoff had to drum up business constantly, whereas Gary really didn't." She put the bowls on the table while Fair cut the bread.

"Harry, this is so good." Cooper swallowed a spoonful.

"Easy to make but time-consuming. It's my grandmother's recipe. I do it exactly as she did. No shortcuts."

"Wonderful." Cooper sighed. "Wonderful to be off duty, too. It's been a day. Started with a false burglary alarm at Ivy Farms. Slid downhill from there. What about yours?" She looked at Fair.

"Not bad. One puncture wound but other than that

mostly paperwork and inquiries from new horse owners about keeping the weight on during winter."

"That should be easy. Feed them more." Cooper buttered her bread.

"Pretty much. Go light on pellets. Use senior food for the older guys. It's more expensive but properly fed those old horses will hold their weight. And a good blanket never hurts. An easy day."

Returning to her most pressing problem, Cooper said, "I called Dawn Hulme, Gary's ex-wife. Wanted to reach her before anyone else did. If you can do that you often get an unprepared response."

"And?" Harry's eyebrows rose.

"Shock. No phony sorrow. She said they rarely spoke over the years. I asked could she tell me why they divorced. She said she started proceedings. He never listened to a word she said and she was sick of it. He didn't beat her, run with other women. He was married to his work; but then, many men are. She repeated again that he never listened to anything she said, asked about her day, what she felt. Nothing. She asked him to go to counseling. He refused and her next call was to a divorce lawyer. And she admitted it was acrimonious."

Fair, spoon midair, remarked, "I listen."

"You do. Really, I'm the one who could be accused of not listening, of being a little dense," Harry confessed.

"A little!" Pewter yelled up from her food dish, painted with her name on the side.

"Now, Pewts," Mrs. Murphy said.

"She never listens to one thing I say. There's a box of rocks upstairs."

Pewter indicated Harry's brain, which did make the other two animals laugh.

"Don't you find it odd that we were standing on the sidewalk and the motorcyclist cruised up?" Harry wondered.

"No. Opportunity equals preparation. I think Gary would have been killed no matter what; and when the motorcyclist saw us there it presented a better opportunity than if he had to park, go into Gary's office, or wait for a client to leave. He might have left a few pieces of thread from his scarf or a tread from his boots, I don't know; but this way, slow down, drive over, pull the trigger. Nothing is left for forensics to pick up. Whoever did this can think quickly. At least that's my idea now."

"I would have never thought of that," Harry admitted.

"You don't need to." Cooper smiled.

"And it could have been a woman?" Fair inquired.

"The tinted visor of the helmet covered the whole face. Motorcycle clothing tends to be leather and given the wind, especially now that it's cold, I think anyone would wear a heavy leather jacket, leather pants, and boots. You wouldn't know gender from the clothing."

"Coop, I never heard one word about him running around after Dawn. That divorce must have throttled any thoughts of another relationship."

"Women do kill and, Harry, how do we know that wasn't a professional killer?"

"That's outrageous," Harry blurted out.

"So it seems, but I have to consider everything no matter how seemingly absurd. One thing I do know and that is that murder makes sense. The killer has a good reason to him or her. The only time I would waffle on that is impulse killing—you know, two guys are loaded at a bar, one thinks he's been mocked, a fight ensues, etc. That's impulse killing and the truth is that stuff happens mostly among the uneducated, the young. Of course, publicly I can't say that but generally an impulse killer is not too intelligent. Someone who kills in cold blood is."

"Ah," Harry murmured.

"Ah and don't try to solve this. Your curiosity does not serve you well." Cooper was firm. "Are you in danger? No, probably not. This killing was planned and worked out totally in the killer's favor. You start poking around, things might turn ugly."

"Hear, hear." Fair seconded Cooper.

"She doesn't listen to me. She won't listen to them," Pewter prophesied.

4

November 1, 1786

Wednesday

Still a bit warm, some leaves waved slightly on the trees as Ewing Garth with his two beautiful daughters walked west from the imposing brick house in which he lived. The girls, as he called them, each married to a good man, lived in identical clapboard houses one quarter of a mile from the main residence. Catherine was twenty-two, the elder by two years. Her house's back side faced west, the Blue Ridge Mountains. She could watch sunsets from the back porch. Rachel's home, opposite her sister's by perhaps another quarter mile, also faced the mountains. Rachel could repose on her front porch with her blond husband, watch the birds, watch the colors of the mountains change. For Catherine and Rachel this enticing vista made even the hard days worthwhile.

Ewing, a touch portly, stepped out briskly. He stopped at the edge of the harvested cornfield.

"Good year." He beamed.

"We have plenty stored along with oats, barley, and sweet, sweet hay," Catherine chimed in, happy, for she took charge of the extensive stables.

"Father, when are you coming with Charles and myself to see the progress at St. Luke's? You will be astonished at how much he has accomplished since the Taylors' funeral."

The Taylors, husband and wife, were buried October 15. Respected, liked, their mutual passing from lung disease brought everyone together. To these two people belonged the honor of being the first to sleep in the lovely cemetery roughly a hundred yards behind the church structure. Set off with stone walls, it seemed to promise peace.

The entire church, constructed of fieldstone, was topped with a slate roof. Quads behind the church reflected the central quad between the two wings, which resembled each other. A covered arched walkway on both sides connected the two buildings at the ends with the church. Even with the protection of the stone arches, if the wind blew the weather would hit you. The church itself sat smack in the middle, large lawns behind and in front of it. The exterior was complete. Now the fastidious interior work occupied Charles West, Rachel's husband.

"I will visit, I promise." His eyes swept down to a timber tract beyond the cornfield.

"You're still shocked that I've become a Lutheran," Rachel teased him.

"No, no, my dear. Your sister and I will uphold the Episcopal faith." He grinned.

Catherine slyly inserted, "Uphold not necessarily believe."

Ewing chuckled. "What would your sainted mother say?"

The two sisters looked at each other and laughed.

"I've seen regiments of woolly bears." Catherine cited the furry caterpillars seeking safe harbor to spin their cocoons.

"Yes, quite a few. Will be a hard winter. They portend such things." Ewing began to walk again. "I've heard that Roger Davis has been asked by Mr. Madison, James not William, to assist him with his voluminous correspondence and writing. Mr. Davis can speak Latin as fluently as Greek."

"And he never lets us forget it." Catherine grimaced for they were the same age but taught by different tutors.

"Too much Cicero." Rachel smiled. "I quite liked the poetry though."

"You're good with languages." Catherine complimented her younger sister. "I'm good with numbers."

"Ah yes," Ewing said. "I received a letter today from Baron Necker, my friend in Paris. It's interesting the people a young man meets on his grand tour. My father was wise to send me. Here it is thirty years later and the baron and I still write, he's somewhat younger, full of ideas. He told me the royal treasury is almost bankrupt, the French deficit is over a hundred million livres, and repayment of their debt is two hundred fifty million in arrears. Payment to the Army and Navy is now erratic, as it is for government ministers. You have a head for numbers, my dear, but clearly Louis XVI does not." He looked at his elder daughter.

"The numbers are so big it's hard to fathom." Rachel shook her head.

"We have domestic and foreign debt enough. Virginia is faltering at paying down her war debts. Indeed our leaders during the war appear not to have been able to add or subtract." Ewing relished the long slanting rays of the sun on his face. "I think we will discharge our debt but what about the other states? Then what?"

"Well, it can't be as bad as France." Rachel took some comfort in that, plus she wasn't too interested in politics.

"The king must call an assembly. There's no other way." Ewing sighed, for an assembly would bring problems of its own.

Any time a group of men gathered to decide upon weighty issues, little good rarely came of it, in his opinion.

"All France has to do is declare a war on Austria or Spain, march in, and steal whatever that nation has lying about. That's the way they do things over there." Catherine shrugged.

"Now, where did you hear that?" Ewing turned to her.

"From you, Father. You've always said they are a lot of squabbling children with an idiot at their head."

"Did I really say such a thing?"

"You implied it. You are much too gracious to be as blunt as I." Catherine reached for his hand and squeezed it.

"Well, no one in their right mind will lend France money." He stopped at the edge of the timber tract. "And if we don't set our own house in order, no nation will lend us anything either. No credit. You can't move forward without credit."

"Father, you have vats of credit." Catherine, who worked with her father, admired his business acumen.

"But I am not a nation. I can see to our increase but I can't manage the affairs of thirteen states, each of them so different from the other."

"We'd be better off if you did." Catherine praised him.

"Now you sound like your mother. She was always puffing me up." He grinned.

"Speaking of puffing up. Have you heard that Maureen Selisse Holloway"—Rachel used both her married names for Maureen's first husband had been murdered—"is rumored to be trying to buy a title for Jeffrey?"

Jeffrey was the second husband, divinely handsome, perhaps fifteen to twenty years younger than his fabulously wealthy wife. She wasn't telling.

"What?" Catherine's jaw dropped.

"Yes. DoRe told Bettina." Rachel mentioned the head of Maureen's stable, a middle-aged widower who was courting their head cook and head slave woman, herself a widow. All crossed their fingers that this would work out and each feared, but kept silent, that Maureen would find a way to hold back DoRe.

"We don't have titles here," Ewing forcefully said.

"She's painted her coat of arms from her birthplace in the Caribbean on her coach. She'll buy him a title then pretend it's of no consequence, but we will be expected to address them as Count Pooh-bah," Catherine predicted.

"Foolishness." Ewing turned for home.

"But amusing to watch." Catherine slipped her arm through his as did Rachel on his other side.

"Father, if DoRe asks Bettina to marry him, you will have to buy him. It's only right."

"Yes, yes."

"And you will have the two best coachmen in Virginia. Won't that give Yancy Grant hives."

Catherine mentioned their head coachman, Barker O., as well as another horse breeder.

"Maureen will make it difficult." Rachel knew how petty and vicious Maureen could be.

"Oooh," Ewing drawled, "if the baronetcy or dukedom is dear enough she'll sell and sell quickly."

"How do you feel?" Rachel asked her sister, changing the subject.

"Fine. I'm only in my third month. This is it. No more. Two children is enough."

"Three," Rachel announced. "Three and I also have three."

Rachel had two girls.

"No, I am not having three children."

"You have John and I have Charles." Rachel laughed out loud as she mentioned their husbands.

"You girls go to the same school. Your mother used to say that about me. She'd call me her 'old boy.'"

"It is true, Father? Men don't grow up." Rachel pinched him as she said that.

"I feel old enough. My bones creak," he complained.

"Pfiffle. You can wear out men half your age. You're trying to work on our sympathies," Catherine remarked.

They all laughed as arm in arm they strolled back, the air chilling now that the sun had set. Three people bound by blood, by the times, by deep love. How fortunate that they could not see the future, but then no one can.

5

"You have a sharp eye," Cooper noted.

"I don't know about that but I try to notice things." Harry stood in the small foyer of Gary Gardner's office. She'd been asked to meet Cooper there as she knew his office work habits well.

"He worked alone. Small operation. He was the creative one. He really didn't need other people, especially with what computers can do now."

"That's what he always said. That's why he moved here. The company became too big in Richmond, too many layers of people piddling in his work. He was happy here."

"The way of the world these days. Nothing gets done quickly, that's for sure. Everyone wastes time covering their ass." Cooper noticed the framed photographs on the walls. "So I've been talking to former clients. No one has had a bad word to say about him." Cooper turned to face Harry. "How often would you say you've been in his office?"

"A lot. He came here in the mid-eighties. I was a kid when he moved here, but he and Mother got on so I'd accompany her to his office. He designed homes or additions for friends; as I got older I'd see him socially. He did a beautiful job for Nelson and Sandra Yarbrough, also Sara Goodwin. People saw his work. He helped Tazio Chappars and our group with the old school buildings we're returning to their original state but with modern plumbing, etc. They researched old photographs, building materials of the time, really the late-nineteenth century. He made it fun and since neither one could design anything new, they didn't butt heads. I doubt that they would have anyway."

Tazio Chappars, in her late thirties now, moved to the area after graduate school. Her family and college friends, Midwesterners, warned her that Virginia, a Southern state, would not be welcoming. They were wrong. Then again Tazio, warm, good-natured, could win over most people.

Cooper returned to the expensively framed colored photographs. "I'm not an architectural historian but I do read. Mostly everyone around here wants the Georgian or Federal look, he seemed more influenced by the French."

Harry smiled. "Gary swore there were enough people in the area to design à la Palladio. He went his own way. He teased me and said I needed to expand my history mostly in the direction of the French."

Cooper smiled back. "So is anything different in here?"

"The office?" Harry moved into the large room with his big computer, the drafting table in the middle of the room, also large, a regular desk, and the square bookshelves all along one wall.

"My plans are still on the table." She looked up and around, walked over to the bookshelves. "Coop."

The tall deputy came alongside her friend. "What?"

"These shelves were packed. Some books are missing."

"Could he have taken them home?"

"No, because when we met, I was here at the drafting table. The shelves were full."

"Can you remember any of them?"

"Beautiful picture books. They're still here." She pointed to large coffee table books of French architecture, a few on great American houses. "His Vitruvius's *De Architectura* is still here."

Cooper pulled one off the shelf, as there were ten volumes. "It's in Latin."

"Gary said it was easy to read because it's so technical. Little has changed. He went to an expensive prep school, St. Paul's, I think. The boys had to take Latin. Said it was the best thing he ever did."

"You took a language, didn't you?"

"French. Four years in high school, four at Smith, and I'm still lousy at it. Occasionally he'd say something in French just to tweak me. Gary was a highly educated man."

"Think. What's missing?"

Harry slowly walked along the shelves, stopping at the

gaps in the lined-up books. "Did you look in his computer?"

"Our tech wiz did. The only thing he mentioned was that Gary kept records of his recent work but nothing concerning Richmond."

"I would guess Rankin Construction Company has records of his designs there. And as far as I know no one here ever complained about his work in Richmond."

"No."

Harry stopped at a gap on a lower shelf. "Mmm."

"What."

"He kept boxes, you know those boxes like extra-large fat books. He kept building codes in them. They're gone."

"Building codes. I'll have his house double-checked but I don't remember them."

"You know the big orange kind, looks like hard cardboard, old books. I can't imagine anyone stealing them because you can get all that stuff online." Harry was puzzled.

"Did you ever look in them?"

"No."

"Then you don't know what was in them."

"You're right. But I do remember what was printed on the spines: codes and the years they were updated or changed from before he moved here. The recent changes he got off the computer. Every county has their own codes. Confusing, to me anyway."

"Anything else?"

"No," Harry replied as she returned to her design on

the drafting table. "But you all secured this office. The files are missing. Did the department take them?"

"No." Cooper frowned. "The files were taken after the scene was supposedly secured. I'm not familiar with this office, but you are. I just felt something was off."

"Let me ask you a question. How many Ducatis are registered in Albemarle County?"

"Very few. Six and one is from the late 1950s." She paused. "We've spoken to each of the owners. No one was riding yesterday. We'll send Dabney out"—she named a young fellow officer—"to double-check the models, but since we don't really know the model of the bike on which the killer rode all we can do is gather stats and wait." Cooper glanced outside as a light snowfall was starting. "How'd you know what the bike was?"

"Motorhead. And I read all the car and bike magazines. That was a brand-new Ducati XDiavel. Cost about fifteen thousand dollars. No license plate."

"That bothers me." Cooper frowned. "You'd think some traffic cop would have noticed."

"You would, but then again maybe the killer didn't ride far. Maybe that bike is in a garage or maybe he towed the bike here in a closed trailer from who knows where, unloaded, did the deed, loaded it back up again. It's not too far-fetched."

Cooper had known Harry enough years to appreciate her logic if not her curiosity. "I guess not if you're determined to kill someone. If only it were his ex-wife," she ruefully admitted.

"Cooper!"

"It would make this a lot easier."

Harry changed the subject. "I don't know why it gets me, but it gets me that my plans are on the drafting table. Like he just stepped out."

"He did." Cooper sighed. "He did."

6

"*She'll ruin her eyes,*" Pewter predicted.

"*She doesn't use her computer that much,*" Tucker countered the gray cat. "*It's Fair who will ruin his eyes, with that big screen in his office here and the same kind at work. He checks his patients, he checks medications and X-rays. I'm surprised he doesn't have a Seeing Eye dog.*" Tucker flicked a large left ear.

Both her ears were large, her hearing proved excellent.

"*You could do it.*" Mrs. Murphy sat on Harry's desk in the tack room so she, too, could view the screen.

"*Too low to the ground. He'd trip over me,*" Tucker sensibly replied.

"*What is she doing?*" Pewter could hear click, click, click.

"*Jump up and see for yourself,*" Mrs. Murphy suggested.

Grumbling, Pewter did rouse herself from the tack trunk, stretch, then leap onto the desktop. As it was an old teacher's desk from the 1950s, sturdy solid wood, her weight barely registered. The desk had been Harry's father's. He didn't believe in wasting money when used furniture could do the job. Finding a teacher's desk was easy. He paid fifteen dollars, sanded it smooth, then stained it.

A small bright red propane stove with a glass front kept the tack room warm. Last year, after exhausting research, Harry had bought one, a Swedish model, for no matter what she tried, the room temperature barely got above sixty degrees. The space heaters sucked up electricity like mad, plus they really couldn't evenly warm the room. The flames at this moment flickered at half-mast. Full blast really threw out the heat. When she went home at night, she'd only leave on the pilot light, but come morning she'd turn up the flame and the room would be perfect in about fifteen minutes. Harry wondered how she'd lived all those years in that miserable cold room. And she knew Gary was a hundred percent right to design space for one in her dream shed. She had just wanted to fuss with him a little bit.

The door to the center aisle, closed, had a large glass window in it. Because Crozet was near the mountains, the sun set earlier than the Farmer's Almanac listed for central Virginia. She was so wrapped up in her computer she didn't notice that the sun had set, twilight was deepening at 5:45 PM.

The horses, blankets on, began to doze in their stalls. The doors at both ends were shut as were the hayloft doors up top. Every now and then a big barn door would rattle when the wind hit it. She heard it but paid little attention.

"That's it."

Pewter peered at the screen. "Is."

"Is." Mrs. Murphy echoed her friend then looked down at a curious Tucker. *"The motorcycle. She's got a picture of it."*

"A beast. This thing is a beast." Harry whistled. "1262cc. And they make faster bikes but this is their cruiser. Some cruiser."

"Does look scary. Well, it was scary," Mrs. Murphy spoke.

"Big Harley?" Tucker, living with a motorhead, had absorbed some of her human's nomenclature.

"No. It's a Ducati XDiavel. That's what the caption says," Pewter remarked.

"Pewter, you can't read." Tucker doubted her report.

"She's whispering stuff," Pewter called back. *"Stuff like this is for the American market. It's not the pure Italian bike. She thinks that's important. She's scrolled that information three times."*

"She's falling in love. You know how she is with anything with an engine in it!" Mrs. Murphy laughed.

Harry tapped her fingers on the desktop, rattling against the wood. "Whoever shot Gary knew bikes and could ride them. No license plate. Who the hell is this? Who would think of such a thing?"

"Someone with a lot to lose," Tucker murmured.

"Or gain," Mrs. Murphy responded.

Hitting the off button, Harry slumped in her chair. "There can't be too many of these in all of Virginia. Cooper can get the state DMV records."

Pewter, shrewd in her own way, brushed against the

screen. "But maybe it's an out-of-state bike. If someone was smart enough to pull this off, I bet they'd be smart enough to know how scarce a XDiavel is."

Tucker, thinking hard, nodded. "You've got a point there."

"Does his ex-wife ride bikes?" Pewter wondered.

Mrs. Murphy swept her whiskers forward. "The ex–Mrs. Gardner is a big BMW girl. She is a woman who takes her makeup seriously."

"Why would he marry a woman like that?" Tucker was puzzled.

"He was a lot younger. And she is pretty even now with all that paint on her face." Mrs. Murphy was fair about it. "I'm not sure men think clearly about these things when they're young."

Pewter quoted Harry's work partner from the old Crozet post office. The wonderful Mrs. Miranda Hogendobber was now in her late seventies although she wasn't advertising. "Miranda always said, 'Marry in haste. Repent in leisure.'"

They giggled as Harry rose, flicked off the lights, turned the stove down to the pilot light, pulled on her beat-up Carhartt Detroit work coat with the wool flannel lining, rummaged for her gloves. "Let's go, kids."

As she opened the tack room door to the center aisle the cold hit her. It wasn't that bad in the barn, probably mid-forties. Being in a warm place, then stepping outside, the cold was so noticeable, it took time to adjust.

Simon, the possum, peeked over the side of the hayloft. His nest, hollowed out of a hay bale, backed to the west, which helped blunt the cold, even though the barn was closed up. Remnants of old blankets and towels kept him warm, plus he could fluff up the hay and snuggle in his blanket surrounded by sweet-smelling hay.

"*I'm going to eat fallen grain. Too nasty to go out.*"

"*See you tomorrow,*" Mrs. Murphy called up to her odd-looking friend.

"*Try to get her to bring some cookies, will you? Anything with molasses in it.*"

"*We'll try,*" Tucker promised.

Harry slid open the barn doors, squeezed through as did the animals. "Great day!"

She'd been so focused on her bike research she hadn't gotten up to look around. Three inches of snow had fallen thick and fast, blown sideways by a stiff wind.

The four ran to the porch door but the animals allowed Harry to go first. She'd make a trail for them that would be easy for them to walk in.

Harry stomped her boots on the porch, then wiped her feet on the rug and opened the kitchen door, grateful for the warmth. Even dashing that short distance, her cheeks were red, cold. The dog and cats shook their paws.

Hanging her coat on a peg by the door, she walked into the living room, knelt down, started crumpling paper. Then she built a good log pile, starting with a square of logs, the center open. She put the paper in that center, crisscrossed logs on top of the square, remained on her knees, jammed fatback under the newspapers. She stood up, brushed off her pants' knees, plucked up a box of long matches, struck one, knelt down and touched the flame to the papers.

"*You know, it's work building a good fire,*" Tucker noted.

"Well, she won't turn up the thermostat. The wind will drop the indoor temperature. This way we'll stay nice and cozy." Pewter loved her creature comforts.

"Did the weatherman predict a storm?" Mrs. Murphy didn't remember that.

"No," Tucker replied.

"Well, we've got one," Pewter announced.

A big diesel motor rumbled, drew louder, then cut off. The outside porch door opened and closed, the kitchen door opened. Fair stepped into the kitchen, breathed deeply.

Harry walked over to kiss her husband. "Glad there weren't any traffic problems."

"There will be." He removed his coat. "I think I got out just in time."

She made him a hot cup of ginger tea, sat across from him at the kitchen table, the same table her parents had used.

"Are you hungry?"

"A little." He put his hands around the cup.

"I'll warm up the potpie."

"Food like that makes winter, mmm, almost desirable." He smiled. "How was your day?"

She filled him in then finally got to the Ducati XDiavel.

"Remember my old Norton?" He sipped, felt a little jolt when the ginger hit.

"Sure do." She then cited all the stats on the powerful Ducati motorcycle.

"Well, tell Cooper. 'Course, she may have already researched that herself."

"Fair, this murder was well thought out and I so adored that man. Seeing him crumple like that, losing such a talented, kind person, I feel awful and really angry."

"That's natural. He was a wonderful man and he adored you as well. However, you are not a law enforcement officer." Fair stopped his lecture right there.

"Don't worry."

"*Ha!*" all three animals said at once.

"What torments me is what did he do to anyone? Nothing that we know about. You'd think something would have leaked out over the years. He wasn't rich, comfortable but not rich. He was well known in his field but he wasn't, what, a star? He would get good designing jobs but he never rubbed in his success. Anyway, there's enough work and money in this county to go around. I can't think he had an outraged competitor. No debts that any of us heard about and no political stuff. He'd vote but politics bored him. I certainly never heard him in an argument. Usually, he'd shrug his shoulders. He was a social drinker. Never once heard him talk about drugs and, well, he wasn't the type. He was a good man."

"Yes, he was." Fair took a deep breath. "Maybe it's middle-age. Maybe it was always around me but I didn't notice before. But, honey, what I see are good people getting screwed every day."

"Screwed, yes. Murdered, no."

7

November 7, 1786

Tuesday

Yancy Grant inhaled the odors of delicious food. Much as he loathed the long three-day journey from Albemarle County to Richmond, ninety miles east, once he arrived at Georgina's, a marvelous tavern with a few rooms available for special guests, a wave of contentment would wash over him. The beautiful girls, some served food, some did not, were also available. Occasionally Yancy would hire the services of one, but since his kneecap was shattered in a recent duel, pleasures became more difficult and his temper could fray with the constant pain.

Seated across from him, Sam Udall, a financier who could supply certain functions of a bank as well as more discreet monetary exchanges, also inhaled. "Lifts the spirits." He held up his glass of expensive French wine to his companion.

Yancy replied in kind, although he needed to be careful since too much alcohol made him impulsive and violent. That was the reason his kneecap was shattered. He foolishly accepted the challenge to a duel from a man, Jeffrey Holloway, he considered his social inferior and therefore not a good shot. Middling men rarely achieved the refinements of horsemanship, shooting, or musical accompaniment, if so gifted, that a man of parts took for granted. Yancy considered himself a man of parts. He was. He risked his fortune to back the rebels as did Ewing Garth. Had the former colonists lost that war, they would have been hanged. But like so many men who raised regiments, paid for food, temporary housing, and firearms, the state of Virginia had barely begun to repay those large outlays of cash. Other states were even worse off, although that was hard for the Virginians to believe. When you need money and aren't getting it, it doesn't matter if someone in North Carolina, a state whose only marketable products were pitch, tar, and turpentine, is worse off.

The two men pleasantly chatted. Yancy would be owing Sam a tidy sum of loaned cash come April.

Georgina, the proprietress, glided over to them. "Yancy Grant, you live too far away. How wonderful to see you and looking so well. As for you, Sam, how could I thrive here without your wisdom?"

"Ah, Georgina, you flatter me." Sam nodded slightly.

Sam and Georgina did talk business. Both impressed the other as each responded to public events without a leaning toward the philosophy of Mr. Jefferson or Mr. Adams. The difference between a strong centralized government and a looser one was not of too much concern. Profits motivated them. The concern was the unpaid debt, credit difficulties, the signs of financial insecurity in France, plus an abiding fear of England.

Europe craved products from the new United States. Except for England, other countries wanted to deepen relationships with the former colonies, free of the economically restrictive hand of England. Merchants in England wanted favorable terms with the new country. Parliament teetered one way then the next, although the anger against Lord North, prime minister and architect of the war, diverted some attention from commerce.

Georgina left them to chatter in peace. A new girl, Sarah, delivered their food.

Yancy cut open his chicken pie, a plume of steam rising upward. "You know, Sam, much as I enjoy those sauces and fripperies the French can concoct, I do so love chicken pie. My mother used to make it."

"Solid food for the cold." Sam savored a lamb chop standing straight up, stuffed with a thin glaze of mint jelly. Eudes, the cook and a free man of color, dazzled the clients with his specialties. An ordinary cook would have basted the lamb chop, then put a glob of green mint jelly by its side. Not Eudes. He stuffed the thick chop, stood it upright on a fine china plate, a small helping of tiny potatoes next to it, sprinkled with parsley and sitting in a light butter sauce.

Both men enjoyed the food, the wine.

Occasionally Deborah would serve in the afternoon but usually she did not. So great was her beauty she was reserved for the nights only and then to sing next to the fellow playing the pianoforte. But if a powerful client, new, arrived in the afternoon, usually brought by a regular customer, Deborah would appear. She made men crazy. She made Georgina money. She made herself money, too.

The beauty walked by the two men, smiled, kept walking toward Georgina's office.

"Aphrodite." Sam grinned.

"A Venus to be sure, but I always think of the goddess as a Greek, when the Greeks were blonds, you know?"

Sam, an educated man, laughed. "When the Romans conquered Athens they took all the beautiful ones back to Rome to teach their children perfect Greek."

Yancy, educated at William and Mary, had some basis in Latin, in Greek. One was not considered educated without the ability to understand Latin. Greek was desirable but Latin was essential. "Odd, is it not? That if you are upper class you don't speak the native tongue, that's vulgar." He used the Latin word for common people, which transformed in English to mean still common but with a stray whiff of dirty, stupid, not worthy of consideration.

"Well, it is. Fortunately, we are not so afflicted. The Russians speak French." He paused. "But then everyone speaks French to an extent. It truly is the language of diplomacy."

"What then, Sir, is the language of finance?"

"Ah, English. Without a doubt. The French have had rich episodes in their history, but for business it's hard to beat a practical, intelligent Englishman. Which we once were," Sam slyly said.

"I have my doubts about us," Yancy glumly replied, then, not wanting to be dour, added, "If we can resolve these current monetary difficulties, I think we will be fine."

"Difficulties?" Sam's eyebrows raised. "Our government has no monetary policy."

"Hamilton is trying."

"One man. And one man who seems to divide others. Some like him. Others loathe him. We need men of acumen to step up and support him as his ideas are the correct ones. Men like Gouverneur Morris." He named a wealthy man from New York.

"If we could just get together the men of means from Boston, from Charleston, Philadelphia, even New York, which is growing." Yancy, hotheaded though he might be, was a solid businessman.

Sam leaned forward. "Yes, and do you know what I really think? We'd better clean up these war debts both internally as well as foreign. We must have a unified Army and Navy. Militias won't do."

"But we won the war." Yancy was surprised.

"My good Sir, our resources are beyond a European's imagining. But once they truly understand, they will be back."

This hit Yancy. "Oh, I hope not."

"Think of it, Yancy. The great rivers we have depositing all that rich soil as they flow to the sea. The impossibly long seacoast and now the Ohio territory is opening, and that is vast, vast. More riches. In Europe a day or two in a coach and you are in another country. Here you can travel for weeks in a coach and you are still in the United States. And who are our neighbors?"

"Spain to the south and England to the north. Both could attack us through their colony." Yancy's mind was spinning now. "And Canada is large, difficult climate but still more resources than any other foreign country."

"They could but England must ferry their Army across the Atlantic and then live off the land. That will be quite difficult because we will fight them as the Indians fight. They have no inkling of that, nothing. Look how they fought our glorious war for independence."

"They nearly won." Yancy felt that time acutely.

"Until we pulled together. And we have Washington." Sam spoke the name with reverence.

"Sam, you always give me much to think about."

"We live in a tumultuous time." He paused, finishing the last of the magical lamb chop. "By the way, I was surprised that you paid a thousand dollars against your loan."

"Hemp. My hemp crop proved lucrative." Yancy knew he was interested in that.

"Ah. Have you been down to the river yet? New warehouses for hemp, for tobacco, much in demand. I heard Ewing Garth is betting on apples and installed an orchard. New. Not really yielding much yet. Too young. He is uncommonly shrewd."

"He spreads the risk. Tobacco land in North Carolina as well as south of the James. Some hemp and so much hay. He has large tracts of established fields. He does not reveal his holdings, but it is rumored in Virginia that he owns eighty-eight thousand acres."

"An impressive man." Sam's eyes followed Deborah as she carried a package back through the tavern.

"Very. His elder daughter is also impressive. She inherited her father's brain." He paused. "Beautiful girl. Her younger sister, Rachel, is also beautiful but it's a softer beauty. She is much like her own mother, excels at gardening, setting a good table, putting people at ease, and I've heard she's been helping her husband set up St. Luke's Church. Funny, isn't it, how we can be so different from our brothers and sisters while retaining qualities in common?"

"Yes." Sam considered his sister, much like him in her focus on the practical, on getting ahead. "It's the older sister I wish to talk about. She breeds good horses, does she not?"

"Yes. She has the eye and she memorizes bloodlines."

"And will she race this spring, do you think?"

"I don't know."

"Talk to her. Convince her there's money to be made." Sam paused. "A great deal of money. I can arrange a betting network." He held up his hand. "But no one will know that you and I are behind it. A percent will flow to us regardless of who wins. See to it, Yancy."

"There will be money for the winner?"

"Of course. Think of England, the races there. Those who bet on the winning horses will reap a handsome sum. The betting agents, their tickets stuck on their bet boards, should make some money. But we will make the most. We take a percent from each agent, we sell tickets to the race, too. We run the race in pairs per horse and we charge an entry fee. In other words, we can't lose if the right horses are running."

"Where?" Yancy simply asked.

"The Levels by the James." Sam smiled.

That would be the only level thing about this proposed contest.

8

December 31, 2016

Saturday

The rich twilight blue seemed to make the falling snow even whiter. The silence, broken only by the horses munching in their stalls, promised purity, a time to think, a time to cleanse. Harry strolled down the center aisle checking on everyone. Shortro, a young gray, lifted his head from the feed bucket, looked at her with soft brown eyes, then returned to the delicious food.

Mrs. Murphy and Tucker kept Harry company. Pewter remained in the warm tack room. Why be cold?

The possum, curled up in his luxurious hay bale, snored slightly. The great horned owl, nesting in the cupola, also closed her eyes. Tonight was a night to stay indoors.

Harry turned the stove down to the pilot light, checked her notes on the desk, and slipped out of the tack room, closing the door behind her, Pewter in tow.

The little family used the small side door at the corner of the stable. Harry knew pushing open the huge double doors with the snow on the ground now would be difficult. As it was, enough snow had fallen in the two hours she was in the barn that she needed to put her shoulder on the door to push it open. The new snow piled up on the old snow.

"I'll be digging that out tomorrow morning."

Once inside the house, the kitchen felt wonderful. She refreshed the fire she'd built in the living room, checked the propane heater in the bedroom, quite a large room. Thank heaven they'd installed the fireplace last summer. A regular fireplace commanded the center of the room. During a night like this one would prove to be, Fair would build a fire there but neither one needed to feed the fire anymore. That propane fireplace in the corner kept them warm.

The old clapboard farmhouse, elegant in its simplicity, had a fireplace in most of the rooms. The walls, stuffed with horsehair, proved the old way of insulating worked. But the windows, handblown, couldn't keep out the cold. Harry thought it would be sacrilege to remove them. The cold air seeped under those windows no matter what. As to the attic, when they were first married, Fair insulated that space. All in all, considering that the house was built in 1834, it testified to the wisdom of her ancestors.

The twilight deepened to Prussian blue, the snow looked like a curtain. In the distance to her right she saw diffuse headlights, heard the truck. Fair pulled into an old shed that served as a makeshift garage. No point digging out his truck. He walked from there to the house, stopping to look skyward.

Then he reached the porch, stepped inside, stomped his boots, took off his cowboy hat, shook it, opened the door. "Honey, I'm home."

"*We* know," Pewter replied.

Tucker bounded up for a pet, Harry for a kiss.

"How bad are the roads?"

"Snowplows are out," he answered. "It's coming down so hard they won't be able to keep up with it. Coop's working tonight, isn't she?"

"She is. I worry about her on New Year's Eve no matter what. This makes it worse."

"Sensible people will stay home."

She smiled. "Fair, it's New Year's Eve. Will anyone young be sensible?"

"I sure hope so." He draped his arm around her shoulders. "I don't mind staying in. Susan and Ned always have their New Year's Eve party at Big Rawly with her grandmother and mother, but surely they'll cancel. It's off Garth Road, a ways back, and no one is going to plow the private road."

As if reading his thoughts, the phone rang.

"Susan."

"Oh, Harry, I'm canceling. But you know in all the years my family has held their New Year's Eve party I think they've only canceled maybe three times. 'Course when granddad was alive he'd go outside and do whatever needed to be done or he'd call someone. I'm sorry."

"Well, it will be a quiet way to start 2017. We'll make up for it somewhere down the road."

"I think so, too. Ned and I texted everyone except for Mom and Grandmother. Called them and I'm calling you. Have you made any New Year's resolutions?"

"Not yet. Have to think about that. You?"

"Yes. I'm not going to watch the news in 2017. Just makes me crazy."

"Hey, that's a good resolution." Harry smiled. "Maybe I'll borrow yours."

"Well, Happy New Year, Sweetie."

"Back at you." Harry hung up the old wall phone, told Fair Susan's resolution.

"She's got a point there. How about if we sit in front of the fire? I'll make you a light hot toddy. For the season."

"Okay."

"I'll have chicken and catnip. For the season," Pewter meowed.

Fair, seeing an upturned gray face staring intently into his own, opened the cupboard dedicated to pet treats, distributed bacon bits.

"It's not chicken and catnip but it's not bad." Pewter stuffed her mouth.

"Good way to celebrate." Mrs. Murphy also grabbed bacon bits.

Tucker chewed on a large bacon strip, too big for the kitties. Conversation could wait.

Harry stoked the fire, threw on another log, settled into the old sofa as Fair joined her with the promised hot toddy.

"You, too?"

He nodded. "Cold night. Hot drink."

Shoulder to shoulder, watching the flames jump, listening to the crackle and pop, they put their stockinged feet on the old coffee table.

"This old house has welcomed one hundred and eighty-three New Year's," Harry mused. "Some were hopeful and I'm sure some were not. I can't imagine what they felt in 1859."

"Mmm, all that tension. It exploded soon enough." Fair knew his history. "Do you think countries go in cycles?"

"I do. Seneca and a lot of the Romans thought so. The Stoics. I'm not as clear on my philosophy as I should be, but they wrote a life cycle for nations, for people. There's nothing new. New technology, but nothing new about people or cultures. They rise and they fall."

"Sobering."

"I guess. It's the way of the world. Every now and then I'll go back through the family Bibles, the birth dates, the death dates, the notes. I am proud of my people. They worked hard. Some thought backward, I guess, others were forward-thinking, but they did their duty; they knew life promised you nothing."

"Not a current attitude." He sipped his drink.

"Fair, we had a frontier. We could always go west until we hit the Pacific. I think attitudes began to change. We started to look inward. Industrialism began to affect everyone and everything. Cities grew large then huge."

"Now that you mention it, you're right. Once we hit the West Coast there was no longer an escape valve."

"You know, honey, we're just too big. Too many people. We're starting to get in one another's way."

"How about China or India? Talk about getting in one another's way." He jumped slightly when a log popped loudly. "Sounded like a gunshot."

"Did." She laughed then changed to a more somber mien. "Hearing that gunshot, a pop like the log . . . I've grown up with rifles and guns, I know the sound, but to hear a pop then see Gary crumple. I can't get it out of my head."

"I wish I could tell you something helpful. I hope in time the memory will fade. Sometimes I think all the violence in the media, news, films, TV stuff, I feel like we've been narcotized to violence. It makes me wonder why violence is entertainment, you know?"

"I do, Sweetie. We've had friends die in car accidents, some to cancer far too young. Central Virginia is not a particularly crime-ridden area but stuff happens here. This was a friend, someone I admired and liked. It haunts me," she said.

They sat in silence for a while.

"Coming down harder." Fair glanced out the window.

"It's so dark."

"The light reflects out a bit. This storm is bigger than the weatherman predicted." He sighed. "Life in and by the mountains. We have our own weather system."

He drew her closer to him. "Can't get cold if I'm close to you."

She smiled. "Flatterer. Have you made any New Year's resolutions?"

"No. I should but I never keep them." He smiled sheepishly. "One year I vowed to go regularly to the gym."

"I never could figure that one out. You're in great shape."

"My work keeps me pretty fit, so does farming, but there's muscles you don't use, and I never stretch. I figured the gym would keep me limber. Oh, then there was the year I promised to read *Remembrance of Things Past*. That lasted two chapters. Better to forget the whole thing."

She put her head on his shoulder. "My resolution is to live every moment. No plans for the future. Live in the here and now. Be grateful for you, this farm, my friends, my four-footed friends. Be grateful for my health." She snapped her fingers. "Could be gone like that."

Harry, five years out from breast cancer, felt she was cured, but she no longer took health for granted.

"Good resolution. I'll try it, too."

Harry rose, stirred the fire, walked to the window. "I can barely see the ornamental cherry tree by this window. Must be coming down two or three inches an hour."

"I'm sure The Weather Channel will know."

"Are you hungry?"

"No. I'll be hungry in the morning," he replied.

"I hope we have power in the morning. All it takes is one car to skid off the road, take out a pole."

"Maybe that will happen on the other side of the county, not our side."

"Yeah, sure." She grinned, continuing to look out the window. "Hope all the foxes, deer, bear, birdies are tucked up."

"You know they are. They're smarter about the weather than we are. Come on and sit back down. I miss you already."

She snuggled next to him. The cats each claimed a lap, Tucker flopped in front of the fireplace.

Cooper, snug in a large county SUV, parked in the lot where Routes 250 and 240 separate, one going straight into Crozet and the other veering slightly south of that. Fortunately, there wasn't much traffic. After a few hours of this, her shift about to end, she turned for home, driving west on Route 250. Sheriff Shaw told her not to worry about getting the car back to the station. Just take it home, come back out in the morning.

Heading down 250 she passed the small shopping center with Harris Teeter and the BB&T bank, kept going. As she kept heading west, she noticed across from Legacy Market and the BP station, a car halfway down the road. She called in the site. It would need to be towed off the road. She put on her flashers, got out, pulling on her jacket, took out her flashlight. No one in the Toyota Yaris, brand-new, too.

Eager to get back in the county SUV, she called out, "Anyone here?"

The wind drowned out her voice. The snow fell so thick, so fast. She could barely see her hand in front of her face. Nonetheless, she walked along the roadside on both sides in both directions for fifty yards. Nothing. She couldn't even make out the lay of the land. If anyone had turned off the road, she'd only see them if she came right up on them.

She called as she walked. No response.

Finally she gave up, returned to the SUV, gratefully opened the door.

There had been a few accidents. She hoped it wouldn't be hours before a tow truck showed up. Luckily Jason Harvey, down on Route 151, just finished up a small mess at the 151 and 250 stoplight, took the call, headed east on 250 for Cooper.

She saw the tow truck, whispered, "Thank you, Jesus." She got out of the car.

"Hey, Jason. Happy New Year."

"You, too, Coop," he called out the window as he maneuvered the big tow truck to hitch up the Yaris.

"While you're lining that up, let me check the glove compartment. I should have done that in the first place." She opened the door, nothing locked, read the papers, flashlight in hand.

The new vehicle belonged to Enterprise Rental, rented by Henrietta Bolander, address in Church Hill, Richmond.

Coop trained the beam on the front seat, nothing there. Then she checked the rear. Nothing. The keys, still in the ignition, had a button to unlock the trunk. She figured she'd better check it. So she pressed it. The trunk lid popped open.

Walking around she shone the light.

"What the . . . ?"

Gary Gardner's file books were stacked in the trunk. She wasn't entirely certain as to the number of files he had in the first place, but the trunk was full of them. Wearing her gloves she opened one box. Papers. Building codes.

"Jason, take this and impound it, will you? Lock it up and give your dad the key. I'll pick them up from him tomorrow or whenever the roads are okay."

"All right."

"It's not exactly county policy but I don't want to take a chance with this car."

"What's back there. Gold?"

"I don't know," she answered honestly. As she climbed back into the car, she noticed all the lights went out. Total darkness except for her headlights and those of Jason's tow truck.

She wondered if she should have put the file boxes into her SUV, then realized they should be fingerprinted first as well as the trunk. Who was to say when the power would come back on?

Well, that was life in the country, but she knew it would be a long, cold night.

9

Snow curled off the snow blade, a white cascade. A large blade attached to the 80 HP John Deere tractor handled the eight to ten inches of snow from last night. The snow stopped but the mercury edged ever downward and the sky remained dark gray. The depth varied according to wind exposure. Fair needed to go over the long drive twice, clear out the path to the barn. Then he went out on the road, no traffic, performed the same clearing for Cooper, who rented the old Jones place. That farm, two miles from Harry, was considered a close neighbor in the country. No lights shone in the kitchen, the electricity was still out. Horse chores done, Harry slowly followed her husband in her 1978 Ford F-150. Old, no computer chips, you had to turn the hubcap centers to lock the wheels in four-wheel drive, the gearshift was in the center of the cab. Thanks to an extra-low gear, almost a creep gear, she churned through the snow. She could pretty much get through anything with the old truck. Also the ground clearance was helpful. Even with plowing off two inches, snow packed in places, stuck to the roads.

Parking near Coop's back door, she moved the cats, who were grumpy about it, to grab two large shopping bags filled with food. She put them on the snow for a moment, lifted out the cats. Tucker had already jumped down. She waved to her husband, who waved back.

Knocking on the door, the four waited. The temperature wouldn't budge off twenty-two degrees, Fahrenheit. Well, it was better than below zero.

The door opened. Cooper, in a heavy sweater, smiled. "Happy New Year."

"Happy New Year. I figured you worked late last night. Brought food. You can heat the casserole on your stove."

"Thank God for gas." Cooper eagerly took the two bags as Harry unburdened herself of a few layers of clothing.

A fire heated the room. All the old houses built before electricity had fireplaces. With a steady wood supply, a person could still get through winter without other sources of heat. The trick was keeping the fire going.

"*Tuna puffs?*" Pewter eagerly asked.

"*I'll take a Milk-Bone. Cold makes me hungry,*" Tucker chimed in.

Cooper smacked the casserole onto a burner after spooning a lot out into a large frying pan. Frying anything pasta that had been cooked, to her, was better than eating a dish fresh.

"I feel faint." Pewter flopped on her side, eyes imploring pity.

"Harry, you know where the treats are. I'd hate for your animals to perish in my house." The tall woman laughed.

Harry opened the cabinet door, handed out enough to shut everyone up.

"Your husband is the best. I did manage to crawl down the drive last night, snow halfway up the wheels."

"Lots of wrecks?"

"No. Surprisingly most people had the sense to stay in. I would have called you but no power, no phones, and my cell's not working, either."

"Neither is mine. Sometimes the weather is bad and the cells work. Other times not. I have no idea why." Harry handed out a second set of treats then sat at the tiny kitchen table.

"First question. Do you remember how many of those file books, the big ones with the marbled exteriors, Gary had? The ones on the lower shelf."

"A lot. Other than that, I don't know."

"Found the file books."

"Where?" Harry sat upright.

"In a car, looked as though it had slid to the side of the road. With all the snow I wouldn't swear to that. No driver. No personal items. It was a Yaris, a rent-a-car from Enterprise. The stuff was in the trunk."

"Any name?"

"Yeah, the paperwork was in the glove compartment. Henrietta Bolander from Richmond had rented the car.

Well, I hopped on that, holiday or not." Cooper paused. "Her license was a fake and a damned good one."

"Weird." Harry pursed her lips. "You looked in the files?"

"Gloves on, I opened a box. Building codes. Like you said. We'll need to go through all of the boxes just to be sure. A lot of building codes, I can tell you that. For just about any county in central Virginia and the counties around Richmond. Year after year. Dabney will go through it along with me once we can get to work. But I am not sure of the number of file boxes or books. Sure look like big books."

"Easy. Once you've gone through everything, bring it all back to Gary's office. We'll put them on the shelf. If one is missing we'll know."

Cooper smiled. "You are so smart."

"*No she's not. Neither are you. Humans just think they're smart.*" Pewter, full, jumped on a kitchen chair.

"*I wouldn't insult someone who just gave me a treat,*" Mrs. Murphy corrected Pewter.

"*Oh la.*" The gray cat preened. "*They don't know what we're saying. You can call a human a fat, disgusting pig. All they hear is a meow.*"

It was on the tip of Tucker's tongue to ask who was calling who fat. She thought better of it.

Harry asked, "Did someone have a key to Gary's office or break in? That can't be classified information."

"No key. Whoever got in there had locksmith skills. Some marks marred the outside door, the metal surround also, but not much. They knew how to push back the tongue. Whoever this is knows things, practical things, and is bold."

Fair knocked, opened the door. They'd heard him cut off the tractor a few moments before.

"Happy New Year."

Cooper, dishing out casserole, said, "Happy New Year back. I'm feeding you your wife's cooking. Bet you two are hungry now."

"Cold makes you hungry." Fair unwound his scarf, pulled off the heavy lined gloves, unzipped his Filson winter jacket, unzipped another layer under that. "The thing that gets me about winter is how long it takes to dress and undress."

"We move like snails." Harry smiled. "Coop, want help with that?"

"No, I've got plates. You can pour the coffee. Shenandoah Joe."

"Sure smells good." Harry rose, lifted the coffee pot off the burner, pulled down heavy mugs. "We've got some good roasting places now. Even Lovingston has one." She named the county seat of Nelson County, southwest of Crozet.

Nelson, not a popular county, was growing like every other place in the area. The views of the Blue Ridge thrilled people. The counties north of Albemarle and east were growing faster than those south or west on the other side of the mountains. East lay Richmond. North lay Washington. People commuted. A few owned small planes, which certainly made for an easier commute if you could afford it.

Fair sat down, a plate put in front of him of hot casserole: fresh tiny potatoes, chicken, parsley, carrots, peas, tiny bacon pieces. Harry loaded the casserole up.

Pewter, chin on the table, worked her adoring but hungry look. Her long dark gray whiskers twitched forward.

Tucker, by Harry's chair leg, whispered to Mrs. Murphy, "God, what a ham."

"I heard that," Pewter snapped.

"Pewter, be quiet or I'll make you get off that chair." Harry glared at her.

Pewter glared back but she did shut up.

Cooper told Fair about the file boxes.

"I vaguely remember those boxes in his drafting room. Beautiful, those old things, aren't they? Now people stuff files in plastic boxes. They can't have been too valuable, they were left in the car. Some people don't even keep paper anymore. Everything is on the computer. 'Course, they don't think of days like today. No electricity. No satellite signal."

"Fair, we don't know if they were all in the car. I expect we'll know this week as your wife has made the sensible suggestion that we take them back to his office, put them on the shelf, and see if any are missing."

"Were they missing when you were there to see his plans?" Fair asked his wife.

"No, everything looked like always."

He paused. "Someone came back. After Gary was shot. There must be something in them more valuable or dangerous than building codes."

"That thought had occurred to me." Cooper remembered she hadn't put out napkins. "But we will search the office more thoroughly now." She pushed back her chair, opened a drawer, pulling out nice paper napkins.

"Thank you." Harry unfolded hers. "Candles next?"

"Well, if it grows any darker, yes," Cooper replied. "I haven't checked the weather. Can't. I use the weather app on my cellphone all the time."

"Same for us. I bet we're in for more snow but how much, I don't know." Harry cleaned her plate. "Wanna bet?"

"With a country girl? No." Cooper held up her forefinger. "No."

"Well, I thought I'd beat the odds there. A big win." Harry appeared disappointed then changed the subject. "No Henrietta Bolander. A fake name but a woman. Women attract less attention than men."

"That depends on the woman and what she's wearing," Fair posited.

Both women looked at him, then each other and shrugged.

A hum began. The lights came on.

"Hooray. The rest of my house is about fifty-two degrees, Fahrenheit," Cooper told them.

"You're very precise." Fair smiled at her.

"Thermometer for outside and inside in the upstairs bedroom. Helps me know how to dress."

"It's fifty-two degrees. You have a fireplace up there," Harry added.

"Yes, but I was so pooped out I slept straight through the night. It went out."

"I do that sometimes, too," Harry confessed. "Put a proper stove up there."

Fair leaned back in his chair, finished the bracing coffee. "Fake driver's license, files still in the car. Puzzling. Murder. Astonishing."

Cooper thought, then said, "Millions of dollars are made in construction. Perhaps one of those early projects violated a code."

"It would have to be one hell of a violation."

"Whatever, if the files are the answer, I don't know, but Gary was killed. We know it wasn't for love." Cooper shrugged.

"Millions?" Harry's voice rose.

"If one of those buildings he worked on has a huge structural flaw and people die, it's possible the construction company could be sued for enormous sums. The other possibility is that someone took money under the table to look the other way during construction or the company paid money under the table to get the job in the first place. Big jobs like office buildings, hotels, even converting the tobacco warehouse and apartments are usually bid. Money under the table could save a bid. Given the millions of dollars to build, the millions in profits, that's a big incentive."

"When I think of government I am reminded we are in this mess because government gives contracts to the lowest bidder. If that's the case, and supposedly it is, why are we billions of dollars in debt?" Harry threw up her hands in frustration.

"Because every time money changes hands it sticks to them." Fair's lip curled upward slightly. "Applies to private enterprise even more than government, but it's more shocking when government corruption is unmasked."

"Should we be like Diogenes? Go through the streets of Athens holding a lantern looking for an honest man?" Cooper shook her head.

"Well, you see where it got him. He wound up living with the dogs," Fair said.

"*Hey*," Tucker barked.

"He was right. Dogs never lie to you. The powers that be in Athens were like the powers that be everywhere. You can't trust them, but I can trust Tucker."

"*Me, too*," Pewter interjected.

"*Pewter, you don't care.*" Mrs. Murphy flicked her tail.

"*I didn't say I cared but you can trust me.*"

"*True enough.*" Mrs. Murphy laughed at her sidekick.

"Let me get home before it turns even darker. Thank you." Fair got up, carried his plate, cup, and saucer to the sink.

"I'll wash them," Harry offered.

"No. I'll do it. When we've gone through everything in the boxes, fingerprinted stuff, I'll call you."

"I'll be there." Harry checked the window over the sink. "Little snowflakes. Just started." She put on her scarf and coat. "Coop, whatever this is it seems to be well thought out, doesn't it?"

"Does."

"The impulse killings are easy, aren't they?"

"Sure are."

"I think you've got your work cut out for you." Harry kissed Coop on the cheek. "I'll help any way I can. Happy New Year."

10

Maureen Selisse Holloway determined to live life as a blonde. Catherine couldn't help herself, she examined the middle-aged woman's coiffure without Maureen noticing when she flounced her stunning royal blue brocade, cut low over the ample bosom with a sheer cover of Belgian lace.

One must keep up social converse and it was the turn of the Cloverfields women to invite Maureen and her young husband for an intimate dinner.

Bettina, as always, cooked a dinner of splendor. She could have cooked for any king in Europe and held her own with one of those chefs there. She'd heard there were Africans at the courts of Europe. The czar of Russia, or the czarina when a woman was in power, is guarded by two enormous ebony-skinned men, not brown, not light brown but ebony. Russia. Never. No matter what she might be paid should she ever be free, Russia was too cold. It was cold enough in Virginia.

One thing about the cold, you could cook in the house kitchen. The summer kitchen, thirty yards away, connected by a herringbone brick–patterned walkway created the problem of how to keep the food hot as the girls ran it into the house. Still better than firing up a huge stove inside in July.

Serena, twenty-five, worked closely with Bettina, observing everything the older woman did. Could she duplicate it someday? Yes. But Serena knew she would never reach Bettina's creativity. The head cook would stare at a brisket of beef, tenderize it a little with her wooden square studded with wooden teeth, stare at it again, suddenly pull out spices, bay leaves, other things. Bettina would sing as she worked.

The ladies sipped a light sherry while the men drank port in the library. Every now and then Bettina and Serena could hear Ewing or his sons-in-law laugh, and occasionally, Jeffrey, Maureen's husband.

As for the women, Serena would sneak down the hall to listen, tiptoe back. "Maureen swears the French court is the height of fashion. The English Queen is dowdy."

"How does she know?" Bettina dried her hands on a dish towel woven at Cloverfields.

Cloverfields was as self-sustaining as possible.

"Guess she's been over there. Mr. Garth visited England and France when he was young. Charles came from England." Serena dreamed of seeing the world, a dream followed by the inconvenience of travel as well as the fact that she was a slave. But certain indispensable slaves traveled with their master or mistress.

Both women wore head rags. Bettina's tied in the front with a square knot. Serena's tied in the back. Neither knew why they did it that way, but it was what their kin taught them. They stuck to it.

The kitchen, everything put in place, sparkled. The fire in the small hearth gave off the odor of hardwood. Bettina tossed in two oak logs.

"Sit down, Serena. Let's catch our breath." The older woman sighed. "It's been a long day."

"You outdid yourself tonight. No wonder you're tired."

Bettina smiled. "I do so love to put that bitch in her place. And this new girl that attends to her, Elizabetta, isn't much better than that damned Sheba. I hope she's dead." Bettina meant Sheba, who had disappeared about a month ago, along with a fabulously large pearl necklace.

"No one's heard anything. Big Rawly's a hard place to live. Hard." Serena sighed. "And Marcia, you'd think she'd be sweet like her real mother. Hellion. I am tempted to hit her upside the head."

Laughing, Bettina swatted good-naturedly at Serena. "Just wait. It'll get worse." She paused. "Why can't that girl with Maureen be called Elizabeth? Elizabetta." She twirled her hand in the air. "My, my."

"I guess if you work close with Maureen you turn into a snot, too." Serena laughed.

The little girl, Marcia, already an exotic beauty, was raised by Rachel as her own. Marcia was two years older than Rachel's daughter Isabelle. Marcia's mother was an escaped slave from Big Rawly, accused of killing Francisco Selisse. That he needed killing was never in doubt, but Ailee didn't do it nor did her lover, Moses. He was helped to York, Pennsylvania, where he was safe. Ailee had been hidden at Cloverfields, gave birth to Marcia. When she looked at the baby, who looked white, which meant she was Francisco's, Ailee hung herself. The slaves knew, as did Catherine, Rachel, John, and Charles. Ewing did not, nor did anyone off the estate.

Bettina felt if the child could pass for white, they should all protect her. She'd be free. Well, she was free and a handful.

Bettina hummed.

"What's that?" Serena asked.

"I hear Rachel and Charles sing it. 'A Mighty Fortress Is Our God.'" She hummed some, and Serena, a good ear, picked it up with her.

Footsteps alerted them.

Catherine stepped into the kitchen. "I had to walk away just for a minute. You know, I would consider drowning Maureen if I thought I could get away with it. She's in there carrying on about how dreadful Yancy Grant is and moreover she knows, knows in her heart, that he wants her. That's really why Yancy and Jeffrey fought that silly duel." Catherine put her hands on her hips. "Wonderful meal." Then she smiled slyly. "Just kills her. Her cook is, shall we say, serviceable."

The three laughed.

"Is it true Maureen is trying to buy a title for Jeffrey?"

Serena looked up into those astonishing eyes of Catherine's.

"How did you hear that?"

"DoRe." Serena named the head coachman at Big Rawly, courting Bettina, as both were widowed.

"Now that you mention it, he did refer offhandedly to it, but I really didn't pay but so much attention. Rachel is the one mesmerized."

"Miss Catherine." Bettina's voice hit the singsong register, meaning she knew Catherine was interested.

A moment of silence, then Catherine admitted, "Well, it's just so absurd." Then she burst out laughing. "All right. Back to Purgatory. They're discussing the merits of shirred velvet versus heavy satin for winter balls. But Maureen did say that Yancy called on them to sell a horse. He promised this spring will be a banner race season, much money to be won."

"Hmm." Bettina wondered if DoRe counseled his mistress or if he'd let her throw her money about to make a big show.

"If he visited Big Rawly, you know he'll come calling," Serena predicted.

"And if he visited Big Rawly he must be desperate," Bettina shrewdly asserted.

"You're right." Catherine considered Bettina's insight.

More footsteps. Rachel stepped into the kitchen. "Your turn. I need a small escape."

Bettina rose. "Miss Catherine. Here. This will help." She reached into the cupboard and pulled out a jar. "Raspberry jam. She loves our raspberry jam."

Catherine took the jar. "Good thinking. I'll tell her it took me a while to find it."

She turned and left.

Rachel sat down on the wooden bench. "Is it true Jeddie's mother insists he marry?"

"He's nineteen. Isn't he nineteen?" Serena asked. Bettina nodded yes, he was.

"He doesn't want to get married." Rachel liked the young horseman who worked with Catherine.

"Says she's going to throw him out." Bettina clucked. "And you know how Felicia can get."

"There's an empty cabin near the weaving cabin. He'd be close to the women when they work. I mean if he came home early or something. That could be, well, you know." Rachel was sensitive to such things.

"He hasn't found the right one. He's not going to chase the girls or he'd be doing it already," Bettina wisely noted.

"I'm sure that's the case." Rachel smiled. "I'll talk to Father to see if he'll allow Jeddie to live over there alone."

"It's not good to live alone. Remember Noah's ark? We're supposed to go two by two." Bettina said this with authority, biblical authority no less.

Serena gave the older woman a sideways glance then started to hum an old song about love.

Rachel smiled. "Two by two." She grinned at Bettina, got up to rejoin the endless talk with Maureen. All about Maureen, of course.

Serena, voice low, said, "We all know you've got your eye on DoRe."

"Honey, it's better if DoRe has his eye on me. Tell you

what, if there's one thing I've learned in this life it's that for a woman to make sure she gets what she wants . . . well, let's just say it has to be the man's idea."

Serena, who married at seventeen, nodded. "It's a lot of work."

11

 "One missing." Coop crossed her arms over her chest.

Harry, walking along the row of file boxes, nodded. "1984. The year he moved here."

The two, in Gary's office, had placed the file boxes back on the shelf. All the contents had been examined, the boxes fingerprinted, scanned. The little rubber dinosaur toys, some tins, wooden boxes were replaced, not being considered important. He kept odd little things: animal teeth, old feathers, cat's-eye marbles. Given the shock of the public death, Sheriff Shaw called other law enforcement people in for a few days' help. The work flew along gratifyingly fast. But no fingerprints on the boxes other than Gary's and few at that. He must have rarely consulted these papers. Whoever lifted the materials wore gloves.

Given the cold surely they'd wear gloves outside but the books had been inside. Forethought.

The bad weather kept most businesses closed. The two women observed no foot traffic, not much car traffic, either. The silence was unusual.

Cooper stood scanning the inviting work space. "Nothing else was touched. The ceramic bowl on his flat work desk contained forty-five dollars in neatly folded bills. Still there. His bathroom, no medication. Of course, that could have been stolen."

Harry responded, "The only pill I ever saw him take, ibuprofen. He hated medication. He'd always tell me if I ever had another operation the drugs could be worse than the disease. I argued back but then again, when my breast cancer was discovered, it was a small tumor. Not advanced. No radiation or chemo. I was lucky. Five years, clean." She took a deep breath. "Sorry. This is about Gary, not me."

Cooper waved the apology away. "Your operation affected him enough that he worried about you. And doctors push drugs. Maybe he had past experience."

"I don't think so but perhaps his ex-wife did." Harry offered that thought.

"I guess I'll drop in on the ex–Mrs. Gardner, now Hulme. Never hurts to do that anyway." Cooper sat down in the desk chair while Harry sat on the stool in front of the impressive antique drafting table.

The dog and two cats sniffed at the back door.

"*Faint. Grease. A hint of grease.*" Tucker lifted her nose.

Mrs. Murphy checked out the faint line just inside the door. "Car grease or motor oil, you think?"

"Gary parked his car in the back. Could have been on his boots." Tucker sat down. "Nothing on the door. Sometimes a door will brush against a person and you know where they were last, like, at the supermarket. Supermarkets always smell the same."

"They use the same cleaners." Mrs. Murphy looked at the doorknob. "If the person came in the back door, the person who removed the files, they had to leave their scent. It's been too long. Nothing. Just nothing."

"They knew how to open locks or had a key." Tucker listened to the two women talking in the workroom. The back door opened onto a small entrance, a coatrack and bench against the wall. Just a small square space, a bathroom there, and then the door into the workroom.

Pewter, uninterested in their door examination, batted at the floor along the wall. "A major spider!"

The ground spider, not a web spinner, lifted its front legs, ready to fight. Pewter took a step back. The other two came over to look at the spider.

"That is a biggie," Tucker agreed.

Pewter batted at the eight-legged creature again. It moved with speed to the back door before she could catch it. Although she didn't really want to catch it, she did want to chase it. A small chip in the baseboard gave the spider safety. She ducked in.

"Bet she has a nest in there," Mrs. Murphy said.

"How could Gary work here and not know he was keeping a big spider?" Pewter questioned.

"The spider could hear him walking. The floor would tremble, right? So she could always hide." Tucker was right about that.

Pewter watched the little chip in the baseboard, tapped it, then moved a few feet to the bottom of the door.

"Here's another little space." Pewter flattened, squinted, fished at the small space with an extended claw. *"A dime."*

Disappointed, she dropped the dime, wasn't exciting. The three walked into the workroom. The door between the small back entrance and the workroom was kept closed to conserve heat. Harry and Coop had parked in the back, entered through the back, and left the door to the workroom slightly ajar.

Harry looked at her friends, who walked in to sit at her feet.

"Spider patrol," Pewter announced.

Harry smiled at the gray cat as she pulled out pencils from a jar clamped on the right side of the drafting table.

"Clever. This way he didn't have to get up and down for pencils. The drafting board is on a slant. He was always coming up with ideas." She read the inscription on the pencil. "Sanford Design Ebony Jet Extra Smooth 14420. All the same." She lifted each one out. One was worn down a bit. The others sharp. "This must have been the one he was using that day. He sharpened them every morning." She carefully replaced the pencils. "Makes me sick. Just sick. And it makes me mad."

"That's understandable but emotion clouds judgment."

"Does," Harry agreed with Cooper. "It can also be a motivator."

"Can, but you'd better not be too motivated. I asked you

here because you knew his office and this work space. You can't whiz off and try to find his murderer."

"Coop, I have no idea. I have no place to whiz off." She threw up her hands. "Stymied."

Out of the corner of her eye, Pewter saw the spider emerge, race across the little space, go under the bathroom door. She took off into the small back room. The others followed.

"It's in the bathroom."

"Pewter, don't disturb it. Maybe it has to go," Tucker teased the frustrated cat.

Pewter, pupils large, dashed over to the baseboard from which the spider had emerged. She couldn't reach in with her entire paw but she could extend two claws. She hooked a tiny metal triangle.

"Ha."

Mrs. Murphy got up, examined Pewter's find.

"Look. This spider's like Simon, a hoarder."

The possum in the barn didn't hoard, but he kept treasures.

Mrs. Murphy cocked her head. "Looks like a little spike from a dog collar."

Hearing "dog collar," Tucker peered into the space. "Could be."

"Or it could be a stud from a motorcycle jacket." Mrs. Murphy remembered the black leather jacket on the killer. They barked and meowed until Harry, irritated, came to them. She knelt down with the three to stare at this small shiny object.

Harry, picking up the stud, said, "Coop."

The deputy walked in as Harry dropped the little stud in her hand. "The animals had this on the floor. Don't know where they found it."

"I know our team went over this place with a fine-tooth comb." Cooper was frustrated by the breaking into Gary's office.

"I'm sure they did but this might be easy to miss depending on where it was."

"A spider had it," Pewter announced.

"You don't know that," Tucker grumbled.

"Well, you could open the bathroom door and ask her," Mrs. Murphy ever so helpfully suggested.

Neither woman said anything about the small stud. Cooper reached into her pocket, pulled out her clean handkerchief, and folded it inside.

"I found it." Pewter stood on her hind legs to bat at the handkerchief in Cooper's hand.

Harry reached down to push the gray cat back a little. "Could be anything."

"Could, but just to be sure I'll take it to the lab. Could be off a dress, one with stud patterns, could be from a dog collar. Old Gringo makes a boot with a kind of swirling stud pattern over the toe. I'd love to buy that pair of boots. Too expensive."

"Or it could have come off a motorcycle jacket." Harry exhaled through her nose loudly.

"Could, but it would be a stupid killer to come back here wearing the same jacket."

Harry turned to go back into the workroom. "Noisy, obvious, and how could he carry the file boxes? That's the only thing that was missing from here."

"1984. I'd better start digging into 1984." Cooper had no idea how literal that would be.

12

"Marvella, how are you?" Harry spoke on the phone to a new friend in Richmond, Marvella Rice Lawson.

The elegant older woman, a power in the art and African American communities, replied, "Good. The snow is beautiful, the main streets are plowed. Big piles of snow everywhere, but Tinsdale and I," she mentioned her husband, "bundle up and take our walks. What about you?"

"Same story. Main roads plowed. Fair plowed out our farm road, paths to the barn, and outbuildings." Harry looked out the window. "Right now the snow is blood red. The sun first turned it gold but now it's setting, blood red. Quite a sight."

"You know, Sotheby's for the last few years has been selling collections of Russian art. Lots of snow scenes, troika rides, that sort of thing, but some of the work is lovely. And it's the first time we've seen any of it."

"Isn't it strange to think how politics affects the arts? Of course, there's the good side, like those wonderful Renaissance painters giving us all their versions of the idealized Madonna."

"Usually their mistresses." Marvella laughed.

"Well, yes." Harry laughed with her. "I was hoping you would be free next Friday and we could go to the Museum of Fine Arts. Have you seen the Architectural Etchings exhibit? They call it 'Remnants and Revivals.' Very uncommon work."

"I have, but I'm happy to go again. Shall I meet you there in the lobby, say, at high noon?" She paused. "Unless there's another snowstorm. I've dutifully watched the projected weather report for the next week but one can't go by it."

"There is that. Can you tell me where I might find a book containing some of those Russian paintings?"

"I can do better than that. I'll give you a thumb drive I made. I've been leaning on my friend, Sean Rankin of Rankin Construction, to sponsor an exhibit of Russian art. So I made one for him. Made extras. If Rankin won't sponsor it someone else will. After all, look at all those incredible Fabergé eggs the museum has in its collection."

Hearing the surname Rankin, Harry replied, "Rankin Construction? The firm that began building the early high-rises in the seventies and beyond?"

"The same, and they're still doing it. They're already digging the deep foundations for the Cloudcroft Building. On the site of an earlier building."

"Too many big buildings. They cut off the sunlight." Harry gauged.

"And they suck in the money." Marvella paused. "Oops, here comes the UPS man. I'll see you next Friday."

Harry, in her tack room, hung up. Speaking to Marvella put her in a good mood. Marvella, an art collector with the means to buy very good work, second-string painters from the nineteenth century, her favorite era, pulled Harry back to her college major, Art History. She wondered what had taken her so long.

Harry dialed Coop's cell. "Where are you?"

"Office. Why?"

"Oh, just wondered if you were out cruising around."

"No, I'm desk bound today and glad of it."

"Do you think I could retrieve my plans from Gary's office? If I can't have the originals, may I make a copy of the work he's done?"

"Wait a minute. Lisa Roudabush asked for Nature First's design." She pushed hold and in five minutes, which seemed longer than it was, her voice came back on. "Rick says he had duplicates made of current projects. But not today. The roads aren't good. Let's see how Monday is."

"He had to be working on other commissions, not just mine and Nature First's."

"He was. One of them is a huge house for Gare Galbraith and Alex Ix. They're transferring their project to

Cathy Purple Cherry." Cooper named a sought-after architect, offices in Annapolis, D.C., and Charlottesville.

"That will be something. She'll be as faithful to his work as Gare and Alex wish, but whatever she does, it will be the best."

"Could you live in one of those big houses?"

"No. Mine's big enough." She waited a moment. "Just spoke to Marvella Rice Lawson. She says Richmond is pretty in the snow but only the main streets are open. I should have asked her if she knew Gary. She mentioned that she knew Sean Rankin. Rankin Construction."

"I'll check him out. Actually, I need to ask Rankin Construction a few more questions. Just double-checking."

"I would imagine Sean is either old or the son of the Rankin that ran the firm then. They must have tons of money because Marvella is going to try to get Rankin Construction to sponsor an exhibit of Russian art at the museum."

"Well, why not?" Cooper evidenced little interest in painting or sculpture. "And I'm not going if they do it, by the way. My feet still hurt from when you dragged me through the exhibit of still life painting, much of it by women from the seventeenth and eighteenth centuries. The flowers were beautiful but I can look at flowers in my garden. Well, actually yours." She laughed.

"Neanderthal. I am shocked," said Harry, who was not.

"Hey, Rick is buzzing me. Must be important. Talk to you later or tomorrow." Cooper hung up, buzzed her boss.

Driving carefully, Cooper headed to Crozet as she followed Rick's instructions. First she stopped at Barbara Barrell's used tack shop, Crozet Tack and Saddle.

She opened the door. Barbara glanced up. "Are you looking for something for Harry?"

"No. I'm glad you're open though. The weather has kept a lot of businesses shut. I'd like to ask you a few questions."

"Sure. Come sit behind the counter with me. I doubt we'll be interrupted. I really opened the shop to get out of the house."

Smiling, Cooper asked, "Were you open December twenty-seventh, Tuesday?"

Barbara nodded. "Had a lot of after Christmas customers looking for bargains."

"Do you recall what you were doing around one PM?"

"I can't be exact but I had two ladies trying on jackets, formal jackets. It had to be roughly that time as they both discussed what they'd eaten for lunch."

"Did you see or hear anything unusual about that time?"

Barbara answered, "No. When the ambulance roared by, maybe one-twenty PM, that alerted me."

"So before that, no traffic. Say a motorcycle?"

Thinking hard, Barbara weighed her words. "Like I said, I was dealing with two women trying on formal jackets. I think I heard a buzz. Maybe a motorcycle, but my attention was on the two ladies for whom this was a monumental decision."

Cooper smiled. "Thanks, Barbara."

"I haven't been helpful. I wish I could be. Hearing an ambulance I assumed there'd been an accident, someone had a heart attack at work or home. I didn't think about it. Of course, when I heard about Gary I was shocked. He was a good man."

"Yes, I think he was, too." Cooper stood, thanked Barbara again, and left.

13

Catherine and Jeddie rode back to the main stable having exercised Reynaldo and Crown Prince. Mother Nature bequeathed to them a gloriously sunny day, mercury in the mid-fifties at eleven in the morning. When they started out the air, brisk, invigorated them and the horses. It warmed somewhat, plus the workout calmed the two boys, energetic fellows.

Riding toward the paddocks, they looked down the two long rows of slave cabins, orderly, gardens in the back. Smoke curled upward from chimneys. The cabins boasted glass windows, an outrageous luxury for slaves as well as poor whites. Ewing, not one to display his wealth as did Maureen Holloway, evidenced it in more subtle ways. Building his own sawmill, a large weaving room, installing glass windows in every building, putting in real brick fireplaces bespoke money, lots of it. Yet the man wore only two pieces of jewelry, a ruby cravat pin his late wife gave him when they married and a gold watch his daughters gave him for his last birthday, April 2nd. Carrying time in his pocket irritated him slightly, but he wore the watch to please his girls.

The front porches of the cabins, swept clean, had wooden chairs on them. Bettina's had two heavy rockers and a swing. A small attached shed housed the dried firewood. The men cut firewood year-round. What rested in the sheds had been cut either last year or in the spring. Cloverfields would never run out of timber. Ewing owned two thousand acres in western Albemarle County. He was ever on the lookout for productive land, the closer to his main holdings the better. As for the North Carolina land, he would visit once a season. Catherine accompanied him, soaked up everything.

Down the second row of cabins, in the distance above the creek, really on a bluff, reposed the large weaving cabin.

"Jeddie, I hear your mother wants you to marry. Now," Catherine said this flatly.

"Every day she mentions someone, lists her good qualities." He shrugged.

"I'm sure each of those girls does possess good qualities. Your mother is hard to please. She's looked them over." She paused. "But you have not."

"Miss Catherine, I like being by myself."

"I understand that. I did, too, until I met John." She decided not to discuss how her heart knocked her ribcage when he lifted her down from Reynaldo the first time she'd met him. "If I can arrange with Father for you to have your own cabin, do you think you can keep it up? It's a lot of work, cleaning, keeping the fires going, cooking for yourself, tending the garden. Life truly is easier if there's two."

"Do you think he might . . . might give me one?"

"Let me work on him. Right now there's only one empty cabin, down near the weaving cabin. You wouldn't be around as many people as you are now. It's at the end of the row and the weaving cabin isn't but so close. You truly will be alone."

"I would like that." He smiled. "I'd rather be with the horses."

"Yes, I understand." She smiled her dazzling smile at this young man she adored.

Working together with the horses, playing with the horses as children, they'd grown close, could almost read each other's thoughts. Jeddie was better at it than Catherine, three years his senior. Jeddie's being a slave never occurred to Catherine. She took him and his station for granted. He, on the other hand, was far more careful. Being young, Jeddie deferred to all the older people whether it was Ewing, who in fact owned him, or Bettina. Jeddie watched, kept his mouth shut except with Catherine.

"I don't know if I could be married. Look how Bumbee always fights with Percy. He lies to her all the time. She throws him out. Takes him back. And my mother. She and my father get along but I don't think they love each other anymore. I don't want to be like that."

"Does make you think, and I suppose it's as easy to marry the wrong person as the right one. But then, my father and mother were devoted to each other. You see my father visit her grave, bring her flowers?" He nodded, she continued. "Bettina and her late husband also cherished each other. And now she's found a spark, something with DoRe. I do believe it's mutual. Jeddie, you just never know."

"I guess," he replied without enthusiasm.

Smiling, Catherine promised, "I'll see what I can do." Looking toward the stable she sighed. "Yancy Grant. I see Ralston leading his horse into the stable."

"He's a hard man." Jeddie pegged him. "But he rides, still rides with that smashed-up knee. Bet it hurts."

"Bet it does," she agreed.

They reached the stable and Ralston ran out to help Catherine down. Tall and skinny, he would soon be seventeen. While not a gifted rider like Jeddie, he was a good hand with a horse. Cleaning tack in the center aisle was little Tulli, intent on his task. Next to him, Catherine's two-year-old, JohnJohn, handed him a clean rag he had dipped in water. JohnJohn performed this with great seriousness.

"You're learning, JohnJohn. And Tulli is very good at what he does."

The little boy, the spitting image of his father, grinned, then babbled, "I'll be the best."

"We'll see, but if you are, son, don't brag about it." Catherine placed her hand on his head.

She loved him but she felt she would be more interested in him when he was self-sufficient and could read and write. Unlike her sister, Catherine did not feel she was a natural mother. But she truly loved JohnJohn and, in her way, she loved Jeddie like a younger brother. She didn't think about love much, really.

"Tulli, where's my husband?"

"He walked up to the house with Mr. Yancy. He lent Mr. Yancy a walking stick, too. Should I go down and fetch Ruth?"

Ruth was everybody's mother and she took care of Catherine's son and Rachel's two daughters, as well as any other child sent to her.

"Finish the bridle, clean up. Then you can walk him down there." She addressed JohnJohn. "JohnJohn, you clean up, too. Have you seen Sweet Potato today?"

JohnJohn nodded.

"Ralston put him up top, held him, and I led Sweet Potato around." Tulli beamed.

"Good. Very good." Catherine brushed her short jacket, snapped a towel at her boots. "Well, I'd better go up to the house. Was Yancy in a good mood?"

Ralston pursed his lips. "For him."

"I see. Well, boys, I'll ride tomorrow. Jeddie, I'll expect you, let's go early."

When she left for the house, Ralston turned to the young man, a few years his senior. "News?"

Jeddie fudged it. "She'll try to get Momma off her marriage ideas."

"I'd sure like to get married." Ralston's smile grew wider. "Keep me warm at night."

"Ha." Jeddie shook his head.

"Your dog can keep you warm," Tulli opined.

"Oh, Tulli, you don't know nothing." Ralston also shook his head.

Up at the house, Ewing, John, and Yancy enjoyed the comfortable chairs in Ewing's library. Serena brought featherlight biscuits, fresh-churned butter, various jams, hot coffee as well as a pot of tea. Ewing offered spirits but Yancy declined.

"I am trying to moderate my habits."

Ewing, hands now clasped over his chest, nodded. "Wise."

"Ah, Catherine." John stood as his wife entered, followed by Yancy, who bowed, and Ewing who kissed her on the cheek.

"Have I disturbed a conference?"

"No, no dear. Do sit down. Yancy was outlining a race program for next spring."

She took a seat offered by her husband. "Mr. Grant, I believe we could all use a diversion. You've come up with a good one."

Expanding with praise from a beautiful woman and a renowned horsewoman at that, he lowered his voice. "Perilous times. You go to the blacksmith, people are arguing. Pestalozzi's Mill. Arguing about prices, the value of money dropping, Mr. Jefferson's ideas about how we should proceed and then those ideas of others, in the opposite direction."

Ewing, conciliatory, per usual, offered, "You're right, Yancy, right. But then you foresaw much of what was to pass before we fought England. Perhaps it is in the nature of men to argue. Each man thinks he has a better plan."

"True. Think of our neighbors who returned to England or fled to Nova Scotia rather than join the rebellion, as they put it. But that was clear. The wrong done to us was so clear. This, I don't know. I was talking with Sam Udall. His focus is that without a national monetary policy we are doomed."

"Yes," Ewing simply replied.

"That is why your plan for sport, for shifting people's focus, is so wise." Catherine smiled at Yancy. "Perhaps their mood will lift. People will become more cooperative simply because the burden has been lightened for a short time. They've needed a good time."

John, not a political bone in his body, paid little attention to this, but as a former combat major in the Army, he worried about future bloodshed. "Gentlemen, you know far more of the intricacies of this than I, but I do not want to be called to fire against my fellow citizens."

Catherine reached for his hand. "Dear, surely it won't come to that."

"Let us pray that you are right, Madam." Yancy leaned forward, a crunch could be heard in his knee. "What I propose is we host races, match races as done in England. An owner can pay a fee to run against a horse he feels is well matched with his own. Both owners must agree. We can't promote lopsided races. As this is so new we would race only one day, let us say a card of four races, the last one being the highest contest."

"Spring or summer?" Ewing inquired.

"Late spring perhaps. Early spring can be so wet," Yancy replied.

"Where would you hold the races?" Catherine's curiosity rose.

"Along the James. The Levels. We might need to do a bit of work but that seems the best place. The soil has much sand." He took a breath. "Sam Udall knows the owner. Of course, he would need compensation, but I do think this is possible. I come to you because you own one of the best horses in Virginia. Reynaldo. If you would consider running him, I think great interest would be aroused."

Catherine, silent, waited for her father to speak. She actually owned Reynaldo, Crown Prince, and Serenissima, a wonderful brood mare. Ewing, not ignorant of good horseflesh, lacked his daughter's gift, but this being business, appearances had to be kept.

"You flatter us, Yancy." Ewing nodded slightly.

"Might you express some interest?"

"I am intrigued. I will need to discuss this with my daughter, of course; she is the one training the boys, as she calls them. But I am intrigued and I do think your idea of some form of entertainment valuable in these times. We are spread so far apart. This would bring us all together."

After he left, John, arm around his wife's waist, said, "You shouldn't be riding close to the summer. I wonder should you be working so hard now?"

"Honey, it's only twelve weeks." Catherine had known for twelve weeks that she was pregnant. "Don't worry."

"I'll keep an eye on you."

"What would you like. Another boy or a girl?" She put her arm around his waist now.

"A little girl who looks just like her mother, her beautiful, radiant mother." John, not the most verbal of men, came up with *radiant*, which impressed his wife.

"You." She kissed him.

Ewing walked back having seen Yancy to the door. Roger, the butler, escorted Yancy down to the stable, glad to be out of the house for a bit. He offered the walking stick for Yancy to keep, compliments of Ewing, but once mounted Yancy handed it back.

Up at the house, Catherine and John sat with Ewing for a moment.

"What do you think, dear?"

"If I'm going to run a horse, Father, it has to be for a big purse."

"Should we win, it would bring people here to breed, would it not?"

"Yes. It is a good idea but I would like to see The Levels before agreeing to anything. And I want to hear about purses."

"Yes, yes." Ewing nodded. "I expect Yancy is trying to see who might be interested and then he and Sam will gather the monies for handsome purses. Silver cups, too, I should think. We can't let the English outdo us on such a pursuit."

John smiled. "We can't let Yancy outdo us."

This made Ewing laugh, then he stared at his son-in-law. "John, do you think there might be violence? Do you think you might be called should this come to pass?"

"I pray that won't happen but yes, I would be called. We fought so long and so hard to free ourselves from the king. We can't fall apart now. We must hold, find some agreement."

"Ah, John, I fear fighting is the way of men."

"Perhaps we can be different. We must be different," John said with feeling.

Catherine, sitting down and sampling a biscuit for she was hungry, listened. "The solution to these competing ideas is to let the women organize the men."

"My dear." Ewing's eyebrows shot upward.

"*Lysistrata*." She giggled.

Ewing explained to John, not a well-educated man, about Aristophanes's play in which the women go on a sex strike to knock some sense into the men.

John laughed, turned to his beautiful wife. "That would work. Yes, it would."

The three laughed then Catherine, as though as an afterthought, pounced. "Father, if we do race, it will be Jeddie who rides. He will need quiet, good sleep. He does not have that under his mother's roof."

"Felicia can be strong-minded. Rachel mentioned this to me the other day." Ewing raised his eyebrows again. "Jeddie's situation must be more pressing than before."

"Felicia wants him out of the house so she's pushing him to get married. That's what I think," Catherine posited.

"I see. Well, he is of an age. What is he now?"

"Nineteen, Father."

"Ah yes." A smile spread across Ewing's face. "No girl in sight?"

"No. He needs proper exercise, needs to exercise the horses. I must work with him. He bursts with talent but he's raw. He's never run in a true race."

"Yes, yes." Ewing wrinkled his brow as John watched his wife maneuver her beloved father.

"You have an empty cabin at some distance from the weaving cabin. That's a possibility."

"Well, we can't have Felicia"—Ewing exhaled—"causing a loss of concentration. I'll ask Charles to look at the cabin. Is it tight? The boy would need wood. Does he know how to cook? It is quiet down there."

"What a wonderful idea. I'm sure Charles is the right person to make certain it is suitable."

Ewing said, almost as if to himself, "Nineteen and not a girl in sight."

"Don't you start," Catherine chided him.

"I was just remembering being nineteen." The corner of his mouth turned up. "Yesterday. It seems like yesterday. I can recall the moment I saw your mother as though it were yesterday. I loved her the moment I saw her. Perhaps it will hit Jeddie that way, too."

"Thank you, Father." Catherine rose, leaned down, and kissed him. "Thank you for helping me with the horses, for helping Jeddie."

Catherine and John left. Ewing, lost in memory for a time, did recall every detail when he first beheld Isabelle.

He had returned from the Grand Tour, his father had some resources but Ewing wished to strike out on his own. A gala affair at Williamsburg, his best friend from college was getting married and he was invited. Who couldn't have a good time in Williamsburg? There with the bridal party was a goddess, a true goddess. Isabelle, slender, hair in a modest becoming coiffure, somewhat loose around her face to frame it, glowing in a rose silk dress, ribbons woven into exquisite lace around her bodice. He was introduced to her by the groom's family. He couldn't speak. He stammered. She touched his forearm, remarking how dry the day was. A bit of punch would help. Music. Her cultivated voice was music. As he escorted her to the monstrously large silver punch bowl, he vowed he would win this woman if it took him years. She had beaus far more handsome than he, rich men, sons of rich men, military men, men fell all over themselves to court her. He listened to her. He listened with all his heart and he spoke from the heart. She fell in love with him. He wanted to know her, not possess her. She, young as she was, felt the difference. Loving Isabelle was the best decision he had ever made. He hoped it would happen to Jeddie. A man, slave or free, thrives with love, grows with love, becomes a better man.

Yes, he would see to the cabin.

14

Crouching down at the chink in the back door of Gary's office, Pewter whispered, *"I know you're in there."*

"That spider isn't coming out," Tucker advised.

"Why would you want her to? She's big. Let her be." Mrs. Murphy's whiskers swept forward.

"So I can chase her."

"Ugh," the tiger replied.

"Look, we chase mice and they're bigger than this spider." Pewter felt bold because, of course, the spider wasn't coming out.

"Mice have four legs. Spiders have eight. Gross."

Tucker, agreeing with Mrs. Murphy, said, *"She does have a point, Pewter. Eight legs. Too many legs."*

Pewter edged just a little closer to the chink, squinted.

She could see the spider in there. Seeing the cat so close, the spider lifted her two front legs, the long ones. Pewter backed up.

As the animals discussed the merits of chasing mammals versus insects versus spiders, the three people in Gary's workroom hovered at the drafting table.

Tazio pointed to the corner fireplace in the drawings. "The big wood-burning fireplace has the far outside corner, the small propane fireplace sits in the corner near the bathroom, smart. You need the steady heat by your pipes. He thought of everything."

"Propane isn't cheap. Prices go up and down. I can cut my firewood. Storms bring down branches," Harry stated.

Tazio came back. "The cost of filling the propane tank will vary. Let's say, since you have a big tank, fewer trips out for Tiger Fuel." She named a local company. "Eight hundred dollars. Will that last the entire winter? Who knows? We've had bitter long winters and surprisingly short ones, but for the sake of argument, let's say your winter propane bill totals sixteen hundred dollars. That's a small price for unfrozen pipes, a small price for you to walk into the work space, which will be reasonably warm. You build a fire in the traditional fireplace and soon enough you can remove your sweater, inhale the wonderful aroma of a wood fire. You're being perverse. You have a propane stove in the tack room and you told me you have one in the bedroom. Just do it."

"She's right." Cooper nodded.

"Well, okay." Harry knew perfectly well Tazio was right, just as she had known Gary was right. "So will you take the drawings, turn them into blueprints? And I am happy to listen to ideas you might have in addition to Gary's."

Tazio smiled sadly. "He was a mentor to me. Whatever I might suggest would be or will be something small, perhaps something decorative. How he wanted to build you Le Petit Trianon."

The three, silent for a moment, heard the animals at the back entrance. Brinkley, quietly attending to Tazio, rose to investigate.

"What's going on?"

"Brinkley." Pewter's voice carried excitement. *"I have trapped in the chink the world's biggest ground spider. We need to get National Geographic here."*

The yellow Lab laid flat down, nose to the floor. *"I can kinda see her."*

That fast the spider popped out, waved her forelegs at the big dog, scooted back in. The dog wiggled backward, scared.

"She's dangerous," Pewter warned. *"I've been keeping her at bay."*

Mrs. Murphy and Tucker looked at each other. Best to keep quiet.

"Pewter, that spider's almost as big as you are." The kindly Lab complimented her.

"She doesn't scare me."

Tucker dropped her eyes. If she looked at the fat gray cat, she would burst out laughing, and then the fur would fly, literally.

Tazio, noting that her dog remained in the back room, craned her neck. "Something's going on."

"Well, three of those freeloaders are mine. I'll check." Harry walked to the back room, door half open.

"*I have a monster trapped. The world's biggest spider. And she has multiple eyes, too!*"

Looking down at the gray cat, Harry remarked, "Your tail is puffed up."

"*Make her think I'm big, too.*"

"*You are,*" Tucker slyly commented.

"*Careful,*" Mrs. Murphy said quietly.

Brinkley, innocent and sweet, asked the puffed-up cat, "*How do you know the spider has multiple eyes?*"

"*When she gets close to the opening, the light shines on her eye. Little red dots. Oh, it's creepy.*" Pewter pronounced judgment.

"I don't know what you all are doing back here, but if there's pawprints on the walls or worse, big trouble. Big trouble." With that, Harry turned on her heel to join her friends. "They're fussing about something. I can't see a thing."

"Political argument, I'm sure." Tazio laughed. "Everybody else is having them."

"Taz, the animals are too smart for that."

"You've got me there," Tazio replied as she searched for a big round tube in which to place the large drawings. "For now should I leave the work he's done for Galbraith and Ix? The notes of Nature First's offices? The original drawings Lisa's coming for?"

"Yes."

They heard a knock on the back door, then it opened. Lisa Roudabush called, "Cooper, I'm here."

"*Don't take another step. You will be attacked by a rabid spider!*" Pewter warned.

"Harry." Lisa spoke loudly. "Your gray cat is having a fit."

Harry walked into the back entrance. "Pewter, you're big as a horse. What's the matter with you?"

"*You're lucky I'm here. I have the killer spider at bay.*"

"*Spiders don't get rabies,*" Mrs. Murphy coolly corrected a large Pewter.

"*This one does! That's why her eyes are red. Her eyes should be black.*" Pewter made it up as she went along, growing ever more emotional.

"Come on, Lisa. Walk past her."

"Well . . . all right. I'll be glad when Pirate is full grown. He can go first."

"*Ha. Even when Pirate is full grown I will terrorize him. Death to spiders! Death to dogs!*"

As the two women walked into the large room, Mrs. Murphy advised, "*There are two dogs here, Pewter. You've insulted them.*"

"*Tucker and Brinkley are the exception that proves the rule,*" Pewter proclaimed.

Tucker turned, walked into the big room followed by Brinkley. "*Sorry, Brinkley, she's so rude.*"

The yellow Lab smiled. "*I pay her no mind. She's mental.*"

Mrs. Murphy tagged after the dogs.

Lisa asked Cooper, "You said I could take our drawings, right?"

"You can. We have what we need."

"I'll grab another tube. Lisa, your drawings are already

rolled up on the bookshelf." Tazio pointed to the middle shelf.

Lisa picked up the Nature First designs, pausing to look at the snow globes, rubber dinosaurs, trinkets. Her eyes scanned the large squared spaces.

"A file box is missing," Lisa noticed.

"Did you ever read his files?" Cooper asked.

"No, but I wondered about them," Lisa replied. "Big and heavy."

"One is missing," Cooper admitted. "We have no idea where it is or why it's gone."

"Odd." Lisa took the proffered tube, placing her rolled-up designs in it.

"You never looked?" Cooper pressed.

"No. He said they contained building codes, year by year. As long as he knew what was in them, that's what matters."

A howl from the back entrance sent them to the room.

"She attacked me! Jumped right in my face. I'm lucky to be alive!"

"Where is she now?" Mrs. Murphy sensibly asked.

"The bathroom. She's holding the door shut, I know it!"

Harry, beholding a dramatic Pewter, suggested, "I don't know what's going on back here but let's go into the big room. Come on, Pewter!"

Tucker slyly whispered, *"I bet the spider has the missing file."*

Cooper wanted a better look at the weather so she peered out the window in the back door. "Slush. And it's going to freeze."

"We're better off with snow." Harry half believed that,

then quizzed Cooper, "You never said if you found any-thing interesting in his desk."

"Why would I? Nothing but bills, inquiries. One letter from his old employer informing him about the hearings in Richmond over the Kushner Building. He was part of the project. Nothing electrifying."

She continued. "All right, ladies. Let's pick it up and let me lock up. We've got about an hour before the sun sets and everything will freeze in a heartbeat. You all go home."

"What's your shift?" Harry usually knew but, thanks to the weather, county employees were all on different shifts now, the sheriff's department doing extra duty.

"Off at seven."

They each got into their cars. Before Cooper could pull away, Harry got out of her Volvo station wagon, tapped on Cooper's window.

"Left my reading glasses on the drafting table."

"Yeah. Yeah." Cooper got out, unlocked the office door, walked in with Harry as Mrs. Murphy, Pewter, and Tucker, noses to the car window, observed with displeasure. Why were they left in the car?

Harry snatched up her reading glasses, put them on, walked over to the shelves.

"You rarely put on your reading glasses in public," Coo-per tormented her.

"You, Taz, and Lisa are not public. And guess what, Smarty, it will happen to you."

"Come on, I need to get back to HQ."

"One little minute." Harry read the bio of Gary's great-great-grandfather under the sword on the wall. It was a small square under the impressive man's photo. "I never took the time to read this. You don't think this could be related to the fact that his great-great-grandfather was a Confederate soldier?"

"No. He'd need to be sitting on a statue for that."

"Very funny." Harry took a moment to look down at the returned files then up to the small trove of treasures, the large tooth, the heavy globes, a few old antique hand tools, the rubber dinosaurs.

"Harry!"

"All right."

The answer to Gary's death was staring them right in the face. There was no way they could have known.

15

"How do you remember everything?" Harry tagged after Marvella, clipping along.

"Good sense of direction," the imperious woman replied then smiled just slightly. "And I am here two times a week, if not three, and I studied the building plans before the addition was added."

"Um. I'm still impressed." Harry was.

"I should think you would have focused on sporting art when you were an Art History major."

"Sporting art hid under a cloud, plus I was at Smith. Everyone wanted to discuss modern art. And there was always the Impressionist contingent. I never fit in."

"Good for you. People who never fit in are more interesting."

"You fit in. Marvella, you run Richmond." Harry laughed.

Marvella stopped at the top of the stairway, a stairway baffling to Harry because she didn't remember it. "Yes. And no. The color of my skin, a factor over which I have no control, same as gender, created a standing outside, for lack of a better word, view. I certainly wasn't embraced when Tinsdale and I, newly married, moved here. But times change, we change. Being outside, having to think twice, so to speak, made me more resourceful, better able to look into people's motivations."

"I never thought of that."

"You didn't need to." She reached for Harry's hand as they descended the steps, Harry's other hand on the guardrail. "I often wonder would I be the person I am if I had not endured institutionalized oppression? I doubt I would be. I think I'd miss more. Pierre and I used to talk about this all the time." She named her recently deceased brother.

"He didn't leave detailed directives concerning his art collection, did he?" Harry knew how good Pierre's collection was, and it was a hundred-eighty degrees opposite his sister's tastes.

Marvella sighed. "I've been working on it. There are places one would like to donate a fine painting, but the school or small gallery doesn't have the means to support it, protect it."

"Aren't you tempted to donate his collection to the Virginia Museum of Fine Arts? Especially after all the work you've done here." Harry and Marvella reached the bottom of the stairs, Marvella dropped her hand.

"I am. I will, but I still must sort through it. I'd like

some works to go to Howard, our joint alma mater. The Art History department is excellent, but everyone wants to be a lawyer, a politician, or a businessman now. I can't stand it," she said with feeling.

Harry tweaked her. "You're married to one of the most powerful lawyers in the mid-South."

Marvella twirled her hand. "Don't I know it. When he talks to me like one of his business partners I let him have it." She grinned. "I tell him he can go home from his business partners but he'd better pay first attention to me. Talk to me like your wife. He hears that."

"Bet he does." They walked toward the dining room on the second floor.

Once again Harry wasn't sure how they had arrived at this point. She was certain that the sporting collection, one of the finest anywhere in the United States, was on the same floor around the corner. It wasn't.

"Do you ever have to put Fair in his place?"

"No. It's usually the other way around. I drift."

"You know what Mae West said. 'I used to be Snow White but I drifted.'"

The two women laughed as the maître d' inclined her head, showed Marvella her table. No waiting. No anything. When Marvella showed up, people jumped.

After ordering a light lunch, Marvella looked out the expansive windows. "I like winter. You see the bones."

Harry knew exactly what she meant. "Me, too."

"All right. Back to Smith. You focused on Medieval Art."

"Not very many of us but the purity of it drew me. Most all of it is religious, or paintings of kings and queens.

I love the colors. I love that each work should tell a story or celebrate a king. It's right there in your face."

"True. I never thought of that." A smartly dressed man, perhaps mid-forties, walked up to the table. "Sean." She extended her hand. "This is Harry Haristeen. She was invaluable in solving my brother's murder."

"A sorrowful task. Pierre was a man of many parts." Then he beamed at Marvella. "As is his sister. I didn't mean to disturb you but I have been thinking about your idea. Talked it over with Dad. We are very interested. Dad's not getting around too much these days. Would you come over to the house?"

"I'd love to. I've put some of the available works on a thumb drive. Do you have a way to show him the paintings?"

"Do." He picked up her hand, lightly kissing it. "You could talk a dog off a meat wagon, you know."

"You flatter me but, Sean, something like this does have political value. Especially in these times. You understand these things."

Pleased with the compliment, he subtly raised an eyebrow. "Tuesday? I'll call. Dad is free Tuesday."

"I'm very excited. I think you will be, too."

"Pleased to meet you, Miss Haristeen." He slightly bowed to her, very slightly, very Southern, and left.

Marvella glowed. "I'll give you a copy. Said I would. Some of the work is quite extraordinary. One thinks of Russia separate from Europe, languishing in the far northern latitudes. But over the last three centuries, even with the interruption and destruction of the arts by the

Soviets, the artists were as polished as any European nation. It's quite extraordinary." She paused. "A thumb drive is easier than all those catalogs." She then said, "That was Sean Rankin."

"I figured that out and I forgot to tell you when we spoke by phone that a fellow who used to work for Rankin Construction was murdered last week. Gary Gardner."

"I'm afraid I don't know him, but I'm sorry to hear he was murdered."

"He was designing a special workshed for me. He said he wanted to build Le Petit Trianon but I was too practical." Harry smiled. "Anyway, he was an architect, obviously, and designed some of the early high-rise buildings here. Left in 1984 to come to Crozet. Said he grew tired of building big boxes."

"Sean's father was one of the early proponents of modern architecture, modern materials. Of course, the early stuff was and remains hideous. Just hideous. Not just here but everywhere."

"The fads turned me away from perhaps appreciating the work as much as I might. When I was in grade school the rash of reflecting buildings began. Shiny windows in bronze or light blue or like mirrors. They are still being constructed," Harry said.

"Well, who is to say that flying buttresses weren't a fad? However, they have stood for more than a thousand years."

"They have." Harry smiled.

"Given Richmond's building codes, the new structures will stand. Unfortunately, most are undistinguished."

"Everywhere, don't you think?"

Marvella nodded. "One of the ways I know buildings are well constructed here is when the Kushner Building was torn down it proved difficult. It was built by Rankin back in the eighties. They will be building the replacement, the Cloudcroft Building. Forty stories. A Z shape. Very unusual with green space along the spine of the Z. At least it's imaginative." She exhaled.

"Was there resistance?" Harry's curiosity awoke.

"On traffic problems, the time it will take to build the thing. A tax break for Cloudcroft for bringing business to Richmond has some people infuriated. They want tax breaks for themselves. We even have a group that is opposed to changing the Richmond skyline. I was unaware that there was one." She slyly smiled.

"The Federal Reserve building." Harry smiled back. "That really is about it. Take comfort in saving the tobacco warehouses."

"I do, but they are rarely above two stories. I take that back, some were large, down by the river where the tobacco was held before being shipped out. I quite like them."

"Save the skyline," Harry mused, returning to the skyline complaint.

"Almost forgot. There is an environmental criticism but I don't know their exact problem. I would think we've done all the environmental damage we can do." Marvella laughed.

On and on they talked, bouncing between current events, the spiritual meanings of colors in medieval art,

Marvella's urging Harry to travel to other museums, perhaps even to once again take classes.

They became quite entranced by the thought of what perspective in art meant, how it changed painting, the movement of the eye.

After all this, Harry followed Marvella to the gorgeous, understated old home that she and Tinsdale owned right on Monument Avenue, where she picked up the thumb drive.

As Harry stood by the door to go home, Marvella encouraged her. "Now you call me the minute you see them. I must hear what you think."

"I will. You've made me curious about Cloudcroft. A Z structure."

Marvella waved her hand. "You'll see for yourself. Next visit. If the weather's good we'll walk to the excavation. On the outside wall Rankin has painted the building's exterior, the landscaping for the green spaces. The wall surrounds the big dig. Each side has a painting. One is the interior, a look at the glamorous lights. Another is the penthouse. The last one is the Richmond skyline with the Z lit up. That word again. Skyline."

16

Bleak, windy, raw, a typical March day kept Ewing inside, fire roaring in his library. Catherine, showing signs of her pregnancy, remained with him, sorting letters. Correspondence on the left, financial interests on the right.

She sat across from her father, her shawl loose around her shoulders. The warmth from the fire proved sufficient.

"You'll want to read this one." She handed him a letter, paper heavy, well laid, gorgeous handwriting on the envelope.

He reached, checked the front. "Ah, the baron. He's in the middle of everything."

When a young man on the Grand Tour of Europe, Ewing, in France, had met Baron Necker, also young, in-

terested in the New World. The two men, eyes to the future, hopes high, became friends. Both became important in their nations. As for Baron Necker, he was born to it. Ewing made his own way, although his father gave him the advantage of a superior education and at his death bequeathed to him the tobacco lands south of the James. The baron would always compliment Ewing by saying that the Virginian had made his own way.

Perching his spectacles on his nose, Ewing read, gasped.

"What is it, Father?"

"The Comte de Vergennes has died. The powerful foreign minister. A bad time to take leave of France no matter what one thinks of him. The king has summoned the Assembly of Notables. Necker writes the hall of the king's Menus-Plaisirs, not one empty seat. Those most powerful sit in the front, vigilant of their privileges. But listen, my dear. The Comptroller General of Finance, Charles-Alexandre de Calonne, began a speech insinuating that he, only he, wooed the king to call this assembly. Furthermore, he, again alone, has restored confidence in the nation's finances, which when he was appointed in 1783 languished in a disastrous state." He looked over the rim of his glasses. "That's a broadside against Necker."

"His predecessor?" Catherine did her best to keep abreast of events in England, France, and the various Germanies. As to Spain, rich though it was, Catherine considered it a shot bolt. She and her father would discuss these things, each finding reasons for the stagnation of Spain, the arrogance of England, the foolishness of France. Then they would examine the new nation in which they lived. The comparisons could be sobering.

"Well, Necker's *Account Rendered* ultimately brought about his dismissal, but listen. This is fantastic. I cannot think of another word. The treasury collects four hundred seventy-five million livres a year. France spends six hundred million livres a year. At the end of 1786 the deficit was thirty-seven million livres, but, oh, this is shocking. Shocking." He took a restorative breath. "By the end of 1786, twelve hundred and fifty million livres had been borrowed—twelve hundred and fifty million livres! Dear God. Furthermore, Calonne laid the financial abuses not just on the former Comptroller, my friend, but at the feet of the most privileged, who benefit from many special financial levies. Certain agricultural goods benefit some members, but not others. The purchase of salt. Good God, this is a most depressing list, but here is the insult, the outrageous insult."

His face reddened. "The raving toady declares that France has given birth to America!" He slapped the letter on the desk. "Was their assistance invaluable? Yes. But the citizens of the colonies gave birth to this nation, not a gaggle of raving aristocrats and royals of questionable intellect. Just wait until I show this to my friends!"

Catherine picked up the letter, read quietly, then laughed. "Well, there is humor in Paris. The baron quotes from a pamphleteer or some form of writer. Now listen." She raised her chin, glanced at her father, and began in her captivating, beguiling, cultivated rich alto: "'Among the blessings attaching to this great age, France will soon be able to count the joy of embracing to its bosom the illustrious author of so many fine pamphlets against the Water Company.'" She laughed.

"That is an elegant humiliation."

"The baron wishes you to know he did not inform you last year of Calonne's pamphlets, thinking them of no interest to a man of the New World, as he puts it. And he wishes you to know that Calonne wrote those pamphlets. The Water Company. France was aware, forgive the pun, of screeds against the Water Company. A project for which Calonne was offered no livres under the table, which may have triggered his resentment." She handed the letter back to her father.

"Something must be done over there, but each of those men at the Assembly will fight tooth and nail for his special privilege. And from this letter it appears the Comptroller has overplayed his hand."

"I forgot to look, who wrote the scathing comment about the joy of embracing?"

Ewing scanned the strong handwriting. "Ah, here he tells us. Mirabeau. A man on the make, a man intelligent enough to make fools of the Assembly." He again looked at his daughter. "That can be heady stuff but remember this is a country with a king. It is possible a man can lose his head. Not here." Then he paused. "Not yet anyway."

"Do you think we should call an assembly?"

"My dear, neither France nor we can go on. Should we add up all the war debts from the thirteen colonies, I don't think it would touch the debt over there, but we are so new, our commerce small compared to theirs. We have some products the world desires. They have more ways to make money or coerce it out of others than we do. But do we need our own gathering?" He thought. "Sometimes putting men of education and wealth in a room is not a good idea. Leaven it with some military men, working men, still not such a good idea, but better. Fill it with lawyers and you are doomed, everlasting doom."

Knowing of her father's disaffection for lawyers, she kept silent.

He placed the letter on his desk. "I don't mean to distress you, my dear, but I wonder if we are in a better state than France. Every state, like every prince, comte, duke, whatever, is out for itself. Petty. Selfish and retarding commerce. This can't go on any more than France's borrowing can continue."

"Someone has to take the first step. Washington?"

Ewing shook his head. "The general will stay above the fray. But if some form of assembly is called it will only work if he blesses it." He rubbed his forehead. "I wish I had answers. And, my dear, we had best prepare ourselves for losses from our French clients. I doubt we will be paid for our large tobacco shipment. I hope I am wrong, but we will face large losses."

"The English?"

A lip curled slightly. "Convinced though they are of their superiority and that we are traitors, they will pay. Actually, I suspect the ire of the educated has been splenetic, focused on Lord North. We are somewhat off the hook."

"We sent much tobacco there."

"Safe. For one thing they sit around in those coffee-houses, talk politics, and smoke. I would question English industry in the cities. Too much talk."

"Perhaps they save the coffeehouse for when work is done. Consider their power," Catherine countered.

"I do. I do." Ewing folded his hands over his chest.

Two sets of small footsteps echoed in the polished hall. Bettina's echoed behind them. JohnJohn, Tulli, and Bettina stopped at the library's open door.

"I rode today!" JohnJohn, tipping over two years old but a big boy for his age, much like his father, loudly announced.

Tulli, nine, kept a close watch on the child, loved him, really. "He did. Cold as it is he rode all by himself."

"I'm going to be a soldier like Father." His little chest puffed out.

"That's wonderful, JohnJohn." Catherine stood, walked to the door, picked up her son.

Ewing laughed. "Next thing you know, he'll be in the irons, racing against you and Jeddie."

"I will."

Tulli, turning into a good little rider, said nothing, but Catherine, sensitive to such things, put her hand on his shoulder. "He'll have to catch you, won't he, Tulli?"

A wordless grin followed this statement.

"All right, you two beggars. Back to the kitchen. Never know what you'll find in there." Bettina turned to walk down the hall.

"A pie?" JohnJohn shouted.

Bettina threw up her hands as she kept walking.

Catherine remarked, "I'd find out if I were you. No one can cook or bake like Bettina."

The little fellow ran, not terribly well but he did run. Tulli skipped behind him.

Catherine returned to her seat, then stood up, carried a log to the fireplace, an upward shower of molten sparks emitting dots of color and light.

"Roger can do that," Ewing said.

Roger, the butler, performed many services. Like Ewing, age was encroaching. He was training his son, Weymouth, to succeed him since being butler is a position of responsibility, power. A good butler understands the politics of any situation. He is also the head man among the slaves. Weymouth, obedient but unmotivated, did not have the makings of a good butler. Roger tried to hide his disappointment.

"I know he can but I like to keep a fire going. And I'm sure Roger is back there in the kitchen with Bettina. They're solving some problem on this place of which we know nothing."

He nodded. "They're uncanny, those two. By the way, how do you think Bettina's romance with DoRe progresses?"

"At a stately pace." Catherine laughed. "They're in their forties, lost their first mates, and DoRe works for that holy horror." She meant Maureen Selisse Holloway.

He shook his head. "Holy horror she is, but she is uncommonly shrewd about finance. She obviously picked up a great deal from her father."

Maureen's father, a powerful banker in the Caribbean,

made money both honestly and dishonestly, but make it, he did. As did Maureen.

The fire hissed, cracked. Ewing inhaled the pleasing odor. His desk, at a right angle to the fireplace, allowed him to view the fire as he worked. In summer's warm weather he would have his desk turned so it faced the fireplace, which would have been scrubbed out, a large brass fan put in the middle with another fan of huge turkey feathers in front of the brass fan.

Catherine, too, watched the flames.

"Sometimes the world weighs on my shoulders. Then I listen to JohnJohn or watch Marcia and Isabelle together. The world vanishes for a time." He smiled. "Then again, bad as it seems it's not as fearful as when I could have been hanged for supporting the rebellion."

"It's God's grace that we won." Catherine, not given to religious sentiments, believed that.

"Indeed." He inquired, "Feeling all right?"

"The baby's not due until July. I'm fine."

"Well, you know anytime you wish to nap or rest, tell me."

"I will. Given the baron's letter, should we not seek other sources of revenue?"

"I have been doing so. I have tried to create sources of income that cannot be wiped out at once. Hence the timber, the apple orchard, the tobacco holdings south of the James and in North Carolina. The only other things I can conceive would be a flour mill, a sawmill, a foundry."

"All needed. But we would have to build them, find people with the knowledge to run them and run them honestly."

"Pestalozzi has the best flours, cornmeal," Ewing added. "I doubt we could do better."

"I've been putting off a decision but given our potential losses, I will contact Yancy and agree to race Reynaldo against Black Knight."

"Is that wise? You would be training as you grow closer to birth."

"True, but I will be on the ground. Jeddie will be breezing him."

"He's a good young man."

"He is. With Jeddie working the blooded horses and Barker O. training the driving horses, we are formidable."

"You're formidable. I sit back and watch."

"You can ride."

"Not well and I don't love it," he admitted. "You have always loved it. And it looks as though JohnJohn may grow into that also. I haven't asked but I can't help myself. Do you want a boy or a girl? If I've heard the answer I don't remember. I think I would remember."

Catherine laughed. "A girl. I live with two boys now, my husband and JohnJohn. I need an ally."

He laughed with her. "Now you know how I felt surrounded by you, Rachel, and your mother." He paused. "I believe I learned more from your mother than anyone else in my life. She was an uncommon woman who could see around corners. She perceived things I missed. She felt things. I would try to be logical and she'd kiss me on the cheek and say, 'Husband, people are not logical. They pretend to be.' She was right."

"She'd say that to me, too. She'd point her finger at me,

usually walking in the garden. 'You are just like your father.' I'm glad of that." Catherine complimented him.

He smiled. "I have many shortcomings."

"Don't we all, Father? But as to being logical, it seems to me, we can try to be so. The French could use a bit of bracing logic and so could we. We do need an assembly. I say nothing. It's not my place and in some ways that gives me an advantage. I can listen to the conversation of your friends and absorb it all. Some people can peer into the future better than others, but no one really knows, do they?"

"And they never will," he declared with finality.

17

"Ninety-one billion dollars. Ninety-one!" Harry exclaimed as she wrapped the snow globes in tissue paper before carefully putting them in a sturdy box. She was helping Tazio reorganize Gary's office, now her new office.

"I never think of agriculture and forestry. I know I should but . . ." Tazio shrugged as she taped up a filled carton.

"Small farmer that I am, I sure do." Harry set one globe aside, the flamingo looking skyward with shock. "Agriculture is Virginia's largest private industry and forestry is third. Everyone is bedazzled by dot-com and coding but, Taz, Mother Earth remains the source of all wealth. Undergirds everything."

"Well, I do remember you telling me that one large

walnut tree can be worth from two to five thousand dollars, depending on the market when it is harvested."

"Susan owns a fortune in walnut, those bottom slopes of the Blue Ridge behind my farm."

"Didn't her uncle will that to her? The one who was a monk?"

"Did. She pays me an annual fee to monitor the walnuts. Personally, I wouldn't cut but a few of them. Too beautiful, too big. I feel that way about a lot of trees, like the big oak at Oak Ridge Estate. It was standing there when Tarleton raided the Upper James during the Revolutionary War, burning and looting while he searched for Patrick Henry, whom he had every intention of hanging."

"I thought there weren't many settlers this far from the Tidewater then." Tazio, from St. Louis, knew a little Virginia history, starting in 1607.

The history of the New World as written down by its colonizers actually started before 1607, with Sir Walter Raleigh's colony at Roanoke on the Albemarle Sound in what is now North Carolina. But those people disappeared. The 1607 group hung on, they starved, froze, did what they could, prayed a lot, but ultimately they did survive.

"Over one hundred fifty years later, Patrick Henry's mother lived this far west. Remember, Dolley Madison's mother was Patrick Henry's mother's sister."

Tazio blew out her cheeks. "How do you remember all that? What I remember about Missouri history is Mark Twain was raised at Hannibal, and T. S. Eliot, Marianne Moore, and Maya Angelou at St. Louis. For a Midwestern state we haven't been slack in the literary department." She laughed.

"How do I remember?" Harry picked up the flamingo, turned him upside down, the snowflakes twisted down. "This cracks me up. He did have a wonderful sense of humor. Oh, back to memory. I attended public school in Crozet. Virginia history was drummed into our heads as was civics. I hear they don't teach civics anymore, pretty much anywhere."

Tazio, close to ten years younger than Harry and therefore in her early thirties, stopped oiling and wiping down her new large drafting table. "I was taught civics. You know what I think? You can chalk this up to me being mixed race if you want, but I truly believe this. Civics was yanked out of the classroom so people of color wouldn't really know how government works at the local, state, and national levels. You're much easier to manipulate if you're ignorant." She took a deep breath. "Guess that applies to whites, too."

"What you don't know can really hurt you, and for those who are poor, uneducated, they become dependent on government. That's truly dangerous, in my book anyway. Docile people give way to a dictator. To anyone who promises them food, clothing, and shelter as a baseline. Not much work involved." Harry added to the thought.

"I have to consider the baseline." Tazio stepped back to admire her rubbing, changed the subject. "What a beautiful table, my drafting table is maybe half this size and not nearly as well made."

"Taz, forgive me if I'm overstepping the line. We've

known each other for some years, we work together to preserve the Colored School, to keep our history truthful. But we've never discussed race. I always figured if I made a mess, you'd tell me."

"I would. The only thing I can tell you is it's never far from my mind. I try not to dwell on it but there are things you can take for granted that I can't. There's always a bit of wariness there."

Harry turned to face her friend. "I'm sorry. I'm sorry you have to spend your time on that. With all your creativity I would wish that would consume all your thoughts, time." She then said, "Sucks, doesn't it?"

"What sucks is that Gary was murdered. Is there still institutional racism and sexism? Sure. Probably not as bad as it was for Mom, who married an African American. But it's there. You don't wipe out centuries, or in the case of women, millennia of prejudice in a generation or two. That's reality. But Gary, what was that? A talented man, a good man, a really helpful fellow. Poof." She snapped her fingers.

"Haunts me. But it's wonderful that you have rented his office. He would have liked that. He just adored you. He'd brag about your work."

"He did?"

"All the time." A big smile crossed Harry's face. "He was a Virginian, remember. He wouldn't tell you to your face. Didn't want you to get the big head."

Tears filled Tazio's eyes. "I thought I was a pest."

Harry came over, put her arm around Tazio's waist. "Honey, he thought the world of you. He'd say, 'If she wants it, she'll become a famous architect, a society architect. She has it all.' Then again, you are a beautiful young woman, and I think working with you, mentoring you, made him feel young."

Tazio couldn't hold back the tears. "Oh God, if only I could tell him what he meant to me. I never did. I never, ever did."

"We forget to tell people we love them. I do it all the time. I couldn't live without Susan. Do I tell her? No. But I'm there when she needs me or when Ned needs someone to help him canvass. I dutifully visit her grandmother and mother and I love them, too. Why is it we just keep our mouths shut?"

"I don't know but I feel guilty."

"Don't. You've taken over his office. You've kept up some photographs of his work. You're keeping most of his books and the old files. Your touches make it more colorful. He was pretty Spartan."

"Funny. He could create such exquisite detail for his homes. Even your shed."

"He could." Harry kissed her on the cheek, then returned to the shelf. "He must have a million rubber dinosaurs and snow globes here. Say, do you mind if I take the flamingo to have something of his?"

"No. I'm keeping the one of Monticello in the snow. But all those knickknacks would drive me crazy. I don't want to dust them. I'll keep the dinosaurs, though. They make me laugh. Plus the dust won't show so much."

Laughing, Harry picked up a globe with a polar bear in it, blew some dust off it. "He didn't dust."

"Coop hasn't found the 1984 file, has she?"

"Coop's questioned everyone. She's also tracked down every Ducati owner in Virginia. She works hard," Harry remarked. "She doesn't have a lot to go on. No, she hasn't found it."

"Ah."

A scuffle by the back door sent Harry to the area. "What are you doing?"

"*Protecting you.*" Pewter, claws unleashed, sat in the middle of the small space.

"*It's the spider,*" Tucker helpfully added.

Brinkley, sweet fellow, stood next to the gray cat. "*It really is a big, big spider.*"

"*I am fearless!*"

"*Obsessed is more like it,*" Mrs. Murphy dryly commented.

"Come on. Into the big room. I'm closing this door. I don't know what you all are up to but it can't be good with all this hissing. Come on." She shepherded them into the room, closed the door tight, which she thought she probably should have done in the first place to keep out that wedge of cold air.

"What was it?"

"Goblins," came the terse reply.

The two women worked for another two hours. What Tazio wished to keep was placed in the carton with tissue paper and newspapers.

"Keeping his pencils and T-square?"

"You bet. I'm keeping the files, too, as I said. It's not a bad idea to have the building codes. He made marginal notes that would be helpful if I ever need to rebuild something built in 1979. I can download the codes but his notes are on the papers. A computer stores tons of material but you never get the marginal notes, the squiggles. And who is to say that a former client might not come in here someday and want an addition? It's just a good idea. If we had building plans for the Colored School I would have pored over them. I mean, I haven't studied them but I did notice odd citations regarding stresses, insulation ratings, new materials. Small initials, but I don't know what they mean. Still, I'm keeping the files."

"Well built, those three frame school buildings."

"Sure are. I love the floor-to-ceiling windows. Natural light is always better than artificial. There was no electricity. Gary was right about structures from the past." She sighed. "He was right about a lot of things."

"What do we do with the cartons?"

"No inheritors. Well, no one wants his work things. I shouldn't put it that way. No children. I'll save stuff. You never know when something might be needed. There isn't much storage space here. I can rent a storage unit for a hundred dollars a month, a small unit is less. This won't even fill a small unit."

"Think it will stay dry?"

"Oh sure. Can you imagine the lawsuits if those U-Stor things were sloppy? But this way it's near but not in the way."

Harry walked over to his desk. "I always like the blue light on his atomic clock."

"Me, too."

"And you've moved the tooth over here. Why are you keeping the tooth? It's a big tooth."

"It's a dinosaur tooth."

"No kidding."

"I take it you weren't one of those kids fascinated by dinosaurs?"

"No. I take it you were and Gary must have been if he kept a tooth."

"I think this is from a meat-eater called Acrocanthosaurus. Big but not gargantuan compared to some other meat-eaters. I'll find out when I have time."

"*Big. Big is the spider.*" Pewter spoke from the floor.

"*Spiders don't have teeth,*" Tucker said.

"*No, but their mouth is sideways. Like little pincers.*" Mrs. Murphy had observed spiders and other little crawlies. "*Can bite you and inject poison.*"

"Ugh." Brinkley closed his eyes.

"Are we done?"

"We are. I'll be open for clients next Monday. This location is so much better than where I was stuck in that cubbyhole at the edge of town. The rent isn't bad."

"Are you keeping his sign?"

"I'll put it in here on the wall. Virginia Signs will hang mine tomorrow." She was pleased. "It's beginning to feel just right."

They locked the door to the back as well as the front when they left. Cold air smacked them right in the face.

"This doesn't only tighten your pores, it tightens your eyeballs," Harry observed.

"Feels like snow, doesn't it?"

Harry nodded, hurried past the space where Gary was shot. For one brief moment she, too, had been looking down the barrel of that gun. Then the killer slipped it back into his motorcycle jacket.

Harry didn't know anything worth killing her over. Not yet.

18

March 18, 1787

Sunday

The glow of the fire behind her snatched some years from Maureen Selisse Holloway's face. Very feminine, narrow nose, full lips, blond hair maintained with a secret remedy, she proved attractive. In her youth she exuded a potent allure. Two sumptuous perfect breasts added to this, as well as a very sizable inheritance. Now perhaps fifteen pounds heavier, in her early forties, she remained attractive but no longer devastating. She vowed to regain her girlish figure but those French sauces, the piecrusts so light they might fly away, and the fine wine. Too much temptation.

Sitting across from her in her petite parlor as she called it, was Catherine. Unlike Maureen, she didn't much care about looks or allure. Yes, she wore beautiful clothes because her sister and Bumbee worked her over. No one

would describe Catherine as warm, friendly but not especially warm, whereas Rachel was so warm she drew people like a magnet. In ways, Catherine frightened people.
She was too beautiful, too logical, too in possession of
her emotions. She loved the horses, loved commerce.
People she endured. Working with her father opened the
world to her.

Maureen, shrewd, silver quick with money, appreciated
Catherine's qualities although she wished the younger
woman was less beautiful.

"Have you ever attended mass?" Maureen asked as a
well-dressed young servant poured tea.

"Yes. Mother took me once when we visited Philadelphia. Very dramatic, colorful, magical for a child."

"Your mother must have been a woman of wide interests."

"She had such curiosity about the world. She'd whisper
to me that an Anglican was just a Catholic with an English
accent."

Maureen laughed. "There's truth to that. Of course with
Mother being Irish and Father Spanish not only did I go
to mass, I was schooled by nuns. Oh, they were so strict."
She shook her head. "Much of the Caribbean is Catholic,
most of the New World is except for America and Canada."

"This room shines. You have a touch."

Maureen beamed. "Color, fabrics, furnishings. Mother
trained me to look for proportion, color, harmony. She
would say, 'Fashion is one thing but be cautious. You don't
want to look like everyone else!'"

"Indeed." Catherine liked that thought.

"Did you, John, and Ewing go to church this morning?"

"Roads were treacherous but we managed. Father says it makes him feel close to Mother." Catherine nibbled a tiny meat pie. "Wonderful."

"High praise from a woman who has the best cook in Virginia. Bettina is a treasure." She paused. "A treasure with many opinions."

They both laughed for Bettina was not shy, but she was smart enough to keep much to herself. Then again, people expected an outgoing cook.

"Do you know, driving over here, I realized you and I have never been alone to chat," Catherine remarked. "I have always been curious as to your farsightedness concerning things like the foundry down by the James, your surprising and successful importation of French fabrics, even some Italian ones."

"Father entertained ships' captains. He would pose questions to the Englishman, the Frenchman, the Spaniard, his countrymen. He would inquire about where the aristocrats were putting their money. This provoked a laugh because have you ever met an aristocrat or a royal who could turn a profit? But of course their managers must or they would get the sack. And my father was trusted by these captains to handle their money. I listened. I was usually in the next room pretending to embroider with the governess, after they would leave, I asked my father questions."

"Seems we both learned from intelligent men. Quietly, of course."

Maureen nodded. "It would never do for a woman to discuss business but I learned how to work through Francisco." She inhaled. "That could be a chore. My late husband thought he knew everything." She lifted a bit of crust with her fork. "My current angel has no head for business. I tell him what to do and he readily does it. I must add that he does understand timber whereas I, from the islands, am weak in that crop, if you will. He is a sweet man, Jeffrey."

"And so handsome. The two of you together make a fine pair," Catherine complimented her, and it wasn't an outright lie.

"You are too kind." She changed the subject. "What do you and your father hear from France?"

Catherine knew Maureen had her own sources as they both did business with the French. Maureen was double-checking.

"Great uncertainty. The foreign minister, de Vergennes, has died. Those with whom we trade are beginning to ask for us to extend their terms. And my father's friend from his Grand Tour, Baron Necker, writes that Calonne, all bombast and twaddle, his exact words, can't settle the crown's debts."

Maureen stared at Catherine, her hazel eyes bright. "No one can, my dear. Not even Crassus could solve their problems."

She named the richest man in Rome during the time of Julius Caesar.

"Ah, so you, too, have heard."

"My father did brisk business with bankers in Paris and I have kept many of them as friends. Mostly through their wives, of course, but one does learn, one does learn. This king is unkingly. Now, Louis XV was every inch a king."

"So I have heard."

"Mother and Father took me to Paris as a young girl, just on the cusp, so to speak, and I saw the king. Impressive, as were his mistresses." She lifted an eyebrow. "No wonder the treasury is low." She couldn't help but laugh.

"We may well have to endure losses, but strange to say, Yancy Grant wants to create horse races down on The Levels with large purses. He mentioned in passing to Father that we had best find other sources of income."

"Did he now?" Maureen loathed Yancy, who insulted her husband and wound up in a duel with him.

"You have suffered from his drunken rage." Catherine meant that. "But he may have come up with something worth examining, which is looking to ourselves as opposed to Europe."

Maureen, turning this over in her mind, nodded but said nothing.

They ate in silence until Catherine said, "You know that Bettina and DoRe are courting."

"Yes."

"We shall have to hope for the best."

Noncommital, Maureen shrugged. "We'll see. I have endured enough uproar on this estate from slaves." As Catherine said nothing, she continued. "But I will bear in mind what you have said about not looking toward France or England."

"Well, I think you have the answer right here."

"I do?"

"Look at the beautiful coach Jeffrey built. He borrowed ours, reproduced it, and made one even better."

Maureen's eyebrows shot upward. "Yes, he did."

"To find a good coach one must go to Philadelphia or import one from England or from the Continent. Much too expensive and now unreliable. If you can keep a foundry going, this ought to be easy."

Maureen, shorn of sentiment, knew better than to ask "What's in it for you?" but she circumnavigated the direct questions. "However did you come up with this idea, which I must think about?"

Catherine smiled. "We are both women who understand profit, one must grow. And I think Yancy is right. What beautiful horses will pull your coaches, phaetons, gigs?"

"Ah."

"A thought."

Catherine left knowing she'd put a tantalizing idea in front of Maureen. She could breed coach horses. They wouldn't be in business together. Catherine couldn't abide that, but one would bolster the other.

As she was helped into the coach by Barker O., who had stayed in the stables with King David and Solomon, the elegant coach horses, she smiled at DoRe.

Barker O. and DoRe, while competitive, had great respect for each other. Discussing horses, training methods, enlivened them.

William, a young man Jeddie's age, nineteen, quietly listened. It wouldn't do to interrupt one's elders.

As Barker O. drove the coach away, William said to DoRe, "Is it true she memorizes bloodlines?"

"She knows them back to the old king, Charles II: He had a mare, Creme Cheeks."

Still watching the coach, putting his hands in his pockets, William looked from the coach to the formidable DoRe.

"A man good with horses can go anywhere in the world."

DoRe stepped back into the barn, William behind him. "Maybe. Maybe not."

"You go everywhere." William's lower lip jutted out.

"I drive the Master and Missus. I see things." He shrugged.

"I want to ride. I want to make money. I hear they race all the time in England and France and jockeys grow rich."

"You think the Missus will send you to France? She won't even send you to Richmond or Williamsburg. She cares nothing about racing. Best you keep your thoughts to yourself."

"Your son got away from here."

DoRe rounded on William. "My son was falsely accused of murder. If he hadn't run, that bitch"—he couldn't help it, he used that word—"would have seen him hang."

DoRe, circumspect, was grateful no one else was in the barn. Maureen set her people against one another spying.

Someone might have tattled on him, receiving money or preference. Trust was in short supply on Big Rawly.

Defiant, reckless, William glared. "I'll be free even if I have to kill someone."

"Don't be a fool, William. Don't ever say that again. You know she has eyes and ears everywhere."

"I'll get away and you'll watch me."

With that William returned to the tack room to clean a bridle.

DoRe shook his head. *The young,* he thought to himself, as he also thought best to keep his distance from a hothead.

Rocking in the coach, feet on a brazier, wrapped in a fur blanket, Catherine felt a tingle of excitement. Risk pushed her on, provoked her to do better. Not a fearful person, she'd try new things. And she wanted to make money, pots of it.

She hoped France would pull things together, honor debts. Then again, she hoped other states would honor debts.

If one couldn't make a profit, if one couldn't get credit, commerce would be strangled. Catherine rarely wished to be a man, but when it came to business, she felt she knew more than many of the men she had observed. And she knew she could never let them know that. She would fight the anger rising in her throat by realizing how easy they were to influence. Maybe it evened out. Who was to say?

But she wanted to win and win big.

19

January 23, 2017

Monday

Square holes cut in the safety walls around the Cloudcroft Building allowed people to watch the progress. Renditions in color of the imaginative Z building covered the high wooden safety walls.

Harry and Marvella peered through two squares.

"This thing is huge," Harry exclaimed.

"Is. Sean said they must dig out the entire foundation, go down to bedrock, sink in the enormous support beams to about eight feet, fill it in to finally realize the Z shape for the foundation. It's complicated." Marvella scanned the heavy machinery for sight of Sean. "Ah, come along, Harry. We need to go to the other side."

The two hurried along watching for icy spots on the temporary sidewalk. Reaching the two-lane road into the cavernous excavation site, they waited. The heavy machinery was kept in the pit but foremen needed to drive their cars into the area.

Marvella checked her watch. "Ten. He's good about time."

Indeed he was.

Her cellphone rang. "Marvella, it's Sean. Stay where you are. I'll pick you up."

Within minutes he drove up the incline in a bespattered Range Rover, the beast Rover not the pretty Velar. He hopped out, opened the door for Marvella first and then the back door for Harry.

"Ladies." He smiled as he turned around the expensive SUV, drove them down, down, down. "Before you endure the cold, let me explain." He pointed to the digging. "The basement, the underpinning of this structure, will of course bear five hundred thousand tons of weight, as much as the Twin Towers did. The I-beams will bear a great deal of weight. We're building this the old way. The Twin Towers were pods affixed to a huge central steel core. When the planes hit, the spokes under the floor crumpled. The floor folded almost like a round filter in a coffee machine."

"What an awful thing," Marvella said.

"It's perhaps the main reason so many people and firefighters were killed. Everything collapsed. Here we have designed supports that transverse the Z. So the ends of the Z sink deep into the diagonal. Other than that this is a conventional structure. A series of crossbeams, squares. It's still the safest way to build a high building, a true skyscraper."

"And you will light the top and the bottom?" Marvella had studied the design.

"We'll use thick translucent glass cladding on top of the Z as well as the bottom. So, for instance, on St. Patrick's Day the Z will glow in green, an inner and outer outline."

"Sounds wonderful." Harry loved the idea.

"One of the advantages of Richmond growing now as opposed to the early twentieth century is we are freed from building big boxes. Even if you cover them in bronze mirrors, they are still big boxes."

"The Virginia Commonwealth University's Institute for Contemporary Art opened all this up, don't you think?" Marvella asked.

"An exciting design and a well-executed one." He smiled. "It really is my hope that with all the new young people pouring in, and more companies, we will architecturally become one of the most visually interesting cities in America. Come on, ladies. Allow me to escort you through the giant trench."

They stepped out. Sean led them over to one excavated spot with heavy wooden posts holding up the sides.

"To keep it from caving in?" Harry wondered.

"Right, and to give us a visual checkpoint. This end of the Z is almost finished; it's much wider than it will eventually become. We thought we knew the earth underneath but there are always surprises." He pointed to a gray section of this area. "Rock. Solid rock. Hard as the devil to get through even with all the equipment available to us today. We thought the rock was deeper but not in this spot. We need level bedrock for stability. Come on over here. Oh, wait a minute. I forgot. Let's go back to the Rover."

They trotted back with him. He reached into the spacious back seat, handing each lady a construction helmet.

"Forgive me."

Harry put hers on.

Marvella remarked, "Fetching." Then she clapped her hard hat over her silver hair.

Even with her sheepskin-lined gloves Harry's hands tingled cold. She jammed her hands in the pockets of her heavy coat.

"How long do you think this part of the work will take?" Marvella asked.

"Mmm, it's going well. Two more months, if we're lucky."

"I can't thank you enough for inviting us down here, Sean. Harry has looked at the thumb drive of Russian art. She was an Art History major at Smith."

"What do you think?" he asked as he led them over to where men were using spades for more careful work.

"I was surprised at the high quality and I was also surprised at their foray into modern art before all that was squashed."

Sean nodded. "And millions of people squashed with it. The Soviet Union only lasted seventy years after all that looting, killing, destruction."

"Ah, Sean," Marvella said. "We all look through the shadow of the guillotine."

Before he could reply, they stood at the edge of another

trench. A young man put his foot on the spade, sunk down, lifted up a load of earth.

"What's that?" Harry, sharp-eyed, pointed to something white exposed when the dirt was removed.

"Keith, hold off a moment. Look at whatever that is." Sean pointed.

Keith dutifully did what the big boss said, brushed it with his glove. He pulled a pocketknife out of his zipped chest pocket, and began digging carefully, then in earnest. The three watched as he wiggled from the earth a skull, top jaw, no bottom.

Sean immediately hurried next to Keith, who held the skull, and was bewildered and a little spooked.

Harry and Marvella now came over.

"I wonder how long this has been down here." Sean blinked.

"Well, not too long. This isn't an indigenous person or a casualty of the war." Harry pointed to the teeth still intact in the upper jaw. "Silver fillings."

"Harry, how observant you are," Marvella exclaimed.

Sean, already on his cellphone, called the city police. Then he clicked off.

"Keith, where's Tony?" He mentioned the foreman for this entire operation.

Keith lifted his arm, pointing back toward the ramp. Tony, in a Rankin Construction work truck, a brand-new RAM 1500 painted white with the lettering, large, in script.

Sean waved. Tony saw the boss's Range Rover, then the

boss. He parked next to the SUV, got out, moved quickly over to Sean. One didn't keep a Rankin waiting.

"Boss."

"Look." Sean picked up the skull, which Keith had set down on the earth as he had no desire to continue holding it.

"What the . . . ?" Tony whistled.

"Harry, oh, Tony, this is Mrs. Haristeen and Mrs. Lawson. Harry pointed out there are silver fillings in the teeth."

"So it's been here at least since silver fillings replaced gold." Tony knew something about gold fillings because his grandfather flashed gold teeth.

"Better stop work. For now. The police need to get here."

"Shouldn't we see if there's the rest of whoever this is?" Tony sensibly asked.

"That's police work."

"You mean we shut this down until they clear everything?" Tony's face blanched.

Sean nodded. "No choice. Once the police get here, assess the situation, I can make some decisions."

"Sean," Marvella quietly said. "Harry and I will leave you. It's important this comes before anything."

"Ah." He turned to Tony. "Drive these two ladies up to the top, will you? No, actually drive them home."

"No, please," Marvella insisted. "You are going to need your foreman."

Once up on the sidewalk again, the two women took a deep breath.

"Harry, your car is at my house. Let's have a cup of tea."

As they walked to Marvella's stately home, built at the end of the nineteenth century, the two discussed who could be under the dirt. A vagrant whom time forgot. A murder victim, come back to claim his revenge. Their imaginations roamed all over the place.

Once at the house, restored by tea, they reviewed everything once more.

Marvella, holding her cup in both hands for the warmth, looked at Harry. "You know, we're all sitting on someone's bones."

Speaking of bones, Susan Tucker, Harry's best friend, had delivered fatback kindling to her grandmother at Old Rawly, the family estate still in Holloway hands. Susan's grandfather was a Holloway.

Putting the fatback in a huge brass kettle, Susan brushed over her jeans.

Mrs. Holloway's dog, Duke, chewed on a huge bone used as a doorstop.

"Susan, Duke is dedicated. How many generations of Holloway dogs have chewed that bone?" The eighty-plus very healthy woman smiled. "You know the story."

"Sort of. When Marcia Garth married Jeffrey Holloway, she brought her corgi. Did I get that right?"

"Since you breed corgis with those bloodlines, yes." She sat in a wing chair facing the fire.

"The Garths always had corgis. Since the Revolutionary War."

"Piglet," Mrs. Holloway said with emphasis. "All I know

is Marcia's corgi, Parson, took this old bone from Clover-fields. How long it was there I don't know, but your father's people felt it made an excellent doorstop and so do I." She was slightly startled when Susan's cellphone rang. "I hate those things."

"Forgive me, Gran. It's Harry."

"Tell her hello."

Harry, now on I-64 heading west, told Susan what had just transpired. When the call ended, Susan told her grandmother.

The older woman thought a moment. "Susan, I have known Harry since she was an infant. She has always had a nose for trouble. Who else would be standing in a dig hole when a skull is unearthed?"

"You're right."

"I would prefer not to be right in this account." She lifted her hand but did not point a finger at her granddaughter. "Mark my words, no good can come from disturbing a body. Let the dead rest. Honor their bones." Mrs. Holloway noticed Susan looking down at the big bone. "Perhaps we should even honor nonhuman bones."

"Well, Duke certainly is, in his own way." Susan laughed.

"Honey, do what you can to blunt Harry's formidable curiosity. I promise you no good can come of it."

Susan nodded in agreement but knew it to be an impossible task.

20

"You won't believe this." Lisa charged into Felipe's office. "Raynell, come in here."

Raynell left her computer, walked into Felipe's tidy office. "Must be good."

"It is." Lisa leaned over Felipe's desk. "They found a skull while digging for the Cloudcroft Building."

"What?" Raynell's hand flew to her chest.

"Kylie called from Richmond." Kylie Carter was head of Nature First for all of Virginia. "It was on the six o'clock news this morning, Channel 6. The camera showed the spot where the skull was found, interviewed workmen including the foreman, Tony Vicenzo. He said hand work was being done to square off an area, and Keith Dodge unearthed the skull with his spade."

"You're good at remembering names." Raynell was impressed.

"Actually, Kylie wrote them down. Anyway, the police were called, showed up, and now the excavating is shut down while they dig to see if they can find more of the body."

"Whoever it is had to be under there at least since the Kushner Building and maybe before." Felipe knew the construction history of that particular area, as did all the Nature First people.

Lisa cupped her chin for a moment. "True."

"This will cost Rankin Construction a fortune. And Cloudcroft." Raynell thought in practical terms.

"Well, the cops can't really treat it as a crime scene until they unearth whatever is down there, if they can. And if there's no evidence of wrongdoing, they'll start up building again."

"That doesn't mean we can't rouse people to picket the place, carry signs." Lisa was excited.

"Lisa, they have the building permit. Picketing isn't going to do any good," Raynell sensibly told her.

"She's right." Felipe backed Raynell. "But what we can do, do it with Kylie, of course, is write a press release about our goals, why we oppose hasty granting of permits, and why Nature First and other groups should be consulted before there is work. We have to frame it in a way where the construction companies realize it's cheaper in the long run to hear us out, do some of the things we ask about the environment, history."

"Good idea." Lisa now sat on the edge of his desk. "But what if that is a murder victim?"

"Changes things," Raynell replied. "A larger area will need to be carefully sifted. At least I think it will."

"The police will ask for personnel records from that time, from the first building. What if someone was fired? Someone missing?" Lisa was thinking out loud. "If we can just get them on graft, on payoffs."

"That's a big jump," Raynell replied.

"The codes are strict now. If we jump to conclusions we'll undermine our credibility." Felipe raised his voice.

Lisa's voice rose. "Credibility. The big companies have no concern for history, whether after Europeans arrived or before."

"Lisa," Raynell addressed her superior, "all that is true but we have to establish it, establish a time line if remains are suspicious. We have nothing to gain by intruding on this."

"How do we know this isn't the remains of a drunk? Someone who fell into the foundation of the old Kushner Building or the building before that, and earth trickled down on him? Could really be anything." Felipe folded his hands. "We need to think this through."

Lisa ordered, "Raynell, see if you can pull up anything on the old Kushner Building and the building before that."

"Right." Raynell left for her small office.

"You know what would really be perfect?" Lisa smiled. "If there's an old cemetery under there. Like a pauper's cemetery."

"I kind of hope not," Felipe murmured. "One body is bad enough, if they find the body."

"Why?"

"Because cemeteries are sacred ground." Felipe was Catholic.

"Oh, Felipe, don't be medieval."

"Lisa, you don't disturb the dead."

21

"I've gotten the codes for 1984," Harry told Cooper.

"What are you doing?"

"You've been tracking down Ducati XDiavels in the mid-Atlantic. I thought I'd save you time." Harry pushed the paperwork across Cooper's kitchen table as the cats and dog snoozed on the floor.

Cooper opened the folder. "Pages and pages of rules. God, I hate this kind of stuff."

"That's government. It's even worse now."

"Did you read all this?"

"I did, and I made a copy for me. Here's the thing. I downloaded this. Right?" Cooper nodded so Harry continued. "Someone lifted the 1984 file from the rented car, and I am assuming whoever did that killed Gary. Could be wrong but it's not a big jump. Why couldn't they simply download this information?"

"There had to be something else in the file box."

"Right? Contraband? A gold bar?" She held up her hand. "Bear with me. Drugs, which would be easy to hide, do not take up much space. Do I think he was a dealer, no, I'm just running with this. So what could it be?"

"Well, Harry, if we knew that we might nab the killer."

"If it wasn't something of material value then it has to be information." Harry folded her hands on the table.

Cooper thought about this. "That makes sense but information about what? Was he a spy? An informer? Now don't laugh. We are too close to Washington. And of course, Virginia and Maryland are loaded with retired foreign officers, diplomats, senior military officers, and CIA, always the CIA. What cracks me up is the CIA people think you can't spot them. It's not that hard. Nor is it that difficult for the FBI unless someone is in deep cover, and seems to me they ought to be in Chicago or Phoenix for that."

"Why?"

"Organized crime. It's everywhere but it is especially powerful in those cities. Anyway, I can't see that in this case. Gary's murder was so public. Organized crime is more intelligent than that unless it's one of their own."

"I really doubt Gary was one of their own. His murder was anything but hidden. Brazen. Absolutely brazen!" Harry clapped her hands for emphasis.

"Yes, it was." Cooper inhaled. "You read the codes?"

Harry nodded. "Pretty clear. Now could a large construction company or, say, lumber supplier pay off city officials? Sure. Maybe Gary uncovered corruption, felt he would be in danger, resigned, and moved here."

"Well, he wouldn't be the first." Cooper glanced down at Pewter. "She snores."

"Yes, she does." She looked down, had to crane her neck to see the rotund gray cat fast asleep. "She's such a bad kitty at times but I really do love her. Can't help it. Mrs. Murphy, on the other hand, is an angel. Well, anyway, back to this mess. What have you found out about Ducatis?"

"Sweeping the mid-Atlantic. Not many. Wherever I have found the DiavelX, or is it the XDiavel, I have contacted the police department, asked for records. Nothing much jumps out at me. If I can ferret out a connection to Charlottesville or Gary, that's a different story."

"This is what I think: The motorcycle was driven here in a closed van. Taken off. The job was done. Back into the van and driven to wherever home is."

"Not a bad idea, but why use a motorcycle?"

"You can weave in and out of traffic. It's easier to hide. There was no license plate, which is why I think it was taken off the road after the murder. Whoever it was knew his schedule, pretty much. Had it not been snowing, my hunch is they would have parked in the back, come in, killed him, and sped down the alleyway. The weather, all of us walking out onto the sidewalk, perfect. I bet he was heading for the back. Anyway, we're not dealing with a shrinking violet."

"Right." Cooper dropped her head in her hands for a

moment then looked up, sat up straight. "Back to the codes."

"He must have kept paperwork about a violation, a pay-off, or maybe an accident. I truly believe it's information not drugs, diamonds, you name it. He saw something or knew something and kept a record. When your team sifted through the files, they found notes on building projects. It makes us hope there's other information somewhere."

"Well, if that's true surely he didn't tip his hand when he left." Cooper blinked. "I would hope not, but then who figured this out? And why now?"

"Monday a part of a skull was found. You saw the tele-vised reports. Accidents happen a lot in a job like that. Maybe someone was crushed by materials. Hit by a swinging crane. I don't know. But what if Gary knew?" Harry said.

"Wrongful death." Cooper hummed. "That's a big jump. I can't think this has anything to do with the mur-der here."

"That's the only thing I can think of." Harry threw up her hands.

"If you're right that information is the key, then his death isn't as bizarre as it seems. The file box is the key." Cooper inhaled deeply. "Now I'm getting as crazy as you are. If I had to take a bet, it would be payoff. Enough for Gary to retire."

"But he didn't retire. He went to work. And, Cooper, he was an honest man."

"There is one other nagging detail. And yes, I think, I

hope, he was honest," Cooper remarked. "Whoever killed Gary was a good shot. You watch TV and films and it looks easy to kill someone. It's not. People who aren't good shots spray bullets everywhere. Often it takes more than one shot. This was one simple shot straight to the heart."

Cooper warned her friend, "Gary is dead. The stakes are high. Few people kill for a thrill. I appreciate you getting the building codes, your thoughts. You are very logical but, Harry, you stumble onto things. Leave this to me and the department. None of us knows who, what, why, or how close the killer is. Don't put yourself in danger. Yes, a dear man we all liked very much was killed in front of both of us. You are not going to avenge his death. We're bumping around in the dark. Just let it alone."

"I will."

22

"Wow." Harry once again admired the work already completed for Nature First.

Lisa, excited, leaned toward Harry, sitting across from her desk.

"One of our biggest projects, which we haven't made public yet. We need more work, really, and to see if we can convince those at Monticello and Montpelier to return those places to their natural state."

"But they are. The work has been spectacular and accurate." Harry loved both of those gifts to America.

"Sorry. I'm not being clear. The wildlife, the trees, shrubs, the obvious botanical archaeology, so to speak. We also want to encourage the return of the wildlife at the time."

"Oh, Lisa, with all those visitors, most of them city

people, how can you revitalize, say, bobcats? It will scare them to death."

"Now see, I disagree." She smiled as Pirate slept at her feet. "If we explain the life cycle of the animal, do not disturb their dens or nests, I think all can coexist. Obviously we will need to feed them. We wouldn't want your pussycats to be lunch."

"Lunch! Why I have Odin, a coyote, for a friend. I'm not afraid of anything. I have battled a giant spider!" Pewter immediately shot off her mouth, waking the puppy.

"Spider?" The Irish wolfhound blinked.

"You're scared of that spider. Big as a teacup, that thing." Tucker grimaced. "Don't worry, Pirate, the spider's not here."

"I am not scared of the spider. Not scared of a bobcat!" The gray cat puffed up to twice her size, unpuffed she was a large lady, puffed she truly needed Jenny Craig.

"You go right ahead and infuriate a bobcat. I am not messing with our larger cousins," Mrs. Murphy sensibly chimed in.

Lisa, hearing the commotion, cocked her head, looked down. "Are they always like this?"

Harry laughed. "Such strong opinions. Well, I don't mean to take up your time. Thought I'd drop by."

"You're not taking up my time. Before you go, Kylie has been investigating the Kushner Building, which will be the Cloudcroft Building, for six months now. The minute word got out about a forty-story replacement she started research. Finding a skull is a godsend. TV coverage was extensive. The newspaper actually wrote about the history of the Kushner Building. Have you read today's Richmond Times-Dispatch?"

"No," Harry answered.

"Nature First took out a full-page ad suggesting city leadership include Nature First in all planning activities for buildings and parks. Of course, there is not one plan for a park."

"Bet it cost a lot."

"Four to five hundred dollars, maybe more."

"Why now?"

"The skull," Lisa replied with ill-concealed glee.

"I was there." Harry then relayed why she was at the pit, the condition of the skull.

"Why didn't you tell me!" Lisa nearly shouted. "Felipe! Raynell. Come into my office."

The shouts upset Pirate. *"What's going on?"*

"Human drama." Pewter smirked.

Pirate put his head on his paws, keeping his eyes wide open.

Harry recounted her story.

"Do you think there's more down there?" Raynell asked.

"I do. I doubt there would be a disembodied head. Of course, the police will be very careful. You almost need an archaeologist for something like this."

"Toothbrushes," Felipe added.

Lisa, a bit overenthusiastic, said with confidence, "If we can delay further construction for a while, cost Rankin and Cloudcroft millions because they'll have to keep everyone on payroll, all those big companies will take us seriously. Listen to us before they dig." Lisa gloated.

"You might be right but I wouldn't want to test those waters," Harry quietly replied.

"Why not?" Raynell wondered.

"There's a dead man in that ground. Who knows why. If the authorities find out maybe it means those big companies played hardball then and they would now."

"That's ridiculous," Raynell blurted out. "Sorry, I didn't mean to offend. It's just big companies are so powerful why bother to kill? Anyway, it's just a skull."

"For now." Felipe folded his arms across his chest.

"Buy a *Times-Dispatch*," Lisa counseled.

As Raynell turned to go back to her office, a small spider dashed across the floor. "Lisa, we need Orkin!"

"Why?"

"A spider."

"Raynell, if I called Orkin every time I saw a spider or a stinkbug, I'd blow our budget."

Raynell grimaced, did not reply, headed to her office as Lisa shook her head. "Really. Would blow the budget."

"That would be interesting on the annual budget: spiders, stinkbugs, water bugs." Harry looked down at her buddies. "Come on, freeloaders. See you, Lisa."

The four left Nature First, walked down the hall to Over the Moon.

Harry pulled open the door. "How can you keep your floors clean with all the snow outside?"

Anne de Vault pointed to a mop leaning beside the door just a bit out of sight. "Woman power."

"Keep you in shape but then you always are." Harry walked up to the sales counter, cats and Tucker in tow.

Anne might once in her life have carried one extra pound but that would be it. Willowy or lean, depending on your vocabulary, would best describe her.

"You're too kind. I have a wonderful book by Harold Evans, *Do I Make Myself Clear?* Put it on your pile?"

"Sure." Harry could rarely resist a good book. "Have you seen the work at Nature First?"

Anne nodded. "Lisa Roudabush pops in every day to say hi, look at what's new."

Another customer, a woman in her twenties, knelt to pull a book off a shelf.

"I suggested that Lisa visit Sandy McAdams at Daedalus. He would have vintage books, some hand bound, to augment her research at his used bookstore. Not only can he find you anything, he remembers everything. Everything. Knocks me out."

"He is a wonder," Harry agreed. "So no new books on fashion or biography? I loved the one on Loulou de la Falaise. Boy that was expensive, too."

"Big book. Anytime a book is oversize it's more money, plus the paper was very high grade. Lisa sticks to environmental books, animal books. What you would expect. She'd never buy a fashion book. Most of what I sell or anyone sells today is cheap paper, by the way, thermographed. Awful, really, but cheap." Anne returned to a favorite theme, cheapness of things.

"Doesn't hold up."

"Doesn't hold up because Tucker chews it," Pewter tattled.

"I don't know if spiders poop, but I hope the teacup spider poops on you!" She bared her teeth.

"Will you two stop?" Harry glared, then returned to Anne. "They were noisy at Nature First."

"Harry, they're usually noisy. Forgot. Lisa loves books about dinosaurs. She's like a kid."

"Well, I recall she had some in her pile just after Christmas. I thought maybe I'd get her a book. I love to give books."

Anne advised, "Even if someone receives a book about something different, not a special interest, I think it feeds their curiosity."

"That's a good idea. Let me get that book, paperback, about von Humboldt. Susan will be intrigued."

"Bottom left shelf."

Harry, Tucker with her, found the book. The cats sat behind the counter.

"Did you ever see *Jurassic Park*?" Harry asked. "Given Gary's collection of tiny rubber dinosaurs, Lisa's interest, maybe we should watch it again."

"No," Anne emphatically said. "Those little raptor dinosaurs in the kitchen were horrible."

"Made me want to keep the lights on," Harry agreed.

"Not a bad idea." Anne nodded. "Who knows what's out there?"

"I know Gary came in here. He'd tell me what was new on the table."

"Glad you dropped in."

"Me, too." Harry walked outside.

23

Lowering clouds, clearly seen from the huge arched panel windows in St. Luke's Lutheran Church, promised cold, snow, or sleet. The windows, a daring design by Charles West, started at four feet off the floor, soaring to top stories, nearly to the high ceiling. The back part of the church contained a balcony. The effect was one of grandeur, soaring hope. The cost for glass proved outrageous, but it did look sensational.

The exterior of St. Luke's, the stonework, had been finished for months now. Interior work took longer. The two-story buildings at the ends of the arched walkways from the main building echoed the main building. They would contain offices, housing for visitors, perhaps even some students of the faith. The pastor's house, clapboard as opposed to stone, at a distance from the church itself, sent up smoke from the large fireplace in the parlor. Men continued to work in the home, finishing touches. They could work faster if warm.

The interior of the church at this moment was not warm. Given the size of the space, two enormous fireplaces proved necessary. One heated the front of the church, placed in the right corner, and one at the rear, in the left corner. The balcony also had a small fireplace, which would keep the choir and those in the balcony reasonably warm. This tapped into the main flue from the left fireplace.

The large panel windows, three sections cleverly made to look like one, could be tipped outward in hot weather. Charles sited the church for the wind flow off the Blue Ridge Mountains. Although not trained as an architect, studying the buildings in the mid-Atlantic, a few from the late seventeenth century, gave him a freedom he would not have felt in his native England. However, living with castles, churches, abbeys, and stables, some built right after the Norman Conquest, provided a useful education. He grew up with structures made to last, and he hoped to create a church that would last long into the future of this New World.

As it was, St. Luke's was anchored to the past with the arches recalling monks walking from the cloisters. The proportions of the church carried a hint of Norman grandeur, but the interior was quite modern.

Charles designed pews to be as comfortable as possible. They would be topped off with long cushions. Most of the carpentry work was complete. Pulling his scarf a bit tighter around his neck, he stood with Rachel, who helped sort out decisions and copy his drafts, for her hand was good. However, no one's hand could match Charles's. His penmanship would have put a royal clerk to shame, and he could imitate anything.

"The organ will sound heavenly." She smiled as Frank Ix sanded down the pulpit one more time.

"Cost a fortune. The men to install will demand a high wage. Rooms will be ready for them. We will pay, for no one here can do what those Germans can do." Charles crossed his arms across his chest. "This is not a thriving congregation, as you know. They have given so much. I have never met a group of people so united in their faith, so determined that their children should be brought up Lutheran."

"And neither of us were." She slipped her arm through his because she liked being close to him, but he would warm her hand even though it was gloved.

"I did as I was told. Trudged to chapel at Harrow, same at Oxford. Never really thought about it. For my father, church was another social obligation. A way to stand above, since as a baron, he would be called upon to contribute and seated in front in the family pew, which has been there since the fourteenth century."

"And now your brother?"

Charles's father had died. His older brother, Hugh, inherited the title, along with massive debt since Baron West had denied himself nothing. To his credit he did see his two sons to a good education, then packed off Charles to the Army. Well, the young man had to learn something, and he certainly wasn't cut out for the church. So like all younger sons in England, Charles found himself socially desirable but impoverished.

"Hugh will try." He sighed. "He keeps borrowing against the estate. We have no mines, a source of wealth. All we have is land, and father proved a poor manager. He always overrode the true manager. So my brother struggles. He is not profligate but one does incur heavy responsibilities in his position. I am grateful to God that I was captured at Saratoga, sent down here. The long march from Saratoga to Virginia opened my eyes to the future. Someday, my love, you will see the country of my birth. It is beautiful and yet, here, here I can do and be as I wish." He beamed at her. "And I met you. There aren't women like you in England, sweetheart. One marries according to one's station. Love has little to do with it, although over the years a couple can learn to care for each other."

"No love matches at all?"

"A few, but in the main, no. One must raise troops for the king if so commanded. One must attend at court, especially if one wishes a political career. I did not, but there are times when one must go for the good of the family. And the social season. Endless balls, empty chatter, a fortune spent on clothes, men as well as women. A good wife advances her husband, the family. Here I can come and go as I please, and I can use my mind. I've found work I love, a woman I love. I have two beautiful and noisy daughters. I have Piglet." He looked down at his faithful corgi, who survived war and capture with him. "But someday, when the girls are older, I would like them to know their father's land." He stopped a moment, grinned. "And I would like some of my old chums to see the woman I married."

"You'll have to teach me how to address people. I know that's very important over there."

"I will."

Karl called down from the pulpit. "We can't paint and we can't gild. Too cold. I had hoped for an early spring, as did the Missus."

"Karl, if there's one thing Virginia has taught both of us, it is that the weather is variable."

Karl had been in the prisoner-of-war camp at the Barracks with Charles. Although Karl was a Hessian they struck up a friendship, as did Charles with John Schuyler, his captor. Fate. Charles believed in fate.

"Indeed." He dusted off the pulpit with a chamois cloth. "Well, we will be down there looking up, but at whom, I know not."

"Oh, the pastor will appear." Charles smiled. "In good time."

"Aye."

Charles looked out the windows again. "Karl, might as well stop. Looks ominous."

Karl followed Charles's gaze. "Does. Miles for us to get home."

"Let's hope we make it before the heavens open."

Cloverfields, seven miles from Wayland's Corner where St. Luke's was being built, was at least on a decent road. Mostly it was straight with a curve or two. It wasn't until one drove or rode just east of Cloverfields that the road twisted, dipped, dropped over Ivy Creek, and became churned mud or slick ice quickly, too quickly.

They made it. Karl worked and lived at Cloverfields. Ewing, like others, used the prisoners for temporary workers during the war. Highly skilled, the only impediment proved to be language. In time that ironed out.

Charles drove Rachel to their door then turned, driving Castor and Pollux, two large horses, to their stable.

Tulli dashed out. "Mr. Charles. Gonna be hateful mean." He pointed to the sky.

"Well it is. I'll help you unhitch and wipe down so you can go home before the worst."

Jeddie walked into the draft horse stable. "I'll do that, Sir. You go on home. If it gets too bad we can bunk up here or maybe make it down to my cabin."

"How do you like living alone?"

"I like it fine. People keep giving me things. Bumbee gives me blankets and Barker O. brought me a chair. And I have my own bed."

"Can you keep it warm?"

"I stoke the fire before I go to sleep and the first thing I do in the morning is stoke it again."

"Good, and I'm glad you can keep warm. Thank you, Tulli. You, too, Jeddie."

It would never occur to Charles not to thank the two boys—well, Jeddie was a young man. He hated it as a child when he'd watch the monied people treat those beneath them, and they literally were beneath them, rudely. Charles, like his father in this regard, thought human society a pyramid. No matter where one is in that pyramid, everyone needs one another.

He walked into his home, Piglet at his heels.

"Tea?"

"Oh, what a wonderful idea."

Just as he said that a fist of wind hit the side of the house, shaking it.

Rachel joined him. No sooner had they sat down when John burst through the door.

Charles stood up, seeing his friend in distress, for he knew John well. "What's wrong?"

"I don't know. Come quickly."

Within minutes they were in John and Catherine's house. Father Gabe and Bettina were there along with Ruth, good with all children and with the gift of healing.

Rachel walked into her sister's bedroom. The men hovered at the door.

Catherine smiled at Rachel. "I'm such a bother."

"What's wrong?"

Bettina, on the other side of the bed, held Catherine's hand. "She started bleeding."

Ruth brought a pan of warm water. Shooed the men out except for Father Gabe.

"I can get up."

"No," Bettina forcefully commanded.

As Father Gabe gently lifted her up, the two women washed her. Towels rested under her on the bed. Rachel removed them, hurried down the hall for more.

When she returned, Father Gabe lifted Catherine again. Rachel placed clean towels underneath her.

"The bleeding slowed." Ruth squeezed out a wet rag, placing it on Catherine's head.

"I'll be fine," Catherine said weakly.

"Of course you will, but you do as Bettina and Father Gabe and Ruth tell you. And me, too." She smiled and Catherine smiled back.

"Listening to them will be easier than listening to you."

"Are you in pain?"

"No. I was climbing down the stairs and I felt the sharpest pain I have ever felt in my life. Then blood gushed out of me. I could barely reach the top of the stairs. I called for John. I could see from his face . . . well, anyway, he carried me in here, ran for Father Gabe then ran for you. Father Gabe brought Bettina and Ruth. That's all I remember."

"Did you pass out?"

"I don't remember." Catherine closed her eyes, then opened them. "I don't hurt at all now."

John and Charles tiptoed into the room.

Catherine turned to face her husband. "Come by me, John."

He did. "I should fetch a doctor. The new fellow. The one who put Jeffrey and Yancy back together. He'll know what to do."

"The weather isn't good. Wait until it clears."

Rachel looked to Father Gabe, then the two women.

Bettina spoke up. "Fever. We got to watch for fever."

"I don't feel hot."

"No, but it might come on," Bettina wisely said.

"Let me sleep. Go tomorrow." She fought to stay awake.

Catherine, always healthy and strong, had never felt pain like what seized her on the steps. Weakness and drowsiness overtook her.

Bettina sat with her, as did Rachel, as she fell into a deep sleep. Under the circumstances, the sleep was a blessing.

Father Gabe and Ruth motioned for John and Charles to go into the hall.

The older man put his hand under John's elbow. "She's lost the baby."

John sagged, then straightened. "Does she know?"

"Not yet," Ruth answered. "She may suspect. We can tell her when she's stronger. We'll see how she is tomorrow morning. If there's no fever, we can tell her."

"I want to be with her." John couldn't help the silent tears.

Charles, feeling helpless, touched John on the shoulder. "We'll take JohnJohn. You keep close."

John nodded his head in agreement.

Father Gabe motioned for Ruth and Charles to withdraw.

When they did, he counseled John. "It may be some time before, before you can be physically close to her."

"Yes," John whispered. "Father Gabe, I will gladly sacrifice anything for her, to keep her healthy. I will do anything. Anything."

Father Gabe nodded. "Love her."

24

"A baby brontosaurus." Harry lifted up a small rubber dinosaur as she sat on the floor of Gary's, now Tazio's, office, which she had opened Monday, January 23rd.

"I thought you came in here to go over your plans?" Tazio, perched on a stool at the drafting table, reminded her.

"Well, I did. I want to, but Fair downloaded all the building codes for me going back to 1980."

"The sheriff's department combed through every file box."

"I know." Harry held up her right forefinger since Pewter wanted the brontosaurus. "This doesn't belong to you."

"It doesn't belong to you, either." The gray cat sniffed. "Since

Gary's dead the toy should be given away. He liked me so give me the dinosaur."

"You've been rifling through 1983 for an hour now. All you've found is one rubber toy. If it were important the department would have kept it."

Harry scrambled to her feet, lifted up the file box, walked over to the traditional desk, not the drafting table, placing it on the top. "Come here for a minute."

"I will if you'll come to go over these plans with me."

"All right but look at this."

Brinkley nudged his human. *"Indulge her."*

"Here I am." Tazio pulled up another chair on rolling casters to sit beside Harry, who was just burning to show her the files.

Carefully lifting out the papers that she had dog-eared, she pointed. "Okay. Here's a job on West Broad Street. Big car dealership. Look at the note in the margin."

"'Replace steel I-beam on northwest corner.'" Tazio read aloud then said, "So?"

"I have 1983 downloaded, remember. On the page regarding steel qualifications, stress, elasticity, that stuff, there's no such memo."

"Harry, why would there be? The code is just the code. There isn't feedback."

"I know, but did he report this, or did the construction company find the problem and simply replace it?"

"You'd need to go through Rankin Construction's files."

"That's exactly what I'm going to tell Coop. And this little toy. Look on this sheet. More jobs. More notes."

Tazio peered at a paper for an office building, very

modern, right on the Henrico/Goochland county line. "Little dinosaur footprints. Harry, he obviously was wrapped up with dinosaurs. This is a doodle, not a note."

"A doodle with a rubber dinosaur in the box. He put his dinosaurs on the shelf. Put them in the box. I need to go through every file box to see what's in the margins and what toys are there."

"You're obsessed. Number one. Number two. The sheriff's department had to cite whatever they found in these file boxes. I'm sure the dinosaurs will be noted. It can't be that important or questions would have been asked of all of us close to Gary. Okay, I've looked. Now come and look at the drawings."

Harry left the box on the desk, trudged to the drafting table to go over the plans.

"I'm going to slay the dragon," Pewter grandly announced. "Besides, we can't sit on the drafting table. It's on a slant."

Mrs. Murphy, Tucker, and Brinkley followed to the back room, door to the bathroom shut. Mostly they tagged along because they, too, were somewhat interested in the spider. However, the two dogs and the cat did not aspire to murder. For one thing, she was so big the squish would be too gross. For another thing, it was live and let live.

Pewter slunk to the little hole in the baseboard.

"I know you're in there."

Nothing.

"You can't fool me."

That fast the large spider blasted out of the hole, shot through Pewter's legs to disappear under the slight space under the bathroom door.

"*She attacked me!*" Pewter screamed.

Harry appeared quickly. "What is going on?"

"*A spider. She's as big as a crab. She attacked me!*" Pewter's pupils looked like big black marbles.

"Let's all go into the workroom. Pewter, you look like a porcupine."

"*You know, it was scary,*" Brinkley admitted.

"*Huge!*" Pewter meowed.

"*It was,*" Mrs. Murphy agreed. "*But you're being a Drama Queen.*"

"*The spider knows that.*" Tucker tormented Pewter. "*She wants to hear you scream.*"

"*You'd scream, too, if she came after you. The world's biggest spider.*"

Tazio glanced up from the papers. "And?"

"I have no idea." Harry joined her again. "They did find a triangular stud in a crack when Cooper and I came back here after Gary's murder. I thought it might be important. Apparently not. Who knows how long it was in that crack?"

"*The spider took it. Probably tore it off a jacket or someone's purse. I bet she knows more than she's telling.*"

"*Pewter, spiders don't talk.*" Mrs. Murphy sat by Harry's chair.

"*You don't know that. I bet they talk to one another.*"

"*How can they talk when their mouths move like pincers?*" Tucker asked.

"*Our jaws are long and we can talk,*" Brinkley offered.

"*We also have tongues. Spiders don't.*" Tucker would have none of it.

"*That doesn't mean they can't hum. They can communicate. I just* know that giant spider has told all her friends about me." Pewter's ego, inflated again, irritated the others.

"I'm sure," Mrs. Murphy dryly said.

Tazio, her left hand resting on Brinkley's head, pointed to the loft with a pencil. "Do you want planed but unfinished oak or something else?"

"It's just storage." Harry shrugged.

"So it is, but it does give you an opportunity to make another work space or even a bedroom. Why don't you put in planed oak and stain it, put drop cloths over it, and then put whatever you want up there? This gives you more options if your needs change, and Harry, you know as well as I do, building never gets cheaper. Do it now."

That struck home. "Well . . . maybe."

"This isn't much square footage. An upgrade won't be expensive. Maybe you'd like something other than oak."

"No. Oak. I need hardwood. Need hardwood in the downstairs, too. Even though there won't be much traffic. And even though the uneven-width heart pine in my kitchen is beautiful, it scratches up all the time and I'm rubbing it all the time."

"Right." Tazio smiled, knowing she'd swung Harry to a more versatile decision.

The two worked for another hour, going over everything. The little Napoleon clock struck five.

"Where'd the time go?" Harry exclaimed.

Tazio looked up at the graceful hands. "Somewhere we can never retrieve it. Do you know I read about air? I thought the article was going to be about pollution, but it wasn't. Air doesn't disappear, and the article said that every two thousand breaths we inhale air that Julius Caesar inhaled."

"No kidding." Harry, impressed, then tidied up her pile of notes. "Let me put back the file box and head home. Dark already. I actually like winter but dark at five, not so much."

"Me, too."

Once home Harry called Cooper, told her everything about the file box for 1983 and what she thought. She urged Cooper to call Rankin Construction.

"I will but I want to go through the boxes myself before I do that. The research team mentioned marginal notes and rubber toys. No one thought it important, and I don't know that it is, but I want to see for myself."

"Can't hurt."

"Hold on one sec." Cooper squinted at a message intruding on the computer screen.

"Harry, when you get home turn on the news. Forensics in Richmond has retrieved the rest of the skeleton and are laying it out on the spot." She read more, looked at photos. "Male. Middle-aged. A bullet lodged in his left front rib. I doubt the news will show you what we see."

"Front rib?"

"Probably shot from behind with a light caliber bullet. Stuck in the bone. Murder."

"You were the one who told me amateurs spray bullets or fire too many."

"I did."

"Another marksman." Harry's heart was racing.

"A good shot at any rate." Cooper sighed. "I don't know how you do it, but you turn up at critical moments."

"Dumb luck."

"Let's hope it isn't bad luck."

25

Using the date Harry had given her with the dinosaur footprints, Cooper tapped into the newspaper reports from the *Richmond Times-Dispatch* for Thursday, June 2, 1983. She liked to circle around a subject to people who were involved. In the case of a fresh murder, of course, she zoomed straight for suspects like Dawn Hulme, Gary's ex-wife. The spouse or ex-spouse looms large in any murder, but Dawn was clear. Then again, the divorce, years ago, lost much of its venom, not that Dawn had much good to say about the late Gary Gardner.

A column on the front page, "Accident on Broad," caught her eye. The office building, the very one cited by Harry with notes in the margin made by Gary, had been the site where a worker died leaning next to his excavator. The victim, forty-three years old, Ali Asplundah, stepped down from the giant backhoe. No one saw him drop as he was on the other side of the large machine, other large pieces of equipment were running in the square space that would provide the foundation. When the machine, in neutral, continued to run for over an hour, one of the other heavy equipment men cut his motor, climbed down, walked over. He found Ali sitting on the dirt, slumped against the machine, dead. The medical examiner proclaimed it a heart attack.

Cooper read about Ali, highly skilled, an early Muslim resident of the city. Muslims had come to Richmond in the eighteenth century but in tiny numbers. Little by little a small population gathered. Those interviewed concerning the deceased all testified he didn't touch alcohol, had a sterling work record, got along with everyone, and loved soccer.

She pulled up subsequent days, a few more reports, then months later the results of the investigation. Nothing was wrong with the backhoe. Mr. Asplundah had never evidenced any signs of heart trouble nor did his medical records indicate the same. It was a simple, unexpected heart attack.

She then researched murder for 1984 in Richmond. Nothing on work sites. She checked the obituaries for the year. That took one and a half hours. Nothing there either. Finally she pulled up missing person reports.

There was one for a construction worker, a welder. His wife reported he had not returned from work. He'd been welding a bent front fender for a friend. His day job was working on the Kushner Building.

Cooper knew the Richmond Police Department already had done what she did, were probably recording right on the site.

She had something. Just what, she wasn't certain. She called Richmond's department, identified herself, her search.

A young man confirmed they were looking for the son of Edward Elkins, the welder reported missing in 1984. They needed DNA.

She'd spent most of her workday in the office. Given the cold, it was better than cruising the streets, picking up drunks, examining bumper benders.

Dark already, she drove home, thinking as she drove. Driving helped her think.

She paid attention to Harry as much as Harry irritated her.

Her neighbor—whom she did love—could insinuate herself into affairs that were none of her business. To make it worse, Harry had no training in law enforcement but she'd become obsessed with something. Gary's murder would arouse a friend's sympathy. Being there, Harry was galvanized. Much as Cooper tried to tell her not to get involved in her soft-soap way, she knew it would do no good. If she told her off, Harry would become more devious, and that would be even more dangerous.

She parked near the side door. Often a walk outdoors cleared her mind. She opened the back door, picked up a box of dog treats and a small jar of corn oil. The temperature, according to the large outdoor thermometer, hung at 26°, Fahrenheit. Her face tingled. Walking into the

shed, which doubled as a garage when she felt like parking there, she went over to a hole under the back wall. It
opened on both sides of the wall and was not the only
den opening. A tidy gray fox lived there. She broke up the
treats, placing them in a pie tin saved for this purpose.
Then she drenched them in corn oil. The fox would love
it. Cold as it was in the shed, it provided protection from
the elements, plus the little fellow had straw, rags, old
towels to curl up in, along with his luxurious double coat.

Leaving, she pushed through the snow to the Jones
family graveyard. The Very Reverend Herbert Jones rented
the farm to Cooper, as he lived in the lovely clapboard
pastor's house at St. Luke's. With Harry's help, Cooper
kept everything tidy. The snow on the gravestones added
to the silence and beauty of this spot, a large gum tree in
the middle of the place, and sleeping Joneses who
stretched back to 1810.

Heading back to the kitchen warmth, she thought about
how many Virginia farms cherished their dead. Gary had
been cremated, spread over a pasture he had always admired. People's last wishes ought to be carried out, but
she liked reading headstones.

Lisa Roudabush, leash secure in her heavy mittens, walked
down Mt. Tabor Road. There were no cars on the road,
which was good as the roads could still be slick. "How are
you doing, Pirate?"

"*Okay.*" The large puppy skipped through the cleared
snow.

He had learned to avoid the piled-up snow.

"We're almost home, buddy."

"Good." He looked up at Lisa.

"Stop." She stopped.

He did, too.

"Good boy."

About five minutes later they reached the small brick house that Lisa rented. Once inside, she emailed Kylie Carter. They congratulated each other on the continuing saga at the excavation site in Richmond.

"Now this will really cost Rankin Construction and Cloudcroft a fortune," Kylie crowed.

"Murder. We couldn't have asked for more." Lisa was exuberant.

Be careful what you ask for.

26

Reynaldo, Jeddie in the stirrups, trotted up and down the hill on the north side of Cloverfields. A true March wind cut through his heavy sweater and short leather jacket, cowhide. Catherine, arms wrapped around her body, stood in mud laced with silver streaks of ice, watching. A week had passed since her miscarriage. Though a bit weak, she felt fine. Working lifted her spirits.

"Walk back down, make him walk." Jeddie nodded, halted the powerful sleek horse, turned him. They walked. Reynaldo pinned his ears but he listened. Jeddie then trotted the horse back up the hill.

"Don't you want me to breeze him?"

"No. Let's walk back to the stable. Make him walk, Jeddie. If you aren't the boss, he'll be the boss. He's strong-willed and very, very smart. Right now we're working on balance. We'll work on wind later."

"Yes, Ma'am." Jeddie grinned.

A handful he was, but Reynaldo possessed rare quality. He had lovely movement from the shoulder, powerful hindquarters, and an abnormally long stride. He was born to run. Catherine's emphasis on his wonderful balance was as much for his mind as his body. Easily bored, which he would let you know, he was intelligent and very alert to his environment.

Jeddie, quiet, supple in the saddle, walked Reynaldo on a loose rein, a vote of confidence in the horse, which Reynaldo liked. He loved Catherine and he loved Jeddie. He tolerated Tulli and Ralston, and thought Baxter O. was decent enough, but there was no way he was ever going to pull a carriage. Never. Reynaldo had a high opinion of himself. But then so did the carriage horses King David and Solomon.

Once in the stable, Tulli ran up to hold the 16.2-hand horse while Jeddie easily swung out of the saddle.

"Tulli, wipe him down. Rub some liniment in his muscles. He likes being rubbed. Put his blanket on him and turn him out," Catherine ordered.

"Yes, Ma'am." Tulli nodded.

"Where's Ralston?"

Tulli answered, "With Baxtor O. in the carriage barn."

"I'll help you, Tulli." Jeddie never shied from work.

"Sit with me for a minute, then you can help Tulli. He's big now. He can take care of himself."

Music to Tulli's ears.

Catherine and Jeddie walked into the large tack room, a small iron potbellied stove keeping things warm as it squatted on a thick piece of slate that rested on packed earth. The wooden floor started a foot and a half from the slate.

Catherine sank in an old wooden chair.

Jeddie pulled up a small wooden tack trunk to sit.

"When it's slick like today you can still do hill work. The hill isn't that steep, but going down is less appealing than going up. And don't do anything without me."

"Yes, Miss Catherine."

"We've got close to eight weeks until the races. Yancy couldn't run them in early spring. Too much planting and calving. People won't be there. Some city people would attend, but for big crowds we have got to get on the other side of spring chores. By the time we race, Reynaldo's wind will be good, his stamina strong. I mean to win this race, I'm sick of hearing how great Yancy's Black Knight is."

"People say Reynaldo's hot. I won't be able to rate him."

"They don't understand horses. I smile, say little. I don't waste time on fools."

"Yes, Ma'am."

She inhaled the aroma of cleaned tack, drying chamois cloths. "Your leather jacket cuts the wind. Lem sold you a good skin and Otto made a nice jacket. You were smart to do that."

"Lem let me scrape the hide, clean up in his tannery for a week. Did all kind of things. Sold me the hide for five dollars. I didn't have it, but my father gave it to me from his secret hiding place."

"Hiding from whom?"

"Mother."

"Ah." Catherine shrugged. "He does extra things. My father will let him do chores on another farm. Well, you know that, but your mother never sees the money? How is she now that you have your own place?"

He lifted his shoulders. "Glad I'm out of her house but she's still at me about getting married." He paused, looked straight at Catherine. "You knew Mother before I was born."

"I was small, but yes."

"Was she ever happy?"

Catherine took a deep breath then exhaled. "No. I don't think Felicity has ever been happy. The irony is her name means happiness in Latin."

"I'm happy. I like the horses. I like the work and I like my cabin. It's big enough for me and easy to keep warm as long as I remember to stack up the fireplace. The nights stay cold."

"I hate that moment in the morning when my bare feet touch the floor." She shuddered. "Wakes me up though. Well, you did good work today with Reynaldo. I'm going up to Father. Feels like rain, sleet, or snow. March is so unpredictable. Just is. If it's clear tomorrow we can work him more. If not, he still gets a rubdown." She stood, put her hand on his shoulder, patted it, then left the stables.

Catherine opened the back door, stepped into the kitchen. The odors and the warmth lifted her spirits. She hung up her heavy shawl, wiggled out of layers, opened the door to the hall. She heard voices in the parlor.

Walking down the polished floor, she then walked into the parlor filled with Hepplewhite furniture, a large good painting of her mother over the fireplace.

"What are you all doing in here? Thought you'd be in the library."

"Sit down, my dear." Ewing patted the brocade sofa on which he sat.

John had folded himself into a large stuffed chair, as had Charles, while Rachel sat on the other side of Father.

"I wish you wouldn't go outside," Ewing chided her.

"I'm fine. I can't sit in my house one more minute. My strength is coming back. Really, I'm fine."

"You aren't riding, are you?" Rachel knew her sister well.

"Not yet." Catherine sounded vague.

John, rare for him, said, "We'll make that decision together. But she is much stronger and see the color in her cheeks."

Charles, fingers like a steeple, opened his mouth, but Rachel spoke before he could.

"Charles received a letter from his brother, Hugh, the baron. He is mired in their father's debts. Sees no way out of the quagmire."

"How much debt?"

"Close to a million pounds. My father lived a profligate life," Charles said without rancor. "He had no discipline. Lived for society. Pookie is left holding the bag."

"Pookie?" Catherine's eyebrows lifted.

"His nickname. He actually has some sense. He tried to marry a few heiresses, but better placed men than he snapped them up, including one dissolute duke. Well, dissolute he may be. The beautiful Amelia Marlin is now Her Grace. Seductive, that title."

"Can't he sell and leave?" Rachel innocently asked.

"He can but he would never have a place in society again. I know it's hard for you to understand, but place is so important. One's entire life revolves around it. And those who make money, commercial men, practically kill themselves trying to become ennobled. A baronet is better than nothing. All this uproar about a coat of arms. People pay fortunes under the table for false quarterings going back centuries. I know it's hard to fathom."

"Your brother needs a way to survive?" Catherine asked.

"He does. Being a younger son, I have nothing with which to help him. I live such a different life. He couldn't understand. Having said that, I do want to take my wonderful wife to England someday."

John spoke up. "The flintlock your father gave you. It has gold and silver mountings. Made by Nicolas Noël Boutet. Might that bring in money?"

"John, it would bring in ninety pounds, perhaps a bit more. A drop in the bucket. You won that from me. Spoils of war. It's your gun." He smiled. "My father gave that to me. I'm not giving it to Pookie. Let's say we spare the Boutet."

John nodded. The flintlock was exquisite.

Catherine sat upright. "Don't despair, Charles. Let me think on it."

He looked at his sister-in-law. Charles respected Catherine's mind, her business acumen.

Rachel, too, stared at her sister. "You're cooking something up. I can always tell."

"Mmm." She wiggled her hand, which to Rachel meant that whatever it was, it was outrageous.

Later, as Catherine and John walked back to their house, Bettina and Serena looked from the kitchen window.

"Too thin." Bettina shook her head.

"Sorrow. Such a sorrow."

Bettina nodded. "The fate of women. We birth stillborn children, those that live, you thank God for their lives. Take two brothers. Both come down with the cough. One lives. One dies. Why? I know of no woman who has raised all her children to adults. Not one."

"Even Mrs. Ewing?" Serena was a child when the mistress had died.

"Even Miss Isabelle. She had a son who lived four days." She threw up her hands. "You never forget the ones who slipped away. You can still remember their voices, the light in their eyes, the way they smelled in your arms when you held them. You carry them forever."

She knew of what she spoke, having lost two children. Bettina looked back at Catherine. She was strong. She'd go on. But there'd be questions now in the back of her mind.

The front of her mind was a different matter.

27

January 30, 2017

Monday

The small staff at Nature First answered phones, sent emails, talked to anyone who would listen. The *Daily Progress*, the Charlottesville paper, which though small had won many awards, called Lisa for a comment on the one-page ad in the *Richmond Times-Dispatch* about why city council needed to be serious about city planning, about including Nature First and other groups into early discussions.

"Every city should do this. Our environmental future is too important to be left to mayors or city managers." Lisa spoke on the phone to a reporter from what locals called "The Daily Prog." Those who were not liberal—for it was a liberal newspaper—called it "The Daily Regress."

The young man on the other end of the line fed her an easy lob. "Even Charlottesville?"

"Especially Charlottesville. The University of Virginia is one of the architectural treasures of our nation. What has been allowed to be built in the city is a disgrace. Ugly doesn't cover it."

"I see." And he did. "And habitat?"

"We're intruding on other species. Building without any consideration for their highways, so to speak, and their food supply. Suburbanites get hysterical about a bear in the garbage can. The bear lived there first."

Another half hour of this and the young man had more than enough material. Lisa hung up the phone.

Felipe stuck his head in her office. "Need a break? It's been a madhouse."

"*I could use a potty break,*" Pirate suggested.

Lisa glanced at the atomic clock on her desk. "Eleven o'clock. Have I been on the phone that long?"

"We've all been answering emails or the phone," Felipe replied.

"Well, let me walk my guy here. He's been very good." She picked up the leash hanging on the back of her chair, snapped it on his collar, grabbed her coat, and walked out. "I won't be long."

And she wasn't. Within twenty minutes she was back. "Anyone else need a break?"

"I can pick up lunch," Raynell offered.

The building contained two food places, one a stand-up place and another offering fuller service. Both Lisa and Felipe gave Raynell their orders. Lisa asked for a sandwich for Pirate, as he'd earned a treat.

Once Raynell brought back lunch they repaired to the small meeting room to eat, go over all that had transpired.

"The ad was worth it." Lisa fed Pirate his sandwich tidbits.

"It will be worth it if we do get invited to the planning meetings." Felipe thought the cost outrageous.

"We'll know in time. Those planning commission meetings usually take place once a month." Lisa bit into a hot sandwich.

"*Food.*" Pewter raced into the room followed by Mrs. Murphy, Tucker, and lastly Harry.

"Sorry." Harry picked up the fat gray cat, placing her outside the room, closing the door.

"*I am starving. I'm going to call the SPCA!*" Pewter hollered.

"She has good lungs." Felipe laughed.

"Sit down, Harry. Would you like half my sandwich? It's huge."

"No. I stopped by—don't stop eating, by the way—I stopped by to tell you your ad has everyone talking, as does the skeleton found in Richmond. Kind of worked in your favor, didn't it?"

"Not that we wish anyone murdered, but since that happened even before there was a Nature First, we might as well use it," Lisa realistically answered.

"Yeah." Harry knitted her eyebrows for a moment. "First Gary is killed."

"Awful," Raynell loudly spoke.

"He once worked for Rankin Construction. If he were still with us he might have some insight." Harry continued her line of thought.

"Like what?" Raynell asked.

"Did anyone have an argument with, say, a foreman, or did anyone steal something?"

"Even so. Doesn't mean he was murdered. And the medical examiner hasn't yet established a time when he died or how long he was there," Felipe said.

"I know, but there's something about this that just eats at me. Something I can't identify."

"Harry, we all lost a friend. Someone who designed wonderful spaces for us. Eats at all of us," Raynell said.

"*I hear you talking about eating!*" Pewter banged on the door.

"Well, I'd better go before I have to replace your door."

"It's terrible the way you don't feed that cat," Lisa teased.

"*You don't know the half of it,*" Tucker chimed in.

Pirate replied, "*She's mean to me.*"

"*Don't pay any attention, Pirate. She thinks the universe revolves around her,*" Tucker said.

Harry, her hand on the doorknob, paused. "I'm going to Over the Moon. Need anything?"

"See if *Books for Living* by Will Schwalbe has come in," Lisa asked.

"If it has, I'll set it on the table by the front door."

The book had come in. After a bracing discussion with Anne, Harry walked back to Nature First, quietly opened the door. They were all on the phone or at their computers. She placed it on the table by the door.

Two hours later, Felipe called to Lisa. "Hey, your book is here."

"Been there for hours." Raynell looked up from her computer.

"I'll take it to her." Felipe picked it up, placed it on Lisa's desk, as she had the phone to her ear.

She was bored so she opened the volume, began licking her fingers as she turned the pages. She leafed through it, she knew she needed to work but she couldn't help peeking into the book she had ordered.

At five, Raynell wrapped her scarf around her neck, pulled on her coat. "Felipe, I'm going home. Lisa's still working, I think."

"Okay. I'll tell her."

A half hour passed. Felipe didn't hear any phone conversation. He stuck his head into Lisa's office, the door was always open. Pirate was licking her hand.

"*Something's wrong*," the handsome fellow cried.

It was. Lisa was dead.

28

January 30, 2017

Monday, 7:00 PM

Felipe and Raynell sat in the conference room with Cooper. Pirate sat with them, confused as his human's body was wheeled out of her office. The sheriff's department crime team arrived at Nature First within twenty minutes of Felipe's call. Cooper, across the street at the large post office investigating a tampered P.O. box, stepped into their office within seven minutes of Felipe's call to the department.

Ashen-faced, Felipe stared straight ahead with his hands folded on the table. Raynell kept wiping away tears.

Notebook open, Cooper gently asked questions. "First, I am not assuming this is an unnatural death but, given the ad in the paper, Nature First right now is in the public eye. Did either of you notice any health problems these last few days?"

Both shook their heads. "No."

"Her mood?"

"Exuberant. Finding the skeleton in Richmond gave us an opening to insist for more involvement in city planning, environmental issues, history stuff." Felipe took a deep breath. "You know."

"I think I do. But she didn't seem stressed?"

"The reverse." Raynell found her voice. "She was energized."

Cooper dropped her hand, placing it on the puppy's head.

"Did I do something wrong?" Pirate asked.

Cooper patted him, turned to Felipe. "Tell me again what you saw."

Clearing his throat, he replied, "Lisa and I were working late. It had been a crazy day. She'd been giving interviews much of the day on the phone. Also she must have checked in with our state headquarters in Richmond every two hours. She and Kylie Carter, state director, work closely together. Anyway, I looked up from my computer at about five-thirty and realized I hadn't heard any talk or noise from her office. Of course, I assumed she was working on her computer but something told me to check. That's when I found her slumped over her desk, computer on. She'd knocked a book she'd just bought onto the floor. Oh, Pirate was pawing at her."

"No signs of, say, a convulsion? Great pain?"

"No. And no one had been in the office since after lunch. It was just the two of us. Raynell left at five. I walked behind Lisa's desk, shook her a little, and she didn't move.

I was horrified but I could still think. I took her pulse. No pulse. That's when I called the sheriff's department."

"Did you touch anything?"

"Just Lisa. I didn't even pick up the book. I brought Pirate back to my office."

"Who did you call after you called the department?"

"Kylie first. She kept me on the phone asking a million questions, none of which I could really answer. I can give you her phone number."

"Thanks. Anyone else?"

"Just Raynell. She'd just gotten home. She came back immediately, which took about fifteen minutes."

"I rent a room in Cascades subdivision," Raynell offered.

"So when did you arrive here?"

"Maybe one minute before you did."

"Did you look at the body?"

"Yes." Raynell's tears flowed again. "It doesn't seem real."

"Did you touch anything?"

"No. I only stood in her doorway."

"Are either of you aware of any condition she might have had?"

Felipe said, "She had an irregular heartbeat. She'd joke and say if anything ever happened to her make sure emergency services knows."

Raynell let out a small sob. "Now she doesn't have any heartbeat at all."

"I don't want to disturb you, but what you can recall so

close to the event of her death can be very helpful. Did she take drugs?"

"Like recreational drugs?" Raynell asked.

"Anything," Cooper tersely answered.

"No," Felipe said. "Once or twice she might tell us she smoked weed at a party, but Lisa wasn't really a user. Sometimes she'd get a headache and take an aspirin. We keep the aspirin in the medicine cabinet in the bathroom."

"Drink?"

"A glass of wine. Sometimes at the end of the day we'd go down to Fardowners Restaurant and have a glass. I never saw her tipsy." Raynell provided that information.

"Have either of you ever been to where she lived?" Cooper continued.

"Once," Raynell replied.

"Well, I've worked here longer than Raynell so I would pick up stuff from her house at times. I don't know, maybe five or six times a year I'd stop by." Felipe unfolded his hands, then folded them back again.

"Did you ever go inside?"

"Sure. Tidy. Not too much furniture. She was renting down Mt. Tabor Road and she was actually looking for a place to buy."

"Raynell."

"I didn't go inside. I picked up a pile of stuff from the Nature Conservancy that she wanted me to read."

"Will we know how she died?" Felipe asked.

"I think so. It appears to be natural causes, but we need

to be careful. The body will go to the medical examiner in Richmond."

"You think she died of a heart attack?" Raynell asked.

"I have no medical expertise whatsoever. But given recent events, we need to be sure she did die of natural causes."

"Who could kill her? We were here working all day. Harry came in for a minute, brought the book that Lisa had ordered from Over the Moon. No one else came by and that was around lunchtime. Who could have killed her? She was just slumped over." Felipe was trying to make sense of a young person's quiet passing.

"Well, it certainly appears natural, but the department has to make sure. When we know you will know, of course."

"What will happen to Pirate? I can't take him," Raynell asked.

"Me neither. Irish wolfhounds are the biggest dogs there are, even bigger than Great Danes," Felipe added.

"I have just the place for him. No point in taking him to the SPCA, good as they are. Don't worry, he'll have a nice home."

"Where am I going? What's going to happen to me? What happened to Lisa?" the puppy cried.

At nine that evening, Tucker let out a bark. *"Cooper."*

Harry and Fair, sitting on the sofa in the living room, heard the corgi.

"I'll go see." Fair volunteered.

He reached the back door as Cooper knocked on it, then opened it. "Fair, please help."

Fair looked down at the forlorn puppy. "What are the symptoms?"

"Heartbreak," Cooper replied.

Harry came into the kitchen. Mrs. Murphy and Pewter, luxuriating on the sofa before the fire, didn't move.

"Pirate." Harry knelt down to pet the fellow.

"You know this dog?" her husband asked.

"Pirate. He belongs to Lisa Roudabush. He's gorgeous, isn't he?"

"Harry, I hope he now belongs to you," Cooper explained. "Given my hours I can't take him. Lisa's dead."

"What!"

Cooper told her what she knew.

"Oh, this is terrible." Harry held the big puppy in her arms.

Pirate was already getting too big to pick up.

Tucker, such a sweet dog, licked the puppy's face when Harry put him down. "*It will be all right.*"

"If I take him to the SPCA he will get wonderful care. They'll call the Irish wolfhound rescue people, but Lisa, well, I believe she would want her puppy to be with someone she knew. And he couldn't have a better home. Harry, please take him."

"Puppy, you've had a terrible shock." Harry looked up at her husband. "Honey?"

Fair knelt down to pet the fellow. "I can't really say no now, can I? But I think we'll need a saddle for him someday."

Tucker ran into the living room to tell the cats.

"*We'll manage.*" Mrs. Murphy shrugged.

"*Another dog. Living with you is bad enough!*" Pewter wailed.

Harry led Pirate to Tucker's bed, realized that wasn't a good idea. She hurried into the bedroom, returned with an old blanket that she placed next to Tucker's bed. She encouraged the puppy to investigate, put a little cracker on it.

Fair poured Cooper a drink. "Here. You've had a long day."

"Thanks." Cooper watched the puppy curl up.

Mrs. Murphy, Pewter, and Tucker came into the kitchen. Worn out, the little big dog had already fallen asleep.

"*Gross. I don't want to live with another dog.*"

"*Oh, Pewts, it won't be so bad.*" Mrs. Murphy sniffed Pirate's head.

"*Bad. It's the worst. Why does everything happen to me?*"

"*If I were you, I'd be good to this puppy,*" Tucker advised. "*He's going to be huge.*"

"*If I'm not afraid of the world's largest spider, I'm not afraid of a disgusting dog,*" the gray cat spat.

"She's got the bottle brush tail." Cooper observed Pewter.

"She'll settle down." Harry sat at the kitchen table. "Lisa was only in her early thirties. Too young to die."

Fair agreed. "Mother used to say 'When the good Lord jerks your chain, you're going.'"

Harry looked at Cooper. "You don't think anyone helped jerk her chain, do you? I mean, you and Gary, the day he died, talked about Lisa getting an Irish wolfhound. You said Nature First disturbs vested interests."

"Did. Anything is possible, but no one walked into the office after you dropped off Lisa's book. I doubt she was killed, but for the sake of argument, if she was, it was incredibly clever."

Indeed.

29

April 4, 1787

Wednesday

"Think the worst is over?" A light wind out of the west blew Rachel's hair.

"You never know," Catherine answered as they both walked through their mother's garden.

Isabelle had lavished her attention on the large formal garden to the rear of the house. On each side of the house, a narrow band of English boxwoods hugged the outside walls. In front of those she had planted annuals that would peep out of the ground for each season but winter.

The two sisters strolled through the formal gardens that were impeccably kept by Rachel with help from the slaves, those with a green thumb. Percy, Bumbee's husband, cussed daily by his wife if she saw him, evidenced just as much creativity with color, plant height, even statuary for gardens as Bumbee displayed in her weaving room. They were two artistic souls who couldn't agree on anything. If Percy said "apples," Bumbee answered "oranges." Better for both that she now lived in the weaving room.

"Did Percy come up with that low serpentine wall?" Catherine asked.

"He said too many straight lines create fatigue." Rachel laughed. "I never know what that man is going to say or do. He talked me into camellias and I don't like camellias, but when they first bloomed, the white against the dark waxy green leaves, he was right. Just set off the front gardens."

"Hmm. Well, the daffodils have broken through the ground. Mother always said, daffodils first, then tulips will follow. Once the tulips have bloomed, spring is truly here. She had such a gift." Catherine sighed. "You've inherited it."

"I don't know," Rachel murmured. "When I asked do you think the worst is over, yes, I did mean winter, but allow me to ask it again. Do you think you are all right?"

"My body has recovered. John holds me at night but we don't yet mingle. He's fearful. He's more fearful than I am. Still, I should perhaps wait a bit."

"Yes," Rachel simply replied, then stopped to admire a forsythia, buds swelling, ready to open in a riot of yellow. "You've heard about Maureen? You and I haven't had a minute to catch up."

"You've been at St. Luke's every day." Catherine smiled.

"What a beautiful job Charles has done. I can't wait for you to see it. We're almost there. The men can begin painting as soon as the temperature stays fifty degrees or above and we're almost there. But I digress." She smiled sweetly because Rachel, like her mother, could wander off on tangents. "Maureen is allowing Jeffrey to begin a carriage business. He will build everything. The tools alone will cost plenty. She will build him a shop impervious to all weathers."

"Where did you hear that?" Catherine's eyebrows lifted up.

"DoRe."

"Bettina?"

"Well, yes, but DoRe told her the shop alone will be huge. He swears it will be fifty by fifty yards. There will be room for ironwork, copperwork, even gilding. Gilding!"

Catherine put her hand on her hip. "Help us dear Lord. She will build herself a carriage of gold."

"I believe you're right." Rachel burst out laughing.

"He is good. Once people see how well crafted his work is—look at the carriage he imitated from ours—I think people will come to him. Especially people from Philadelphia and Charleston. God forbid they don't own the latest or the best." She paused, grinned widely. "Including matched pairs as well as four-in-hand horses. Hard to find. Hard to train, and we've got Barker O. No one can make a carriage horse like that man."

"DoRe?"

Catherine considered this. "Close. A terrific whip." She used the correct term for a coachman who drives. "Uncanny. I wish I had both men. What we are losing to France we would recoup here. Nothing we can do about DoRe until he asks Bettina to marry him."

"He will, won't he?" Rachel frowned for a moment.

"He will, but he's a cautious man who works for a difficult but clever woman." Catherine stopped to examine a green daffodil shoot. "Isn't it a miracle how plants know when to grow, when to open their blooms? It really is a cycle of life and then death."

"Yes." Rachel changed the subject. "What have you heard from Yancy? Of course, he will want the last race to be Black Knight against Reynaldo. I certainly wouldn't leave Reynaldo alone in any stall down by The Levels. Nor would I allow anyone else to touch him."

Catherine smiled. "Jeddie and I have thought of that. No one will get near my boy. But Yancy did put in writing—the letter came yesterday—that whoever wins their race takes the entire purse. He also said the entry fee will be one hundred dollars."

"What! That's an enormous sum."

"It is. I expect he thinks this will weed out the bit players and really pump up the purses. John, Jeddie, and I will travel down to The Levels next week. I'm not agreeing to anything until I see the place."

"You don't trust him, do you?"

"Not one hundred percent," she confessed. "But I do know he has more to lose than I do if I don't race or if my horse is mysteriously injured. He needs Reynaldo."

"I suppose . . ." Rachel's voice trailed off.

"Aren't the mountains ravishing." Catherine shielded her eyes, for the sun had just touched the rim of the Blue Ridge.

"I never tire of gazing at them." They turned to go back to their respective homes.

"Has Charles heard more from his brother?"

"All dismal." Rachel grimaced.

"I have an idea. You will need to broach it with him."

Rachel, knowing her sister well, held up her hands, palms upward. "Catherine?"

"Just listen. If Hugh becomes bankrupt he will be ruined in more ways than one. No heiress will marry him now. Think what will happen if he loses everything? By the way, is he good-looking?"

"I asked Charles that. He said it's hard to judge one's own brother, plus women look at men differently than men do. So I asked, 'Do you all resemble each other?' To that he answered 'Yes.' He can't be all that bad-looking."

"No. You must convince your husband to convince Hugh to adopt Jeffrey Holloway."

"Catherine, you can't be serious."

"Hear me out. Maureen, after I talk to her, which means after Hugh agrees, will bail him out plus give him a monthly allowance. Jeffrey will visit once a year but stay here. However, he will be the son of a baron."

"How do you know or even think that Jeffrey will outlive Hugh? They aren't that far apart in age."

"Doesn't matter. He is the heir."

"I don't think Jeffrey wants any of this." Rachel's lower lip protruded slightly.

"He doesn't. He is a sensible man in many ways, but she wants it. She can't stand the fact that people think she married a nobody. A handsome nobody, but still. He could at least come from a Tidewater family."

Rachel weighed this. "Well . . . yes, but it is absurd."

"Nothing is absurd if she gets her way."

"Catherine, how rich do you think Maureen is?"

"Millions. She is one of the richest people in our country, certainly in the Caribbean. All we know of is the money her father made honestly. God knows where she's got the rest of it stashed. She learned from her father. She told me as much and she, like a smart dog, buries her bone. In fact, I would not be surprised if Maureen isn't playing politics quietly. Slipping people money, you know, like Alexander Hamilton. She wouldn't give Jefferson a penny. She believes he spends what he doesn't have and knows nothing about money. As she once said, 'He lives in the clouds.'"

"I wouldn't know."

"Rachel, we don't want to know."

Rachel looked into her sister's intense light eyes. "Why would you do this?"

"First, I would do it for Charles. He's distressed."

"He is," Rachel admitted.

"Secondly, Maureen will owe us."

"You're going to charge her?" Rachel was aghast.

"No. Consider this, Sister. If France goes to hell we lose a great deal of money. Father has spread the risk. We aren't going to be in Hugh's position thanks to father's business acumen, but we may well be in tightened circumstances. If need be, Maureen will be our banker."

Stunned, Rachel stopped in her tracks. "Dear God."

"God doesn't care about our finances. Listen to me. Our beloved father will not live forever. For decades I hope and pray, but someday you and I must carry this estate."

"We have our husbands."

"Neither one of our husbands is a businessman. My husband is a war hero. He commands great respect and I respect him, but he comes from poor farmers in Massachusetts. He knows nothing about money, how it moves, what it truly buys, which is power. Your husband knows a bit more but he is an artist, an architect. He would have to walk away from what he has learned to love and learn a new business. He'd be an innocent among rapacious, greedy men. Not every businessman is without conscience but many are. After all, our father takes care of his people, is unfailingly generous, backed the colonials during the war. But our father is an extraordinary man. We must run this place when that sad day comes."

"Catherine, I know nothing. You're the one. You've inherited our father's brain. Plus you work with him."

"I may be the one but both of us must work through our husbands. I don't think John will balk, and I do know the shrewd men among us know he is no businessman, but they can't cross him nor try to make a fool of him. I will destroy them."

"Catherine."

"Sister, it's kill or be killed."

Rachel remained silent for a long time. "What is it that I must do?"

"What our mother did. Be beautiful. Be sweet. Host

wonderful parties and soirees. Invite everyone. Look up into the eyes of the gentlemen who visit. Be adoring of their achievements. Men like you. You are exactly what they want a woman to be."

"Well, you're far more beautiful than I am."

"No, I am not, plus I struggle to flatter their vapid egos. I do it but you are an angel. Men adore you. Children adore you. Even other women adore you."

"Now, now, you're laying it on thick." Rachel put her arm around her sister's waist.

"It's the truth. And the truth is I am somewhat dazzling. Men fall over when they see me but I frighten them. You draw them. And Charles is a wonderful husband. You work well together. His manners are Old World, aristocratic, and he is a kind man, a very kind man, as is my John. I worry about both of them. They lead with their hearts."

Rachel sighed, pulled her sister with her as they walked down to Ruth's cabin, where the children stayed many days, playing with one another. "They do."

Catherine smiled. "Some days I fear I may need to guard against them as well as rivals. It is possible to be too good, you know." She laughed.

"What is it really that you want me to do?"

"Listen to me. We can argue. We are sisters after all, but when it comes to business, to profit and to power, listen to me."

"Do you ever wonder what it would be like if you were father's son instead of his elder daughter?"

Catherine threw back her head and laughed. "I'd be in

more duels than the men around us. Thank the Lord I am a woman. And truthfully, Rachel, it's so easy to work through men. Takes a bit of time but it is so easy."

Rachel smiled. "We had a mother who taught us well."

"Walking through her gardens, which you keep so beautifully, I miss her. If only she could see her grandchildren. If only she could see Father and he her. I don't know as any love is perfect but theirs came close."

Rachel, voice low, said, "I don't understand love. I try but I don't. But I feel it."

"Yes, I do, too. I just don't talk about it."

30

"Another month if there are no more delays." Sean spoke to Tony as both men observed the work site now that Rankin Construction could resume operations.

"Overtime?" Tony asked his boss.

"No other way."

The foreman folded his arms over his chest, his flannel-lined overall helping to keep him warm in the February cold. "You'll have to hire more men. These guys aren't going to work around the clock. They'll pull some overtime but not a solid month."

"I know. Fortunately, when we create a budget we try to factor in these things. I'm not worried . . . yet." Sean grimaced. "Damnedest thing finding Elkins."

"You know what I remember? He was a whiner. 'Course

I wasn't a foreman then. He was above me but nonstop bitching and moaning. I couldn't stand the guy."

Sean half smiled. "Obviously someone else couldn't either." He looked skyward, and it was getting darker at midday. "Well, it was a long time ago. We were both wet behind the ears. Dad made me work from the ground up, literally. Best thing he ever did. What I do remember is less the whining because Elkins was smart enough not to look like a candyass in front of the boss's son. I remember he'd make trips to the library, books. Lots of books on Richmond, throughout history, this area. The falls, anyway, books on what it was like. Williamsburg men used to send their recalcitrant slaves here. Pretty rough, I guess."

"Elkins always said Ali Asplundah was murdered." Tony shook his head. "He'd whisper Ali knew too much."

"Ali died of a heart attack, leaning up against the huge Cat he was working. Amazing how much better equipment is today."

"It's easier to operate but all this computer chip stuff drives me crazy," Tony responded.

"Might be right. But when I started in this business, if a track came off a giant Caterpillar, a new one cost ten thousand dollars. That would be dirt cheap today. Forgive the pun." Sean smiled broadly.

"Yeah, nothing ever gets cheaper. Well, maybe computers."

"The hell." Sean spat. "Apple sells a phone now for one thousand dollars. It's nuts and people are dumb enough to pay for it. As for equipment, it's astronomical, but you know we can't do what we do without it. And"—he paused—"the stuff does last longer, just like car engines last longer."

"True."

"So what or why did Elkins think Ali was killed? Never said anything to me. No one did."

Tony felt a snowflake. "I don't think anyone took him seriously. But even if they did, nothing to gain by that kind of talk around someone like you."

"Jeez, Tony, now I wonder what else I missed back in the day."

"Not too much. But finding his body makes me wonder about the complaining."

"Whatever he did, it would have to be a lot worse than complaining for someone to shoot him," Sean sensibly said. "Funny to think that years later that lead was still pressed into his ribcage."

"I sure hope there are no more bodies under this ground or we'll be way, way behind." Sean also felt a snowflake on his nose, looked upward. "I swear February is the longest month in the year."

"We've got at least six more feet to dig. That's much deeper than the base for the Kushner Building. We'll probably find pigeon bones, squirrels, and if we find more humans, I'm willing to bet the remains are much, much older than Elkins's."

"Yeah."

"Any ideas?"

"About what?"

"About what to do if we find anything else?"

"Tony, for God's sake, hide it if it's human. We'll never

get this job done. And we can always put the bones in a box, put it on another site. Preferably one being dug by Franklin Bros." Sean let out a loud laugh.

Tony shook his head, laughed. "Our biggest competitor is probably enjoying every minute of this."

"Yeah, old man Frank Franklin was hot when they didn't get the bid. But we knew this site a lot better. After all, Dad built the Kushner Building." He then smiled at Tony. "We all did. By then you and I knew a little more."

"Yeah, but times are different now. When we started out there was no Nature First, no Save the Bay, all the rest of it. Everyone has an ax to grind and yet everyone wants the city's economy to tick up."

"Doublethink." Sean slapped Tony on the back. "Back to work."

"What do you want to do if I find anything?"

"Hide it. I mean it. Whoever digs up whatever, you take over. Tell him not to worry about it and save the bones. I'm willing to bet if you find the remains of a homeless dog from 1810 the whole damned job will shut down again."

Tony nodded, turned, and headed back to the men standing by their enormous machines.

Sean climbed into the Rankin truck to head back to the office. A review of the files as well as soil types was in order. The police made copies of Elkins's employment record. He wanted to review what they were reviewing. So much had happened, including frantic calls from the bank, from Cloudcroft, he hadn't had the time to check things himself. Rankin had taken no construction loans, of course, but Cloudcroft, for all their braying about their obscene profits with growth of 9.7 percent just last year, seemed reluctant to spend those profits, hence a large construction loan on their part. So the bank called Sean, who reassured them that Cloudcroft truly was good for the loan. They didn't want to risk operating capital, which they had told the bank. Did he think they had lots of money? He did but he also figured they were all a nest of vipers.

Ronald Reagan's quote of an old Russian proverb played in his mind. "Trust but verify." He didn't trust but he certainly verified.

31

"Where's Pirate?" Felipe asked when Harry walked through the door.

"Home with Tucker. I thought it would be too upsetting for him to come back here. He's still looking for Lisa. Breaks my heart." Then she added, since Felipe looked brokenhearted, too, "He's settling in. Tucker adores him. Mrs. Murphy rubs up against him. Pewter, pfft." She flicked her hand.

"Thank you for giving him a good home. I would have liked to have kept him. Such a mellow fellow, but my apartment is small and Pirate will not be small."

"No. He's a loving puppy. He'll be fine in time." She smiled. "I stopped by to see if you and Raynell needed anything? Where is she by the way?"

"Back in Lisa's office. The sheriff's department sifted

through everything. She's trying to get it all back in place before Kylie Carter shows up. Tomorrow."

"Ah. I assume nothing much came of the crime team."

He shook his head. "Well, they're thorough. Actually, I was impressed with them, and we all know Cooper, of course."

"That's something, I guess." Harry unzipped her worn work jacket. "Feels good in here. Are you sure you don't need anything?"

"No, but thank you."

Raynell emerged from Lisa's office, a sheaf of papers in hand. "Oh, hello, Harry."

"Just dropped by to check in on you all."

"We're still in shock," Raynell confessed, putting the papers on the side table by the front door. "I believe Lisa saved everything she'd ever read."

Felipe smiled. "Close to it. She'd research something on her computer, but if she read a magazine she'd tear out pages."

"Her file cabinets are organized. Give her that," Raynell remarked. "Me, I'm paperless if I can help it. Just hit the save button. Takes care of everything."

A colored glossy page caught Harry's eye. "Dinosaurs. Gary had little rubber dinosaurs everywhere."

"When he was working here, sometimes he'd be on all fours." Raynell smiled. "The two of them would be yakking about a 'saurus' this and a 'saurus' that. I know Nature First has an interest in prior periods of life, but pretty much I stick to what's on the planet now."

"Me, too," Harry agreed.

Felipe interlocked his fingers, placing his hands behind his head. "She had this theory that whatever happened before could happen again. Lisa believed Mother Nature moves forward and backward. She'd say, 'Look at how rivers have changed course even in a few hundred years. Who is to say we can't all be dragged back in time to the primordial swamp.'"

Raynell shifted her weight from one well-shod foot to the other. "I guess anything is possible."

"Yeah, but the more we find from, say, the Triassic-Jurassic period to the Cretaceous period up to the Paleogene time, the more we will know about what truly happened. You know, the times of mass extinction. Look at what's happening with these monster hurricanes. Maybe there will be evidence of enormous climate changes we haven't found yet," Harry said, betraying that she had done some homework.

"People are pushing this change," Raynell said with conviction.

"We are, but that doesn't mean that Nature wasn't heading down that path. There's so much we don't know." Felipe looked up at Harry, whom he much liked. "For instance, did you know that where the Blue Ridge Mountains are, our beautiful mountains, there was once a sixty mile by ten mile lake? It was a bit east of the mountains and over the millennia the mountains kept eroding into this lake. Every time there'd be an earthquake or an uplift of the mountains, they'd erode into the lake. So in this former lake, in the muds and that good old Virginia red clay, there is over two hundred and fifteen million years of stuff, of fossils, of footprints, of bones. We're just beginning to understand what we are literally standing on."

"True, but Felipe, dinosaurs and whatever aren't coming back," Raynell calmly replied. "I don't see that happening."

"We don't know. What if the earth permanently tips just one percent more away from the sun or toward the sun? Think what could happen."

"It is fascinating." Harry thought it was.

"I guess it is, but I'm more concerned with saving and improving the environment for, say, hummingbirds, raptors, even elk if they release them into the mountains down in Lee County." Raynell mentioned a Virginia county at its southwestern corner, a poor county but so beautiful.

Harry glanced again at the pile of papers and couldn't help herself. She flicked through a few of them.

"Funny. Gary had this article in his files."

"What's that?" Raynell asked.

"This one." Harry pulled out an article about why frogs survived when dinosaurs died en masse. "This one that states that eighty-eight percent of frogs on earth today began to flourish, just bred their little hearts out, after the dinosaurs died off."

"I haven't read that one," Felipe said, and smiled when Raynell handed the article to him. "Well, I better show frogs new respect."

"I read the article in Gary's file box. Couldn't help my-self. As I recall the theory is that frogs survived because they didn't need so much space to live. When the forests came back they could climb up in trees to escape preda-tors or hide under leaves. Plus they could eat insects and there sure are enough of those, I guess, at any time on earth." Harry laughed. "Chiggers. That's what we really need. An investigation into why chiggers developed."

Felipe and Raynell laughed with her.

"Well, I'd better get back to putting everything in order. Kylie will be here tomorrow with some of her staff."

"I imagine everyone is shook up."

"And then some. Felipe and I want to keep the office running."

"Raynell, they aren't going to shut it down. What we're really worried about is will we get a new boss or will one of us take over? It's easier if it's one of us mostly because we worked closely together, we knew Lisa's methods and she really did teach us political maneuvering," Felipe gratefully said.

A concerned look crossed Harry's even features. "Gary redid your office. He and Lisa got on like a house on fire. Both are dead. Murdered."

"Murdered? Lisa died of a stroke or a heart attack," Raynell objected, clearly upset at the suggestion.

"Well, we don't know yet. But I believe the two deaths are connected."

"Harry, that's nuts," Raynell blurted out.

"Yeah, well, I've heard that before. Maybe I am nuts but

two people who knew each other fairly well, both had an interest in nature in all of its manifestations, both opposed rampant development by builders. I don't know but that little light in my head just lit up."

"Harry, I hope it's a dim bulb." Raynell breathed deeply.

32

April 10, 1787

Tuesday

Ewing strode through the carriage stables, looking for his elder daughter.

She glanced up from King David's hoof, which Baxter O. held between his knees.

"Baxter, thank you, you can put his hoof down."

Ewing, clearly agitated, focused on King David. "Is he all right?"

"Fine. A little tender. A small stone bruise. The pastures are greening up. A little turn out and no work will fix him just fine." She smiled at Baxter O., whose opinion she valued highly; they had talked this over.

"Walk with me," her father commanded. "I need to get the kinks out."

She teased him. "Head or back?"

"Just you wait." He smiled at her. He then launched

into what was on his mind. "Roger Davis wrote Maureen Seli . . . I mean Holloway, to tell her there is to be a convention in Philadelphia in May. Settled. It will happen, and those representatives farthest away from Babylon on the Delaware are already on their way. What an opportunity this will be for endless pronouncements, legal twaddle, and rampaging self-interest. I don't know what's worse: deteriorating as we are or letting those men argue at a convention."

"Father, you're the one who says we have to do something. We can't have export and import taxes between states and that's what the current situation amounts to, doesn't it?"

Grimly, he nodded. "Does, but Jefferson and his minions will be philosophically opposed to Adams and his following. Each will parade his Latin, too."

"Surely there will be more moderate men."

"Hamilton?" Ewing's voice lowered. "Jefferson hates him, loathes him, and I expect it's mutual. So that means Madison loathes him. I don't see how an accord, even a rough accord, can be affected with these intensely self-regarding men."

"When you speak, I am glad I am not in politics." Catherine smiled.

"It's the devil's work. Is. I have lived a long time. I have observed from across the ocean the foolishness of kings, who worry more about their conquests and how they will be remembered than in fostering trade. They know nothing about trade and how wealth is created. They only know how to spend it like the mess in France with the queen's jewelry. It's absurd. And we're absurd, too."

"Will Washington be there?"

"He will. He's probably the only man who can keep order. Franklin is eighty-one. But he has a way of bringing people together."

"I thought Jefferson was still our ambassador to France." Catherine was well informed, but only her family knew this, as well as Maureen, who divined it.

A slight breeze tousled Ewing's hair. The early afternoon burst with spring's promise of renewal. Many trees sported small buds opening to reveal true spring green color. The daffodils still bloomed but on the down side. Next would come the tulips with their wide array of colors.

"Oh, he's in France, but I tell you who will be there, in his clever way. Madison. Madison. Madison."

"Hence Roger Davis's centrality to all this?"

"Mmm." Ewing pursed his lips. "Madison is shifty. Brilliant, yes, but so are Hamilton and others. But Madison leaves little trace of his goings and comings. He's like a tailor using invisible thread."

"I thought you liked his mother."

"She makes Franklin look young." Ewing laughed. "Nell Madison has been dying since the day she was born. Whatever affliction is present or talked about, she has had it or is exhibiting the first symptoms. She'll outlive us all. No wonder James isn't married. She's driven them all away." He laughed again.

"Much as I like John's family, I am glad they are in Massachusetts. And then when we visit them once a year, or they come here, I feel peeved at myself. His mother is a hardworking, loving woman and she never tells me what to do."

"Oh, my dear, who can do that? I've been trying since you learned to walk."

A slight blush rose on Catherine's cheeks. "I listen."

"Now you do but you were a handful."

"Rachel was perfect." Catherine smiled.

"Let's just say Rachel is more like your mother."

"And I am more like you." Catherine slipped her arm through his.

He looked down for a step or two then looked up at an aqua sky. "So they say."

She laughed. "Back to Philadelphia. It's a Quaker city. How can it be Babylon on the Delaware?"

"Don't be fooled by all that simplicity rubbish. A Quaker can spend money as well as the rest of us. Perhaps they're smarter about hiding it. No lavish jewelry or excessive furniture. However, I have yet to see a rich Quaker who doesn't own a handsome carriage."

"I suppose each group of people has their ways and a way to get around them." She drew even closer to her father.

"True. My fear is an agreement that is sensible, focused on trade, the latest farming practices won't be reached. Everyone will question slavery but no state will really do anything. Look how many slaves New York has. It will be a deadlock. And all the disagreements will be on the table."

"Maybe they have to be on the table to get anything done."

He patted her hand. "I don't know, my dear. I believe in letting sleeping dogs lie."

"It is a sensible way to live and yet these are new times. No one ever thought we would throw out King George, defeat the British Army and Navy, dispense with born aristocrats and royalty. I suppose we should all fall on our knees and give thanks for Lord North." She cited the prime minister who most felt misled the king.

"And fall on our knees for Washington. How he kept together the different state militias, most of whom only signed up for three months and weren't paid, I might add."

"Many still haven't been."

"Yes. Yes. That's unforgivable. You see a man begging on a Richmond or Williamsburg street and he lost his legs at Guilford or some other battle. It's a sin, you know."

"I do. John isn't shy about expressing himself when it comes to his comrades. He's not a political man but he feels deeply for those who served."

A sharp smile crossed Ewing's face. "Old men start the wars. Young men fight them. It's been that way since Marathon." He waved with his free hand. "I can't let this affect me so."

"Father, you risked your life not in battle but by working for the cause, by pouring money into it, by raising troops."

"I did and I never dreamed it would come to this."

"Does the future ever turn out as we dream?"

"I don't know, my dear. My future has you, your sister, good husbands, grandchildren. In so many ways it's better than I could have imagined. Politics, national direction, that's a different matter."

"Why do you think Roger Davis writes Maureen?"

He stopped, looked at his daughter. "I don't know. In fact, I didn't consider that until you brought it up."

"You know Maureen never engages in anything that doesn't redound to her advancement."

"Can you imagine if she could be in politics?"

"But, Father, she is."

Confusion, then a ripple of fear followed this statement for Ewing. "How?"

"Perhaps it takes a woman to fathom another woman's methods." She hastily added, "Which isn't to say I approve."

"Well?" His interest skyrocketed.

"I believe, I can't prove, but I believe Maureen has kept all of her former husband's financial friends, bankers, sugarcane planters, shipbuilders, and captains. I believe she has stayed at the center of that net."

"You don't say." He frowned. "She is uncommonly shrewd."

"I believe most of her money remains in the Caribbean. And I also believe she lends it at a high interest from time to time."

"So much for usury." He half smiled.

"Always honored in the breech. It's an easy profit and should the lender fail, you take back whatever he has of value. I have no doubt she owns ships, plantations in the

Caribbean and she's angling for something here. Why else would Roger Davis keep her informed?"

"She's paying Madison under the table?" Ewing was shocked.

"It is possible but I think she's more clever than that, and truly I don't think the highly intellectual Madison is a person of finance or greed."

"I don't know about that. His father wasn't slow and truthfully neither is his mother, although she hides it behind her stream of illnesses. I believe she knows where every penny is. Every penny."

"You know them far better than I, Father."

"Maureen is a formidable enemy, as was Francisco. I always stayed on the good side, did some business with Francisco."

"She's ruthless. She would steal the pennies off a dead man's eye." Catherine used the old phrase. "And she's not above killing a slave."

"Herself!" Ewing was horrified.

"I think if Maureen sets her mind to something, anybody who gets in the way courts danger."

"But personally kill a slave?"

"I think . . ." Catherine almost let it slip about Maureen's attempted murder of Ailee. "Well, I suspect she could."

"One hears of men who kill in a fit of rage, but a woman. Oh, that is unnatural."

"So you think murder is natural?" Catherine loved to talk to her father about anything.

"I suppose I do. Humans have been killing one another

for thousands of years. We just emerged from a brutal war. Look what the British did to our prisoners. They let them die in the holds of prison ships off Boston. Unforgivable. We treated their prisoners with decency. Thanks to Washington. But yes, I think murder, killing, theft, all the sins are part of humankind wherever we are in the world. In deepest Africa, one tribe kills another. In Europe all they do is start wars. China. The hoards of the East marching and killing across the plains. Finally stopped at Vienna in 1683. I'm afraid, my dear, it's what we are. But women. Women are morally superior to men."

She smiled. "Or Father, perhaps we haven't had the chance."

He walked more briskly with her. "You know, Catherine, sometimes you scare me."

"I don't mean to but ideas cross my mind. And thanks to you, I received a good education."

"Do you talk to John in this fashion?"

She shook her head. "John deals with what's in front of him. And remember, he did not have much education, just a bit of schooling in that tiny town in Western Massachusetts. Hardscrabble there."

"Indeed," her father agreed.

"I tell you, he is not a learned man nor an intellectual one, but he is brave, believes in Christ devoutly, far more devoutly than I do. And well . . ." She paused. "I think the early death of the baby has affected him even more than myself. There are times when I look at him, he doesn't know I am watching him, and he's so sad, so deeply sad."

"I am sorry to hear that."

"He wants to make everything all right. But he can't. So he struggles to accept why God would do this to our baby, to me. I mourn the child, of course I do, but in a way women are prepared for these things."

A long, long silence followed this as Ewing stared at the mountains. "Your mother bore her loss with incredible courage. You may be like me, my dear, but you are also much like her."

"It's a woman's lot, Father."

"Yes, yes, it is." Then his voice grew stronger. "In life there is death and in death life. We must endure."

"I am. I am." Her hand slid from his forearm and she held his hand. "The future is not given to any of us. We must fight for it."

33

Rankin Construction, five years ago, built a media room. Just as in a television studio, screens lined the walls, with a large center screen in the middle.

"I built this to combat theft as well as politically motivated vandalizing of construction sites. As you can see, each site has multiple cameras trained on it." Sean couldn't help bragging.

"Do your workers know they're there?" Harry's curiosity bubbled over.

"The foremen know where the cameras are. We try to hide them. Can't always." He sighed. "But our losses to theft and, for lack of a better term, urban terrorism, have fallen."

"Urban terrorism. I've never heard you speak like that." Marvella, sitting in the chair next to Sean, questioned.

"I can't think of a better term. We've got these groups that want to save butterflies, flying squirrels, you name it. Now look, I am not in the business of destroying wildlife but there has to be some common sense. Richmond needs buildings, new buildings. People are pouring in. Businesses are relocating. We've got to build." He took a long pause. "Intelligently."

"Yes." Marvella sighed. "I had no idea all this was going on."

"Thanks to the skeleton being found at the Cloudcroft site, people want to crawl over everybody's building sites. Not just ours," he replied. "And if a company has a Middle-Eastern name, Turkish, anything not European, if you know what I mean, there's even more dissatisfaction."

Dryly, Marvella intoned, "Fortunately, Rankin is quite Northern European."

He smiled sheepishly. "Well, yes. Then again, so is Lawson."

"Touché." She smiled back. "Well, given all this current uproar what better time to put forward Rankin Construction as a patron of the arts and especially as a benefactor to the Virginia Museum of Fine Arts?" She took a breath. "Did you see the paintings?"

"You know I did or we wouldn't be together." He smiled at her again.

Sean knew when he was being managed and Marvella was an expert.

Harry watched in amusement.

"As I mentioned before, these are not well-known artists here or even in Europe. They're good. Not great. We aren't talking about a Russian Matisse but this is excellent work, hidden from all of us on the other side of the Iron Curtain." Marvella stopped again. "Have you ever read that speech given in Fulton, Missouri, by Churchill? Where he first uses the term 'Iron Curtain'?"

"No, I haven't. Unlike you, I'm not a history buff."

"What about you, Harry?"

"No."

"Well, you can read it online. Do. Apart from Lincoln I don't think there has ever been an American leader with a true gift for language."

"Not even Jefferson?" Harry inquired.

"Too busy, and remember, he had a committee, essentially, for the Declaration of Independence. But he certainly was an extraordinary man. So far ahead of his time in some ways and so much a part of his time in others. I guess that can be said of us all in good time. Well, I digress. Sean, what I have been able to assemble with Sotheby's help, they have been wonderful in pointing me in the direction of, shall we say, lost artists?"

"I especially liked Stepan Kolesnikov." Harry watched as Sean pulled up subjects from the thumb drive.

"The wolf?" Sean studied the work.

"Emotional. For me, anyway. A lone animal in a harsh landscape, winter in Russia. Does it get any worse?" Harry wondered.

"I don't know, but I always thought Napoleon's siege of Moscow was where the French developed their taste for horse meat," Marvella said without rancor.

Sean nodded. "He threw away over a million of his own men, and God knows how many of his enemies he killed, but he's a hero. Hitler and Mussolini and Stalin are not. Imagine if an American behaved in such a way?"

"I find it odd a culture with such a rich, elegant appreciation of the arts thinks nothing of mass death." Marvella shrugged. "But I suppose every nation rationalizes its worst decisions. Well, back to the hoped-for exhibit. Sean, was there any artist who you especially liked?"

"This one." He clicked on Ivan Pokhitonov's painting, *Snowy Garden.* "These have sold, have they not?"

Marvella nodded they had. "But with help we may be able to assemble many of them. If you and the board of directors for the company are willing to sponsor this, the first thing I will do is track down former ambassadors to Russia. They will know the right people and a few may even have an interest in the arts. Russia has produced gorgeous items over the years. Their uniforms, court dresses, extraordinary."

"I think we can do this and we do need some positive P.R." He shook his head. "If you take any construction company, there are workers who leave, workers who work a brief time and never return after collecting their paycheck. And remember, this Edward Elkins worked here before drug testing. You'd be surprised what a difference that has made."

"I suppose there's something good about violating your constitutional rights." Marvella laughed.

Sean laughed, too. "I can't say as I like random drug testing. It's a cushy job for a doctor but drugs are rampant not just here, everywhere. And they grow ever more so-phisticated."

"Sports." Harry uttered one word.

"Oh, they've known that for years." Marvella waved her hand. "Just like they've known for years about concussions. Is there a Virginian who doesn't remember Ray Easterling?"

She named a famous and beloved pro-football player, one of those men whom everyone liked, who took his own life in 2012. Turned out he had a damaged brain.

"We don't give money to any form of sporting event and drugs are one of the reasons." Sean leaned back in his chair. "We give to environmental groups, we give to schools where they still teach shop."

"Do they?" Marvella was surprised.

"A few do. We need a big trade school actually. But we give supplies and we'll send, say, an electrician to show them some of the more sophisticated wirings. Everything is connected now. It's not just turning on the lights."

"Never thought of that," Harry commented, then in-quired, "You give to Nature First?"

"We do. Ducks Unlimited gets most of our environ-mental funding, but as Nature First started here, we give."

"Weren't you surprised when Nature First took out a one-page ad criticizing you?"

"I was and I called Kylie Carter that morning. She apol-ogized, said this was Lisa Roudabush's idea, but she did agree that Nature First couldn't appear to be bought off. Bought off!"

"I'm afraid, dear Sean, it's the way of the world."

"I was raised that you don't bite the hand that feeds you." He folded his arms across his chest.

"True," Harry agreed. "But people in nonprofits aren't always the most realistic. Often they're driven by passion."

"Did they find out how Lisa died?" he asked.

"No. The results aren't back from the medical examiner's office. Just found dead at her desk."

"People can suffer strokes at a young age," Marvella said to Harry.

"Heart attacks." Sean chipped in.

"This is a happy discussion," Harry said wryly.

"You're right." Marvella smiled. "Sean, thank you so much for getting behind this. I do think it will be helpful. Cast a positive light."

As the two women took their leave of his office, Sean made a request. "When the medical examiner's report does come back, let me know. It is odd."

It was more than odd. It was murder.

34

Stacked along one side of the coach building wall rested planed maple. Even without veneer, the tight surface of this readily available hardwood glowed.

Jeffrey lost no time in developing a workplace in one of the old outbuildings at Big Rawly. Maureen, inflamed by his excitement, was already having a new building twice the size of this one constructed. Any piece of equipment Jeffrey wanted, she bought. The wheelwright, a very focused slave, also worked in the space so it was convivial, as the two men appreciated a high degree of skills. They had much in common as people. Slavery was the confusing wedge.

"Most impressive," Yancy complimented Jeffrey on the frame for a large coach, one that could handle almost all types of weather.

"My lady is determined that this venture will succeed. I am hopeful as you can see. And I've already received two more orders. One for a phaeton and one for a children's cart."

"Quite a difference in scale." Yancy appreciated the particulars.

"So it is and you, more than anyone, can imagine what will become of my handiwork if the children's cart is hitched to a naughty pony."

Yancy smiled and Jeffrey, remembering his bad knee, offered, "Please sit down." Then he turned to one of his apprentices, a very light-skinned young man of perhaps seventeen, who looked suspiciously like the late Francisco. "Pompey, run to the kitchen, will you, and bring back libations and something to entice Mr. Gates to eat?"

The younger man, considered an easy target, shocked Yancy when he shot the older man's knee in a duel. It was shoot or be shot, so Jeffrey shot.

"No need."

Jeffrey smiled. "Well, I'm famished. Perhaps you'll join me. One never knows what they're up to in the kitchen."

"I am here"—Yancy cleared his throat—"to seek your help. Given our past that may seem most forward of me, but I would not ask if I didn't have something to offer in return." Sensing Jeffrey's interest, he continued. "My lad, Ollie, has broken his leg. One of those accidents. He hit the ground hard and on the wrong foot, so to speak, and now his leg is broken. As the races will be on us in a month, I would like to rent your William."

"He is good, isn't he?"

"Working with DoRe would improve anyone and William has talent, plus he's lean and light. How old is he, by the way?"

"Twenty, I think."

"I would pay a dollar a day for his services, but even better, should Black Knight win his race, I will split the winnings with you and Mrs. Holloway, as well as reward William, of course."

"Very generous." Jeffrey considered how to present his position. "As you know, these are my wife's people. She has known them far longer than I." He paused, clearing his throat. "She evidences a keen interest in their skills." He now held up his hand. "Yes, I know as her husband her possessions are mine but to keep harmony, I defer to her. As I said, she has lived with many of them for close to twenty years."

"Very wise." Yancy nodded.

"What I will do is present your offer to her, suggest it is much to our benefit. Of course, we will arrive at the races in the coach I built from Ewing's model."

"You will be besieged with orders. So many people east of here have not had the pleasure of viewing your creations. Tell me, how do you determine the colors?"

"The coach-in-four, the frame there, Mr. and Mrs. Volpe adamantly want a maroon body with gold pinstriping, black wheels with black spokes and a thin maroon and gold pinstripe on each spoke. As to the interior, we could live in it once done. Mrs. Volpe craves comforts."

Yancy laughed. "The ladies do seem to incline that way. But it does sound arresting."

"It does. My secret fear is one day someone will want a white coach."

"Whatever for?"

"That's exactly why. No one else will have one."

Two ladies in bonnets and aprons carried trays of food while Pompey rolled down a food cart obviously built by Jeffrey. Tea, afternoon sherry, and a sparkling decanter of something a bit stronger was secured to the top of the cart by indentations cut down to fit the various pots. Jeffrey had thought of everything. On the bottom shelf rested heavier food items. The two cook's assistants carried the sweets.

"My word, this is a feast," Yancy exclaimed.

"I really am hungry. Your visit has given me the opportunity to indulge."

The two men ate, chatted, somehow the better for their duel. It was done. Over. Yancy considered Jeffrey socially beneath him, but Jeffrey's marriage to Maureen turned that upside down. As for Jeffrey, he craved male company. Maureen kept him on a short tether.

They talked about the expansion of Pestalozzi's Mill, the number of people coming this far west now that their energies could be directed toward a free future.

"Have you seen Catherine Schuyler?" Jeffrey inquired.

"No. I heard she suffered a loss. She's young and strong. But these things cast heavy sorrows."

"Indeed."

Yancy nodded as he cut a large chicken breast into smaller pieces.

"My lady will visit her. She said she wanted to give

Catherine time and she also said fevers can accompany such a loss. Just carry away the woman."

"Yes. Yes. Fortunately, that time seems to be past."

"That's what Maureen—I mean Mrs. Holloway—says, too. And if she agrees to your offer she will go to Catherine." Jeffrey took a deep breath. "We will be racing against her Reynaldo."

"I promise you, Jeffrey, this will be the best horse race in our new nation. My Black Knight against the Garths' Reynaldo."

"I believe you are right."

"All the talk at the mill today was about this convention in Philadelphia. To start early May, so they say. The last time I remember this much talk was before the war. It's a good thing, I think."

"I hope so but unlike you, I am not political. Even when we fell afoul of each other, I always kept in mind the great risk you took during the war. You are a man of exceptional courage."

"You are kind."

"I often wonder if such a trial occurs in my lifetime will I be equal to it? I was too young during the war and I think my father kept a lot from me. Youth can be inflamed."

"Indeed." Yancy laughed. "I often wonder how we lived through it."

They visited for another half hour then Yancy mounted up with help from DoRe.

Jeffrey walked up to the house, where his wife was giving orders in the garden, shoots popping up, lilacs ready to bloom.

She turned. "My tulips, spectacular though they were, are now asleep."

"You have such an eye for color, my dear." He kissed her on the cheek. "I've had an interesting proposal, an interesting visit."

He presented everything to her.

"Half of the winnings should he win?"

"Yes."

"And does he want us to pay part of Black Knight's feed and training now?"

"No, no. He wishes to rent William, as I said."

She sat on a Chinese-inspired bench. "That really means he gets the benefit of DoRe."

"DoRe will remain here, of course, but yes, my angel, William has been at DoRe's knee since he was about that tall."

She laughed. "Well, he has grown since then."

"An advantage in this case."

"Is." She scanned the garden, eyes falling on the azaleas, some weeks from revealing their treasures. "I have no objection and I do think this is an opportunity for you to do business."

"I hope so." He now held her hand. "I'm looking forward to the races."

"Yes," she simply said, sighed. "I must call upon Catherine. Now is a good time. But I don't want her to think we are actually competing against her. She bought Serenissma, Francisco's blooded mare, for a princely sum. It's important to keep good relations."

"I'm sure she will be grateful for your call."

Maureen picked up his hand, the one holding hers, kissed it. "I always wanted children. You know that but this dream never came to pass. When I see or hear of the sufferings of women I know, I think perhaps I was spared. Oh yes, she has JohnJohn—two, I think—but so many diseases carry the little ones away. It has to have crossed her mind that she can take nothing for granted."

"You would have been a perfect mother." He halfway believed it. "And to be surrounded by children as beautiful as their mother. And who knows, we might yet . . ."

"Oh, now, Jeffrey. Much as I would love to have your child, I am soon out of reach." She lifted her shoulders. "I think there was only one Abraham and Sarah." She quoted the old couple in the Bible who conceived.

"That doesn't mean we can't try." Jeffrey knew just how to handle her.

35

Sweeping out the center aisle in the morning, horses turned out to play in the snow, Harry heard the phone ring in her tack room.

Hurrying in, she picked it up. "Hello."

"Harry, do you know what has happened?" Anne de Vault's voice registered worry.

"No. About what?"

"I opened the store today like always and heard a bit of commotion down the hall. So I walked down there and, Harry, Nature First is blocked off with the horrible yellow crime scene tape."

"What?"

"No one can go in."

"Where are Felipe and Raynell?"

"I don't know but I expect if they came to work today

they are somewhere being questioned again. I mean this is now a crime, right?"

"Anne, the crime is murder. Why else would there be tape up?"

"This is awful. She was found slumped at her desk, no violence. Murder?" Anne couldn't believe it, well, she didn't want to believe it.

Who would?

"There are ways to kill without leaving a mark or at least an obvious mark. Was Cooper there?"

"No. The young lady who noticed me told me they were the forensic team. I told her I owned the bookstore down the hall."

"Anne, I am terribly sorry. This is upsetting and you are right there. Is there anything I can do?"

"Yes. Can you think of a reason the rest of us might be in danger?"

"No. I'm not saying that to pacify you, but we've had two unexplained deaths of two people who knew each other, shared common interests, and worked together insofar as redoing the office is working together. They liked each other."

"Yes," Anne said that slowly. "Other than design, I mean what did Gary and Lisa have in common?"

"Little things. I mean they seem like little things to me. She was obsessed with dinosaurs. He kept little rubber dinosaurs on his shelves."

"Lots of people have a keen interest in dinosaurs."

"Yes, but they are usually eight or nine years old."

A very long pause followed this. "You've got a point there."

"The other thing—again, such a little thing—when I helped Tazio set up her office—well, I really sat on the floor to go through Gary's file books but I did move a chair or two and I polished desks. Anyway, I found an article about frogs surviving dinosaurs. Lisa had the same article."

"It's possible they spoke to each other, suggested books and magazines. It's not far-fetched."

"No, but now they are both dead. Murdered."

"Should I close the store?"

"No. You might want to gather the other shop owners there, discuss it, and go back to business. I always think the worst thing to do is react before you know enough. It's important to keep calm."

"Easy to say."

"I know. You asked me a question and I answered it. Let's take a worst-case scenario. The killer is close by. Don't show panic. Make him wonder."

"That's not the worst-case scenario. The worst-case scenario is he comes after me."

"You're right. But, Anne, you don't share the same interests the two of them did. I mean, you have aesthetic tastes, you like architecture, but that's not front and center. And whatever took Gary, I don't think it was architecture."

"I hope not." She took a deep breath. "What is the saying? Keep calm and carry on. I'll try."

"You'll do it. Thank you for calling me. I'm going to

track down Cooper. She'll tell me to butt out. Always does, but I can read between the lines. If I get even a whiff of generalized danger, I'll call you."

"Thank you."

After hanging up, Harry finished her job, returned to the house along with Tucker, who shadowed her. Tucker felt she was protecting Harry. If she could, she would.

Opening the door, Pirate woke up, bounded over. *"I missed you. I fell asleep. You won't leave me, will you?"*

"What a handsome boy." She knelt down to kiss the puppy, who was growing so fast she wouldn't have to kneel much longer.

"I like you. I like Tucker." The tail wagged.

Tucker whispered, *"Say something good about the cats. Pewter has one eye open and she can be a royal pain in the ass if you get on her bad side."*

The Irish wolfhound whispered back, *"She's mean to me. The other kitty is nice."*

"Pewter is even mean to Harry. She turns her back on her, flattens her ears, and walks away or sits on the bookshelf and kicks off a row of books. She's a terrible cat."

"I heard that!" came a growl.

Now Mrs. Murphy awakened. *"Heard what?"*

"Tucker told Pirate I was a terrible cat."

"Oh, don't pay any attention. She's being dramatic," the tiger cat said to the Queen of Drama.

Oblivious to the swirl around her, Harry reached for the wall phone. She did notice that Pirate was sticking close.

"Coop! Anne de Vault called me to tell me Nature First has crime scene tape on the doors."

"Ah, well, yes it does."

"So this is what I think." Harry ignored the groan on the other end of the line. "Murder. Obviously. No violence. No blood. No bruises or marks. At least no obvious marks. It's possible the medical examiner's office found something. But my money is on poison."

"Yes." Cooper tried to remain noncommittal.

"And it would have to be a fast-acting, colorless, and odorless poison. No arsenic. We'd know because it has a distinct odor. No belladonna. Her pupils would have been enlarged. It appeared she suffered a stroke or a heart attack."

"That's quite a bit of information from someone who didn't see the body."

"Coop, someone would have noticed. This is a small community. I would have heard, so I know I'm right."

"You are. The team is there going over everything, especially the little kitchen and the bathroom. There could be a trace in a cup. A small residue on a counter."

"Tell me. You know I'll dig it out sooner or later, plus what if I'm in danger? I've been in her office many times, and recently."

"If you were exposed you'd be dead," Cooper said with finality.

"What the hell is it?" An exasperated Harry swore.

Resigned, Cooper spilled the beans: "Nicotine."

"Cigarettes?" Harry was incredulous.

"Pure nicotine. It is colorless, odorless, viscous. You can

buy it on the Internet for twenty dollars for fifteen milli-
liters. Those transactions can be traced. We can't find such
a transaction. It's possible the killer has had a supply for
years or stole nicotine from a pharmacy in the past."

"Nicotine?" Harry uttered in disbelief. "How can you
kill someone with nicotine? Force it down their throat?"

"No. It's easy because nicotine can be absorbed through
the skin. Exposure to the air causes some discoloration.
To date there is no discoloration on Lisa's body."

"Could the killer have wiped it on, say, her lips or her
arm?"

"I think he did. Whoever killed her knows chemistry."
Cooper took a deep breath. "The stuff, the pure liquid
stuff, five drops or less, can kill a person in minutes. If it's
a high dose there won't even be the nausea and seizures
that can accompany it. The victim can die almost instantly
of respiratory failure. Five drops for a normal-sized
woman of Lisa's age."

"Dear Lord." Harry gasped.

"She probably suffered a few seconds, knowing she was
dying, but it was so quick. We can't find out how the poison was administered. That's why the team is back. Is
there a trace on her desk? Something like that?"

"Then wouldn't Felipe or Raynell be dead?"

"Possibly. If there was a trace it would have made them
sick. But neither one mentioned illness. And Lisa had to
have had pure nicotine on her body."

"Where are Felipe and Raynell?"

Cooper was exasperated. "They're down at HQ. More
questions."

"I knew it!"

"That doesn't take a rocket scientist," Cooper fired back at her.

"Well, I imagine they're scared."

"Raynell more than Felipe. She kept saying what if she touched something. We told her if she had, she'd know. Tears. The usual. Felipe on the other hand is trying to figure this out. Replaying everything. Stuff like, did someone come in and out and somehow they missed it."

"I don't see how they could."

"No."

"Here's another piece of unsolicited advice. She was killed because of something she has in common with Gary."

"You don't know that" came a too-swift reply that told Harry what she needed to know.

Fortified by that, Harry repeated to Cooper the thoughts she had told Anne.

"I agree the two shared those interests, but what could there be about them that would imperil someone else or someone else's profits? It doesn't add up."

"If you find the connection, it will."

"I'm not as convinced as you are but I do agree there might be a tie. But, Harry, if whatever they shared in common led to their murders, it's a tie they were at great pains to hide."

"Maybe not, Coop. We just don't see it yet, or it's outlandish to us. But I will tell you one thing, whoever used this poison is smart. Knows chemistry. And is bold. Think of how Gary was shot in front of us. This, of course, was stealth. Do you think this might be a professional killer?"

Cooper didn't want to answer directly but she knew Harry would see through any evasion. "It very well may be, which means keep out, Harry. Those people are highly intelligent and ruthless."

"Do they get paid a lot?"

"Yes. Most do, and they take pride in their work."

"It's hard for me to imagine being proud of killing people."

"It's not so out there. What if a killer is a rampant ideologue? Like the Bolsheviks in Russia. They had mass-starvation campaigns, killing millions who they believed would impede the revolution. These are people who kill because they believe that killing will solve the problem, make a better world. Or create more profit—not exactly a better world, but better for whoever's paying them. Ideologues are worse than profiteers."

"The Thirty Years' War." Harry remembered her history.

"Isis. That kind of thinking will never go away. It might be able to be contained but it will be with us because it's so simple. Here's the equation: I will kill all my enemies and then I'll be safe."

"Doublethink," Harry murmured. "But do you think this is the work of such a person?"

"No."

"Why?"

"We'd have hints by now. Earlier run-ins. An ideological killer often has to brag or shows signs of the quality through writing, Facebook, that stuff. Nothing like that here."

"You're right, but is it possible something triggered the response?"

"Something did, but I don't think it's ideology."

"CYA? Someone needs to cover their ass or that of the person paying the bill?"

"Yes. This is too clean. Know what I mean?"

"But there has to be a trigger." Harry was adamant.

There was, underfoot, part of their lives every day. They didn't know it, never looked for it, had no special interest in it.

36

Blue skies, fluffy white clouds, a soft westerly breeze, Saturday seemed the apotheosis of spring. The Levels, groomed, cleaned, the spring grass cut to about an inch and a half proved flat. Teams of draft horses had rolled the sandy loam underneath the early grass to flatten the river deposits even more. The James quietly flowed toward the east, a gift, for it could be turbulent at times. Yancy Grant, Sam Udall, both dressed as perfect gentlemen, walked among the carriages lined up on the racecourse, one straight mile by the river. Few coach-in-fours were in evidence, for the day invited one to sit in the open air. The wealthy were attended by some of their slaves, also decked out in livery or finery. All manner of conveyance lined the racecourse, including carts driven by working men, lining up as a second row. Amidst all this finery, many on foot strolled along. Some remained in their carriages, feeling the bit of height provided a better view. But the lure of passing and repassing, of lurid gossip whispered behind gloved hands sang a song of temptation. Most gave in.

The poor whites and free blacks made up a third row. Anticipation of the competition was high.

Maureen and Jeffrey, arm in arm, walked along the front row, nodding and chatting as they displayed themselves.

The maroon coach-in-four with the gold pinstripes that Jeffrey built for his wife was also on display. Some men even knelt down to investigate the axles. DoRe, reins relaxed, sat in his driving seat, the best seat for the races, he was sure. Barker O. felt the same way as he observed the large crowd from the height of Ewing's coach-in-four. Rachel and Charles attended in their older open two-seater; Charles drove but Rachel would drive for spells. She quite liked it. All the Cloverfields' coaches gleamed navy with mustard pinstripes enlivened by a tiny shamrock in the center of each door. Ewing shied away from brash display.

Many others did not, most especially Georgina and her girls. Pinks, mint greens, aqua silks fit her ladies to show them at their best, and their best, cleavage to the max, was prominently visible. The ladies of quality, high born or low, refused to even glance at the tarts, as they thought of them. The men suffered little restraint, all eyes mostly on Deborah. Naturally, Georgina's girls couldn't mix with the other people, so they stayed together, behaving like the ladies they dreamed of becoming. Mignon and Eudes, fearing trouble, did not attend. The chances of someone identifying Mignon as an escaped slave from Maureen's Big Rawly might be slim, but Eudes wouldn't risk it. As spirits were freely flowing, common at any large event, someone could shoot off their mouth without thinking.

Catherine and John, back at the area for the horses, away from the commotion, paid no attention to the social whirl. Jeddie, tight breeches, high boots, and a navy silk shirt, a navy cap with a mustard button in the middle, fidgeted on a tack trunk. John sat with him as Catherine rested in a campaign chair. Ralston and Tulli sat with Reynaldo, already fascinated with the activity. Reynaldo had never seen this many people, smelled the foods, the liquor, the other horses—some nervous, which, of course, he could smell. Catherine tried to relax. If they needed an extra hand, a strong man, Barker O. could be brought back.

"Got the sweats?" Tulli unhelpfully asked from his seat by the 16.2-hand horse.

"No," Jeddie called back in irritation.

"Bettina made sweet tea," Catherine offered.

"I don't trust my stomach," he replied.

"Smart man. I never trusted mine before a battle." John rarely recalled his time in the war. "You'd think once the fighting started you'd be scared, but that's when I would settle down."

Catherine looked at her handsome husband. "You were in your element, darling."

"Oh, I don't know about that." He grinned.

A roar diverted their attention. The first race was off.

Tulli jumped out of his seat, which brought a snort and a step backward from Reynaldo.

"Dammit, Tulli, you're supposed to keep him quiet," Jeddie cursed.

"Tulli, come here," John ordered.

The little fellow, chastened, walked over to John, who stood up, put his hands under Tulli's armpits, held him up over his head. If anyone around them had a notion to shine on Catherine, that display of raw power dissuaded them.

"Who won?" John asked as he brought the boy down.

"Chestnut."

"Ah, the Maryland people." Catherine nodded. "Good horses in Maryland."

The crowd, lively now, eager to collect their winnings, swamped the betting men, tickets in their caps, boards behind them with odds for each race.

Men shouted, money changed hands. Those that lost the race made less noise. Once the bettors settled accounts, a new group of people stepped up to bet on the second race.

"Doesn't Pestalozzi have a share in the gray?" John asked.

"Yes. Yancy talked him into it." Catherine looked over at her now-seated husband. "You saw the odds on our race, did you not? Even. Gin up the betting," Catherine said without emotion. "I figure gamblers think greed can be satisfied with luck."

"Well, I never thought of that. I'll bet on Reynaldo."

"Me, too." She smiled. "But that doesn't mean I am fond of gambling. Life is a big enough gamble."

Ewing, leaving a small knot of men behind, joined them. John rose, pulling a second tack trunk forward for his father-in-law.

"I think our organizers have a success, a runaway success."

"People need a distraction." Catherine nodded toward her father. "What better than a distraction where you might win money?"

"Or lose it." Ewing smiled.

"Where's Rachel and Charles?"

Ewing laughed. "Dragooned into high tone exchanges with Maureen and her acolytes."

"Well, I am not going to rescue her." Catherine laughed.

"Maureen sends over Elizabetta to bet. She won ten dollars on the first race. Not bad."

"No. It will keep Maureen happy. I know she will probably bet on Black Knight for our race. She almost must, you know," Catherine remarked.

Ewing agreed but John surprised them. "She'll make a show of it. She knows we have a superior horse."

"You don't think she'd bet against herself?" Catherine questioned.

"John has a point. Maureen can be subtle. She wants to win. She'll put a larger bet on Reynaldo and a token bet on Black Knight. DoRe will carry the bet on Black Knight as everyone knows he is the main man at the stable. She'll have some shill we don't know put down the money on Reynaldo," Ewing thought out loud.

"Why not give it to Elizabetta?" Catherine hadn't thought it through.

"People know that's her lady-in-waiting and Maureen would never trust a slave with that much money. I believe she will place a sizable sum on our boy." Ewing tapped his cane on the ground.

"DoRe's a slave," Ralston, silent until now, a slave himself, spoke up.

"Yes," Catherine answered the skinny young man. "But DoRe is known throughout the state as one of the best coachmen. Seeing him put down money will encourage people to follow him as he is placing a bet for his mistress.

"Wonder who the shill is?" Catherine was puzzled.

"Someone we have never seen or someone we discount." Ewing shrewdly pictured the scene.

A second roar went up. Even the loud cheering didn't drown out the hoofbeats.

"Fast one," Jeddie said.

"Sounds like it." John thought so, too.

That race ended with the same drama as the betting men stuffed bills in their pockets.

Yancy, observing this, realized not all that money would be accounted for, but he and Sam would still get a good cut. He had men placed throughout the crowd, but they weren't as noticeable as the bettors. If any betting agent tried to run after the last race, he wouldn't get far, and that nasty lump of money he carried wouldn't, either.

Sam Udall, pretending to be courteous, walked to Georgina with a snap. He touched the corner of his hat with his cane to the madam and turned to beam at Deborah, who shimmered with allure.

"Are you enjoying yourself?"

"Yes," she coolly responded.

"Perhaps someday you would allow me to show you my small but good stable. My horse will be running in the fourth race. I have an interest in Black Knight."

Georgina, hearing all, called out, "We will be sure to bet on him, Sam, just as we bet on you."

He grinned at the double entendre, again bowed slightly, and withdrew. He couldn't be seen spending too much time with the soiled doves.

Sitting on campaign chairs placed on a raised dais, Georgina and her girls could see everything and everybody. Deborah, an elegant fan in hand, sat next to Georgina. Below these two, the other girls walked about or relaxed on the dais next to the main one. Sarah, Deborah's dresser, paid attention to Maureen Holloway, now promenading along the carriages in the front row.

Looking up at Georgina, Sarah tilted her head in Maureen's direction. "They say she is immensely rich."

"She dresses well," Georgina replied.

"I should hope so." Sarah, an escaped slave like Deborah, like most all the girls of color, laughed.

Voice low, Deborah, a sharp commercial mind growing sharper under Georgina's tutelage, said, "The races have been good for business."

Georgina leaned toward the ravishing woman to reply. "I told Sam and Yancy how grateful I am for them praising our tavern. I offered both men a choice, seven specially cooked meals or cash." She breathed in with meaning.

Deborah nodded. "And I will never be a free meal."

"Of course not, dear. I allowed as how the other girls and the new girls they have not yet viewed would deliver the excellent fare."

"And." Deborah grinned.

"Sam took the offering while Yancy took the cash. Shall I take it that he is failing in some respect? He has never discussed such things with me, of course, but perhaps one of the girls?"

Sarah, stepping up on the dais, knelt down to look up at Georgina. "The smashed knee. I think I was the last girl to entertain him. He's in a lot of pain."

"I see." Georgina nodded. "As for Sam, he is—"

"Led by his prick." Sarah let out a peal of laughter. "Such as it is."

This made both Georgina and Deborah giggle. "The Lord endows us in His own mysterious ways. When I look at you all, my dears, endowments are prominent."

"Well, if we ran a Molly house I guess they would be as well." Deborah shrugged, citing the term for a house of prostitution for men who wanted men.

Georgina returned her gaze to Maureen, stopping to chat with everyone. The picture of sociability. "She's shrewd. She may have inherited her wealth but she is shrewd. I can feel it." A deep breath followed this with a narrowing of eyes. "The day may come when we can do business with her."

"What?" Deborah was incredulous.

"Theater, Deborah. Propriety is theater. Profit is real."

Maureen placed modest bets on the horses. The third race, announced by a caller, turned people's attention to the two horses, riders up, being led to the starting line, a thin rope that would be dropped at a signal from the steward. Yancy and Sam enlisted horsemen who raced or knew racing in England. All the conditions were repeated here, including the celebratory atmosphere.

Elizabetta put down twenty dollars on Nestor, a horse in whom Sam also had a small interest. Twenty dollars, a good sum, impressed others, but for Maureen it was an amount large enough to demonstrate her support but not large enough to be taken seriously.

Off they shot, rope dropped; the dark bay, King Baldwin, raced past Nestor, but Nestor found his stride, catching up. King Baldwin's jockey made the mistake of asking for too much too soon and King, not an easy horse, stood up then let out a huge buck behind, and the jockey was launched, not into eternity but launched. The doctor rushed out onto the racecourse while Nestor easily crossed the finish line to Sam's delight.

A stretcher—three had been brought, just in case—carried out by two burly men, was flopped on the ground. They picked up the hapless jockey dumping him on the canvas to a scream of pain as he clutched his ribcage.

"Refreshments," a child called out, pushing a wagon of cakes and cider.

"Boy," Georgina called out. "Come here."

"Yes, Ma'am." He smiled in anticipation, plus though just a twelve-year-old, he thought the women so pretty.

"I'll take ten of your cakes." Georgina reached under her seat for a small purse. "Tell me, do you know any of these spectators?"

"Some."

"Mrs. Holloway?"

"No, Ma'am. I know some of those people like the Garths."

"Ah, would you point them out to me?"

He handed her the cakes on a little tray, which she had the girls pass around. The tray was returned.

"Over there is Ewing Garth. The horseman is his daughter Catherine. She's back in the paddocks, what passes for paddocks. She's uncommonly beautiful. Selects and trains the horses. You can see her sister, Rachel, over there." He pointed to Rachel and Charles, in earnest conversation with Jeffrey Holloway. "She looks much like her sister."

"Ah" was all Georgina said, as she handed him money plus a tip.

"Oh, thank you, Madam. Luck on your horses."

The girls smiled as he moved to the other patrons.

"Deborah, Sarah, take a few of the girls, those with good conversational skills and sharp eyes. Talk to the slaves, as though a brief repass, you know how to do it. Find out if they know of anyone, anyone female, wishing to improve her condition. Young and pretty. I will, of course, assist in a quiet manner."

"What about the freedmen?" Sarah inquired.

Georgina waved her hand. "They wouldn't know."

As the girls walked off, Yancy came up, tipped his hat.

"The course is being rolled again. We'll start up promptly. Best to keep the ground as level and tight as we can."

"Whose idea was the barrels filled with rocks or whatever you've got in there?" She offered him a cake, which he refused.

"Mine."

"You have a practical turn of mind."

"I do."

"And you know so many people, including Maureen Holloway."

"I do, although Mrs. Holloway and I are on speaking terms but little more, as you know. After all, I was challenged by her husband in your tavern."

"So you were."

"Strange to say I get along better with her husband, even though we tried to kill each other." He laughed.

"Fortunately you both proved unsuccessful."

This provoked greater laughter.

He saw the two draft horses pulling the heavy barrels turn at mile's end, coming back. "Excuse me, Georgina. I must see if all is as it should be."

"One more thing. Have you and Sam made money?"

"Without the tally from the races we are at eight thousand dollars."

Georgina smiled broadly. "Excellent. Few things in life are as uplifting as profit." As he started to go, she asked, "Yancy, is it true that Maureen Holloway has lent you a jockey?"

"Yes. Most obliging of her." He touched his hat and turned to check the course.

Georgina watched him walk, limp pronounced, but he wouldn't use a cane. She found it unusual that a woman whose husband faced Yancy in a duel would allow him the use of one of her horse boys, as Georgina thought of them. Her opinion of Maureen rose upward. Surely the lady would not countenance such an arrangement were there not a sizable profit to flow her way.

Catherine, walking toward her father as he sat high now, next to Barker O. on the coach, placed her hand over her eyes to shield them from the glare. Without hesitation, with strength and grace, she swung up to squeeze next to her father and Barker O.

"Soon be time for us," she remarked.

"My dear, I do wish you would not engage in such strenuous activities," her father chided her.

As it was her father she was direct. "Father, women have lost children for thousands of years. I am fine. It would have been worse had the baby been born in his time and not lived but a few days or been stillborn. This is easier to bear." She waited a moment. "But your tenderness toward me"—she leaned over her father—"and you, too, Barker O. Everyone at Cloverfields has been solicitous of me. I am fine. I am strong. I pray for that little soul." She took a deep breath. "I find as I go along in life that I pray for many souls."

Ewing picked up her hand, kissing it. "Ah, my dear. It comes with time, does it not, Barker O.?"

Barker O. mid-forties, nodded. "We must trust in the Lord."

Changing the subject, Catherine looked out at the entire mile-long course, which could be clearly seen from the top of the magnificent coach. "When John, Jeddie, and I took two days last month to come down here and look, it was coming along, but I must say Yancy and his partner—What is his name?"

"Sam Udall, a financier. He is overtaking the Tidewater financiers. An uncommonly prescient man."

"Why so?" She leaned on her father, the solidness of him comforting.

"He foresaw the diminution of the power of the Tide-water families. After the war power has shifted. He has made all the right connections, nurturing what I perceive as a new man, a man motivated by profit alone, not over-throwing a king and starting a new nation."

"Do you not think there are still patriots even among the new men?"

"I hope so just as I hope John Adams can be usefully directed." He shrugged. "Politics and lending are dirty businesses. Yes, I have had to avail myself in the past of both financing others, seeking partners, especially for my western timber purchase, but lately I am losing my appetite. I wish only to deal with friends."

"Ah" was all she could say, then added, "I should like to meet this Sam Udall."

"Why?" came the swift query.

"We can never have enough friends, even if they differ from us in many ways." She noticed the two heavily muscled plow horses finish rolling the course. "What time is it?"

Ewing pulled out the gold, inscribed, birthday pocket watch.

"One-thirty. I see the horses being brought up."

"Mmm. The light chestnut is the Skipwith horse. Small but well made. I'd like to take one of our mares to this stallion. Of course, let's see how he does. The other horse, Maryland people. I only know them by reputation. Finsters. Well, we'll see."

Ewing blinked as she stood up. "You aren't leaving now?"

"I need to get back to Reynaldo and Jeddie. He's so nervous he can't speak."

Ewing patted the seat. "Watch the race. It won't last long. Gives you the opportunity to observe the Skipwith horse."

She sat back down. "You're right."

The two horses lined up, fractious, but the Skipwith horse, Orb, settled first. Two grooms finally lined up Shadows, the Finster horse, then quickly stepped back, and the two men holding the rope dropped it, knowing if they didn't the Maryland horse would act up again.

"They're off," Ewing enthused.

Shadows definitely was off. He stood up on his hind legs, then rocked down on his forelegs, letting out one hell of a buck, then lurched forward with such a leap the crowd marveled that the slender jockey, a ginger-haired white boy, could stick. Stick he did and it was a terrific race. Shadows slowly catching up to Orb, who had a long stride. The two rode next to each other, the jockeys intent on the finish line. Sweat covered Shadows's flanks, a hot horse in all respects. Orb, more businesslike, kept up his steady pace, focused on the finish line. He began to pull away slightly, which forced the ginger-haired young man to use the whip. Shadows paid little attention until he crossed the finish line a nose behind Orb. Then he turned around, tried to bite the boy. After that display of pique, he bucked, snorted, shook his head. A fellow couldn't get him to walk back. Another fellow, this one from the Finster barn, rode out on a calm older gelding, reached over, grabbed the reins. Next to his buddy, the hot horse calmed a bit.

"If he hadn't bucked, we would have won," the jockey bitterly complained.

"Right."

Catherine hurried back to the paddock.

Piglet, truly enormous bone in his mouth, glanced up.

"Now, there's a treasure," she joked, hoping to lighten the tension.

Charles, there to help if needed, praised his corgi. "Could have brought the beast down himself."

"True." The intrepid dog dropped the bone.

Catherine studied this relic for a moment. "Where did he get it?"

Charles pointed to a large pile of rocks and other debris down near the river, where it had been dumped as the course was handpicked then rolled consistently over the last month until the races.

Reynaldo, saddled up, watched everybody and everything.

John gave Jeddie a leg up.

Catherine took Reynaldo by the bridle as John walked on the other side. Ralston walked Reynaldo's pasture mate, Sweetpea. Both Sweetpea and Catherine calmed Reynaldo. She was one of the few people who could ride him, but once her pregnancy showed she stopped. However, Catherine, at the barn every day, talked to him, watched Jeddie exercise him, and never forgot carrots, little treats.

No one spoke. Once at the starting line they waited a moment or two for Black Knight to come up.

"Jeddie," Catherine softly said as she stroked Reynaldo's neck. "You'll do well."

"Yes, Ma'am," he simply said as Catherine and Ralston stepped back. John reached for the bridle until Black Knight was alongside. Then he stepped back, too.

The rope pulled up and William snarled at Jeddie, "I'm gonna leave you in the dirt, boy."

Jeddie didn't reply.

The rope dropped and the two handsome horses took off, riders actually relaxed, in charge.

The crowd watched as this was the big race, the race on which two outstanding reputations hinged. They roared.

Stride for stride the two blew through the first quarter mile. Still stride for stride at the half mile, William switched his whip to his right hand. Jeddie was on his right and he lashed out, hitting Jeddie across the face full force. Blood from the leather edge cut into his cheeks. William struck again and again, then rode into Jeddie, not as dangerous as it might be since the horses were stride for stride. Still, legs could become entangled. Thank God they did not, but with the force of a twelve-hundred-pound animal on his legs, blood in his eyes, Jeddie tried to fend off the whip with his left hand. One more blow, one more push, and he rolled off on Reynaldo's right side. That stunned people. So did the fact that Reynaldo stopped, put his head down to touch Jeddie, who curled up in pain. The crowd screamed in fury. Maureen, standing in her carriage, Jeffrey alongside of her, could barely breathe.

"What is going on?"

"I don't know, my love, but it isn't good. I'll attend to it." Jeffrey climbed down from the carriage as did DoRe.

Barker O. also climbed down from the Garth carriage. Catherine and John were already running out onto the course. Yancy and Sam Udall hurried out from the other side.

Black Knight crossed the finish line. William kept going. John, also out on the course to bring in Yancy's horse and knock the devil out of William stopped, looked at the receding figure in wonderment. Then he turned to go back to his wife.

Catherine, kneeling down as John took Reynaldo's reins over his head, held her hand to Jeddie's forehead.

"I could kill him," she said.

Smiling through his pain, Jeddie replied, "Let me."

"Can you stand?" She put her arm under his back as Charles reached them to do the same on the young man's other side.

Jeddie stood. The crowd cheered. He winced, hand going to his left collarbone.

The doctor reached them. "Let's walk back to the paddock. You must be made of iron, young man. How you survived that without as many broken bones as dominoes, I will never know."

Sam and Yancy now reached them. Sam had never seen Catherine.

Yancy, shocked, stammered, "Oh, I do hope you don't think I would promote such vile behavior."

She shook her head. "Yancy, you are above such things."

Sam couldn't speak and this wasn't the time for introductions. He beheld a goddess. Oh, yes, he wanted to sleep with Deborah, to perhaps make a large financial arrangement with Georgina to keep her as his mistress, but for this woman, at first sight, he felt something he had never felt in his life. Sam was in love.

The two race promoters stood in the middle of the course while Jeddie was helped back to the paddock. Catherine led Reynaldo, who kept reaching with his nose to touch the rider he loved almost as much as he loved Catherine.

Back at the paddock, the doctor told Jeddie to sit on a tack trunk. Ewing, Barker O., Charles, Rachel, and John stood by him as Ralston and Catherine quickly untacked Reynaldo.

"Wipe him down, Ralston. I must see to Jeddie."

She stepped over to see the doctor check Jeddie's ribs as Rachel held a hand towel to his bleeding face.

"No broken ribs, broken arms." The middle-aged Richmond doctor felt Jeddie all over then touched his collarbone to a small yelp. "Uh-huh."

"I'm fine."

"Jeddie, listen to the doctor," Catherine, worry on her face, ordered him.

Rachel asked the competent man, "What must we do or what must he do?"

"The collarbone is a slender bone. I'll make him a sling and he must keep his arm in it. No lifting anything. No reaching or using this arm." He stared at Jeddie. "If you move the bone, which I am going to set, it will heal crooked. You'll never have full use of it again, and the lump will show through your skin. Do you want to keep riding?"

"Yes, Sir."

"Then do as I say." He looked at John. "Will you hold him steady in his seat. This will hurt."

The doctor extended Jeddie's arm then pulled until the bone snapped back into place.

"Dear God," Jeddie gasped, sweat now pouring from his forehead.

"That's the worst. Now I'm going to cut off your good colorful shirt and I'll bind you up. Then I'll put you in a sling. When you go to bed at night you can take off the sling, but you must sleep on your back."

Rachel, hands folded, as Charles put his arm around her waist while Piglet sat by Charles's feet with his prize, asked, "Doctor, what will keep him from rolling onto his side? Won't that push the bone out of place?"

"Yes. He's either got to sleep sitting up or sleep lying flat on his back."

Catherine put her hand on Tulli's shoulder. He had been

watching with tears in his eyes. "Tulli, you'll need to be in the cabin with him and sleep with him. If he starts to roll, you need to stop him."

"I am not sleeping with Tulli. He snores," Jeddie declared while the doctor still wrapped him.

"I do not," the little fellow defended himself.

"Well then, Ralston, you sleep with him." Catherine pointed a finger at the lanky young man.

"Yes, Ma'am," Ralston agreed.

"What about bathing? Can we unwrap him?" Rachel asked.

"Keep this as it is for two weeks. He can't get it wet or the bandage will tighten and that will be painful. But he can sit in a tub, he's got one good wing." The doctor smiled.

"I'm not bathing him." Ralston grimaced.

"You don't even wash yourself." Jeddie was feeling better.

Ralston looked imploringly at Catherine, who smiled at him.

"Ralston and Tulli, go on back to Reynaldo. Give him some treats. He's had a difficult first race, too."

Maureen and Jeffrey carefully approached as the doctor finished the wrap.

"My dear, we had nothing to do with this."

"I know that." Catherine acknowledged Maureen's discomfort.

"Obviously, that fellow planned this," Charles said.

Jeffrey agreed. "Had to. He'll either run that horse to death, or dismount when he feels safe, take the tack off because he can sell it, slap Black Knight's hindquarters. A run to freedom, I suspect."

"Freedom to where?" Maureen grimaced.

"If he reaches New England, he can pass himself off as a freedman." John finally spoke.

"How would they know? They have slaves. Well, Vermont has but a handful but still, who would believe him if he makes it?" Jeffrey replied.

"I don't know." Charles sighed. "He's young, skilled, bold. If he lives, who is to say?"

"I am so very sorry for this. To think it was one of my people. I shall question DoRe." Maureen almost wrung her hands, then stopped.

"Maureen, don't. Please don't trouble yourself," Catherine, quick thinking, told her. "DoRe wouldn't know. William would not have been foolish enough to betray his plan to anyone, but especially not to DoRe, who is faithful to you."

This was a flat-out lie. DoRe hated her, thanks to her accusing his son of murder, but he never gave evidence of such feelings. Catherine had Bettina in mind. If Maureen bore down on DoRe, she might make it hard for him to come calling at Cloverfields.

"She's right." Jeffrey jumped in. "The only thing we can do is post rewards, a description of William as well as a description of Black Knight."

"Good idea." Charles nodded, knowing the flyers produced little effect.

Once Maureen and Jeffrey left, Catherine sat next to Jeddie, his arm in a sling. Suddenly she was tired.

"I'll kill him if I find him. At least Reynaldo isn't hurt." Jeddie had a light bandage on his face, the cut deeper than he thought.

"You'll ride again. I just hope it won't be like this." Catherine smiled at him.

"Me, too," he agreed.

The doctor looked down at Piglet. "My, that is a find. You know these bones get dug up frequently. As far as the ocean. Makes creating pastures a bit of work. You all live by the mountains, am I right?"

"We do," John answered.

"You pick up stones and more stones. From here to the ocean it's stones and bones. Curious. People have theories. I just bend over and clean it all up. But if I had a dog like this fellow, he could do it."

"Where are you located, Doctor?" John asked.

The middle-aged man extended his hand. "Alfred McKay. Goochland County. Sam Udall hired me to attend to the races. It's been quite a day."

"What happened to the jockey in the second race?"

"Ribs. Usually it's a broken arm or ribs. Occasionally a leg. When a man falls off a horse his shoulder often hits the ground first. At least I hope it does. If his head hits he's either dead or confused. Often permanently confused. I'm grateful no one was killed today, no horses, either." He smiled at Jeddie. "Like I said, young man, bones of iron." He put his hand on Jeddie's shoulder. "I have never seen anything like that. Ever."

"Nor have we," Charles chimed in, then extended his hand. "Charles West, formerly of His Majesty's Army."

"Ah. You saw the error of your ways." Dr. McKay beamed.

"I did, Sir, and I also saw this beautiful woman. What man would return across the ocean?"

"Indeed," Dr. McKay agreed.

"John Schuyler." John held out his large hand.

"Major John Schuyler. Yorktown?" His eyes lit up.

"The same."

"I am in your debt, Major. We are all in your debt."

John blushed. "Doctor, I served with good men and I served under Lafayette. God was with us"—he paused—"and the French."

The men laughed, including Ewing, who had been silent, deeply concerned.

As the doctor left, the Garths started packing up. They would make it halfway home by sundown. Stay at an inn called The Ordinary. As they put tack away, brought out soaps, buckets, the oats they brought so Reynaldo would be eating what he ate at home, DoRe strode over.

"You all right?"

"Yeah."

"DoRe, if you did know anything, lay low," Jeddie said.

"I didn't. He's a fool. A damned arrogant fool. But I understand his wanting to escape Big Rawly. I do," DoRe replied.

Jeddie nodded.

Catherine, seeing DoRe, walked over. "Is she hysterical?"

"No, just vicious."

Catherine nodded. "You know she'll offer your stable help money to rat on one another?"

"She will, but I'll give William credit, he kept his cards close to his chest. I hate what he did to Jeddie and I hope he doesn't kill Black Knight, a good horse, but I can't fault him for running."

Catherine leveled her luminous eyes at him. "Do you hope he makes it?" When DoRe sensibly did not reply, she did to her own question. "I hope he does, even though I share the same anger you do. He could have killed Jeddie."

"I'm tougher than that."

"Of course you are." She turned to Jeddie, pale, still sitting on the trunk, his arm in a sling.

Races finished, money settled up, the Garths headed west. Piglet sat in the phaeton with Charles and Rachel. He would not relinquish his giant bone.

Catherine, John, and Ewing rested in the four-in-hand coach. Jeddie refused to sit in it even though asked. He sat with Barker O. while Ralston and Tulli perched behind them holding onto the low rail.

What a day.

37

Pirate, his handsome head on his two huge forepaws, watched at the back entrance to Tazio's studio, formerly Gary's. Beginning to feel part of the group, he played with Tucker, sometimes with Mrs. Murphy, but gave Pewter a wide berth. Observing her he, young though he was, knew this was the right decision. The gray cat, immobile, stayed at the small opening under the baseboard.

"*Give it up.*" Mrs. Murphy sighed.

"*No. I'm keeping her at bay.*"

"*She might not even be in there.*" Tucker lay next to Pirate.

"*I'm not taking chances.*" Pewter sounded tough.

"*If she were in there you'd see eight eyes, red from the reflected light,*" Mrs. Murphy told her.

"*I don't know how big her nest is. It could run the entire way along the baseboard. She's a monster. A prehistoric spider.*"

"*Really?*" The puppy was impressed.

"*Oh, yes. She probably scared dinosaurs. Her kind has been dangerous forever. She is so big she covers a saucer. Big.*"

Tucker whispered, "*Demitasse.*"

"*What's demitasse?*" the puppy wondered.

This brought immediate response from the gray cat. "*Don't listen to Bubblebutt. She undermines me all the time.*"

"*Bubblebutt? Parts of you are so fat they're in the next zip code,*" Tucker fired back.

"*I ought to come over there and bloody your nose, but I can't abandon my duty.*" This was uttered with a superior air of responsibility.

As Pewter grumbled about everyone, Harry sat on the floor, notebook in her lap, one of Gary's file boxes open.

"Harry, how many times are you going to be in here fooling around with those boxes?" Tazio good-naturedly asked.

"Almost done."

"I'm in no hurry for you to leave. In fact, it's good to have company."

"How can you work with someone around?"

"If I'm trying to solve a problem, make preliminary drawings, I can't. But if I'm beyond that, I can."

"You're beyond that?"

"Am." The gorgeous young woman smiled.

"What's this project?"

"Mark and Karen Catron want a large dome over the center aisle of their barn, as well as skylights over every stall and even for the tack room. They're on a natural light kick and they're quite right."

"I didn't know you designed animal habitat."

"Didn't. But Mark can talk a dog off a meat wagon and I started thinking about it; it's interesting. So I asked Paul, he walked me through Big Mim's stables, built in 1882, explained everything. Then he told me to double seal every skylight and the dome, underside and weatherside."

"Done?"

"Close. I'm trying to talk them into partial hay storage overhead with a quarter-inch spacing between floorboards to keep air flowing. They don't want to do it because of the ceiling being lowered. It won't be much, but it will seem like it, and then that mitigates the big dome."

"They're right."

"I know it but they need better hay storage. If I suggest a separate hay shed, covered walkway, then it will look as though I'm drumming up business."

Harry considered this. "Well, I understand that, but if you don't suggest it then you aren't giving them the benefit of your expertise, as well as Big Mim's. She has hay barns all over that farm."

"I don't want them to think I'm churning, you know, what stockbrokers do."

"No one is going to think that. And they're a hundred percent right about bringing in all the natural light. Of course, if they do it and other people see the result, then everyone will want that. Saves on the electric bill."

"Those bills never go down," Tazio ruefully remarked as her yellow Lab, Brinkley, dreamed at her feet.

Brinkley, a loving fellow, could only take so much of

Pewter, especially now that she was obsessed with the spider, who, granted, was large.

"May I see the plans?"

"Of course."

Harry put her legs under her, pushed herself up without using her hands.

"How do you do that?"

"You have to use both legs equally. My mother taught me how." Harry leaned over Tazio at the drafting table. "Wow."

"The wash stall has a bit of heat so it can be used in the winter. Tack room, too. Baseboard heat, but with all this natural light that ought to be most of the bill, that and the light in the tack room and the wash stall."

"What about turn-of-the-century lanterns on the outside of the barn?"

"Be lovely but they haven't asked for touches like that."

"Don't you love the old fixtures?"

"For the most part. Depends on the structure." Tazio put down her soft lead pencil. "What are you doing over there? And why a notebook? You've been through those file boxes and so has the sheriff's department. All it is are building codes. So what's the draw?"

"Forgive the pun." Harry smiled at her. "Look at your shelves. You've kept a lot of Gary's dinosaurs, a few of the globes, and the bone fragment, kind of clunky and heavy. So what do you see?"

"Rubber dinosaurs, some original snow globes, and a big, old bone that I kind of like and, really, so does Brinkley."

"So that's it." Harry laughed as Brinkley, upon hearing his name, opened one eye.

"I see rubber toys. What do you see?" Tazio asked Harry.

"When I go through the file boxes, there are notes in some of the code margins. Just stuff about materials, weight-bearing capabilities, life span for some items. What you would expect, especially from a meticulous man who wanted to learn, to improve."

"Right." Tazio rested her chin in the cup of her hand.

"Some of the file boxes have little toy dinosaurs in them." Harry held up her hand because Tazio knew that. "At first, I just figured he was stashing an abundance of prehistoric creatures. But then I started thinking about that and the fact that Lisa seemed obsessed or enchanted with dinosaurs. So I went back through just now. In every box that contains a dinosaur there is a date noted on an excavation code. And no two dinosaurs are alike, now that I know their names. Sometimes there are initials. Don't know for what."

"So?"

"Well, I think these codes related to jobs on which he was working."

"I still don't see what's going on."

"Tazio, give me a minute. I am beginning to see a pattern. Every code so noted deals with excavation. The notations about steel or joists, nothing. Well, somehow the dinosaurs mean something."

"I dimly remember from one of my geology classes that from Baltimore to just below Richmond, plus a chunk of Pennsylvania, was for millions of years a vast primordial swamp."

"I've been reading about that, too. The other oddity is both Gary and Lisa kept papers from magazines, *National Geographic*, the good ones. They had almost identical papers and I first saw that with an article on frogs. Then I found an article both cut out about mammoths. It had photos of the reconstructed mammoth from the La Brea Tar Pits in Los Angeles."

"In his file box?"

"No. That was in his long center desk drawer. When you moved in and I helped, I went through his drawers. I know the sheriff's department did but I wanted to double-check. So I think there's a pattern. The key is the 1984 file."

"Ah." Tazio's brow wrinkled.

"We need to find that box."

"My hunch, which I have said before, is if you find that box you find the killer." She breathed out. "You'll tell Cooper all this?"

"When I am more sure."

"Harry, this isn't a safe study."

"I know. And I know I get in her way. But I can do things my way. They have to follow protocol, which can often slow things down. I'll tell her, really."

"Harry, he was gunned down in front of everyone in cold blood. If you get too close, whoever this is, whatever this is about, they aren't going to pull back."

"Yeah, I know."

"*ATTACK!*"

Brinkley, wide awake, bounded to the back door.

Harry and Tazio hurried in, for the hissing and growling sounded awful.

Poor Pirate lay flat on the ground, ears down. Tucker stood on all fours, while Mrs. Murphy joined her cat friend.

"*Attack. The giant spider attacked me,*" Pewter, eyes wide, screamed.

Mrs. Murphy, calm, said to the humans, "*The giant spider ran over her tail. Leapt right out of its cubbyhole and ran over her tail.*"

"*She weighed a ton!*" Pewter, tail looking like a bottle brush, told them.

"All right. Let's go into the next room, pick up our stuff, and head for home. Tomorrow's Valentine's Day. Stuff to do."

"*There is a dangerous monster in here,*" Pewter, riveted to the spot, warned.

"*It is big.*" The puppy, feeling a little safer, offered his opinion.

"*Big. It's gigantic. It has long legs and too many eyes. It glares at me. I can see the hatred, and its terrible mouth works opposite ours. Oh, it's a terrible sight.*" Pewter slowly walked into the next room.

Once in the Volvo station wagon, heat turned on but still cold, the four animals sat in the backseat. The rear with the big window was still cold. This way they were closer to the heat.

"*She has no idea how much danger she's in. That spider will come out and bite. Poison!*" Pewter dramatically predicted.

"*How do you know she won't bite you first?*" the corgi slightly maliciously asked.

"I can run fast. Harry's slow. Humans are slow. It's amazing that they survive," Pewter remarked.

"I noticed that." Pirate's bushy eyebrows rose up. "Do you think it's because they only have two legs?"

"That's some of it," Mrs. Murphy answered.

Pewter, breathing deeply, intoned, "That spider will kill."

"Right," Tucker dryly replied.

38

Scarf wound around her neck, Harry peered through the peephole in the painted fence for the Cloud-croft project. With the exception of a small square where the bones had been discovered, the digging neared completion. Hands in pockets, she fished out a small pair of binoculars. Usually these reposed on the kitchen windowsill so she could watch birds if cooking or washing dishes, a towel always handy to pick up the binoculars. Lifting them to her eyes she quickly adjusted them. The picture, crystal clear, revealed the soil, much of it alluvial deposits from the James. Digging in Richmond proved easier than digging in those places where the soil was red clay, baked hard as the bricks made from it in colonial times.

She scanned every edge. If something was going to

show up it would be on the edge. A pile of dirt, not yet removed, towered at the northwest corner, the wind blowing from that direction, even with the wall. Not much could dampen a winter wind. She paused. Glints from soda cans, pieces of plastic bottles, an odd lumber fragment, such things protruded from the dirt pile. If anything or anyone lay in the middle, no one would know.

Her question was if something unusual showed up, would the workers report it?

Cold air tingled in her lungs. She pulled her scarf up over her nose. Days such as this gave Harry new respect for Canadians. Leaning her head against the wall, she scanned again, then placed the binoculars in her pocket as well as her one hand. South by a few blocks, the great river flowed over quite beautiful rapids. Bald eagles soared. Often they flew over Richmond itself to their nests. The avian life on the river blossomed. Ending the spraying of DDT in 1972 had allowed life-forms to again flourish.

On the way downtown she had stopped at each location where a notation had been made in Gary's files. She knew two of those locations involved a death. One was the Kushner Building, the other was years before on a site at West Broad Street where Mr. Asplundah was found dead sitting next to the excavation. The third referred to steel, as well as a new advanced insulating material back in the early eighties. As those structures stood, well built, she could glean nothing except they were big-ticket buildings. Expensive even then, they'd cost twice as much to replace, possibly more, given stricter building codes. Irritating as those codes were, they might save lives and structures in the event of a catastrophic hurricane or flooding. As the weather was changing, she hoped whoever drew up the codes was right. But in her heart she knew cash payments to the right people could circumvent some of this. Meeting new standards cost and it cost more every day.

Here a beautiful building, a hoped-for showpiece for the new Richmond, would cost forty-two million. That was the estimated cost with an undisclosed profit. Any delay, any lost time due to weather or goods not shipped on time would send that figure upward with the profit percentage diminishing. Anyone in construction understood this, which was why a home builder or someone like Rankin Construction tried to fold in such delays. If anything went amiss, no government bailout. Nor should there be. Private enterprise was just that. Harry understood all that, for as a farmer, although her parameters were different, no bailout was available for the small farmer. As to huge agribusiness, well, that could be something different. City workers need cheap food or one gets mass disturbances. Cheap food means mega-farming companies, fiddling with crops, using giant machines instead of people. So now, a man working for a huge company would look at the computer in his tractor or combine. Was there anyone left who knew how to get out, check the seeds, check the seedlings, check the half-grown crop? She could scoop up a handful of soil and know what she had. A computer printout might be helpful but unnecessary. You either knew your job or you didn't.

So, looking at this enormous project, one important to a city on the verge of booming, Harry wondered who knew their job.

Even with fur-lined boots her feet felt numb. She pulled out the binoculars one more time; sighing, she returned them to her pocket, walked to her station wagon. She had called Marvella before leaving the farm, who graciously invited her to drop by.

When Harry stepped into Marvella's home she visibly relaxed.

"You're cold as ice." Marvella put her hand on Harry's cherry red cheek.

"I swear it would feel better if it snowed some more."

"I think you'll get your wish. Here, let me take your coat." Marvella helped Harry out of her knee-length coat. "This weighs a ton."

"Does but it's warm."

"Come into the kitchen. Wednesday is my girl's day off."

Following the slender woman to her kitchen, Harry appreciated the works on the wall. The kitchen, itself modern, spotless, still radiated some warmth, something a bit cozy.

"Coffee, tea, or how about some hot chocolate?"

"Hot chocolate sounds good."

"You know when the Spaniards conquered the Incas, the Aztecs, whoever they conquered down there, they were fascinated by chocolate. No chocolate in the Old

World or bananas or tomatoes. Hard to imagine. Well, no coffee, either."

"Or cocaine."

"You're right." Marvella poured milk into a saucepan. No shortcuts for her.

"All these outlawed drugs have useful applications. They are a natural form of medicine, of painkillers, but . . . well, you know."

"I do. All a government has to do to create illegal fortunes is outlaw a substance or a service. Prostitution, for example."

"Hard work, I would think." Harry inhaled the aroma.

Marvella folded in expensive ground chocolate with the milk, poured that into a cup for Harry. She sat down to join her.

"As you know I was over at Cloudcroft. They've made a lot of progress."

"So have I. I am very close to getting Rankin Construction's agreement to underwrite the Russian exhibit."

"You know Sean well?"

"As you saw, we get along fine but it's a social friendship, not a deep friendship. Given my work for the Virginia Museum of Fine Arts, best I stay on everyone's good side."

Harry laughed. "I'm sure they feel the same way about you."

"I hope so." Marvella smiled. "I truly hope so."

"It's just the two of us and I know I am a newer person in your life, but I have to ask: Do you trust Sean Rankin?"

Eyebrows knitting together, Marvella replied, "I have no reason not to trust him."

"What about his father?"

"When Tinsdale and I moved here, Reg Rankin was slowing down, beginning to hand over, in bits, the company to Sean. I only met him a few times. Older generation. Proper. A man of his time."

"Honest?"

"Well, again I don't know. I've never heard anything to the contrary. Now let me ask you, why these questions?"

"Over the years a few deaths have occurred at construction sites."

"Harry, that's natural. Construction can be dangerous."

"I know, but in going through Gary Gardner's files, his building code files, I've found dates written in the margins for jobs wherein someone died. And 1984's file is missing. That's the year the man whose skeleton we found died. Now Gary is dead as is Lisa Roudabush, both of whom shared a fascination for earlier epochs, for dinosaurs, architecture later, obviously. Somehow it's too close for comfort."

"Be careful. If you mention this without hard proof you have just angered, or at the very least irritated, a powerful man, a powerful company with many employees."

"That's why I came to you. I'm not mentioning it."

She breathed deeply. "I'm old enough to know there are many reasons to kill, a lot to cover up. Illegal transactions, that sort of thing. At least in private business if they have affairs it's usually not fatal. In politics it used to be, but now they cling to Jesus, apologize, cry, and appear to be forgiven." She let out a peal of laughter.

"I've often wondered if God has no sex, no women as partners in his life, how can he forgive infidelity for one?"

Marvella laughed again. "Because he doesn't understand it."

"Well, whatever this is about, I think sex has nothing to do with it."

"But wouldn't it be more interesting if it did?"

"You're awful."

"No, I'm not. I'm honest. Financial misdeeds are dull and those who commit them are dull. Now a roaring sex-capade? The best. Think of the South Carolina governor caught with his pants down. Oh, I so loved it."

Harry laughed. "Too good to be true."

"Too good to be true. You're too young to remember, you weren't even born, when Wilbur Mills, head of the powerful Ways and Means Committee, the most powerful committee in Congress, and always will be . . . Well, the esteemed congressman was found disheveled and drunk at a public fountain in D.C., cavorting, or hoping to cavort with, a stripper who had indeed shed some unnecessary garments. It was so public the press couldn't cover it up. The gentleman's agreement unraveled." She shook with mirth.

"You'd think those guys would figure it out, especially now that the gentleman's agreement is over."

"Oh, Harry, men think they're only as old as the woman they're sleeping with."

"It's not working," Harry shot back, and they both doubled over.

"You know, it's not that I think women are better than men, truly, but I do think we are more realistic, especially about sex."

"Marvella, don't you think we have to be and always will?"

The elegant older woman nodded. "I don't know if I would go so far as to say gender or race or the time at which you were born is destiny, but in many ways it fulfills the definition."

On and on they chatted, delighted with each other's company, then Harry glanced at the superb grandfather clock. "Marvella, forgive me. I have overstayed my welcome. You should have thrown me out."

"I enjoy your company. You are a generation younger than I. I find our exchanges invigorating, and the fact that you were an Art History major is an extra bonus."

"Thank you." Harry stood up, leaned over to give Marvella a kiss on her smooth cheek.

Marvella stood. "Isn't it fate that we meet people whom we feel we have known all our lives?"

"Yes." As she walked to the door, Harry slowed for a moment. "You know, there are many dimensions to existence and we see only one. I think there are more and when we have these feelings, whether it's knowing someone or déjà vu, I think we just get a peep of another dimension."

"I do, too, but we are hag-ridden by logic. Speaking of which, your piecing together these disparate bits of information is logical, but with a leap of faith, if that's what one can call it. Best to remember, that killer is out there and whatever is at stake remains at stake."

"You're right."

"Consider, Harry, and again this is a function of age, anyone in power, whether political or financial, may not use force, but there is always implied force."

"Well . . ." Harry digested this unsettling thought or tried to do so.

"Again, be careful. Maybe it's better you don't know."

"I know you're right, and I know you don't want me to stumble into a nest of vipers, but I think I already have. And I think whatever this is involves both power and money, millions."

"I hope you're wrong. I fear you're right." This time Marvella pecked Harry on the cheek, opened the door, and watched her walk to her Volvo, open the door, and get in.

39

February 16, 2017

Thursday

"Thanks, Felipe." Harry smiled at the slender dark-haired young man. "I know this request is a bit odd."

"No, no. It's always good to see you, and your wildlife people have helped us."

"Takes all of us, I think." Harry felt a tug at her jeans.

"Ask if he has any treats." Pewter effected a sweet look.

"Pewts." Harry looked down at Pewter and Mrs. Murphy. She'd left Tucker and Pirate at home, thinking it might be too confusing and sad for the puppy.

"Hi, Harry," Raynell called from behind her computer. "Holler if you have questions."

"Thanks." Harry walked straight back to Lisa's office, which was as she'd left it.

The sheriff's department carefully checked out everything then put it all back in place. There was nothing in her office or on her computer to give them any clues, at least not clues that they could currently understand.

First scanning Lisa's shelves, with her own notes from Gary's office in hand, she noticed a few books duplicated. One was *The Great Warming* by Brian M. Fagan. Of course, there were a few books on reptiles both extinct and current, one recent bestseller on birds that Harry also had read, and *Why Birds Sing* by David Rothenberg. Gary had most of the dinosaur books, the reptile books, alligators, crocodiles, stuff like that. She pulled a book out, jumped back, then giggled.

"*What's up?*" Mrs. Murphy wondered.

"A big rubber spider behind the books." Harry's hand flew to her chest as though she'd understood her sensible cat.

"*Ha. I have saved you every time we are at Gary's. I battle real spiders,*" Pewter bragged.

Mrs. Murphy jumped on the polished desk, where the book on dinosaurs that Lisa had been reading when she died was closed, sitting on the corner. Harry had pulled it off the bookshelf but hadn't leafed through it yet. She was hoping it would give her a clue as to the dinosaur fascination.

Harry made notes, checked off those books that were the same. Then she sat down at the desk as Mrs. Murphy investigated the dinosaur book. Pulling open a long center drawer, she took out a sheaf of papers. The frog article sat on top. Gary had the same information. A long magazine piece about when the Blue Ridge Mountains were covered with water interested Harry, as well as the receding of the waters and the upheavals that created the Fall Line running throughout the state. The earth had been lowered to such a degree that running roughly southwest to northeast, waterfalls marked the break just like the Continental Divide in the far West. Tidying up what she'd read, she put them back in the drawer in exact order.

"*Pewts. Jump up here,*" said Mrs. Murphy.

"*I'm happy where I am. I smell treats in this lower drawer.*"

"*Come up here. It's important.*"

"*She'll open this drawer. I want to be right here,*" Pewter argued.

"*It's dog treats.*"

"*Doesn't mean I can't lick them.*" Pewter swept her whiskers forward.

"*Dammit, Pewter, get up here,*" Mrs. Murphy growled.

As the tiger cat rarely swore, Pewter figured out this was important so she leapt up onto the desk as Harry ignored both of them. She was accustomed to working with feline help.

"*Put your nose there, right there on the right-hand corner of the book.*"

Pewter sniffed, her eyes watered. "*Eww.*"

"*Something bad is on those pages.*" Mrs. Murphy sounded firm. "*We can't let Harry open the book.*"

"*She can't smell it.*" Pewter took a moment, then realized what Mrs. Murphy was saying. "*Poison?*"

"*It's stung our eyes. We smell something bitter inside. Whatever it is, Pewts, it can't be good.*"

"*Let's push it on the floor.*"

"*No! Then she'll pick it up and open it.*"

Pewter backed off, as did Mrs. Murphy, putting themselves between Harry and the dinosaur book.

Harry reached for the book to page through a bit, see if there were any notes therein.

"*Don't touch it.*" Mrs. Murphy batted her hand away.

"That's enough." Harry reached again and this time both cats swatted at her.

Leaning back in the comfortable chair, the human observed her cats. She knew, as do most people who live close to animals, that their senses prove far superior to human ones. Each time she reached for the book, she met increasingly fierce resistance. She paused, then considered she should leave the book where it was. She wasn't sure why she did this, but she did trust her cats. A human without close ties to a higher vertebrate would think her foolish, but cat, dog, horse owners eventually learned to trust their friends. Puzzled, she closed her notebook, left the office, stopped by Felipe's door.

"Do you know there's a rubber spider behind Lisa's books?"

He nodded. "Raynell told her to put it there."

Raynell called out, "I am not an arachnophobe but I don't want to look at spiders."

Harry laughed. "Few of us do."

"*I know where there is a monstrous spider.*"

"*Pewter, they don't care,*" her friend advised.

"*If they saw her they would.*"

Once in her kitchen, horses still out, Harry sat down. She'd need to bring them in in an hour. Harry cheated by opening their outside barn doors and letting them run into their stalls. One is supposed to put on a halter, walk them in the center aisle, slip off the halter once the horse is in his or her stall. Granted this freedom meant a certain amount of visiting someone else's stall to check that that horse wasn't getting better food. Lasted all of a minute, when Harry would chide the animal, who would walk out, throw a little head toss, and go to his or her stall. This way Harry could perform the chore much more quickly and, in the bitter cold, she was happy to do so. Luckily, all her horses got along, some of the credit belonging to Harry, who knew how to introduce animals to one another. Gazing at her friends, blankets on, playing in the snow, she thought where did we go wrong? When we separated from nature? When we considered ourselves superior to other life-forms? Why were we so destructive, often cruel, killing animals, one another? Something went amiss in the human brain and she prayed it hadn't gone amiss in her own. Then she would think of her friends, good, loving people, and she knew millions of others were also good and loving. For whatever reason those people had not made common cause whereas the brutal, the controlling, the violent had.

An odd idea followed this reverie. She lifted the receiver of the wall phone off its cradle. She got better reception with a landline.

"Cooper."

"Yes."

"Did you read the notes I sent you?"

"I did. You've spent a great deal of time and thought on the books, the file boxes, articles, little rubber dinosaurs.

I admit that Lisa and Gary having so many books, articles, items in common is possibly important, but it's still a stretch and I have no idea where to go with it. I see the common thread, but why would it lead to murder?"

"And you don't know how Lisa was poisoned?"

"Still."

"Do something for me."

"Depends."

"Go to Lisa's office, take the dinosaur book off her desk, and test it. I was there today and . . ."

"Harry."

"I know, I know, but I wanted to double-check her books and stuff against Gary's. Anyway, I have the time, you don't, and this isn't the most promising path to sell to Rick. Our sheriff likes more facts up front."

"Remember, Sheriff Shaw only has but so much manpower. He can't send us off on a whim."

"I do understand but please do this. Mrs. Murphy and Pewter wouldn't allow me to touch that book. Say what you will, their senses are far better than ours."

"Why? Tell me why. You've told me what the cats did, but what's behind this?"

A long pause followed, then Harry replied. "It hit me when I left Nature First. I used to tease Lisa that she was an old lady. She'd lick her finger before turning the page of a book. I said I only ever saw old people do that. She would shoot back that pages stick together in a new book and she didn't feel like rubbing them together or sliding a penknife between them to pop them apart. Check the book."

Cooper didn't argue. "Right."

By the time the deputy reached Nature First, the book was gone. Neither Felipe nor Raynell said they took it.

She left them, walked over to Anne de Vault at Over the Moon.

"Anne, did you like Lisa Roudabush?"

"Adored her. She was a good customer and fun to chat with. Why would you ask me that? You know I liked her. We were all in shock when she died."

"It's not public yet but she was poisoned. We're trying to keep our cards close to our chest."

"Who would poison Lisa?"

"That's why I'm here. Who would poison Lisa?"

"I can't think of anyone who didn't like her."

"Let me show you something." Cooper, a quick study, picked up a book off a display area.

"Yes?" Anne watched as Cooper opened the book, licked her finger, turned a page.

The tall deputy did this a few times when Anne's hand flew to her mouth. "Oh God!"

"I think this is what killed her."

"Oh God. One of the books I sold her. No. No. Who would do something like that?"

"Someone who knew her very well." Cooper then said, "Close up the store and come with me."

"You don't think I did this. You can't."

"I don't, Anne, I don't. But come along. You're going to answer many questions down at HQ. You may have over-looked something that we can pick up. You have a right not to testify . . ."

Unnerving as being considered a suspect was, Anne understood. At police headquarters she endured the grilling because she wanted to find out who killed Lisa. Cooper drove her back to the store.

As Anne opened the door to get out of the car, Cooper said, "Thank you. I know that wasn't pleasant but it wasn't awful, either. Be vigilant, Anne. I mean it. Whoever did this knew Lisa inside and out. Whoever did it was clever enough to use a habit to wipe her out. And now the book is missing."

Anne, shaken by that warning, worn down by the experience, nonetheless had her wits about her. "Deputy, sometimes people can be too clever by half."

40

"What do you intend to do about it?" A puce-faced Maureen pointed her fan at Yancy.

"I paid you for William's services, for each day he was off your estate."

"He ran away. You owe me his value."

Jeffrey, knowing that contradicting his angry wife wouldn't do a bit of good, sat by her side in the lavish tack room in the stable.

DoRe, wiping down one of the fine carriage horses, listened to every word. The other stable hands flitted in and out. He'd raise his eyebrows and they'd dash out again, a flurry of work for the mistress's ever-critical eye.

"Madam, William's defection," Yancy said with a sly drop in tone, "was an affair entirely of his own devising. Posting rewards just as I have for Black Knight is all I can suggest."

"So you refuse to pay me the five thousand dollars of his value?" She inflated the young man's price.

"I do." Yancy knew perfectly well what she was doing, trying to wear him down.

Next would come a supposed compromise.

"Realizing that he was headstrong and did escape using your horse, four thousand."

"Madam, he is not my responsibility. I could just as easily turn to you and declare that your slave stole my horse, and Black Knight is worth ten thousand dollars."

"He is not worth a dime. He didn't win the race," she spat.

"He had no chance. It was bad enough William stole an extremely valuable animal with good English bloodlines, he also savaged Jeddie Rice."

"How is the young man, by the way? I've been meaning to go over to Cloverfields but can't seem to get away." Jeffrey diplomatically did not inform Yancy that keeping Maureen somewhat steady, canvassing the barn men regarding William, had taken a great deal of time, too much time.

"Riding. Nothing hot but he's back up, his arm in a sling. He knew nothing, of course. His face will bear a permanent scar. His collarbone will heal. He's young."

"A whip shouldn't leave much of a scar." Maureen hadn't a scrap of concern over Jeddie Rice.

"You're right." Yancy uttered those golden words. "However, William sewed small lead weights into the end of the whip, a small square flap. I thought nothing of it. But when he would whip Black Knight it stung. Certainly stung Jeddie, who William hit far harder than my beautiful horse."

"Ah." Jeffrey sighed. "Yancy, let's you and I come up with a joint poster, a joint reward? My wife is too distraught by this to carry an additional burden."

"I can be of assistance." Her mouth snapped shut.

He put his hand over hers. "Of course you can, but first you had one worker short in the stables and then this. Too much weight on your lovely shoulders."

Much as she didn't like being slid aside, she basked in the compliment.

"If you think it's not too much for you. You have those coach commissions."

He smiled at her. "All will be well. My first concern is ever your welfare."

Yancy rose with difficulty, bowed slightly. "This distresses each of us and I am heartily sorry that such an event occurred."

"Yes." Jeffrey stood while Maureen remained seated.

The two men walked outside, where Jeffrey helped Yancy into the saddle. "Had you even a slight premonition?"

"None. He labored hard, listened to instruction." A deep sigh followed this. "Thank you, too, for settling your wife."

Jeffrey shrugged. "Other than the last race, how did you fare?"

"Very well. Sam Udall, a shrewd man with many connections, proved a good business partner. I hope we will work together again. I have paid off my debts. If the last race could have been run then I would have enough profit to reinvest in my holdings." He paused. "But we have found a good vehicle for profit."

That meant that a healthy profit was realized. Jeffrey need not have asked more, but he watched Yancy ride away as he mused that two men ready to kill each other could reach an accord. Turning, he felt warm sunshine on his face as he walked to the stable. No word reached anyone concerning the affair in Philadelphia. He wondered if those delegates could reach an accord. Then he thought to himself, *If Yancy and I can do so, surely they can.*

On his way out Yancy passed Charles and Rachel, Rachel driving the phaeton, on their way to Big Rawly. He told them of his recent meeting, they both expressed the hope for a good first cutting of hay, then he rode away.

Once at the exquisite main house, Rachel untied her bonnet, Charles dusted himself off, and the butler ushered them into a large, airy back room.

Maureen, up from the stable, extended her hand, a small glass of sherry at her side. "Please sit. Forgive me for imbibing spirits early but I have endured an unpleasant meeting with that man."

"We do hope our visit will rectify that." Charles inclined his head toward her as he took a seat in a French chair, itself worth a bundle.

Rachel waved away a tray of sweets now placed on the table where the young but not especially pretty serving girl poured tea.

"Autumn, after serving our guests, do make sure my husband is in his shop."

A slight curtsy. "Yes, Miss Maureen."

As the slender girl left, Rachel reached over, took a letter from her husband, handed it to Maureen. "This arrived today."

Maureen beheld the pale blue stationery, deep black ink in a strong man's handwriting on the envelope. She slid out the heavy laid paper, opened it to behold a baron's crest at the top. How fetching. Just the sight of it enlivened her. She read the three pages avidly, then dropped her hand with the letter into her lap.

"Your brother will show us his estate." She nearly cooed. "He longs to meet us. And to his great credit he is forthright about what is owed."

Charles, voice soft, replied, "Oh, Mrs. Holloway, my brother is a good man, which you will see for yourself. Our late father's improvidence has nearly crushed him."

"One million pounds of debt. I don't wonder." Maureen, given her father's banking profession in the Caribbean, was conversant with the true value of pounds, rubles, livres, even drachmas of old.

"May I write him that you and Mr. Holloway will be visiting?"

"Of course, and I will write to him also. Jeffrey needs to finish his big coach-in-four. Then we may be off. He works quickly, my Jeffrey. Then again, he has hired some of the best wheelwrights, coopers, and cabinetmakers, to say nothing of the harness man. The best."

"How will he ever surpass the coach he made for you?" Rachel praised Jeffrey, always a good move.

"Oh, he is endlessly inventive. Can do anything. Solve

problems with wood, iron, copper, even creating spaces for grease in the wheel hubs so they will hold more grease, and the same for the axles. He amazes me."

"He is a lucky man. You have given him the opportunity to work, work he desires." Charles, himself doing work he loved, meant that.

She beamed. "I will accept your brother's offer. I have no desire to live in England, and I assume neither do you?"

"This is my country." He breathed in slightly. "Do I harbor fond memories, pictures of verdant green pastures, of the sparkling rivers lapping at those shores? I do. And I am grateful for my education but . . . well, you know this from your experience, here we are not so bound by birth. It is no sign of low birth to work with one's hands. Ah well, you know these things."

"I do." She carefully returned the letter to the envelope. "Do you think the baron is accurate in his assessment of what he needs to live?"

"Being far away from current costs, I trust his figures. He won't be as foolish as our father, but he has a place, a title, and he must fulfill responsibilities. If there is a war we are expected to raise regiments, supplies. If we are not asked, given a specific goal, then we must work however the king commands to prosecute the war."

"One pays for one's privileges."

"It's the way of the world," Charles agreed. "He will continue to investigate the correct route for an adoption. It has been done throughout the centuries. Well. Julius Caesar adopted Octavius, so there is a long path." What Charles didn't say was that Jeffrey and Maureen would probably not have children. So the title would die in time or Jeffrey, himself, would need to adopt. Charles figured, cross that bridge when they came to it.

"Monies will be needed to cross palms." Maureen tapped the letter on the palm of her hand a few times as though hearing a distant rhythm.

"That, too, is the way of the world," Rachel replied without much intonation, then added, "And we have a small price."

Shocked, Charles's jaw dropped. She had said nothing to him.

Maureen, far more cynical, simply stared. "Yes."

"As I said it is small."

"How small?"

"I wish you to free DoRe."

Surprised, Maureen covered that emotion. "You have one of the best coachmen in Virginia."

"I do and you are kind to notice. DoRe will do as he pleases, I have no knowledge that he would work for us."

"Then why should I free him?"

"Because he is courting Bettina." Maureen knew of this, as did just about everyone. "I hope this will embolden him to ask for her hand."

"What does being free have to do with it?" Maureen was in no mood to assist any slave, especially after William's running away and the loss of other Big Rawly slaves.

"If he lives here and she with us, they will have very little time together. Imagine if your beloved Mr. Holloway lived and worked on another estate. You two belong together." Rachel knew that would reach her, especially the "belong together."

"Well," Maureen asked, "just why is Bettina's happiness and DoRe's happiness so important?"

Charles, eyes wide, observed every syllable, every gesture.

"Maureen, you know how my mother suffered at the end." Maureen nodded and Rachel continued. "Bettina never left her side. She even slept in the bedroom. The two of them shared a special friendship, something rare. I want Bettina's days to be filled with love."

Leaning back in her chair, Maureen held off.

"Rachel, my love, you feel such things so deeply. I had no idea. Oh yes, I knew that Bettina cared for your mother, and your mother asked her to promise to watch over you for Ewing has spoken of it many times." Charles smiled at her. "And now you are watching over her."

Rachel modestly dropped her eyes, then raised them up to Maureen, who cared little for the emotion involved.

"If you will give me time to be certain one of the stable boys can take over."

"DoRe has trained them. It shouldn't take long." Rachel wanted to clap but didn't. "Two months?"

"Three. I won't free him until I have made all the arrangements with the baron. That will be months, for once we are in England I intend to enjoy London."

"Of course, but if there is hope, perhaps DoRe will not wait overlong to speak to Bettina about a future," Rachel said.

Charles glanced at the ormolu-festooned clock. "We

have overstayed our welcome. You, as always, have been gracious. It's such a pleasure to visit you and Big Rawly," Charles fibbed, but did not stand up until Maureen did.

His manners were impeccable, not lost on Maureen or anyone, really.

Rachel kissed Maureen on the cheek. Charles bowed and brushed his lips over her hand. She felt quite regal.

Driving back to Cloverfields, a glorious light breeze tossing her hair, for she put her bonnet on the seat, Charles said, "You think of everything."

"Oh, I don't know. I hope for the best. And I pray the Holloways and your brother will work this out."

"Rachel, he has no choice. It's an heir or ruination. Clearly she has the money. She didn't blink."

"What do you think a dollar is worth versus the pound?" she asked, feeling the soft leather in her hand as King David trotted along.

"The pound is worth far more. Twenty dollars? Fifteen?"

"Then again, a dollar in Virginia, in South Carolina. Just what is a dollar worth?"

He grinned. "A pound, a dollar, a pittance compared to your value."

41

The moon passed half moon heading to a dark moon. As February 20th was Presidents' Day, a national holiday, federal workers and many others enjoyed a day off.

Harry figured to use this to her advantage, especially in the encroaching darkness. Driving to Richmond on I-64, she remembered when people were given Lincoln's birthday on the 12th and Washington's on the 22nd. Schoolchildren loved two days off, as did many adults. Well, commerce first, so both men's birthdays were rolled into one, Presidents' Day. She considered it a gyp.

Tucker, seated next to her in the Volvo, watched out the window as the early sunset turned the snow-covered pastures and bare trees gold, then salmon, finally red, then boom: darkness. The intrepid dog knew her human was up to something, but what? The cats, left behind, complained loudly. And Tucker knew when they returned to Crozet a book would be knocked off a shelf and desecrated or something would be pushed on the floor from the kitchen counter. The cats believed in revenge.

Finally, Harry reached the site of the Cloudcroft construction. Parking the station wagon on a side street, easier in Richmond than in other cities, she put Tucker on a leash, grabbed bolt cutters and a mountaineer's pick, shoved a small flashlight in her pocket, locked the wagon, began walking. Puffs of breath escaped their noses and mouths, little tokens of winter.

In the left deep pocket of her heavy Filson coat, she'd jammed the bolt cutters. Given Tucker's superior senses, Harry thought she would be a help, just in case. The other pocket held her snub-nosed .38. If anyone threatened her, once close she could take care of him; and she believed it would be a him.

This was crazy but Harry felt she owed this to Gary. Not much traffic. No worries there. Even if they saw her, who would report her as she cut the heavy chain around the large double doors that allowed the equipment in and out? The chain, hardened, took all her strength but she got it, quickly slipped inside the crack she opened in the doors, and just as quickly shut them. She unsnapped Tucker's leash.

The excavation had reached all bedrock. Once the piles of dirt and debris were removed the sinking of mighty girders could begin. At least she thought that would be the process, for Gary had once told her how skyscrapers were built. Steel beams would be driven to six or eight feet, the true foundation. Construction had moved on from that, depending on the building, but she didn't know other methods. Bedrock was all she knew. She needed to get to Cloudcroft before the debris piles were removed.

Briskly walking to a large dirt mound, she clicked on her flashlight, took out a small pick from her inside pocket, dug in. Glass shards, different colors but mostly beer bottles, flicked out. Nothing of human remains. She believed if more had been found, say, just a finger bone, that might not be noticed or, if so, reported. Enough time had been lost with the discovery of Edward Elkins from 1984, that number again. If only she could find Gary's missing file for 1984. If she had it she felt she would have the killer, killers, or parties responsible. She had no idea if the deaths noted, well the dates and notes, really, in the columns of the old files had all been committed by one individual, but she now believed these construction deaths were related, cleverly done. She didn't know why, but she felt sure much of the answer might reside in these piles. Not too much in this one, so she moved all the way across to another. More glass, some old pieces of chain, tin cans, then a tooth popped out, a very large tooth.

Tucker, on patrol, kept silent. They were alone and safe for now. Shining the flashlight, Harry stuck the tooth in her pocket. She dug some more through the frost covering the dirt, but the pile, so huge, had not frozen through or she would have had to work harder with her little mountaineer's pick. The tooth spurred her. Digging further in and making a straight line of four feet, her reach, she vigorously dug. Then she saw them—some sort of bones, gleaming in the dirt. She renewed her efforts, but whatever it was, it was buried too deep for her to dislodge. She took a picture with her cellphone.

She had what she wanted. She knew what this was about or at least what lay underneath Richmond.

Looking around, no security guard, no one at all, she felt safe. Then again, why have a security guard for a big hole? That thought occurred to her as she climbed up the ramp to the street. Whoever was behind this was supremely confident. Well, so was she. She had a big part of the answer. Hers was a misplaced confidence. She failed to notice the small cameras mounted on top of parts of the fence and one even on top of a large yellow excavator. She knew about the cameras from that discussion in Sean's office. But so intense was her obsession, she forgot.

Yes, Harry had her evidence, but they had her.

42

Sean Rankin's office offered a fabulous view of the James and the streets leading down to this wide, swift river. Kayakers loved it for they could live in the city, go down to the river, set off, and paddle. The falls might prove a problem for the neophyte but not the advanced. Truly, it was a beautiful river with bald eagles, great blue herons, ospreys, all manner of fishing birds and even a few fishing people, although not on a bitter day like this one.

Marvella, body still terrific, sat next to Sean. Her cashmere dress, a shocking magenta, revealed just how good her body was.

Leather boots completed the outfit along with a golden pin the shape of an Irish harp. Sean, buying his clothes from Paul Stuart on Madison Avenue in Manhattan, looked equally well turned out but less colorful. Both individuals loved fashion.

With a thumb drive in his personal computer, he clicked through Russian artists.

"I do see why this would be good for the VMFA. It complements the Fabergé collection in the sense that this is another way into rich Russia, the sophisticated Russians who were as comfortable in Paris as they were in St. Petersburg. Have you spoken to Alex Nyerges?" Mr. Nyerges was the VMFA director.

"Yes, he has seen the paintings. He is willing to mount an exhibit. The museum, now world class, intends to show us the world. It's thrilling, really."

"How do you propose to get the artworks?"

"The museum has European experts, as you know, quite strong in the eighteenth and nineteenth centuries. And of course, more works from those centuries remain intact. But really, Sean, there isn't a weak department at the VMFA anymore. It truly is world class. Those individuals can call their counterparts at other museums. Most will loan the work. It's undervalued and unknown for the most part. This will help the breakthrough to Russian art. Most people just think of icons."

He smiled. "They're in for a surprise." Then he asked, "How do you propose to get those works that are in private hands?"

"We will need Sotheby's for that. They really have led the way on selling Russian art and artifacts. Sotheby's has specialists in London, New York, Moscow, Paris, even a private client group. It's to their benefit for us to mount such an exhibit. I think they will help us reach private clients who have bought their offerings over the last few years."

He leaned back in the chair, then forward, popped out the thumb drive, slipped another one in. The Cloudcroft bedrock appeared, a shadowy figure with a corgi, picking at a dirt pile. The figure was clearly caught by each camera, although far away and therefore a bit fuzzy. One camera somewhat revealed Harry's face. Her cap pulled down for warmth covered only a part of her face.

"Could this be your friend?" he asked smoothly.

Marvella's stomach twisted into a tight knot. In that instant she knew Rankin was behind, at least, the disappearance of Edward Elkins, who had been found underneath what was the old Kushner Building. Something in his tone, his feigned innocence, told her. She pulled herself together, leaned forward.

"It's difficult to make out features but it could be. Then again, how many women could fit this image?" She prayed that was enough to allay his fears.

"Yes." He folded his hands together. "I'm still waiting on Dad for the exhibit confirmation. I have been working on him and I'll get back to you."

As she left his sumptuous office she knew what he really said was "Help me out and I'll help you out. Discreetly."

Sweat rolled down Marvella's back like an old hot flash.

The minute she reached home she picked up her landline. Much harder to trace the call.

"Harry." Her voice's urgency alerted Harry.

"Marvella, what's wrong?"

"Were you at Cloudcroft last night with your corgi?"

A long pause followed, then "Yes."

"They know. Cameras. Protect yourself, Harry. I don't know what is going on but I feel strongly that you are in danger."

"I could be." Harry told the truth. "Marvella, thank you and watch out for yourself."

"I didn't identify you. I did say it might be you but so many women could fit the description of that shadowy woman in the dark."

"You risked your exhibit."

"That's irrelevant," Marvella immediately replied. "Promise you will protect yourself and not do anything so foolish."

"I will. I found old bones, Marvella. Not human. Older. Much older."

"No good can come from old bones, no matter to whom they belonged," Marvella said with feeling, for after all, one does not disturb the dead.

43

Spring, late this year, exploded. Dogwoods opened, the redbuds bloomed and bloomed longer than usual. The daffodils finished just as tulips popped up. Man and beast breathed in the delicious air, happy the last frost was finally over.

Catherine, watching Ralston ride, stood next to Jeddie.

"He's stiff. His elbows are locked. Tell him to get off," Jeddie criticized.

"He's not the rider you are but the horses need a bit of work. I've seen a lot worse."

"Just let me ride. I can do it with a sling. I only need one arm and I've walked them with this sling. I can trot and gallop."

"No," she sharply replied. "That's final. Walking, yes. The rest, no."

Grimacing, he stared at Ralston, his eyes narrowing. "All he thinks about is girls."

"Well." She decided not to pursue that.

"I can't stand this."

"A few more weeks. They'll fly by. Now stop complaining. Have you any ideas how we can help Yancy?"

"Do what?"

"Well, he's paid off Maureen for William's labor. Actually, he paid double. She was insisting that Yancy pay William's value, which of course she trebled. She did not offer to pay for the loss of Black Knight. Yancy quite rightly said this was a matter for the authorities."

"William can't keep Black Knight, although he could get a high price for the horse. If he's smart and I think he is, he left the horse, started walking by foot."

"Jeddie, there's been so much to do you and I haven't been able to study this. Did William say anything to you when you worked horses together?"

Jeddie shook his head "no," which was the truth. "He bragged on himself. He kept telling me how he would outride me but I paid no attention."

"He's left you a scar on your cheek."

"If I ever find him I'll break his arms," Jeddie hissed. "If he'd hurt Reynaldo, I would kill him."

"I'd help you." She touched his shoulder. "Be careful." As he looked at her, puzzled, she quietly said, "I don't want Maureen's anger to travel to you."

He looked at her. He knew what Maureen was capable of doing to her slaves.

Ralston trotted back, stopped at Catherine and Jeddie, who gave him a withering look.

"He's such a lovely mover. Ralston, when you and Tulli wipe him down, turn him out, go to the carriage house and see if Barker O. needs a hand."

"Yes, Miss Catherine." He smiled, ignored Jeddie, rode toward the stable while Jeddie watched.

"I can go to Barker O."

"Let him do it. We need to sit down and figure out if we're going to breed Queen Esther. Have you studied your bloodlines?"

"Yes."

Before she could answer, the rhythmic clip-clop of two horses working in tandem drew their attention as DoRe drove to the stable. Jeddie stepped forward to hold the matched pair with his good hand.

DoRe easily swung down, winced a bit as his one leg touched the ground. "Miss Catherine."

"DoRe. How good to see you and on such a beautiful day. How did you manage to slip away from Big Rawly?"

He sighed. "She wants to know if anyone believes Sheba is behind William's escape."

Sheba had been missing since October 1786. As Maureen's lady-in-waiting she exercised her power with deviousness, greed, and endless lies. DoRe knew she was dead, but no one else did.

"Sheba wouldn't help anyone," Catherine swiftly replied.

"True."

"Go on to the house. Bettina will have something special. Perhaps we can all come up with something that will satisfy Maureen's curiosity. She has lost five people in the last few years."

"She believes it's a conspiracy," DoRe solemnly reported. "She's offered me money to spy. For now. Who knows what she'll do next?"

"Indeed." Catherine nodded in agreement.

DoRe looked at Jeddie. "Hurt?"

"Not much. I want to ride but Miss Catherine won't let me."

"She's right."

"DoRe, go on, Bettina will be happy to see you," Catherine urged him, then turned to Jeddie.

"Tell Ralston and Tulli to unhitch the horses, wipe them down, put them in a stall. Be a good rest. And don't use your arm, hear?"

"I do."

She left him and walked toward Rachel's house. Her sister was bent over Charles's drafting table.

"Look at this." Rachel called her over once Catherine came through the door. "Charles wants to gild, just one line on the trim between the wall and the ceiling. He wants to repeat the line on the pulpit and the lectern."

"Beautiful."

"He doesn't want the church to look Papist, all that gilt, candles, you know."

"St. Luke's is safe from excess." Catherine folded her arms over her bosom. "DoRe's here." She relayed his mission.

"She never gives up, does she?"

"No. Do you really think Hugh will sell his title?"

"It's that or debtor's prison. Charles says Hugh can't actually vacate the title, but Jeffrey as his son, despite age, would be called lord. When Hugh dies Jeffrey becomes a baron."

"If Hugh dies first."

"Best not to look closely into the future. I have been thinking about Bettina. Until we know for certain that this arrangement has been effected, I don't think we should upset Father. The losses from France and the uncertainty in Philadelphia capture his attention."

"All he has heard from the convention is Mr. Adams pushes endlessly for his idea of government, with which Father is uncertain. He fears concentrating power in a few hands. He says that's why we fought the king. But then he thinks Jefferson's ideas are too loose. He is deeply puzzled!"

"Just so, Sister, we have no say, what we have created isn't working."

Catherine agreed. "A tidbit of gossip enlivened the news. A very pretty young widow who serves food at her mother's tavern seems to have caught the attention of half the delegates. She's Patrick Henry's cousin."

Rachel laughed. "I hope she has better morals."

Catherine laughed, too, for Henry was known for fathering many illegitimate children, a concern for his mother and, of course, the women who bore them.

"Charles says fishing rights might be a difficult issue without a strong central government. One state can accuse another of poaching. He says a House of Parliament doesn't mean there will be a king, but there has to be some form of representation."

"Yes." Catherine shrugged. "Virginia is vast. We should have the most representatives."

"That will never work. Charles declares all the other states will line up against us if they haven't done it already."

"Good Lord." Catherine threw up her hands.

Rachel smiled. "Prayer seems to be in order."

Piglet slowly walked in carrying the huge bone from the races.

"That bone is bigger than he is." Catherine laughed.

"He won't let it out of his sight. We have to put it up if Piglet is to attend Charles." Rachel laughed, too. "He won't even let Isabelle and Marcia play with it. Do you know Marcia can name some flowers?"

"Ah, well let me know when she can weed the garden." Catherine sat down on a bench, suddenly tired.

"Are you . . . ?"

She waved Rachel away. "I've been on my feet since before sunup. Just a little weary."

"Has everything returned to normal?" Rachel, close as she was to her sister, couldn't summon the courage to ask if Catherine had a period yet.

"Yes." She looked into her sister's face. "John was afraid to touch me. He's such a tender man. I told him we are man and wife, I'm fine. But, I don't know if I want more children. I want him so I suppose I will."

"Oh, I would love dozens."

"I don't know. I love JohnJohn but now I fear child-birth, and I hated it anyway."

"Oh, you forget the pain."

"You did. I didn't," Catherine said clearly.

Rachel now sat next to her. "Oh, Catherine."

"I'm fine. It's just that I am asking myself questions, questions one usually doesn't speak out loud. Things like: Do we have men who can lead our new country? I see lots of strutting but I don't know. I worry about Father. He reads me letters from his many business interests. If he gets a letter from Philadelphia he reads it to me. Seems like clouds of talk to me."

"Yes, me, too. And a House of Parliament would en-shrine the talk. We would be as bad as England."

Catherine murmured, "Perhaps, but they are the most powerful nation in the world, king or no king."

"What about the French?"

"Oh, Rachel, they are illogical." Catherine spoke with all the rich prejudice of an English-speaking person.

"I think the world is changing too fast."

"Maybe it always has. The trick is to change with it."

"But what if you can't?" Rachel's voice was plaintive.

"Then you die," Catherine replied starkly.

44

Feverishly writing in her notebook, Harry sat at Gary's desk while Tazio worked at the drafting table. Harry checked and double-checked each file box. One by one she flipped through the pages she had marked with arrows sticking off the paper. Finally she carefully sifted through 1983, satisfied herself, returned the file.

Mrs. Murphy, Pewter, Tucker, Pirate, and Brinkley had wedged against the now-closed door to the small back room. Harry, bringing Pirate along, allowed the puppy to join the others.

Pewter, wide awake, poked Mrs. Murphy, half asleep. *"She's shut the door. Fear. The spider is too much."*

"She doesn't know there's a spider back there." Tucker opened one eye.

"*What do you know? I'm staying right here, on duty,*" Pewter grumbled as Tucker closed that one eye.

The front door opened, Raynell came in with a roll under her arm, the original drawings for Nature First's redo. The wind made it difficult for her to close the door.

"Jeez," she gasped as she pulled it closed.

"Think it was like this when Washington was born?" Tazio looked up, smiling.

"Hope not." Harry chimed in.

"Keeping the fires going had to be a full-time job, plus one needs to be near the fireplace." Raynell unwound her scarf.

"It's easy to forget how much effort it took to keep warm or cool or fetch the butter from the springhouse," Harry added.

"What about cities? Delivering firewood, lighting lamps, then later in time cleaning out gas lamps, gas lines to homes for light. And then what about cleaning up the streets? Can you imagine the tons of horse manure?" Tazio slipped a pencil behind her ear.

Harry laughed. "Actually, I can."

"At least we developed good sewage systems." Raynell studied architecture as well as wildlife for Nature First.

"Can you imagine living in London or Paris, even in the eighteenth century? Had to be noxious even as ideas exploded everywhere, and the arts, too." Harry returned the file to its slot on the bottom shelf.

"How come you're keeping them?" Raynell asked Tazio. "You can get all that information off the Internet."

"His notes in the margins are helpful. He has initials,

question marks, and sometimes these envelope drawings by construction sites. It's better to sit down with a pile of papers instead of scrolling back and forth. I need his notes."

"You're right," Raynell agreed. "So what are you writing?" She directed this to Harry.

"Checking against the notes I've transcribed."

"Harry, what do you need with them? Unless you're going into architecture or construction."

"I am going to find Gary's killer."

"In building codes?" Raynell was incredulous.

"Yes. What if the envelope drawings along with initials in some of the margins mean blackmail?"

"Harry, you have too much imagination." Raynell winked.

Pewter, eyes now open, put her ear to the crack of the back-room door. "I hear her. Heavy footsteps. Eight of them."

"Pewter, you're getting mental." Mrs. Murphy sighed.

"Getting?" Tucker spoke loudly, which sounded like a yip to the humans.

That fast, the rotund gray cat leapt onto Tucker's back, boxing her ears. Tucker, surprised, had the presence of mind to roll over so now fatpuss was underneath the corgi. However, cats on their back are formidable, fur flew.

"Dammit." Harry rose from her kneeling by the bottom shelf, walked over, pulled Tucker off a highly offended cat.

"You always take her part," Tucker whined.

"Tucker, she's not taking Pewter's part she's just separating you, for which I am grateful." Mrs. Murphy spoke as Brinkley and Pi-rate watched, eyes wide open.

"I have been cruelly treated by a tailless wonder," Pewter spat.

In a flash of what she thought was brilliance, Harry opened the door to the back and the animals did go back there.

"I am not protecting you all from the monster spider. That spider is so big she must be a holdover from prehistoric times. She's a dinosaur spider and I don't care if she bites you all." Pewter looked up at Harry, then glared at Tucker.

Harry, hands on hips, shook her head, kept the door open a crack, then returned to the big room. "Sorry."

"They are dramatic." Tazio laughed.

Raynell sat in one of the old ladderback chairs, placing the drawings across her knees. "Back to the codes."

"Oh." Harry plopped behind Gary's desk. "He noted with initials in the margins at the construction sites where workers had died, like Ali Asplundah on June 2, 1983. If I could ever find the 1984 code file I think he would have marked in the margin for the Kushner Build-ing. I think he knew something about Edward Elkins. 1984 was the year Gary left. He put two and two together and got out or possibly was paid off."

Raynell rested her hands on the rolled-up drawings. "Well, what's two and two? I don't get it. I wish Lisa was here. Maybe she would."

"Lisa, I think, had figured it out. Your boss was maybe over the top about her cause sometimes, my opinion, but she was really smart," Harry said.

"I don't think you can do a job like that if you aren't

passionate," Tazio demurred. "The pay is low, the tasks enormous, and a nonprofit person must continually fundraise as well as educate. Has to be exhausting."

"Felipe and I miss her very much." Raynell stood, gave the drawings to Tazio. "We've got copies. Thought you'd like the original."

"Thanks."

The monster is on the ceiling! Pewter hollered.

Sure enough, the spider had crept out from her entrance into the bathroom, stopped, assessed the situation, then crawled up the wall to affix herself to the ceiling, sending Pewter into fits.

"Ignore her." Harry threw up her hands.

"You know, I still don't get it. It's not strange that someone might note worker deaths. If I kept a diary I would. So maybe the codes were his diary," Raynell said.

"Maybe. I think this has to do with what's under the buildings."

"Harry, who cares?" Raynell sounded doubtful.

"Many people would care if they know history, a road map of this area over time is under there. Millions of years of dinosaur bones and some maybe almost intact as whole animals. That's why Gary and Lisa had all those rubber dinosaurs. Yes, they were fascinated, but both knew that area between Richmond and Danville was home to dinosaurs for about two hundred and fifteen million years. Properly unearthed, the fossils, bones, whatever, would reveal a great deal about evolution and about perhaps what really happened to those creatures."

"I don't know." Raynell's eyebrows rose.

"If you study the period, the Jurassic, the Cretaceous, you'll learn that the basin running all the way up to Washington, D.C., even toward Baltimore and down to Danville, is loaded with fossils. The richest area is from Richmond to Danville. I'm pretty sure now and I'm going to drive this over to Cooper at HQ. You know some people would lose fortunes if construction suddenly had to stop or nothing new could be built until this is squared somehow with scientists. Some people have killed and would kill over it. I think those who are dead figured this out, saw bones and wanted some hush money. I really think it led to murder."

Raynell nodded, reached into her purse, pulled out a Glock. "You're right. Now you and Tazio get into the back room."

"What are you doing?" Tazio gasped.

"My job. Into the back room. Now."

The two women, side by side, walked into the back room, where the animals, almost as puzzled as the two women, stared at them, except for Pewter.

"Death from above!" the gray cat screamed.

Raynell did look upward for a moment and she, too, screamed. Her fear of spiders gave Harry and Tazio a split second to leap for the gun, which the woman foolishly pointed up at the humongous spider on the ceiling. The spider, perhaps having a sense of humor, dropped from that height right onto Raynell, who felt the weight on her head and those legs creeping down toward her face.

Tucker lunged for Raynell's calf as Brinkley took the other one. Those fangs hurt like the devil.

The spider evaded Raynell's desperate attempts to dislodge her. Harry, in terrific shape thanks to farming, grabbed the gun hand and brought Raynell's arm down hard over her knee. A snap could be heard, the gun dropped. Tazio pinned her other arm behind her back as Mrs. Murphy batted the gun away.

"*Rabies. The spider had rabies,*" Pewter bellowed for all she was worth.

Raynell, screaming, sweating, begged, "Get that spider off of me."

"Not until you confess. You killed Gary, right?" Harry held her broken arm, giving it a jerk.

Raynell screamed. "I did. I did." Weeping, she pleaded, "Get the spider off."

"*She's going to bite you.*" Pewter relished the moment.

Pirate, although a puppy, stood on the fallen woman's chest.

"Please, help me!" Raynell sobbed.

"Who do you work for? Then we'll remove the spider," Harry promised.

"A company in partnership with Rankin Construction."

"I am not touching that spider," Tazio sensibly said as she kept Raynell's left arm securely pinned.

"I'll move her. God, she's enormous." Harry gulped, kept her hand securely on Raynell's arm, reached over to brush the eight-legged wonder off the sobbing woman's head. The spider, having had her fun, jumped off, scurrying to the bathroom.

"Taz, do you have any rope?"

"Do."

Harry let go of Raynell's arm but stomped it first for good measure.

The jolt of pain as well as residual fear kept Raynell from rising. Harry scooped up the gun, guarded by Mrs. Murphy, flipped off the safety, pointed it at the stricken woman.

Tazio ran to her supply closet, brought out a sturdy roll of twine and tied Raynell's hands in front of her, her right arm limp. Raynell tried to bat at Tazio with her left as the spider's exit gave her a bit of courage, but Tucker and Brinkley kept their fangs secure in her calves.

Dragged to a chair, twine now wrapped so many times, Raynell wasn't going anywhere.

Harry called Cooper.

Pewter remained in front of the bathroom door but the other animals guarded Raynell.

Cooper, Sheriff Shaw, Dabney arrived at the studio within fifteen minutes, sirens blaring. They must have hit seventy miles an hour on those old roads.

Cooper, first in the door, looked at Raynell, then Harry and Tazio. "You okay?"

"Great."

Pewter called from the back room, "*I saved the day. Really, she walked under the ceiling and the monster dropped. Engineered the whole thing.*"

The other animals kept quiet, but Tucker and Brinkley grimaced.

"Blood." Sheriff Shaw followed the dripping blood from the back room to where Raynell sat, then noticed the bloody jaws of Tucker and Brinkley.

"They bit her calves," Harry simply said.

Tazio turned to Raynell. "Out with it."

Cooper retrieved her small notebook, flipped it open.

Raynell kept her mouth shut, so Harry punched her broken arm. "Now! Or I'll break the other one." She looked up at Sheriff Shaw. "Self-defense."

"Of course."

"I killed Gary Gardner."

"Next." Harry moved toward her.

"Next what?"

"Next victim."

"Uh . . ."

Harry raised her hand again. That fast, Harry unleashed a backhand across Raynell's face, the sound of which could have been heard out on the street.

The officers wouldn't stop her. Nor would they report this. Raynell could babble to any lawyer she wished. Harry loved Gary. She was so angry she bordered on the irrational. It was a wonder Harry didn't try to kill Raynell. Raynell got what was coming to her.

"Lisa Roudabush."

"How did you know to try and kill me?" Harry pressed.

"The camera at the excavation site gave you away."

Triumphant, Harry looked at Cooper, Rick, and Dabney. "She's all yours."

Tucker and Brinkley drank water as Raynell was led away.

"*That's better.*" Tucker exhaled.

"*Human blood has a metallic taste,*" Brinkley replied.

Pirate, watching everything, asked, "*Does this happen often?*"

Mrs. Murphy, on the desk, looked down at the hand-some fellow. *"Around Harry it does."*

Tazio dropped into her drafting table chair. "What the hell am I going to do about that spider?"

Suddenly Harry burst out laughing, laughter after a crisis has passed, soon joined by Tazio.

"Feed her dead flies. She saved our lives." Harry laughed until she cried.

"I saved you. Me. Me. Me," Pewter called from the adjoining room, then sashayed into the big room as if to make her point.

"Well, Pewts, now we know why you were so fascinated with the back room." Harry wiped the tears from her eyes.

"I can't kill that big thing. She really did save us."

"Like I said, dead flies. And she won't live but so long yet. While she's here she is impressive." Harry scratched Mrs. Murphy, sitting on the desk, then reached down to pet Pewter.

"Were you scared?" Tazio asked.

"Surprised. And scared now that it's over." She thought a moment. "Spiders. I recall the divine from colonial times, Jonathan Edwards, who wrote, 'We are depraved creatures, spiders hanging over the fire.' Thank God that spider was hanging on the ceiling," Harry said.

"Do you think we are depraved?"

"Some of us are, but no, I don't. What about you?"

"No, but they certainly get all the media attention. I guess that's our Puritan background, exalt misery and suffering. That's all I see from it. Not a hint of joy."

"You know what H. L. Mencken wrote, 'A Puritan is a person who fears that someone, somewhere, is having fun.'" Harry laughed a little bit, having condensed the famous quote.

With that they both exploded in raucous laughter again, truly grateful to be alive.

45

June 15, 1787

Friday

Windows wide open, a refreshing breeze forced Ewing to put paperweights on his desk papers. Spectacles affixed, he read a letter from Philadelphia as Roger brought in afternoon tea.

Pushing his spectacles up, Ewing smiled at his contemporary. "Thank you." He put down the letter then looked up at his butler. "Nothing is going to plan."

"Sir?"

"The convention. It's one argument after another. Roger Davis writes, under the table. I pay him to do so but best no one knows. I think he's also informing others, which irritates me. Anyway, Madison puts forth all his ideas for government giving states much autonomy. These aren't tabled but each delegate appears to feel his thoughts are necessary. Roger, I fear nothing can be done, but one sensible thing has occurred. The members elected George Washington president of the convention. He can vote as a member but he will not express opinions."

Roger, alert to the times, very intelligent, poured tea. "Master, he is not much a talking man, so they say."

"No. But I hear in small groups—especially if ladies are present, his wife in particular—he can be filled with laughter. I can only imagine the burdens he has carried and is carrying now."

Roger folded his arms across his chest. "Indeed."

"I like Jemmy Madison. I like his brother, and I fear their mother. She doesn't suffer fools gladly. Imperious." He shook his head, then laughed. "Well, I've nattered on, but I need be careful because I know Madison and Jefferson, though he be in France, think as one. And I must confess, I differ much from my neighbors, for I think John Adams has the stronger case, but I have doubts."

"Mr. Ewing, you should be there. You understand business. I think these men are mostly lawyers."

Ewing laughed. "Fearful, isn't it?"

A knock at the front door sent Roger to it. Ewing heard a familiar voice, rose, strode out into the hall.

"Ah, Yancy, my dear fellow. Please come in." He nodded to Roger, who stepped aside. "Roger has brought me my afternoon restorative tea. Might you join me?"

"I would be honored."

The two men walked into Ewing's library/office as Roger hastened to the kitchen. Bettina and Serena gathered biscuits, made small sandwiches; then Bettina, her sense of occasion aroused, quickly picked a few flowers and the two women created an early summer arrangement. Roger brought the tray into the office, which was beautiful in its proportions, the light shining on the leather-bound books.

"Tell Bettina she again works her magic." Ewing beamed up at Roger, who discreetly withdrew.

Ewing relayed the contents of the letter from Philadelphia without revealing the author.

"Have we not set ourselves too great a task?" Yancy asked. "We know only kings and queens. Athens is so very far away, as is Rome, though a little closer. They seem to be the ideal. Well early Rome, not late Rome."

Ewing nodded. "We have what they wrote."

"Yes, yes, but times are different. Think of the weaponry we have now, the speed of our ships. The ancients could never have imagined firearms."

"Yes." Ewing took a bracing sip. "I buy the teas but Bettina does something."

"She waves her hand over the tea leaves. She has magic." Yancy smiled then took a deep breath. "I have come to throw myself upon the mercy of an old friend, a friend tried and true in difficult times. Had we not won, you and I would have been hanged together."

Ewing's eyebrows knitted together, he leaned toward Yancy. "What can I do? You have only to ask."

Yancy swallowed. "I found Black Knight. I carted him to the barn, where your most excellent daughter is going over him with Barker O. and Jeddie. He's had a tooth knocked out, has cuts everywhere, and his tendons are bowed. Someone was brutal to the magnificent creature."

"I am so sorry. Is there any possibility to find out?"

"The man who brought him to me is a farmer in Goochland County. Appears educated. He said the animal wandered onto his farm. He patched him up as best he could. A visiting neighbor recognized Blackie from the races. I expect most of Goochland County was there. So I paid the fellow for his troubles." He looked into his friend's eyes. "I can't restore him to health. Catherine can. I am ruined, Ewing, ruined."

"I thought you profited from the races."

"I did. I repaid my debts to Sam Udall. I hired a lawyer since Maureen threatened to sue me for the loss of William. Why in God's name would I be party to a slave escaping on my blooded horse!"

"Runaway slaves are part of life, but I do think many of us would turn away from reporting anyone escaping Maureen. Her cruelty is anything but casual."

"She has backed off her lawsuit, thanks to her husband. The man with whom I fought a duel has become a friend." He inhaled deeply. "But I have no workers as you know. I can't afford to house and feed anyone. I can't afford to pay for an indentured servant from Ireland. I prefer an Irishman for working with horses. And I can't pinpoint where I went wrong. I did think our new country would have settled its debts by now."

"Yes." Ewing nodded. "If nothing else this gaggle of argumentative men in Philadelphia must do that very thing. How can I help?"

"Will you take my boy?"

"Of course I will. When Catherine has him healthy again, I shall return him."

Yancy lifted his hands, palms upward. "I haven't the means to keep him."

"What if she gave you a horse bred by him? He'll never race again, obviously, but when his bows heal he will be able to stand at stud."

"Oh, my friend, I can't race. The time it takes to train. I can't do it. I have just enough for hayseed, for corn. By the time the hay is ready to be cut, I hope I shall have found some workers, day men."

Ewing, voice strong, replied, "I'll send some of my men. You'll bounce back. We've been through war, floundering after the war, which did go on and on, and now we will survive whatever is happening in Philadelphia. We are men of business. Those who live only by books will destroy us all. I pray there are such practical men in Philadelphia, but we are such men here."

Yancy sat a little straighter. "Practicality is in short supply."

"Nicely put." Ewing poured another cup of tea for each of them. "I fear men who do not work for an honest living and I fear even more those men who think they are smarter than those of us who do."

"Lately, I have been wondering were we pushed into the war, did we understand the problems or were we goaded into it? Did England think we could be dashed, humbled then subservient? All profits flowing one way, so to speak."

With certainty Ewing responded, "We were provoked.

We would settle one insult, which would be followed by another outlandish tax. But no matter what, the profits would not flow one way. The English can't get enough of our tobacco, hemp, indigo, cotton, and rum. They have to do business with us and, really, where else in the world is there tobacco? If another nation tries to grow it from our seed it will not be Virginia Burley."

"I hadn't thought of that."

"I hadn't either until you brought it up. Now see here, Yancy. You're tired. You're in constant pain. Your spirits are low. But you are a resourceful man. Let us just get through this growing season. You will make a profit even if Mother Nature is difficult. We can sort things out after that and"—Ewing put his hand on Yancy's wrist—"do not now or ever sell your holdings to Maureen Selisse."

Yancy's eyes opened wide. "What?"

"She is both ruthless and astute. You own highly productive land. She's trying to beat you down. Jeffrey has dissuaded her from a lawsuit but she'll come up with other ideas. You know she's on her way to England."

"I had heard. I gave it no credence."

Ewing smiled broadly. "It's true. She is sailing to meet with Charles's deeply indebted brother to buy a title."

"Fantastic."

"Isn't it though." Ewing laughed again. "Now ease your mind. Black Knight will thrive, as will you. Shall we walk down to the stable so you can say goodbye?"

Yancy's eyes misted, he shook his head. "Thank you, no. Perhaps when time passes."

"Of course. Do you think William was the perpetrator of his suffering?"

"No. I think William dismounted, took off the tack, stored it somewhere, then made his way either downriver or to the coast. Blackie wandered for who knows how long, possibly picked up by someone who thought they had a new horse but couldn't ride him. He's a lot of horse. I expect he was badly beaten and I expect the violence put him further out of reach. Apart from my ill-fated duel, I don't really believe in violence."

"I understand, but I see little hope of men doing otherwise."

"Yes." Yancy stood as Ewing did, the two men walked down the hall to the large door where Roger was waiting, which meant he'd heard the whole thing. Roger bowed as Yancy stepped out, Ewing alongside.

His cart, coming up from the stable, was a sure sign that Roger overheard all, then sent his son down to alert the boys to ready Yancy's cart and drive it to the door. Ewing knew this, of course, but pretended otherwise over the years.

Clasping Ewing's hands in both of his, Yancy said, "I shall never forget your kindness."

"All will be well. Truly, all will be well." He watched as his friend drove his heavy-boned draft horse down the long drive of Cloverfields.

Ewing pulled out his gold pocket watch, checking the time, whispering to himself, "I swore I wouldn't do this."

Placing the birthday watch back into his vest, he walked down to the stable, where Black Knight stood in a large stall,

Catherine on one side, Jeddie on another, and Barker O. in front just in case.

Slowly approaching so as not to frighten the animal, Ewing asked, "How bad is it?"

"Hay, some good oats, he'll fill back out," Catherine replied. "Fortunately his hooves are good, no damage."

Jeddie, out of the sling at last, knelt down holding a heavy warm cloth on Black Knight's forelegs. "Bows."

"Yes, so Yancy said."

"He'll recover. The scar will be prominent but he'll actually be ridable, nothing hard. He's got quality." Catherine admired the fellow.

"He's yours. Yancy has given him to us. He can't afford proper care. Hard times."

Barker O. turned his head slightly.

"Father . . ." She changed her mind, said to the men, "Let's turn him out next to Reynaldo. It's a small paddock. He can walk about and eat. The last thing he needs is to stand."

Quiet for a moment, the skinny Black Knight sniffed then dashed to the end of the sizable paddock. Reynaldo, in the adjoining paddock, let out a holler, which Black Knight returned. Then he ran to the fence line, where the two stallions stared at each other.

"They'll work it out." Barker O. smiled.

"I'm rather glad I don't know what they're saying." Catherine laughed, happy to see an abused animal bright again.

Love could heal most creatures.

Piglet joined them, interested in the new horse and

wise enough not to chase him. Piglet did, however, herd Ewing, Catherine, Barker O., and Jeddie toward the fence line, feeling it his duty to watch over them as they watched the two boys fuss at each other. Lots of flared nostrils, snorts, turning in circles, bucks that finally settled into biting. It was occurring to Reynaldo that he was stuck with this fast horse whom he met at The Levels, just as it occurred to Black Knight he had arrived at paradise.

That gorgeous June day, wind ruffling manes and Catherine's long hair, no one knew if they would have a country that held together, but at that moment the Blue Ridge Mountains promised permanence: the rolling fields, shoots now above the ground offering a form of hope. In time Cloverfields would fall to the ground, the outbuildings and stables dwindle into disrepair.

None of them would live to see that, thankfully, but the mountains would stand. Each of those humans and even the corgi would live full lives, painful, joyful, complete, and their bloodlines would flow through the centuries along with the two stallions'.

Old people would say then as now, "Blood tells."

And so it would.

46

February 24, 2017

Friday

Branches scraped against the handblown panes of the windows in Harry's old farmhouse. Cooper, Tazio, Brinkley, Pirate, Tucker, Mrs. Murphy, and Pewter reposed in the living room. Well, the animals reposed, the humans sat in chairs with Tazio on the sofa, Brinkley glued to her.

"Just never ends, does it?" Harry glanced out into the early darkness as a branch's high-pitched noise captured attention.

"A fire makes everything pleasant no matter what happens outside." Tazio looked into the gathering night.

Cooper, hand on Pirate's head as he sat by her chair, sighed. "You two nearly got killed. I've cussed you before and I'll cuss you now."

Harry defended both of them. "We had no idea. Admit it, neither did you."

"We were closer than you think. The killer of both Gary and Lisa had to know their habits, which meant a close friend or a close coworker. We even hired a handwriting analyst to study people's handwriting, including yours, and that opened the door a wedge."

"How so?" Harry asked.

"The rental car papers for Enterprise. Remember the car left across from Legacy Market in the snowstorm? The papers were under a false name, false but with a really good counterfeit driver's license. Raynell had incredibly well-made false papers for whatever she needed.

"We began to focus on her, Felipe, and the head of Nature First down in Richmond. Each of them had a work record that could be traced. Darla, Raynell's real name, had a great cover. She really did work for other non-profits."

"So she's a professional killer?" Tazio wondered.

"If she has to kill, she will. But she can root out whatever the company that hires her needs. She can also set up stings."

"Like what?" Harry watched the flames edged in blue.

"Trap a rival executive or politician either with a drug setup or a gorgeous call girl. Obviously, she's good at what she does. Born and raised in Des Moines, Iowa. How she got into this business . . . well, she won't admit she's in it." Cooper shrugged. "They never do and their bills are paid by some of their former customers. If she takes the rap she will come out of jail even richer. Some system, right?" Cooper sighed.

"You have the 1984 files?" Harry wanted to know

about the files, since she'd spent so much time going through the other years.

"Yes. September 19, 1984, by the Kushner project was a note, 'E. E. missing for three days. Dinosaur bones found in his trunk. Disregarded as they were not human. Thrown away.'"

"Longer than his other notes." Harry leaned forward. "Wonder why?"

"With Edward Elkins's disappearance, I expect Gary realized Elkins's gossip about Ali being killed may not have been gossip. Remember, Gary was fascinated by dinosaurs. Also he somewhat knew Ali, who died in 1983. An apparent heart attack, but so close to Elkins's. He knew what those bones could mean for research and what it would mean to Rankin Construction or anyone hoping to build in Richmond. He got out while the getting was good. He didn't tip his hand, but he must have gotten sloppy with Lisa. We're hoping we can worm it out of Darla but she's a tough nut."

"The book?" Harry questioned.

"Brilliant. She brushed nicotine on the corners of the pages wearing rubber gloves before taking the book to Lisa's office. In all my years of law enforcement this is the cleverest way I have ever seen to kill someone."

"Bunch of bones. People are crazy." Pewter expressed her opinion.

"People want to know about the past," Tucker replied.

"Who cares? Doesn't change anything," the cat rightfully surmised.

"If humans understand something they feel better. Maybe they feel *safer, even if they can't control anything. They believe it helps them look into the future."*

"I've got news for them." Pewter lifted her chin. "They'll muck up the future no matter what they've learned about the past. They have no common sense."

None of the other animals challenged this view, as there was some truth to it, but why let Pewter jump on her soapbox?

"Did you ever find the Ducati?" Harry would have loved to have that bike.

"No. What Rick and I think, especially after talking to the people who study organized crime, is this some form of highly organized crime? No, but Darla is part of a company, for lack of a better word, that destroys reputations and sometimes destroys people. We hope this may lead us to who those people are. We know they are enormously rich and they may be international. We strongly believe they also operate politically, ruining elected officials who might reduce the profits of their clients." Cooper rested her hands on her knees. "The crime that gets reported in the papers is usually impulse crimes or crimes driven by drugs, lack of money, personal revenge, but drugs usually fuel most of what we see, that or alcohol. The truth is that crimes like this are thought out and carried out by highly intelligent people. It's doubtful that Darla, smart as she is, came up with all of the plan. People higher up created it and, remember, this had to cover up the scientific treasure underground."

"How can people stop building? Really?" Tazio questioned. "Okay, the area is incredibly important, not just for a short time, but as we've been reading at least two hundred and fifteen million years. There's no easy answer."

"No," Cooper agreed.

"So millions really are at stake and not just this project but future projects. Have you thought that Rankin Construction did not act alone?" Harry was trying to put it together.

"It has occurred to us. State agencies will push into our research and future research, and so will the federal government. Our little county sheriff's department is about to be overwhelmed by people who think they're smarter than we are, but we cracked the case. Sean denies everything."

"I did!" Pewter shouted. "I saved everyone!"

"So back to the Ducati." Harry pressured.

"We think the bike was either bought or rented by the parent company, again for lack of a better word, and trailered here. Once Gary was killed, Darla drove it back to a rendezvous place or a garage used by the company, where it would be picked up. Again, clever. Almost impossible to trace especially if a dealership is owned by this company. They have fingers in many pies to cover their tracks. Certainly they have a ready supply of unregistered guns. A great deal of crime money is hidden in purchasing small or midsize companies. Sometimes they are silent partners. Sometimes they take the profits and run. The once-legitimate partner can't report them."

"We're naive, aren't we?" Tazio suggested.

"People have no idea of the extent of organized crime.

One of the reasons they have so much money is they don't pay taxes on the big money makers, like this type of operation or drugs, especially drugs. Not a penny goes back to the public, but if drugs, like alcohol, were legal, monies would be available for rehab. And people might be more willing to come forward for help. If they do so now, they're a criminal."

"That will be a hard sell." Harry had mixed emotions about this.

"You'd think Prohibition would have taught us something." Cooper sighed. "But Darla is a rich woman. She liked her work. She was good at it. Only a phobia saved you all."

"God bless that spider," Tazio murmured.

"The spider really was after me. Darla got in the way. A killer spider. You all are here because of me!" Pewter announced.

Pirate opened his mouth but Mrs. Murphy rubbed against the puppy's chest to distract him.

"You're right, Pewter," Tucker lied.

"I solved the murder. Will I get any credit? Of course not." Her whiskers twitched.

"Well, you solved who killed Gary and Lisa." Harry half smiled at Cooper. "I can't say that I feel good about this but I'm glad I know. Two wonderful, involved people wiped out because of money."

"Money, power, sex, revenge, reputation." Cooper sighed. "The usual. It's almost always one of those."

"What becomes of the scientific treasure under Richmond?" Harry wondered.

"We'll never know." Cooper shrugged. "That primordial swamp also runs under Maryland, the District of Columbia, Virginia, part of North Carolina."

"Wouldn't it be funny if a brontosaurus is under the White House?" Harry grinned.

"That would get everyone's knickers in a knot." Cooper used the old expression.

"Getting back to spiders, I read somewhere that spiders are one of nature's most successful species. You are never more than three feet away from a spider unless you're in the Arctic or Antarctica," Tazio ruminated.

"Never fear," Pewter boasted. "I fought a dinosaur spider, a giant spider with eight big legs and lots of nasty red eyes. I saved everyone. Me!"

Noticing the fire needed more logs, Harry rose, walked over to the special large brass kettle, picked out a log, and didn't a spider, not huge but noticeable, jump off the log.

Harry, startled, recovered, tossing the log on the fire.

"A killer. Rabies. Save yourself." Pewter shot out of that room at top speed.

The other animals laughed at the frightened cat.

The humans beholding the speedy exit, complete with sound effects, just watched.

"What gets into her?" Harry mused.

"You don't want to know," Mrs. Murphy and Tucker replied in unison, as the spider ducked into the bookcase.

Dear Reader,

Buried under our feet from Baltimore to roughly North Carolina rest many bones from millions of years. Given recent discoveries elsewhere concerning things like dinosaurs having colored feathers, one can only wonder what we might learn if we could explore this area.

Kathleen King helped research this primordial swamp and the creatures therein. She seemed to enjoy it.

As to the chemistry of how Lisa was killed, I am indebted to Harriet Phillips, Ph.D., a botanist who works as a process chemist. "Dee" also whips-in to me when I hunt the hounds, as Kathleen rides in the field.

Another foxhunter, Mark Catron—also a biker—did the motorcycle research.

Foxhunters truly are fascinating, super people. I am well served.

Please note: We do not kill foxes.

I do, however, kill people in print.

The eighteenth-century story line touches on the Constitutional Convention. Our characters view it from the standpoint of the great risk they took for us to free ourselves from the king. If you would read the Articles of Confederation you might wonder how anyone thought these Articles could work. But coming after a long war against a monarchy with little regard for our safety, no representation in Parliament, the exploitation of our resources and labor, the Articles make sense. Their failure threw us into a crisis as great as the war. No one knew if the nation could survive. That we did is testimony to open discussion, painful compromises, and the fact that Washington oversaw the convention. Only this one man could have held us together. He was not a big talker, not given to passionate ideological statements. Yet anyone who ever met or worked with him felt a quiet air of command, trust, and good sense. The participants in the convention received most of the attention, but I personally believe without Washington, all would have come apart at the seams.

Had I followed this gathering to its conclusion this novel would be larger than the cedars of Lebanon. The next Sneaky Pie will deal with the conclusion, plus the personal difficulties as well as the joys of our characters. It's so easy when one reads history written decades, centuries, after the events to forget that those people didn't know what would happen, what would work. They hoped, they tried, and their lives had far less comforts than our own.

The salvation of this contentious convention in Philadelphia was the Connecticut Compromise, which solved the problem of representation based on population.

Too often difficult issues were tabled. Slavery, and all thirteen colonies had slaves, we tabled for twenty years. By the time twenty years was up, slavery was entrenched. We were also sliding toward the War of 1812.

The other battleground was our monetary policy. In an

odd fashion this has never been satisfactorily resolved despite some of the institutions we now take for granted, i.e., the Federal Reserve.

Those of you who read *A Hiss Before Dying*, the Sneaky Pie mystery before this, probably recall Sheba's, Maureen's lady-in-waiting, death at the hands, literally, of DoRe.

She was then discovered in our century because someone was poking around in St. Luke's cemetery.

In the Sneaky Pie following this, Sheba's malign influence creates havoc and death in the spring of 2017. This would have been overload for this book. Then again, Sheba liked to strike just when one's hopes were raised. What is more hopeful than spring?

As an aside, such a power hungry, amoral/immoral personality is hardly unique in humankind. They appear in both genders, all classes, all nationalities, all races. They tend to be intelligent, and she was up to a point. Bloated with their successes they always overstep and underestimate others. Sheba was no different from the monsters of the past. Her compass was smaller but those within its circle suffered.

Those who do not know history are doomed to repeat it. If you are an American reading this, our survival, our creating a new form of government (although we did have Parliament as a kind of model) really is a miracle. And if you are an American, you can never take the Constitution or the Bill of Rights for granted. Each generation must fight for these documents and their promises in their own way. I'd say we're in the middle of a good one.

Like Catherine, Rachel, Ewing, John, Charles, Bettina, Jeddie, Serena, Bumbee, Georgina and her girls, Yancy, even Maureen in her fashion, never give up. Never.

Dear Reader,

I quite liked being the only dog but the Irish wolfhound puppy is awfully sweet, and when he grows up he and I can terrorize Pewter, who is insufferable.

Tucker

Dear Reader,

I've thought of saber-toothed tigers but not dinosaurs. Finding out this was once an enormous swamp, and then discovering that frogs survived, makes me wonder. Not that I don't like frogs, I do, but frogs?

As for the spider, there really is a whopper spider in this house. I avoid her and Pewter is truly scared no matter what she says. There are people terrified of spiders, snakes, stuff like that. I say every creature has its domain. I won't bother them if they don't bother me. Pewter's domain is her food bowl.

Yours Always,

Dear Reader,
They couldn't live without me.

Pewter

Read on for an exclusive sneak peek at
Rita Mae Brown and Sneaky Pie Brown's
next Mrs. Murphy mystery

Whiskers in the Dark

Available now in hardcover and ebook
from Bantam Books

1

"Did you kill anybody?" Harry asked as the firelight flickered on her face.

"Do you think I'm going to answer that question?" Arlene Billeaud laughed at her.

Harry Haristeen; Susan Tucker, her best friend; Arlene Billeaud; Jason Holzknecht; and his wife, Clare Lazo Holzknect, sat by the fireplace in the large stone building known as the Institute. Established in the 1850s as the Loudoun Agricultural and Chemical Institute it had weathered many a storm. In 1855 an advertisement claimed that courses would benefit the farmer, the merchant, and the engineer, certainly a broad student base. But the Panic of 1857, a damaging financial depression for so many, spelled the end for the institute. Next came the war. Still the property persevered, today serving as the home of the National Beagle Club of America.

Those people in the inviting room had come from Maryland and Virginia to clean up paths, move downed trees, and repair the kennels, as violent storms had swept through Loudoun County in Northern Virginia.

The impulse for this was that Hounds F4R Heroes would be hosting its annual National Beagle Club Event at the end of the month. Anyone could enter a two-couple pack of beagles, four hounds to hunt, with prizes awarded to the top couples.

The purpose, to raise money for veterans, drew many spectators and competitors. The funds were used to provide veterans opportunites for fishing, hunting, and other outdoor recreation. Hounds F4R Heroes operated nationally and was steadily growing."

The small group had arrived early for tomorrow's work. Others would drive in the next morning. Harry and Susan were staying in one of the first log cabins built in 1917, when the club was just up and running. Other cabins were added later, tight, warm if you kept the fire going, with enough windows to let in the light. Harry's two cats, Mrs. Murphy and Pewter, along with two dogs—Tee Tucker, a corgi, and Pirate, a half-grown Irish wolfhound—were back at the cabin. No dirty paws at the Institute.

"Another drink?" Jason, tall, maybe mid-fifties, offered, pointing to the opened bottle of wine.

"No thanks," Harry, not a drinker, replied.

"A smidge." Susan raised her glass as did the other two women.

Apart from the work they expected to face tomorrow, they talked about packs of hounds, both bassets and beagles, their hunting season, which had just ended, and friends in common.

"Oh, come on." Harry tweaked Arlene. "We know you had a dangerous job before you retired."

"Not as dangerous as you might think, because I was not an undercover agent."

Arlene had recently retired from the Central Intelligence Agency.

"Rats." Harry pretended to pout. "I want good stories."

"Well, this isn't a good story but my area was Russia. So I was responsible for absorbing and digesting information from there."

"From undercover agents there?" Harry was fascinated.

"I would never say we have agents there but I can promise you we have their agents here."

Clare, a former Navy captain, sipped her white wine. "Not only does Russia have agents here but so do our allies. Everyone spies on everyone, and yes, Harry, we too have agents everywhere. One must."

"The best way to look at this is that power is amoral." Jason settled into his chair, having poured himself another glass of wine.

"I know what you're saying is true but it drives me crazy," Susan spoke. "All that money to sift through people's computers, hacking this and hacking that. Following people and I suppose killing some. Harry isn't far wrong."

"So the question is: If one must kill, say, a Nigerian undercover agent who is funneling American funds to a terrorist group and thousands are dying, is the murder justified?" Arlene asked a question back.

"Well, if we aren't being killed, no." Harry was firm.

"What about the terrorists—at least I think of them as terrorists—who kidnapped the girls in Nigeria? It doesn't affect us but you don't kidnap hundreds of children." Susan tried to think this out.

"But sending operatives over there costs a lot of money. Sending troops outright even more," Jason said. "When I was in the diplomatic corps, depending on where I was assigned, we were always told and trained, 'Hands off!' "

Clare spoke again, "The theory is every state has sovereign rights. They may treat their people quite differently than we treat ours but we have no right to interfere in internal issues no matter how repugnant. Hence we have agencies like the CIA, which does not necessarily interfere but provides information to shape our foreign policy that a diplomat going through normal channels may not be able to provide."

"Jason, did you ever feel you were in a tight spot?" Harry's curiosity kept her questioning.

"Not physically. As you know, my longest posting was in Ankara, Turkey. I speak fluent Turkish, know the culture, and have a smattering of some languages of places surrounding Turkey. Enough to be able to read, say, a Russian headline. But Turkey's geographic position guarantees that it will forever be a trade and political crossroads. Any violence in surrounding countries, say, like Greece—remember they've had riots—could spill over into Turkey."

"Greece would invade Turkey?" Harry was incredulous.

"Not today." Jason smiled. "But riots in Greece or, say, in the Crimea might set off those disaffected in Turkey. Every nation has a pool of disaffected people who can take to the streets with or without much provocation. This includes us."

"Unfortunately, it does. Which is why Hounds for Heroes is important." Arlene put her feet up on a hassock. "Those men and women, many of them, have seen service in miserable spots. But if you've worn our country's uniform you deserve some recognition. I'm thrilled that we can provide sport."

Harry knew that Arlene had lost a leg in the Middle East. She did not peer at her foot, but then Arlene had socks, pants, and a good false limb. She'd served in the Army before being recruited, not a word that Arlene used for the CIA. Her analytical skills and her IQ made her particularly valuable. Not that she wasn't valuable in the Army, but while she was recuperating in a Veterans Hospital she was wooed. It turned out to be a wonderful job for her. She liked the Army, but she loved the agency. Then again, she was in no danger of losing her other leg in Washington.

"I predict that Ashland Bassets will win the basset day. Beagles, maybe Sandanona or Ben Venue." Jason sounded authoritative.

"Why aren't we going to win?" his wife asked, raising her eyebrows.

"What do you think?" Jason asked Arlene.

"Since I'm the director of the event for this year, I plead neutral. I'm hoping for good weather whoever wins."

"Ashland Bassets, Waldingfield Beagles." Harry gave her favorites.

"Can't do that, Harry. We know those hunts. Of course, we want them to win, but who knows?" Susan looked at her watch. "You know what, I'm turning in. We should be up and out by first light tomorrow, especially since we don't know how much damage there is. We have five hundred and twelve acres to canvas."

"Glad as I am that the founders of the National Beagle Club had the foresight to buy all this, it is a lot to maintain," Clare posited.

"Is, but there's no place like it." Harry stood up with Susan. "Cold though, isn't it?"

"Going to be a late spring." Arlene knew that she should rouse herself, but she was ready to fall asleep where she was.

Harry and Susan left the building, hurrying to their cabin. Smoke curled out of the chimney as Harry built a solid fire before they joined the others. As the humans opened the door, the dogs awakened and, tails wagging, hurried up to them.

"Oh, I missed you," said Tucker, the corgi, licking Harry's hand.

"Me, too," agreed the growing giant, Pirate.

One eye now open, the fat, gray Pewter grumbled, "Suck-ups."

Mrs. Murphy sprawled on the comforter on the narrow bed and flicked the tip of her tail. "We can at least purr."

Harry carefully placed two more logs on the fire and

adjusted the grate cover. "That should see us through the night."

"You build good fires," said Susan. "I kind of think there's going to be a lot to do tomorrow."

"Yeah." Harry agreed with Susan. "Wasn't Clare in the Navy?"

"She speaks fluent Russian. So she was mostly on a giant ship out in the Gulf of Finland, according to her. Listening to the Russians, not far away."

"I wouldn't have the patience for that, would you?"

"I suppose I could do it, but I wouldn't like it. Well, I wouldn't mind being on a ship for months at a time." Susan took off her shoes and socks, stripped off her clothes, and quickly jumped into bed.

The room was warm, but the bed would be warmer.

"*I am not moving,*" Pewter announced as Harry also stripped down, then turned back a corner of the covers.

"Pewter, I need to get into bed."

"*I was here first.*"

"Come on, move over." Harry pushed the large cat away from where the covers were turned back.

"*Abused. I am being abused!*"

"Shut up," Tucker called out from in front of the fire.

"*Lickspittle!*" Pewter replied.

"*Come on, you two. I need to sleep.*" Mrs. Murphy suggested.

"*Here we are in this cabin, in the middle of nowhere. Nothing ever happens here. I feel bored already. I am a saint to have come along. Really.*" Pewter whined.

"*I would hardly call being in Loudoun County 'the middle of no-*

where.'" Mrs. Murphy replied, as she felt a pair of feet slide under her.

"Isn't it the most populous county in Virginia?" Tucker questioned.

"If it isn't, it soon will be," Mrs. Murphy replied, for she listened to everything Fair, Harry's husband, read aloud from *The Richmond Times-Dispatch.*

"'Night, Harry," said Susan.

"'Night, Susan," she replied. "'Night, babies."

"'Night." Came the chorus.

2

"Wish the buds would open. You can see the color, but so far, nothing." Harry remarked to Susan.

"We have a few warmish days and then bam, cold again," Susan said as she cleared a tree limb from a foot path far from the institute building.

The earth, hard underneath, wore out their legs after time, made their feet hurt. The two had been at their labors all day.

"Jeez, that's a big one." Harry exhaled.

Susan stood, looked up at the massive tree from which the limb had been torn. "I thought *we* suffered horrible wind storms. Had to be worse up here."

"Northern Virginia's weather is different from ours. Well, girl, let's start at the thinnest end and do this in small sections. That way we can pull them to the side of the path."

"Ok."

They worked six feet from one another, wisely placing their chain saws under the tree, cutting up at an angle, stopping as they neared the top. Then each woman slipped her chain saw down and cut from the top. As these were two country girls, they handled equipment—chain saws, post hole diggers, tractors—with ease.

These old friends had been in the cradle together, gone to high school together, then Harry went to Smith, and Susan went to William and Mary. They each adored the other's husband, shared friends and some passions, especially gardening. Susan was the better gardener, Harry the better farmer.

Cutting off their chain saws, they each moved a hunk of tree limb to the side.

"What do you think?" Susan asked.

"Well, beagles and bassets can pass. People, too, if they look where they're going." Harry studied the opening they were cutting through the trees. "You know, the Hounds for Heroes 3rd Annual Weekend Gala is only two weeks away. There will be dozens more people here than on a regular trials weekend. Basset trials on Friday, Beagle trials on Saturday, cocktail parties both nights, a dance party, and pig roast. It'll be quite an affair, but no one anticipated so much damage could happen in the month since the Triple Challenge. The trails will be ready, but it's taking many hands. It's so important. We all want the event to go well."

The Triple Challenge, a three-day event sponsored by the National Beagle Club, tested both hounds and humans. The three phases included the hunting talent of the individual hound, the ability to contribute to the working pack, and the qualities of conformation, movement, condition, and temperament.

Hounds F4R Heroes, a competition later in April, not only showed off the beagles' versatility, but also bassets. The competitions hunted on different days, since one didn't hunt bassets and beagles together. Last year Hounds F4R Heroes contributed $20,000 to veterans.

Beagle packs and basset packs had foot followers. People stayed in good shape, as they walked the hounds in the off season, and ran after them during the season. Both types of hounds chased rabbits. What a thrill that was for the huntsman, the whippers-in, and the people running their butts off behind the hounds.

Harry and Susan followed the Waldingfield Beagles, the oldest pack in America. Harry and her husband also foxhunted, but Susan and her husband weren't much for riding. So Harry started running along with her friend, finding that she loved it. She never could jog. Bored her to tears, but following a flying pack enlivened her.

"How far are we from the cabin?" Harry wondered.

"I don't know. Maybe fifteen minutes," Susan guessed. "Well, girl, I'm about done. Bet the other work parties are, too. Let's head back."

"Sounds good." Harry put her fingers between her lips, emitting a loud whistle.

Tucker, Harry's Corgi, and Pirate, who Harry and Fair had taken in when his owner was killed, lifted their heads.

"Time to go." The obedient Corgi announced.

"Oh, this smells really good." The already large dog waffled.

Tucker ambled over, put her nose to the ground, and inhaled. "Yes, it does smell good, but you don't want to meet this guy. A bear. Even bigger than you when you're full grown."

Pirate's lovely brown eyes widened. "A bear. Like we see on TV sometimes?"

"Not every animal likes dogs." Tucker turned, trotting in the direction of the whistle. "Come on. If we show up late, she'll fret."

Taking a brief breather, the two friends sat on an old fallen tree.

"I'm feeling my age." Susan shook her head.

"At forty-three?"

"Forty-two!" Susan squinted at Harry.

"Just wanted to see if your mind was going," Harry giggled.

"Better be careful. I know how to get even." Susan punched Harry's arm lightly.

"Oh, but Susan, you're such a good Christian."

"You're pushing it." Susan laughed as she noticed the two dogs coming toward them.

"I smelled a bear!" The puppy enthused.

Tucker added, "And a mess of turkeys. I don't know how many rabbits there are here, but you could sure hunt turkeys."

Harry dropped her hand on Pirate's head as Susan petted Tucker. "Isn't this the ridge near where the First Massachusetts Cavalry was slaughtered?" asked Harry. She pointed in the direction of the bend in the old road west of the farm house. Neither the Union nor the Confederate forces expected to encounter one another that 17th of

June, 1863. But encounter they did, and the First Massachusetts was cut to ribbons.

"That's supposed to be it." Susan loved history, being a history major at college. "People don't realize that sixty percent of that war was fought in Virginia. There was a reason we didn't want to secede. We knew those soldiers would cross the Potomac long before they'd get into Georgia or other parts. But this engagement was fought piecemeal. Brigadier General Judson Kilpatrick, in command of the Massachusetts Brigade, never sent scouts ahead. None of the Union commanders did."

"How many men are in a brigade?"

"Varies. A lot of times, the papers reported bigger numbers to try and scare the enemy. Didn't work. But maybe a thousand. There was a curve, we'll pass it once we hit the rise where the Confederates held their position. The Federal's never had a chance."

Harry rubbed Pirate. "There's no such thing as a good war."

Susan nodded. "No, but there are necessary wars. Got my wind back." She stood up.

"There's our little red wagon, waiting for us up ahead. I'll be glad to dump my chain saw. It gets heavy after a while."

The women placed their tools in the wagon. Harry took first turn pulling, while the dogs tagged along.

They reached the kennels, well-built wooden structures for the different packs. A tree limb had smashed right through the roof of one kennel, knocking down the fence, as well.

"Guess they'll get to that tomorrow," Susan noted.

Harry paused a moment. "The main stone building really is impressive. It was a hospital during the war. It seems as good as the day it was built. Yet I feel this tug of sorrow when I look at it."

"What's strange is that so many died when it was a hospital, but no one is sure where they are buried. But the limbs, the amputated limbs, are supposed to be over there." Susan pointed to a long low mound.

"Odd." Harry grimaced.

They trudged to their cabin.

As they reached the cabin, sitting on the front porch were Mrs. Murphy and Pewter.

"*Killed a platoon of mice. We set a world record!*" Pewter puffed up.

As she was given to overstatement, the dogs looked to the far more reasonable tiger cat.

"*Barn is full of them.*" Mrs. Murphy verified.

The mice infestation was the reason the cats had been allowed to visit. Of course, none of the house pets could come to the fundraiser, but they were useful right now, and happy to be along—despite Pewter's complaining.

Once cleaned up, with food put down for the animals, and a fire renewed in the fireplace, for it was really getting cold, Harry and Susan walked over to the stone house for supper.

About twenty people sat at the tables, all talking at once about their work party.

Harry—next to Amy Burke Walker, on the Board of Directors, and a whipper-in for the Waldingfield Beagles hunted by Dr. Arie Rijke—mentioned the mound.

Amy agreed. "Right, no one know where the bodies are, but people say they've seen ghosts out and about. Some have been seen in this building."

Liz Kelly, a young archivist, leaned toward them from the opposite side of the table. "For over one hundred years people here claimed to see Civil War ghosts."

Liz Reeser, the Assistant Treasurer, piped up. "I swear I saw one. A young man who walked right by me in the middle of the night. But I wasn't afraid. I don't know why."

Betsy Park, from Sandanona Hounds in New York, smiled. "Oh, people always say that about a war hospital."

Mary Reed, Master of Bassets for Ashland Bassets, agreed. "They do, don't they? Still?" She raised her eyebrows.

Jason Holzknecht smiled. "When I was in Turkey, every part of any city or little town hosted ghosts. There were ghosts from the fifth century B.C, ghosts from Justinian's time, ghosts from Atatürk's takeover. More ghosts than the living. I never saw one." He laughed.

Arlene tweaked him. "Maybe you scared them off."

He laughed back. "Could be."

Jason rose high in his profession, got good postings, finally ending his career in Paris. He owned a car dealership outside of D.C., in Maryland. He'd made a great deal of money. Of course, Clare helped.

"Well, I wasn't in Turkey like you, but I did see Istanbul," Arlene said to Jason. "But it is exciting. The Russians still lust after it. Always will."

"We have everything in this country," Mary Reed added. "When you travel you realize Mother Nature made us rich."

"True." Susan agreed, then turned to Arlene. "Did you ever see ghosts?"

A long pause followed this.

"I'm not sure. Once I thought I saw a shadow, but. . . ." She shrugged. *"Who knows?"*

As the humans chatted away, the two cats and two dogs sat on the porch of the cabin.

"Who's that?" Tucker noticed a beagle in front of the stone house.

"I thought we were the only animals here." Pewter sat up for a better look.

The little dog stopped. The four friends could see its tri-color, its handsome head, but somehow the animal appeared insubstantial.

Mrs. Murphy, whiskers forward, called out. "Who are you?"

The dog stared at them and did not answer, but turned and headed for the tree line behind the kennels.

Pirate, puzzled, remarked, "You can see through the dog."

All four, now on their feet, watched the disappearing beagle.

Tucker, voice low, declared, "That's a ghost."